# JACK KIRBY'S IN THE DAYS OF THE MOB

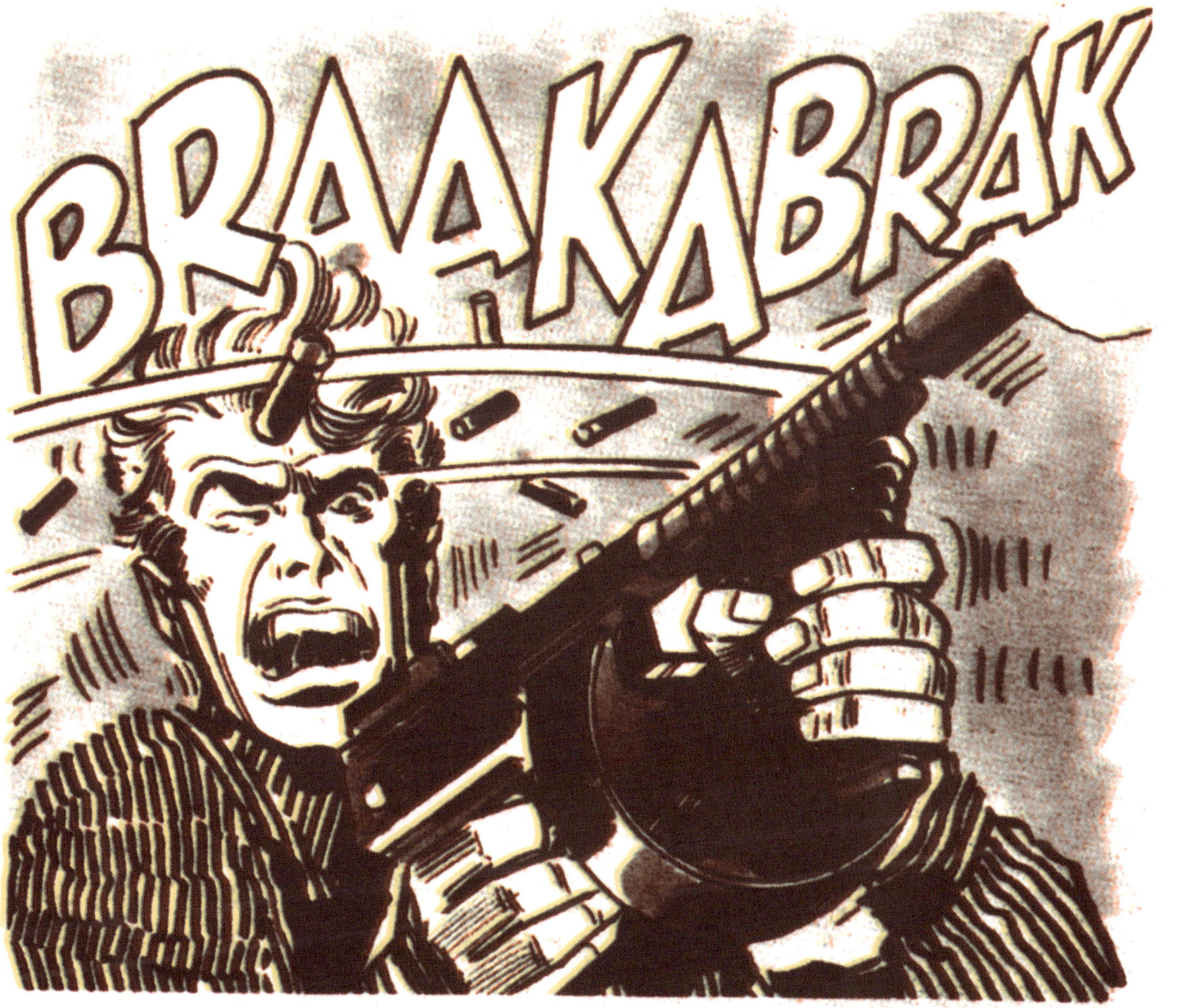
BRAAKABRAK

**Jack Kirby** Editor – Original Series
**Scott Nybakken** Editor
**Robbin Brosterman** Design Director – Books
**Louis Prandi** Publication Design

**Bob Harras** VP – Editor-in-Chief

**Diane Nelson** President
**Dan DiDio** and **Jim Lee** Co-Publishers
**Geoff Johns** Chief Creative Officer
**John Rood** Executive VP – Sales, Marketing and Business Development
**Amy Genkins** Senior VP – Business and Legal Affairs
**Nairi Gardiner** Senior VP – Finance
**Jeff Boison** VP – Publishing Operations
**Mark Chiarello** VP – Art Direction and Design
**John Cunningham** VP – Marketing
**Terri Cunningham** VP – Talent Relations and Services
**Alison Gill** Senior VP – Manufacturing and Operations
**Hank Kanalz** Senior VP – Digital
**Jay Kogan** VP – Business and Legal Affairs, Publishing
**Jack Mahan** VP – Business Affairs, Talent
**Nick Napolitano** VP – Manufacturing Administration
**Sue Pohja** VP – Book Sales
**Courtney Simmons** Senior VP – Publicity
**Bob Wayne** Senior VP – Sales

### IN THE DAYS OF THE MOB

Published by DC Comics. Cover, introduction and compilation Copyright © 2013 DC Comics. All Rights Reserved. Originally published as IN THE DAYS OF THE MOB 1. Copyright © 1971 DC Comics. All Rights Reserved. All characters, their distinctive likenesses and related elements featured in this publication are trademarks of DC Comics. The stories, characters and incidents featured in this publication are entirely fictional. DC Comics does not read or accept unsolicited submissions of ideas, stories or artwork.

DC Comics
1700 Broadway, New York, NY 10019
A Warner Bros. Entertainment Company.
Printed by RRD, China. 5/20/13.
First Printing.
ISBN: 978-1-4012-4079-0

Library of Congress Cataloging-in-Publication Data

Kirby, Jack.
  In the days of the mob / Jack Kirby.
     pages cm
  "The Roaring '30s Come Alive!"
  "Originally published as In the Days of the Mob 1."
  ISBN 978-1-4012-4079-0
  1. Organized crime--Comic books, strips, etc. 2. Graphic novels. I. Title.
  PN6727.K57I5 2013
  741.5'973--dc23
                                    2013009145

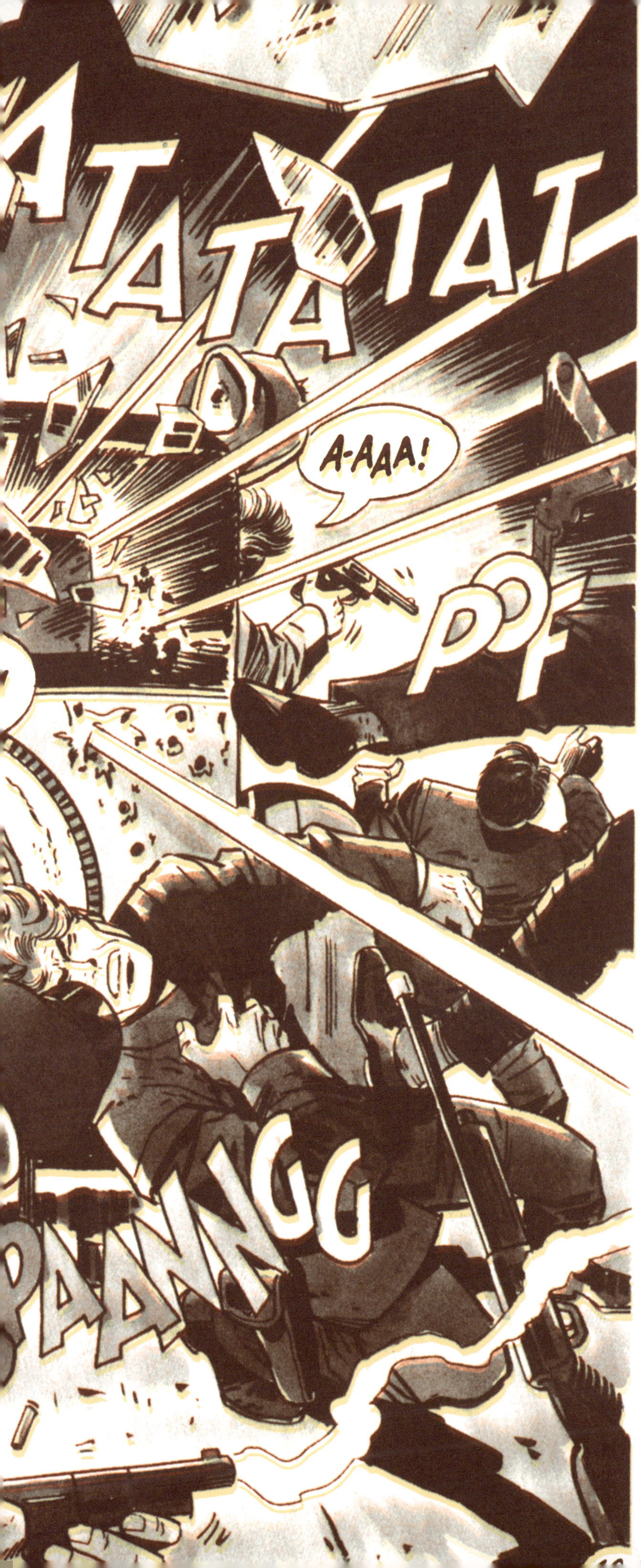
A-AAA!

# CRIME AND ~~PUNISHMENT~~ PINBALL

## AN INTRODUCTION BY JOHN MORROW

Remember pinball machines? You'd insert a coin, pull back a plunger, and shoot a shiny silver ball onto a playing field, where you'd use flippers to try to beat the high score or earn that ever-elusive extra ball or "special." They used to be found in every convenience store, pool hall, bar, and bowling alley on Earth. If you've purchased this book, I'm betting that you're old enough to have played a pinball machine—so here's a little history about them that has relevance to comic book creator Jack Kirby and the stories he created for IN THE DAYS OF THE MOB.

In 1941 there were around 250,000 pinball machines in the U.S., and ten percent of those were located in New York City, where Kirby lived and worked. The United States Treasury had to increase its coin production that year in part to keep up with their popularity. But it wasn't all fun and games; in the 1930s and '40s the pinball industry had direct ties to organized crime, and it was also at the center of numerous cases of local government corruption. There was money to be made from the seemingly harmless amusement devices, and crooks were out to get their cut any way they could.

Because of this, pinball machines were banned in major cities in the 1940s (including New York City), and popular opinion held that they were games of chance rather than skill — i.e., gambling. (Manufacturers added flippers to the games specifically to counteract this perception.) New York Mayor Fiorello LaGuardia denounced the devices for robbing children of their lunch money and instituted raids on pinball dens throughout the city in which cops smashed machines and dumped them into the Big Apple's rivers. The pinball rackets were forced underground into private "speakeasies," skirting LaGuardia's pinball prohibition and strengthening the public's perception that playing the game was a less than wholesome form of entertainment.

Another form of frowned-upon fun in the 1940s and '50s was comic books, and one of the top-selling comics genres was crime, begun in 1942 by editor/writer Charles Biro in his hugely popular title *Crime Does Not Pay.* There were depictions of real-life mob shootings, hangings, electrocutions, assaults... you name it, Biro showed it. Readers ate it up, to the tune of five million copies per issue (if the cover blurbs are to be believed). Success always brings out copycats, and by the end of the 1940s nearly one out of every seven comics was a crime book. Some of the best of those Biro imitations were by Jack Kirby and his partner Joe Simon, in titles like *Justice Traps the Guilty* (a name undoubtedly chosen to capitalize on Biro's similar-sounding title).

Kirby had grown up in the 1920s and '30s on Manhattan's Lower East Side, where he gained firsthand knowledge of gangsters and gun molls. It served him well on these books, as did the time he spent as a kid watching Jimmy Cagney gangster films at his local movie house. In 1947 he even drew a story for *Headline Comics* called "Grim Pay-Off for the Pinball Mob," billed as "A True Crime-Never-Pays Release." It depicts a candy store owner standing up to two mobsters who force a pinball machine on him, saying, "There's a school across the street... I won't have those kids losing their lunch money!!"

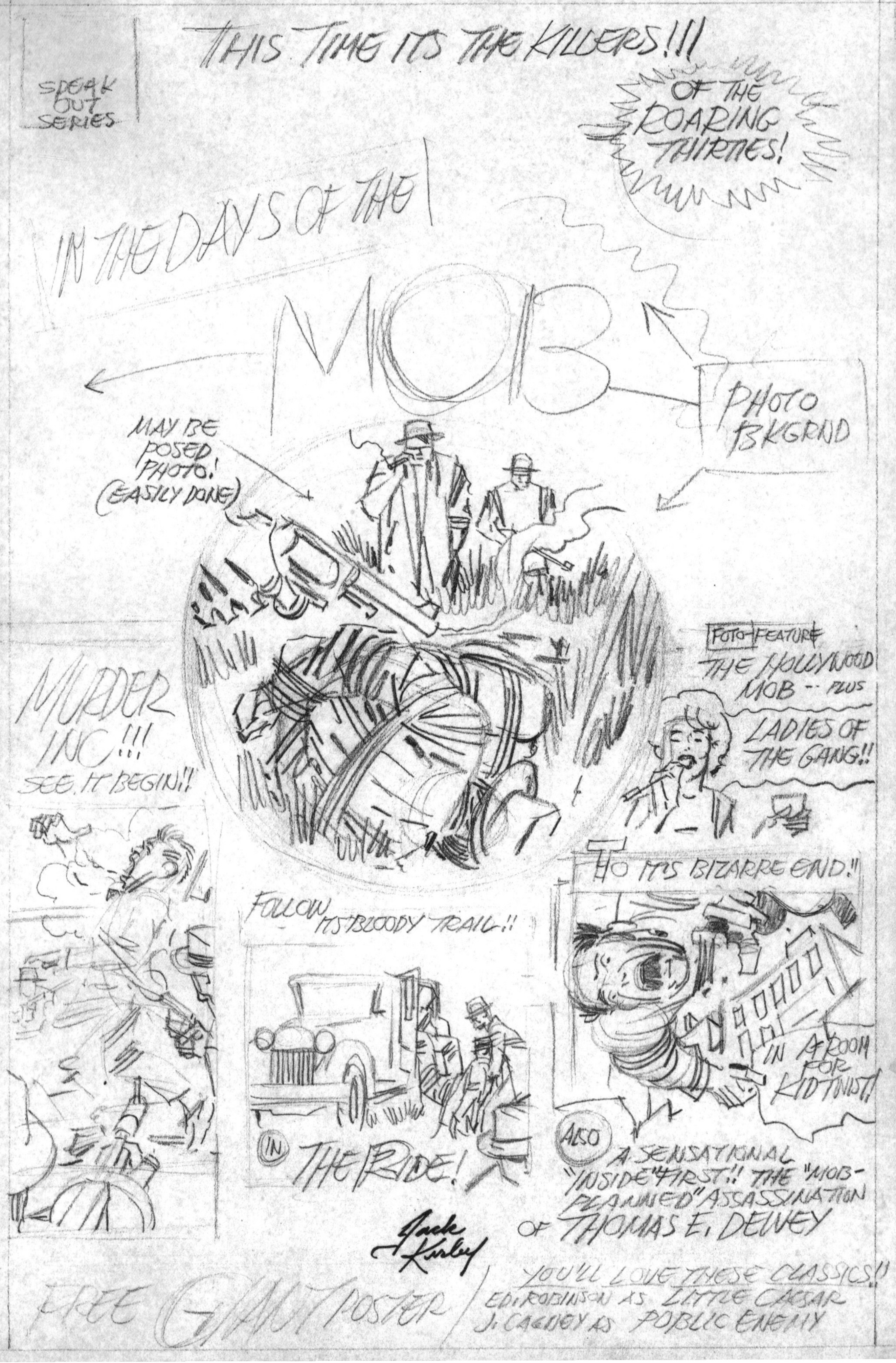
SPEAK OUT SERIES
THIS TIME ITS THE KILLERS!!!
OF THE ROARING THIRTIES!
IN THE DAYS OF THE
MOB
PHOTO BKGRND
MAY BE POSED PHOTO! (EASILY DONE)
MURDER INC!!!
SEE IT BEGIN!!
FOTO FEATURE
THE HOLLYWOOD MOB -- PLUS
LADIES OF THE GANG!!
TO ITS BIZARRE END!!
FOLLOW ITS BLOODY TRAIL!!
IN A ROOM FOR KIDNAPPING!
IN
THE RIDE!
ALSO
A SENSATIONAL "INSIDE" FIRST!! THE "MOB-PLANNED" ASSASSINATION OF THOMAS E. DEWEY
Jack Kirby
FREE GIANT POSTER
YOU'LL LOVE THESE CLASSICS!!
ED. ROBINSON AS LITTLE CAESAR
J. CAGNEY AS PUBLIC ENEMY

(Kirby then showed the brave shopkeeper getting his teeth knocked out for having a social conscience, but after the law eventually raided the mobsters' headquarters he had the victorious proprietor proudly toss the machine on a trash heap in the story's final panel.)

All these gangland exploits may have excited America's youth, but, just like pinball, they infuriated parents, educators, pastors, and one particular psychologist named Dr. Fredric Wertham. In 1948 Wertham started a one-man crusade against comics, using speaking engagements and articles in *Reader's Digest* and *Ladies' Home Journal* as his soapbox. Citing comic books as the main cause of juvenile delinquency, his 1954 book *Seduction of the Innocent* and the subsequent investigations by the Senate Subcommittee on Juvenile Delinquency resulted in most comics publishers self-censoring their titles and agreeing to follow a strict Comics Code.

While other genres (particularly horror) stepped just as far over the line of good taste as their gangster-heavy counterpart, once the Comics Code took hold it was curtains for crime. Biro's books ended by 1955, and Kirby's true crime features had died off a couple of years before that. Not that Kirby was hurting for work, mind you. Pivoting neatly from lawbreakers to heartbreakers, he and Simon had pioneered the romance comics genre, which proved hugely successful (and much more socially acceptable) in the 1950s. Kirby later managed to make another mark on pop culture by co-creating most of the Marvel Universe in the 1960s before deciding to move over to DC Comics in 1970 — which is where this book picks up.

*******

One of the first projects Kirby undertook at DC was an experimental magazine entitled IN THE DAYS OF THE MOB. At the time, Mario Puzo's 1969 novel *The Godfather* had just seared itself into the public's consciousness, and DC figured the time was ripe to resurrect crime comics. Jack jumped at the chance to crack his knuckles on a genre he had left behind 20 years before. Since the title was set up to be a newsstand magazine, it wouldn't be subject to the Comics Code that bumped off its predecessors from the 1940s. Sadly, DC put Kirby's original idea of making it a deluxe, glossy, color publication on ice, and then pulled the plug on the whole project immediately after the first issue was published (an issue that was barely seen, thanks to a lousy newsstand distribution system that was rumored to be heavily mob-controlled). This left Kirby's already-completed second issue unpublished...

... until now, that is. The fine folks up at DC recently asked me to reassemble the art for that second issue, so I set out to settle that score for Jack. Over the years, I had amassed copies of a good number of the unused pages, enough to see that he had written the issue as a sort of four-act play, with recurring characters walking on- and off-stage throughout all four parts. The first act, "Murder, Inc.!", had actually been published in 1974 in the obscure AMAZING WORLD OF DC COMICS #1, while "A Room for Kid Twist!" saw print in an even rarer fan newsletter. While DC had re-lettered most of the original boards, the art I found was missing a lot of those paste-ups, leaving much of inker and letterer Mike Royer's original calligraphy intact. If you see two different lettering styles throughout any of the stories here (even on the same page), that's why.

Kirby was regularly using photo collages in his stories during this era, and the opening page of "A Room for Kid Twist!" had a large white area where he had planned to include one. I found an unused Kirby collage labeled "For MOB #2" and worked it in. Even if it wasn't the exact one Jack planned to use, it was authentic and seemed to fit the bill.

I was still short a number of key pages, however. Kirby's rough layout for the cover included text that referred to a "Free Giant Poster" of Edward G. Robinson as "Little Caesar" and James Cagney as "The Public Enemy," as well as a photo featurette entitled "The Hollywood Mob," presumably similar to the first issue's featurette "The Breeding Ground." I don't know if these two elements were ever completed (they would have run on pages 24-28 of the issue), but they weren't critical to this book. I was determined, however, to completely restore all four of the stories that Kirby wrote and drew, so it was time to assemble my own "gang" to help.

I turned to Rand "The Scan" Hoppe of the Jack Kirby Museum (www.kirbymuseum.org) and "Tommygun" Tom Kraft of whatifkirby.com to help get my mitts on the pages I hadn't yet found. In some cases, the best sources we could dig up were smudgy photocopies, so I called in Tom "CMYK" Ziuko for help in rubbing out the offending areas. The results look nearly as gorgeous as the day Jack and Mike finished them.

Which brings me to the story "The Ride!". *(Spoiler alert: If you know what's good for ya, read "The Ride!" before continuing with this intro, just so's I don't ruin no surprises.)* As the hoods prepare to dump poor Walter's corpse in the lake, what do they use to keep his carcass from floating back up?

Yep, it's a pinball machine, and accurately rendered by Kirby. He even omitted the flippers (they didn't appear on machines until 1947).

"The Ride!" is a virtuoso performance by Kirby. In it, he depicts the brutal slaying of a mobster from the pinball rackets who has been caught with his hand in the till. But like Alfred Hitchcock in his classic film *Psycho*, Kirby knew that "less is more" — all the blood and gore takes place off-screen, which heightens the scene's intensity. You do get a close-up of Walter's ragged torso on page 22, a bit of framing that tends to dehumanize and depersonalize his lifeless form. But the scene a couple of pages earlier in which an ice pick is plunged repeatedly into Walter is one of the most intense I've ever seen from Kirby, with nary a drop of blood shown.

The rest of this issue is filled with more vicious fights, piles of dead bodies, and some of the sexiest renditions of women Kirby ever produced — certainly not the squeaky-clean, superhero-triumphs-over-evil kind of stories that most of us associate with the King of Comics. Based on my research, however, these stories are factually accurate accounts of real-life criminals, and when they get their comeuppance it isn't pretty. The depictions of violence may not compare with what's shown in films like *Goodfellas, Pulp Fiction,* or even the *Godfather* trilogy, but Jack didn't pull many punches in this, his last effort in the crime comics genre.

*******

Nowadays you won't find many crime comics *or* pinball machines around. The "Bally tables" (named after the leading pinball manufacturer of the 1970s) eventually reached a wide level of acceptance and popularity after the 1975 release of the film version of The Who's rock opera *Tommy*, which featured a "deaf, dumb, and blind kid" who could outplay anyone at the game. New York City finally overturned Mayor LaGuardia's pinball ban in 1976, a half-dozen years after these stories were drawn (although even today it's illegal to play pinball on Sundays in Ocean City, New Jersey). But as video games rose in popularity, pinball fell out of fashion, to the point where only one company (not Bally) makes the machines today.

Not many creators still crank out crime comics, either. One notable exception is Frank Miller, whose *Sin City* series morphed into a blockbuster film, with a sequel in the works as of this writing. (A few years ago, as I was planning an issue of my own magazine spotlighting Kirby's crime comics, I asked Frank to re-ink the splash page from IN THE DAYS OF THE MOB #2 for its cover. Miller, being a huge fan of both Kirby and crime comics, agreed without hesitation. I never thought to ask him if *he* liked pinball.)

Let's hope Frank's films, and this collection, spark a resurgence of interest in the genre. If today's creators can tell a story half as well as Kirby does here, I for one look forward to it.

I hope pinball makes a comeback too. After all, neither it, nor crime books, was detrimental to my upbringing or corrupted my young mind, so what's the harm? (Although, come to think of it, I can't begin to count the number of dimes and quarters I've spent playing every pinball machine I could get my hands on. And I did skip lunch at school a few times to save money to buy Kirby comics. I've even owned three different pinball machines over the years. Do you suppose Mayor LaGuardia was right after all?)

Well, anyway, please excuse me while I go knock over a bank or somethin'...

*John Morrow, when he's not playing the Comet pinball machine in his office, is the editor of* The Jack Kirby Collector *magazine — now in its 20th year of celebrating the life and career of Jack Kirby. He's also the founder of TwoMorrows Publishing, which brings new life to comics fandom through its award-winning line of books and magazines about comics history.*

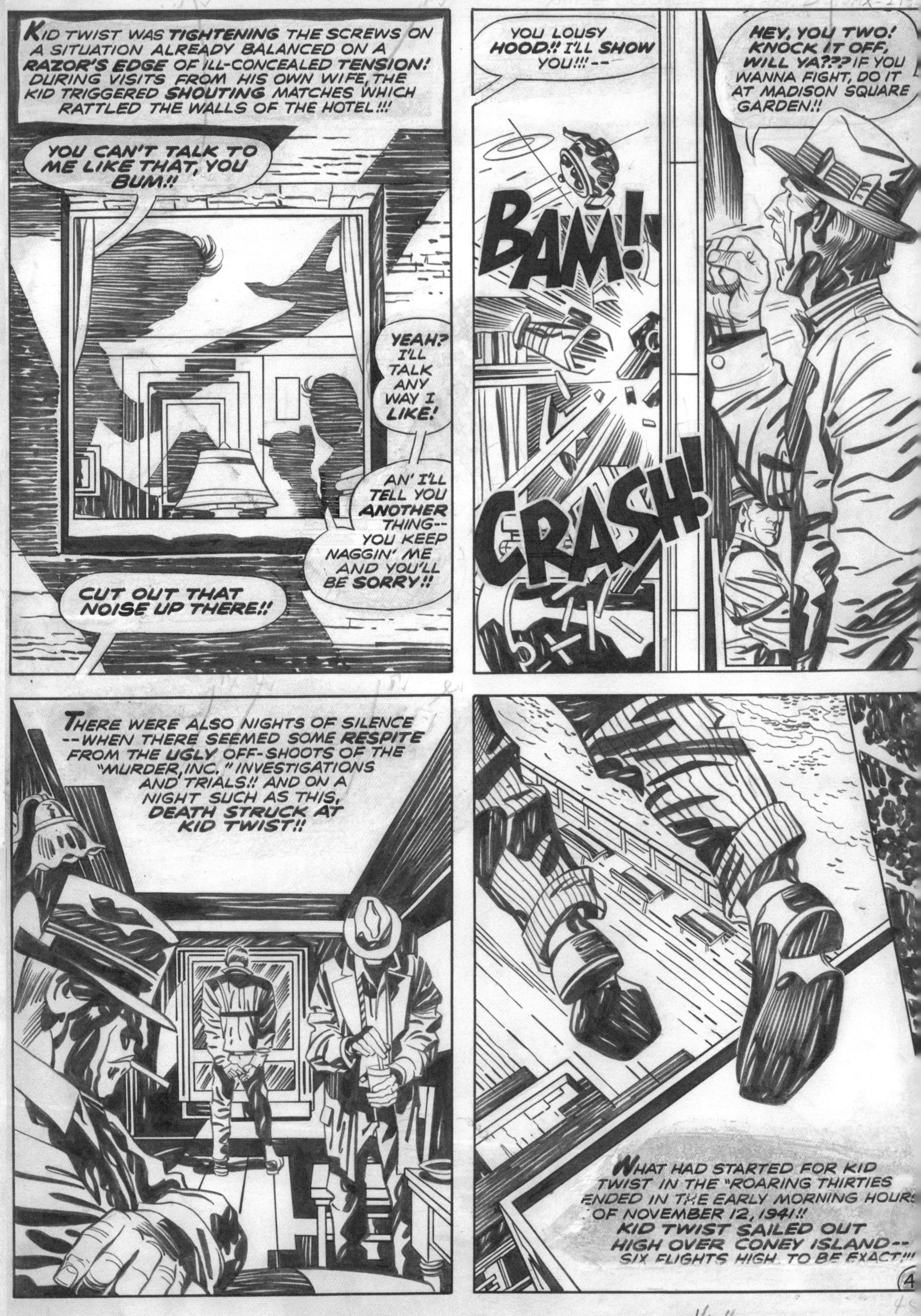
KID TWIST WAS TIGHTENING THE SCREWS ON A SITUATION ALREADY BALANCED ON A RAZOR'S EDGE OF ILL-CONCEALED TENSION! DURING VISITS FROM HIS OWN WIFE, THE KID TRIGGERED SHOUTING MATCHES WHICH RATTLED THE WALLS OF THE HOTEL!!!
YOU CAN'T TALK TO ME LIKE THAT, YOU BUM!!
YEAH? I'LL TALK ANY WAY I LIKE!
AN' I'LL TELL YOU ANOTHER THING-- YOU KEEP NAGGIN' ME AND YOU'LL BE SORRY!!
CUT OUT THAT NOISE UP THERE!!
YOU LOUSY HOOD!! I'LL SHOW YOU!!! --
HEY, YOU TWO! KNOCK IT OFF, WILL YA??? IF YOU WANNA FIGHT, DO IT AT MADISON SQUARE GARDEN!!
BAM!
CRASH!
THERE WERE ALSO NIGHTS OF SILENCE --WHEN THERE SEEMED SOME RESPITE FROM THE UGLY OFF-SHOOTS OF THE "MURDER, INC." INVESTIGATIONS AND TRIALS!! AND ON A NIGHT SUCH AS THIS, DEATH STRUCK AT KID TWIST!!
WHAT HAD STARTED FOR KID TWIST IN THE "ROARING THIRTIES ENDED IN THE EARLY MORNING HOURS OF NOVEMBER 12, 1941!! KID TWIST SAILED OUT HIGH OVER CONEY ISLAND-- SIX FLIGHTS HIGH, TO BE EXACT!!
4

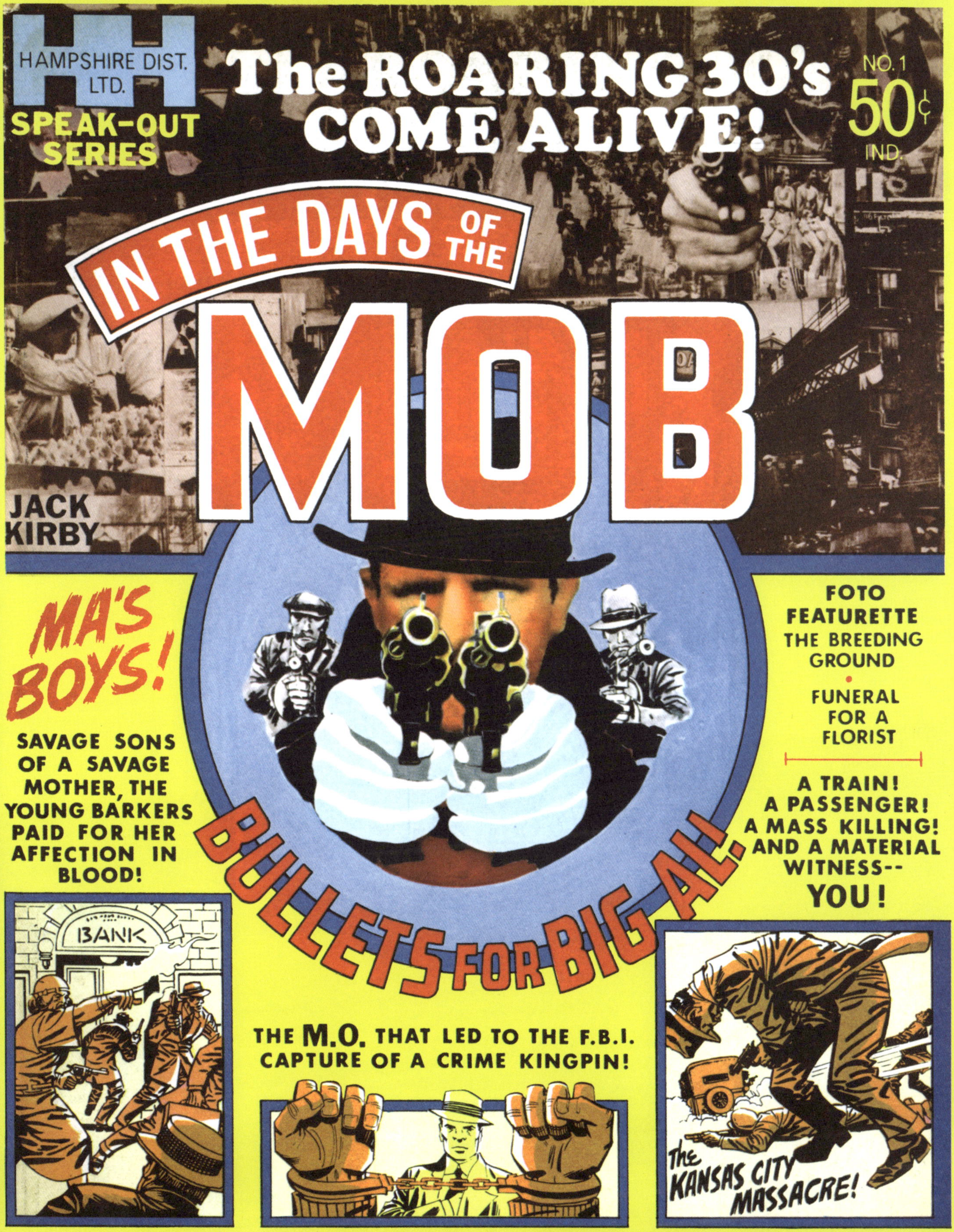

HAMPSHIRE DIST. LTD.
SPEAK-OUT SERIES
The ROARING 30's COME ALIVE!
NO. 1
50¢
IND.
IN THE DAYS OF THE
MOB
JACK KIRBY
MA'S BOYS!
SAVAGE SONS OF A SAVAGE MOTHER, THE YOUNG BARKERS PAID FOR HER AFFECTION IN BLOOD!
FOTO FEATURETTE
THE BREEDING GROUND
FUNERAL FOR A FLORIST
A TRAIN! A PASSENGER! A MASS KILLING! AND A MATERIAL WITNESS-- YOU!
BULLETS FOR BIG AL.
BANK
THE M.O. THAT LED TO THE F.B.I. CAPTURE OF A CRIME KINGPIN!
The KANSAS CITY MASSACRE!
FREE! A GIANT "WANTED" POSTER OF JOHN DILLINGER!

# IN THE DAYS OF THE MOB

## CONTENTS

**MA'S BOYS** .................................................. Page 5
    It was Ma Barker who always got the notices but what about her boys? Who paid in blood for them?

**BULLETS FOR BIG AL** .................................. Page 20
    It was smarter to talk about it—than get killed for trying!

*Featurette:* **THE BREEDING GROUND** ............ Page 32
    America of the Thirties — SICK—BROKE—and WHITE!

*Article:* **FUNERAL FOR A FLORIST** .................. Page 35
    by Mark Evanier and Steve Sherman.

**KANSAS CITY MASSACRE** .............................. Page 37
    Pretty Boy Floyd and MURDER meet a train!

**METHOD OF OPERATION** .............................. Page 45
    How they caught Country Boy!

**KILL JOY WAS HERE** ...................................... Page 47
    Sergio Aragones laughs at crime!

Written, drawn & edited by Jack Kirby
Inks by Vince Colletta

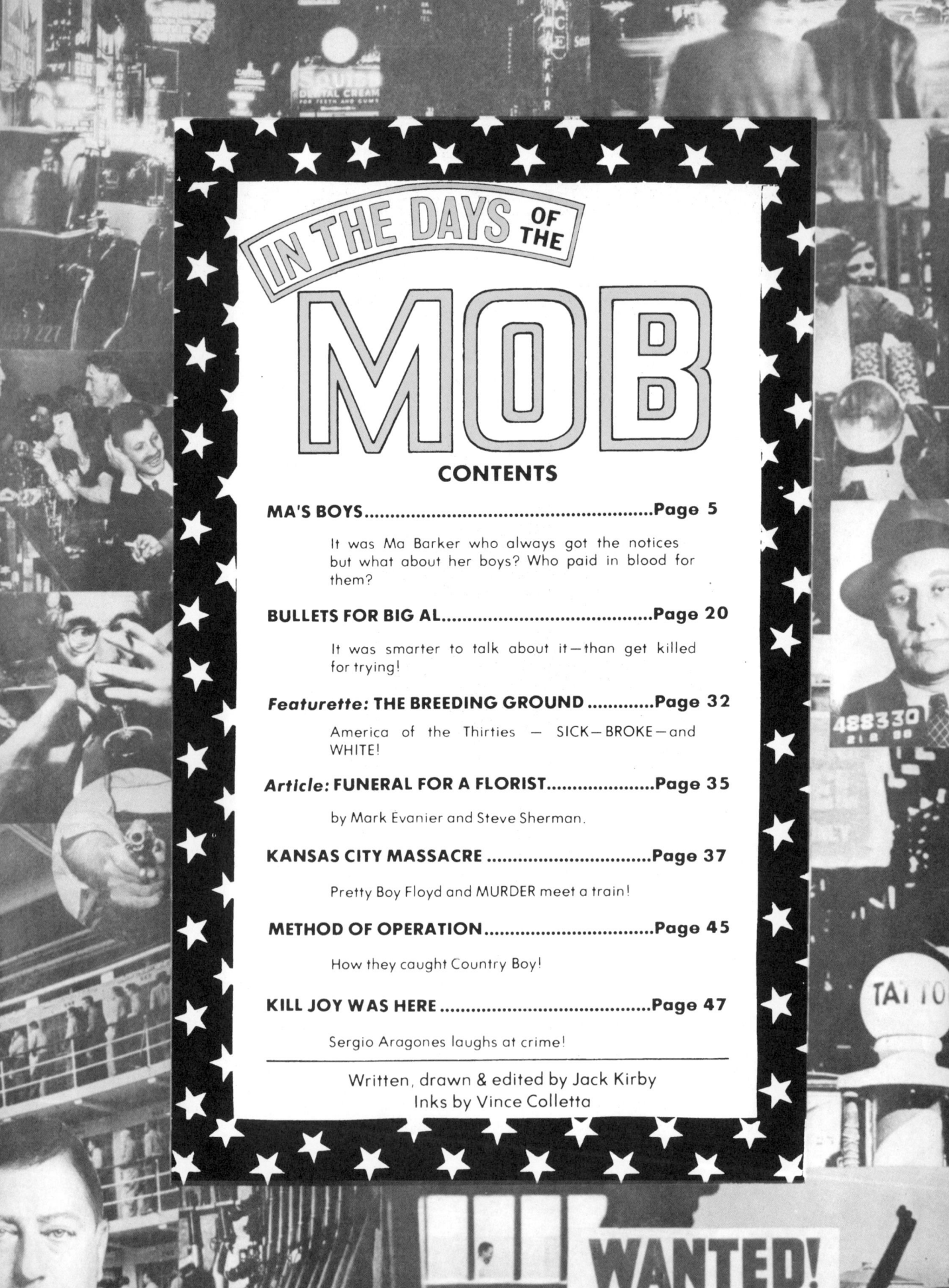

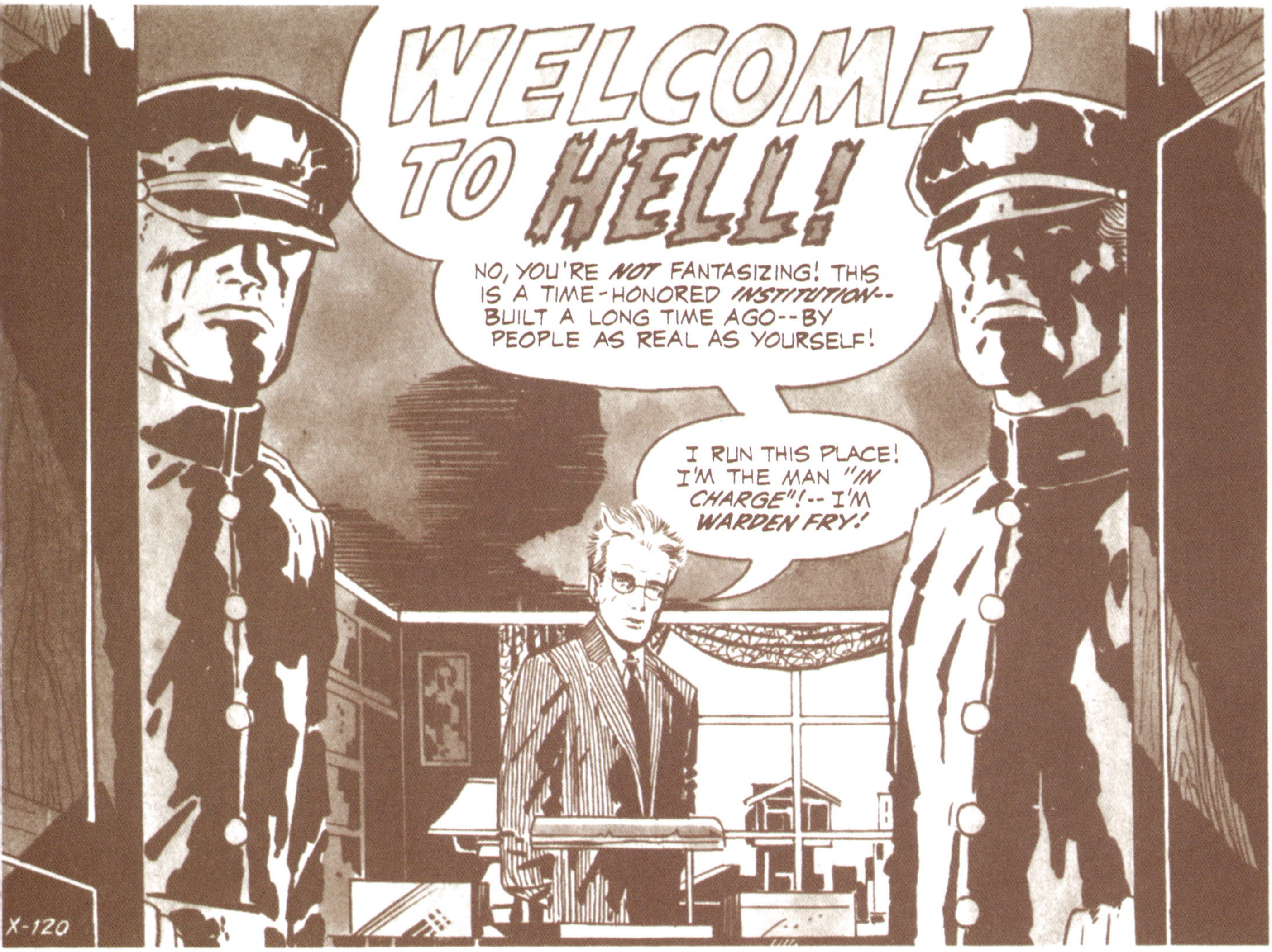
WELCOME TO HELL!
NO, YOU'RE NOT FANTASIZING! THIS IS A TIME-HONORED INSTITUTION-- BUILT A LONG TIME AGO--BY PEOPLE AS REAL AS YOURSELF!
I RUN THIS PLACE! I'M THE MAN "IN CHARGE"!--I'M WARDEN FRY!
X-120

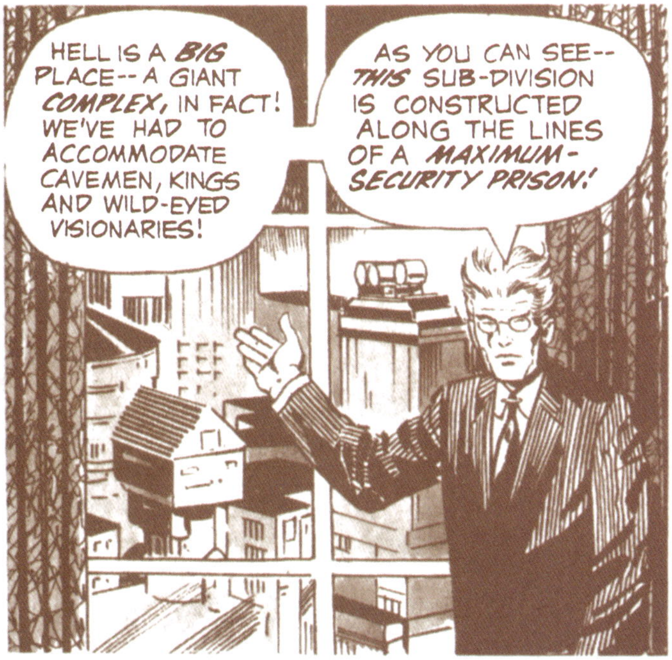
HELL IS A BIG PLACE--A GIANT COMPLEX, IN FACT! WE'VE HAD TO ACCOMMODATE CAVEMEN, KINGS AND WILD-EYED VISIONARIES!
AS YOU CAN SEE-- THIS SUB-DIVISION IS CONSTRUCTED ALONG THE LINES OF A MAXIMUM-SECURITY PRISON!

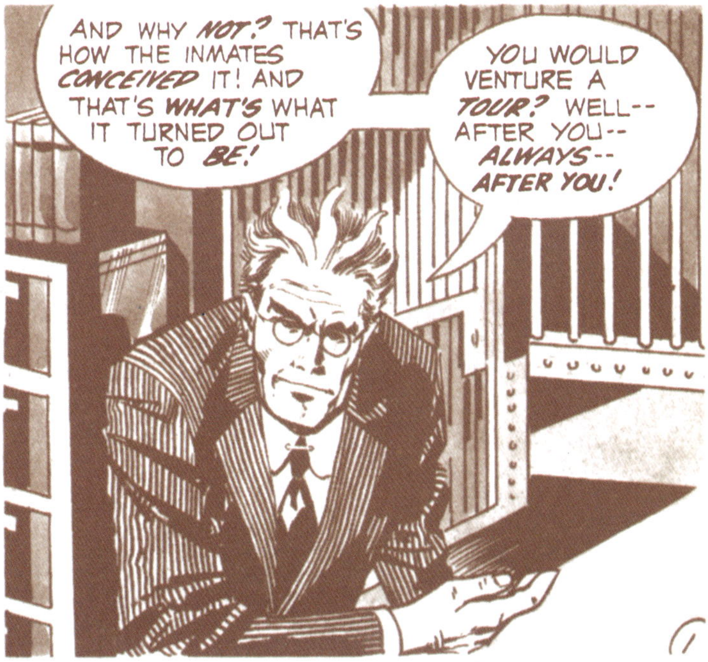
AND WHY NOT? THAT'S HOW THE INMATES CONCEIVED IT! AND THAT'S WHAT'S WHAT IT TURNED OUT TO BE!
YOU WOULD VENTURE A TOUR? WELL-- AFTER YOU-- ALWAYS-- AFTER YOU!

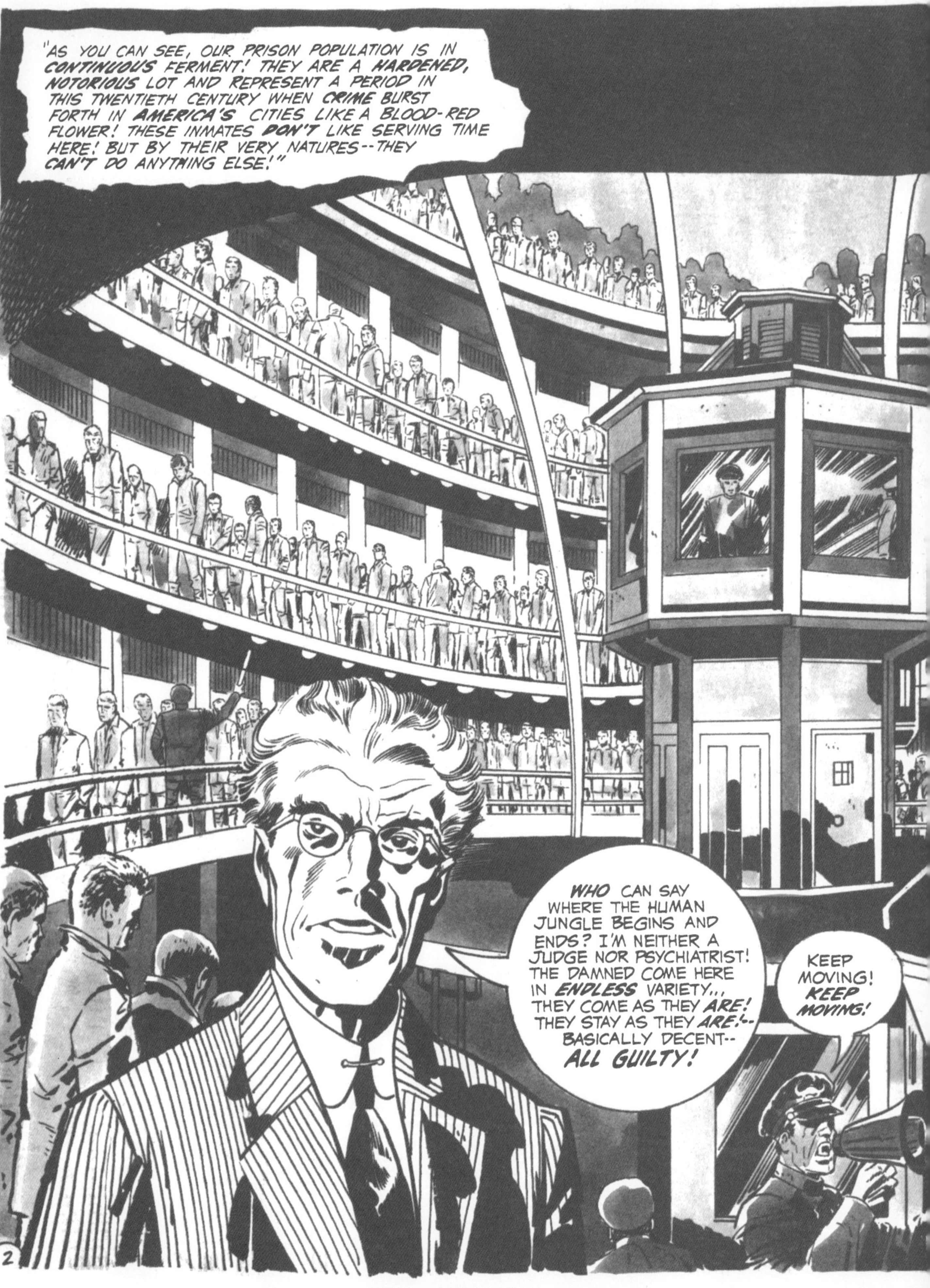
"AS YOU CAN SEE, OUR PRISON POPULATION IS IN CONTINUOUS FERMENT! THEY ARE A HARDENED, NOTORIOUS LOT AND REPRESENT A PERIOD IN THIS TWENTIETH CENTURY WHEN CRIME BURST FORTH IN AMERICA'S CITIES LIKE A BLOOD-RED FLOWER! THESE INMATES DON'T LIKE SERVING TIME HERE! BUT BY THEIR VERY NATURES--THEY CAN'T DO ANYTHING ELSE!"
WHO CAN SAY WHERE THE HUMAN JUNGLE BEGINS AND ENDS? I'M NEITHER A JUDGE NOR PSYCHIATRIST! THE DAMNED COME HERE IN ENDLESS VARIETY.., THEY COME AS THEY ARE! THEY STAY AS THEY ARE!-- BASICALLY DECENT-- ALL GUILTY!
KEEP MOVING! KEEP MOVING!

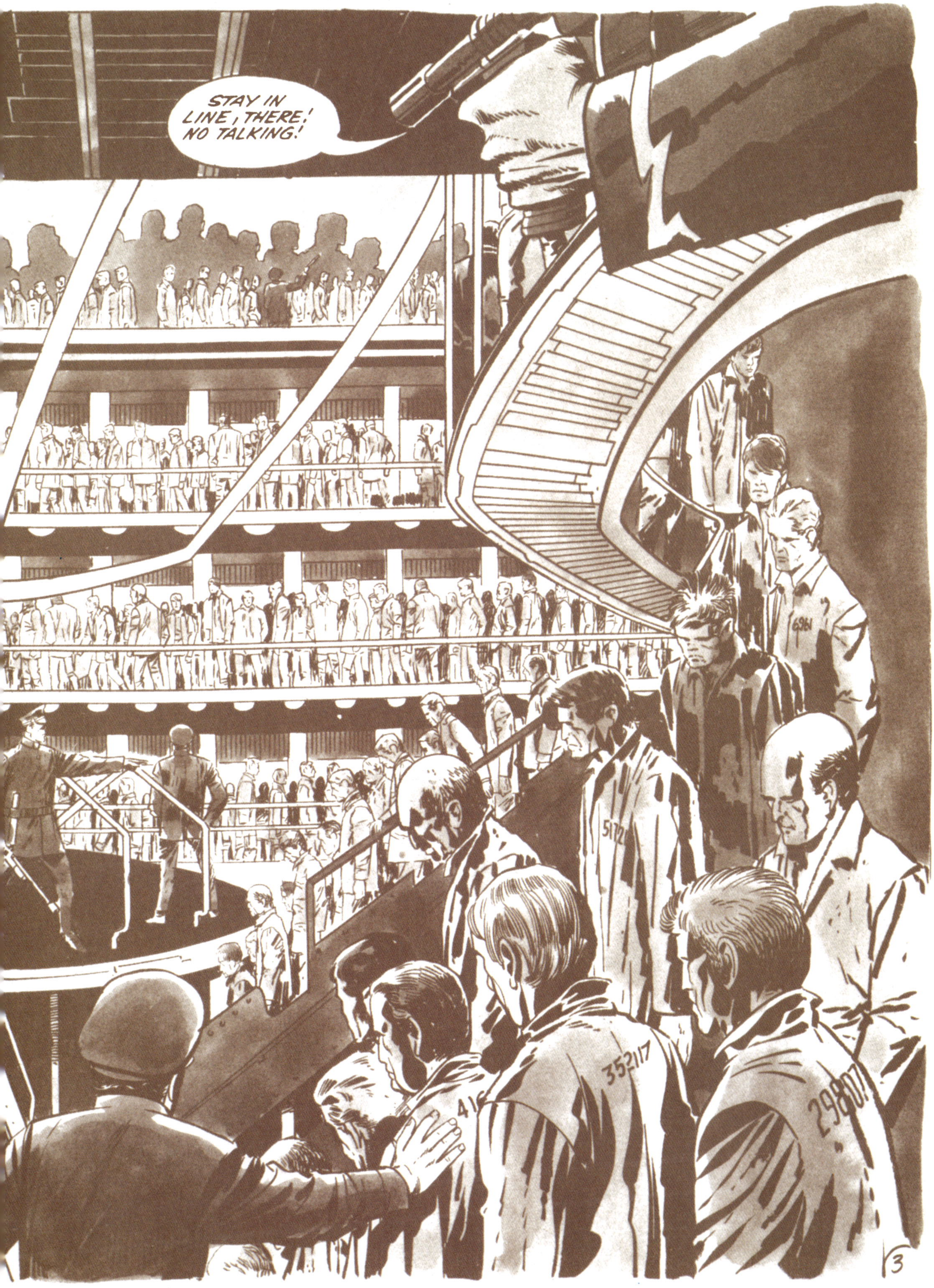
STAY IN LINE, THERE! NO TALKING!
6961
51120
352117
41
29807
3

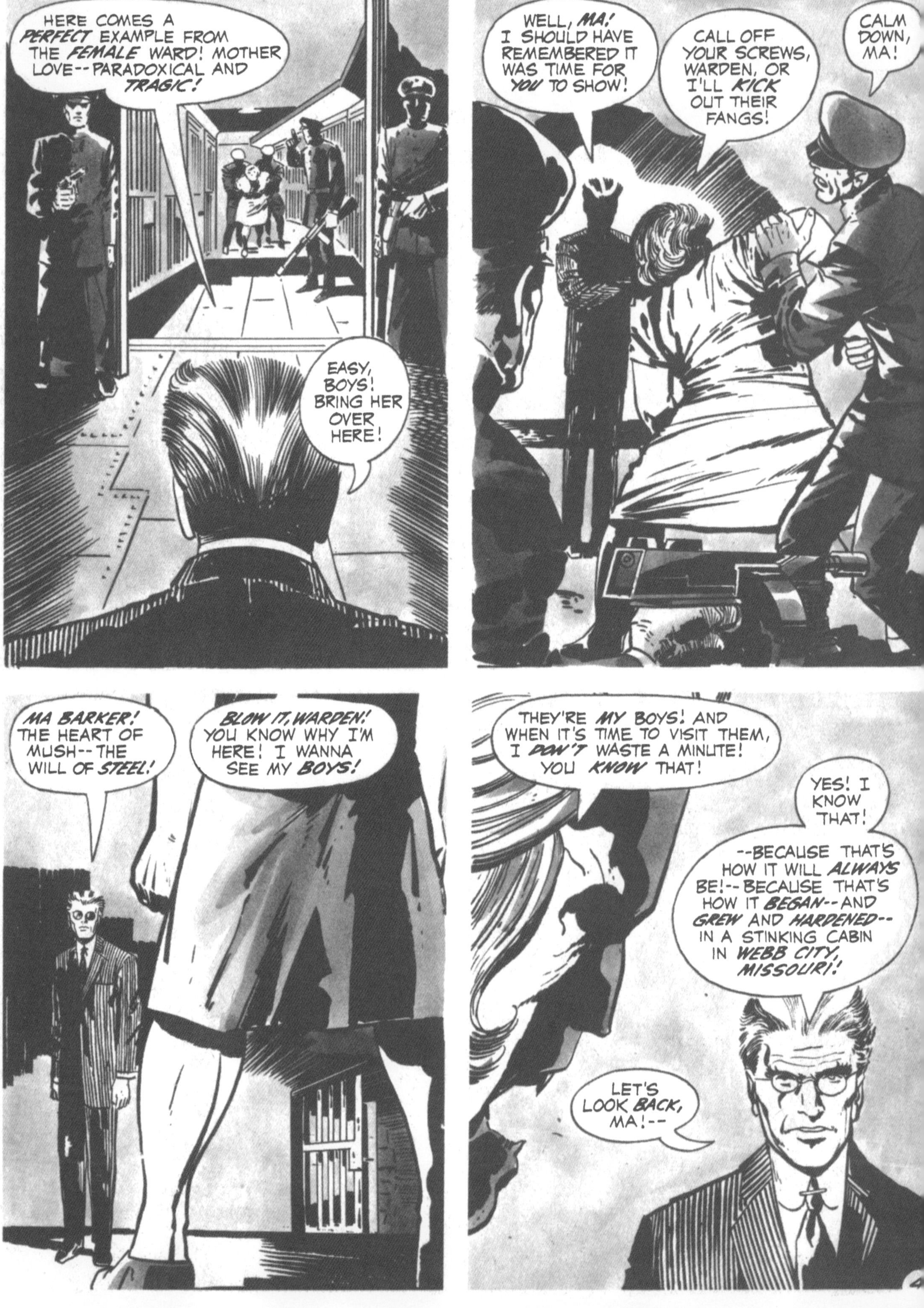
HERE COMES A PERFECT EXAMPLE FROM THE FEMALE WARD! MOTHER LOVE--PARADOXICAL AND TRAGIC!
EASY, BOYS! BRING HER OVER HERE!
WELL, MA! I SHOULD HAVE REMEMBERED IT WAS TIME FOR YOU TO SHOW!
CALL OFF YOUR SCREWS, WARDEN, OR I'LL KICK OUT THEIR FANGS!
CALM DOWN, MA!
MA BARKER! THE HEART OF MUSH--THE WILL OF STEEL!
BLOW IT, WARDEN! YOU KNOW WHY I'M HERE! I WANNA SEE MY BOYS!
THEY'RE MY BOYS! AND WHEN IT'S TIME TO VISIT THEM, I DON'T WASTE A MINUTE! YOU KNOW THAT!
YES! I KNOW THAT!
--BECAUSE THAT'S HOW IT WILL ALWAYS BE!--BECAUSE THAT'S HOW IT BEGAN--AND GREW AND HARDENED--IN A STINKING CABIN IN WEBB CITY, MISSOURI!
LET'S LOOK BACK, MA!--

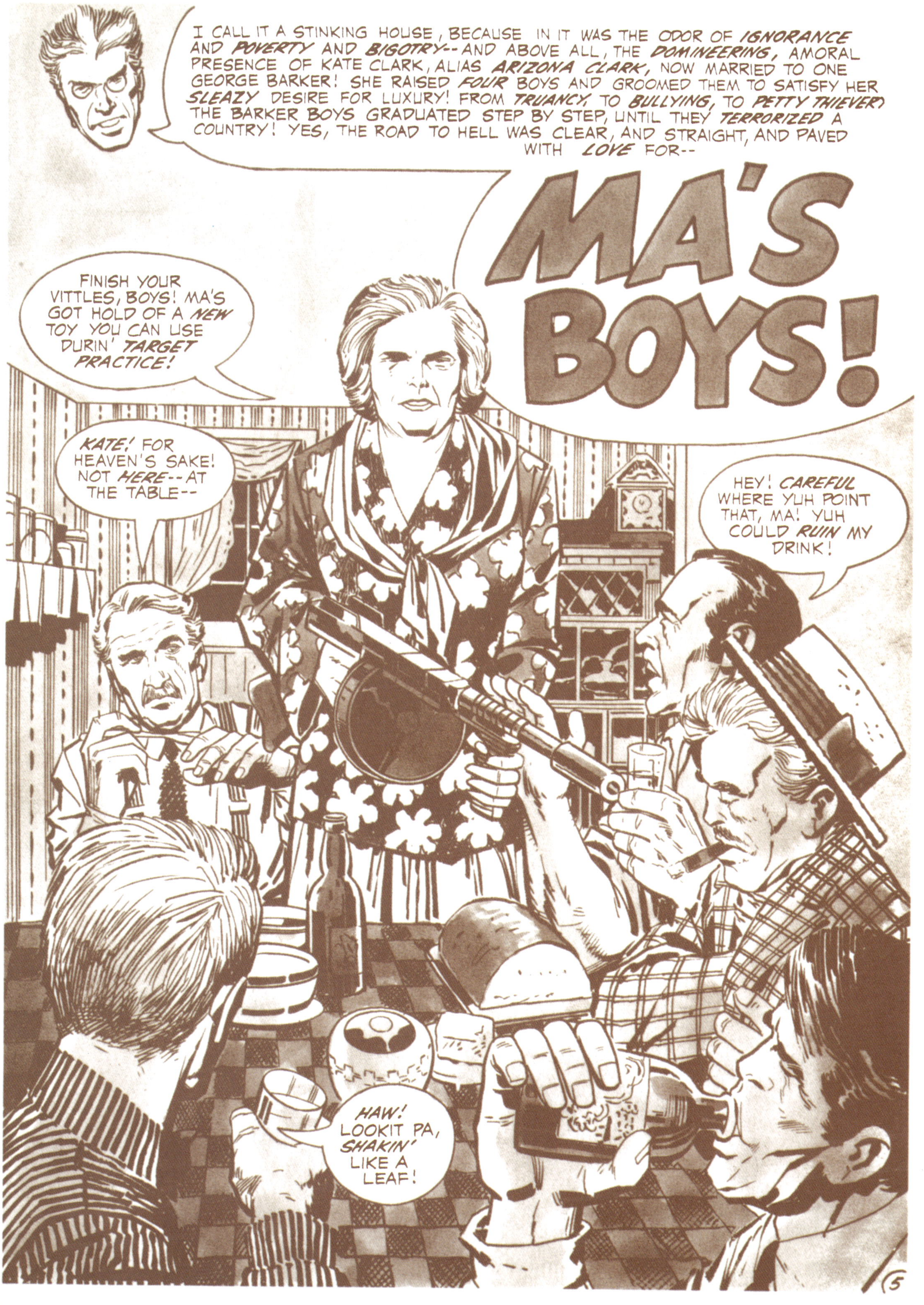
I CALL IT A STINKING HOUSE, BECAUSE IN IT WAS THE ODOR OF IGNORANCE AND POVERTY AND BIGOTRY--AND ABOVE ALL, THE DOMINEERING, AMORAL PRESENCE OF KATE CLARK, ALIAS ARIZONA CLARK, NOW MARRIED TO ONE GEORGE BARKER! SHE RAISED FOUR BOYS AND GROOMED THEM TO SATISFY HER SLEAZY DESIRE FOR LUXURY! FROM TRUANCY, TO BULLYING, TO PETTY THIEVERY THE BARKER BOYS GRADUATED STEP BY STEP, UNTIL THEY TERRORIZED A COUNTRY! YES, THE ROAD TO HELL WAS CLEAR, AND STRAIGHT, AND PAVED WITH LOVE FOR--
MA'S BOYS!
FINISH YOUR VITTLES, BOYS! MA'S GOT HOLD OF A NEW TOY YOU CAN USE DURIN' TARGET PRACTICE!
KATE! FOR HEAVEN'S SAKE! NOT HERE--AT THE TABLE--
HEY! CAREFUL WHERE YUH POINT THAT, MA! YUH COULD RUIN MY DRINK!
HAW! LOOKIT PA, SHAKIN' LIKE A LEAF!
5

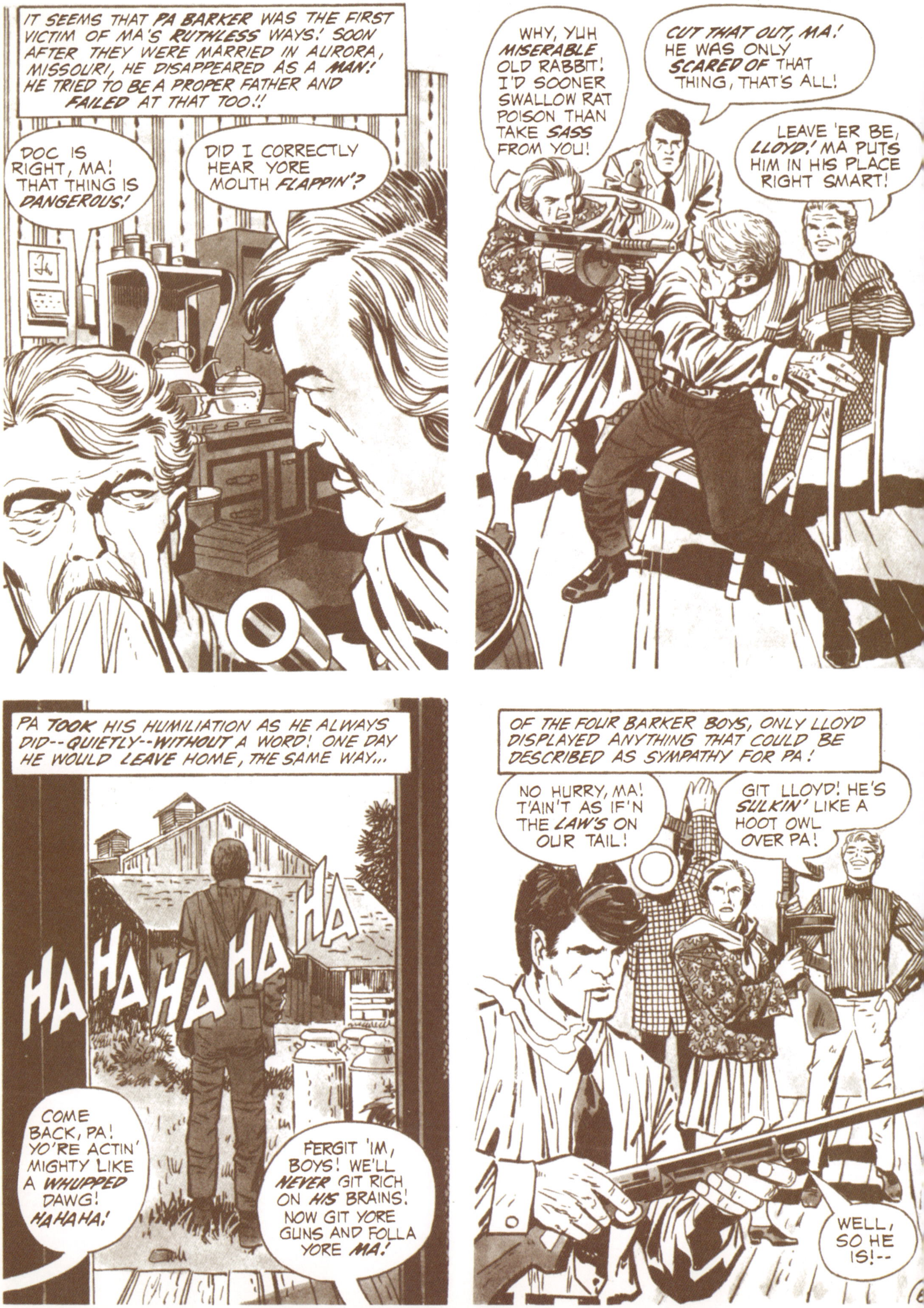
IT SEEMS THAT PA BARKER WAS THE FIRST VICTIM OF MA'S RUTHLESS WAYS! SOON AFTER THEY WERE MARRIED IN AURORA, MISSOURI, HE DISAPPEARED AS A MAN! HE TRIED TO BE A PROPER FATHER AND FAILED AT THAT TOO!!
DOC IS RIGHT, MA! THAT THING IS DANGEROUS!
DID I CORRECTLY HEAR YORE MOUTH FLAPPIN'?
WHY, YUH MISERABLE OLD RABBIT! I'D SOONER SWALLOW RAT POISON THAN TAKE SASS FROM YOU!
CUT THAT OUT, MA! HE WAS ONLY SCARED OF THAT THING, THAT'S ALL!
LEAVE 'ER BE, LLOYD! MA PUTS HIM IN HIS PLACE RIGHT SMART!
PA TOOK HIS HUMILIATION AS HE ALWAYS DID--QUIETLY--WITHOUT A WORD! ONE DAY HE WOULD LEAVE HOME, THE SAME WAY...
HA HA HA HA HA HA HA
COME BACK, PA! YO'RE ACTIN' MIGHTY LIKE A WHUPPED DAWG! HAHAHA!
FERGIT 'IM, BOYS! WE'LL NEVER GIT RICH ON HIS BRAINS! NOW GIT YORE GUNS AND FOLLA YORE MA!
OF THE FOUR BARKER BOYS, ONLY LLOYD DISPLAYED ANYTHING THAT COULD BE DESCRIBED AS SYMPATHY FOR PA!
NO HURRY, MA! T'AIN'T AS IF'N THE LAW'S ON OUR TAIL!
GIT LLOYD! HE'S SULKIN' LIKE A HOOT OWL OVER PA!
WELL, SO HE IS!--

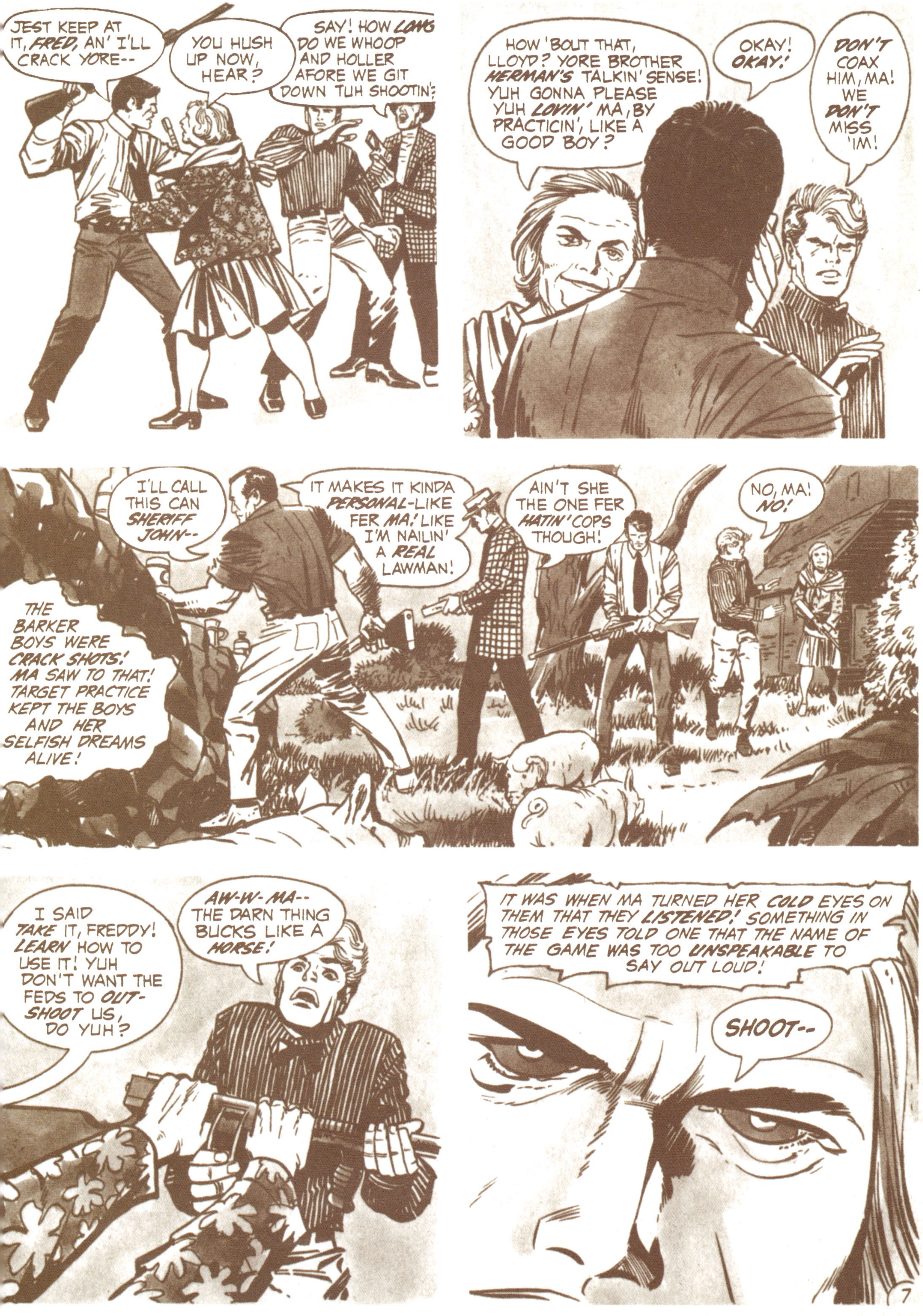
JEST KEEP AT IT, FRED, AN' I'LL CRACK YORE--
YOU HUSH UP NOW, HEAR?
SAY! HOW LONG DO WE WHOOP AND HOLLER AFORE WE GIT DOWN TUH SHOOTIN'?
HOW 'BOUT THAT, LLOYD? YORE BROTHER HERMAN'S TALKIN' SENSE! YUH GONNA PLEASE YUH LOVIN' MA, BY PRACTICIN', LIKE A GOOD BOY?
OKAY! OKAY!
DON'T COAX HIM, MA! WE DON'T MISS 'IM!
I'LL CALL THIS CAN SHERIFF JOHN--
IT MAKES IT KINDA PERSONAL-LIKE FER MA! LIKE I'M NAILIN' A REAL LAWMAN!
AIN'T SHE THE ONE FER HATIN' COPS THOUGH!
NO, MA! NO!
THE BARKER BOYS WERE CRACK SHOTS! MA SAW TO THAT! TARGET PRACTICE KEPT THE BOYS AND HER SELFISH DREAMS ALIVE!
I SAID TAKE IT, FREDDY! LEARN HOW TO USE IT! YUH DON'T WANT THE FEDS TO OUT-SHOOT US, DO YUH?
AW-W-MA-- THE DARN THING BUCKS LIKE A HORSE!
IT WAS WHEN MA TURNED HER COLD EYES ON THEM THAT THEY LISTENED! SOMETHING IN THOSE EYES TOLD ONE THAT THE NAME OF THE GAME WAS TOO UNSPEAKABLE TO SAY OUT LOUD!
SHOOT--
7

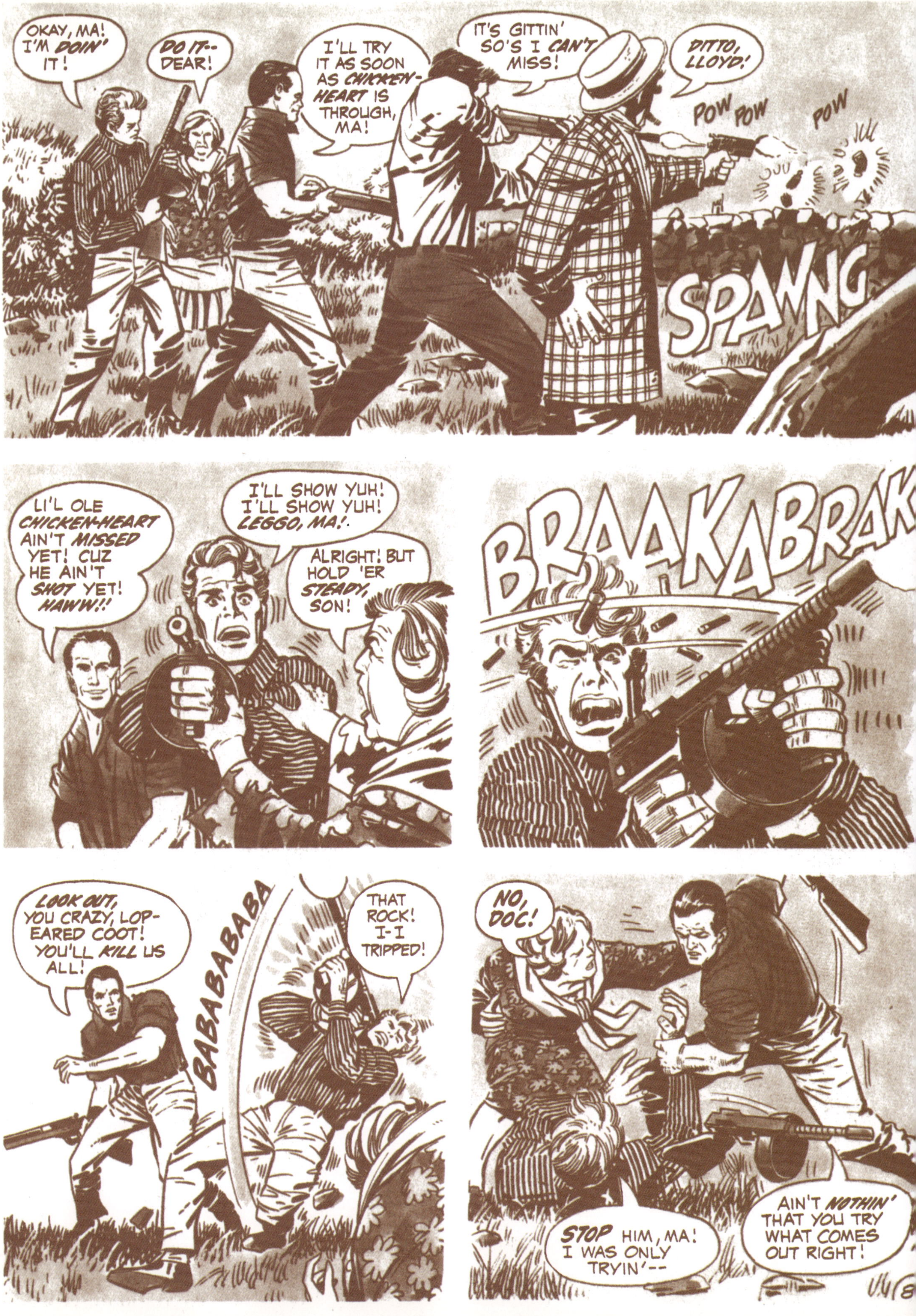
OKAY, MA! I'M DOIN' IT!
DO IT-- DEAR!
I'LL TRY IT AS SOON AS CHICKEN-HEART IS THROUGH, MA!
IT'S GITTIN' SO'S I CAN'T MISS!
DITTO, LLOYD!
POW POW
POW
SPAWNG
LI'L OLE CHICKEN-HEART AIN'T MISSED YET! CUZ HE AIN'T SHOT YET! HAWW!!
I'LL SHOW YUH! I'LL SHOW YUH! LEGGO, MA!
ALRIGHT! BUT HOLD 'ER STEADY, SON!
BRAAKABRAK
LOOK OUT, YOU CRAZY, LOP-EARED COOT! YOU'LL KILL US ALL!
BABABABABA
THAT ROCK! I-I TRIPPED!
NO, DOC!
STOP HIM, MA! I WAS ONLY TRYIN'--
AIN'T NOTHIN' THAT YOU TRY WHAT COMES OUT RIGHT!

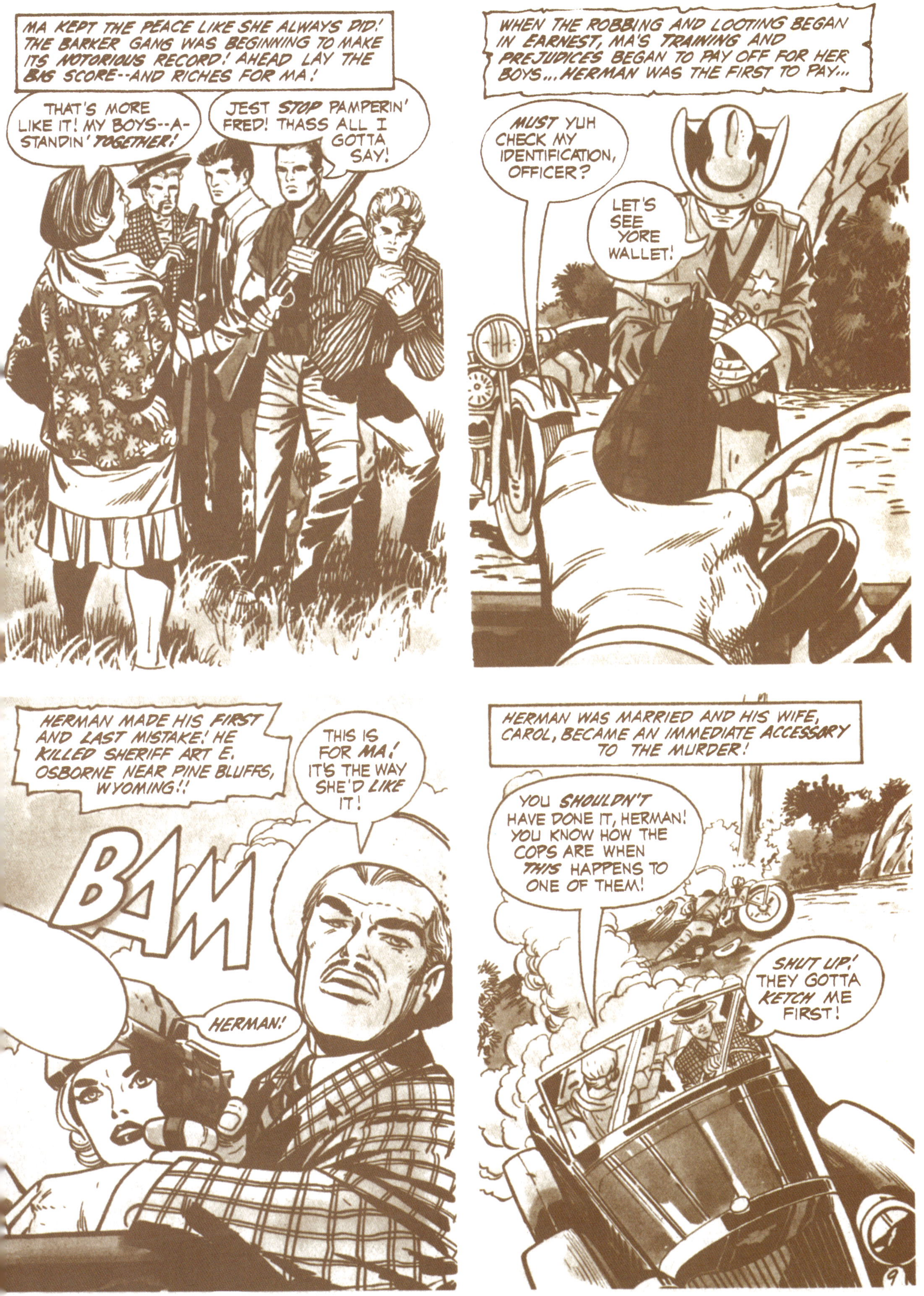

MA KEPT THE PEACE LIKE SHE ALWAYS DID! THE BARKER GANG WAS BEGINNING TO MAKE ITS NOTORIOUS RECORD! AHEAD LAY THE BIG SCORE--AND RICHES FOR MA!
THAT'S MORE LIKE IT! MY BOYS--A-STANDIN' TOGETHER!
JEST STOP PAMPERIN' FRED! THASS ALL I GOTTA SAY!
WHEN THE ROBBING AND LOOTING BEGAN IN EARNEST, MA'S TRAINING AND PREJUDICES BEGAN TO PAY OFF FOR HER BOYS... HERMAN WAS THE FIRST TO PAY...
MUST YUH CHECK MY IDENTIFICATION, OFFICER?
LET'S SEE YORE WALLET!
HERMAN MADE HIS FIRST AND LAST MISTAKE! HE KILLED SHERIFF ART E. OSBORNE NEAR PINE BLUFFS, WYOMING!!
THIS IS FOR MA! IT'S THE WAY SHE'D LIKE IT!
BAM
HERMAN!
HERMAN WAS MARRIED AND HIS WIFE, CAROL, BECAME AN IMMEDIATE ACCESSORY TO THE MURDER!
YOU SHOULDN'T HAVE DONE IT, HERMAN! YOU KNOW HOW THE COPS ARE WHEN THIS HAPPENS TO ONE OF THEM!
SHUT UP! THEY GOTTA KETCH ME FIRST!
9

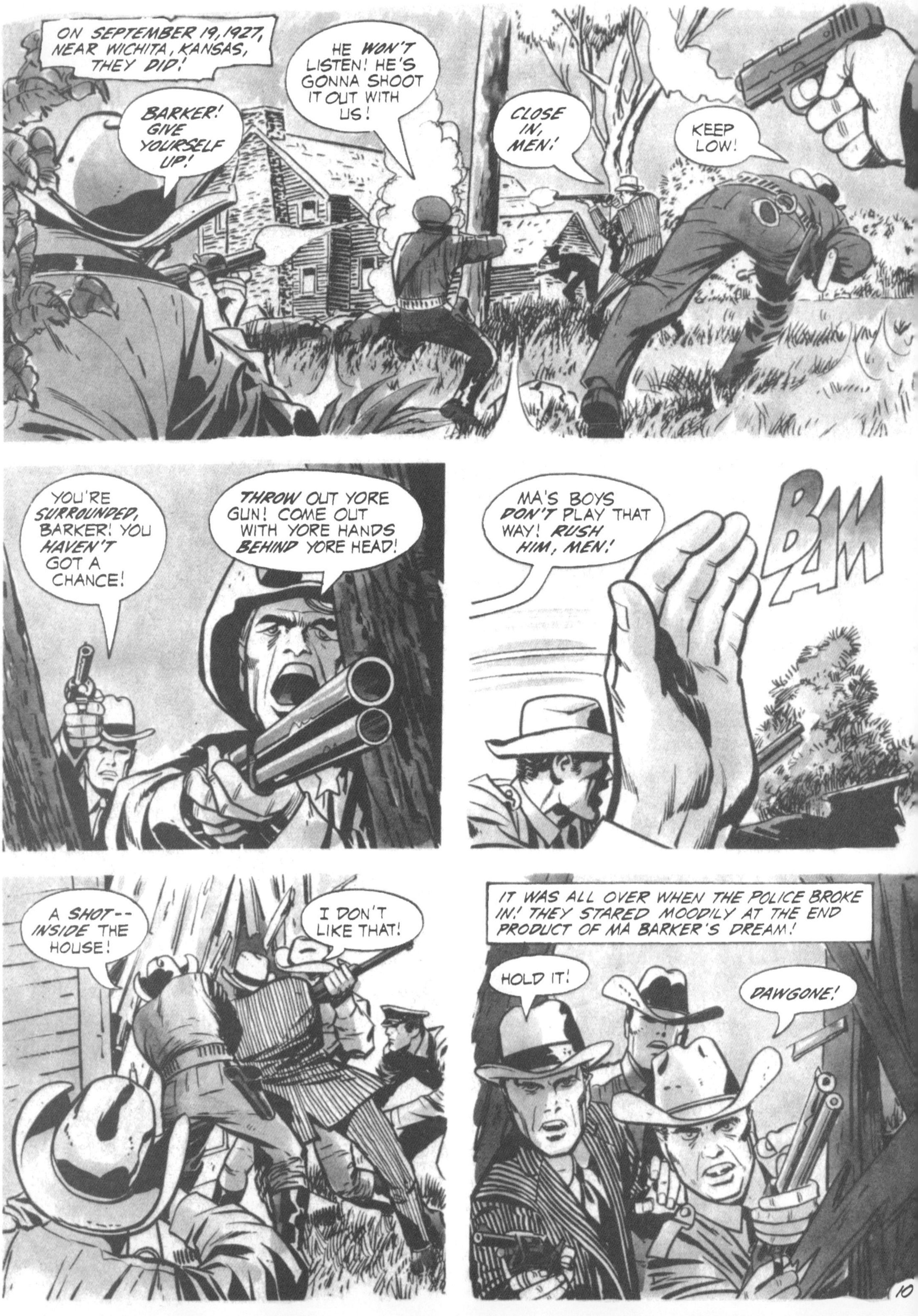
ON SEPTEMBER 19, 1927, NEAR WICHITA, KANSAS, THEY DID!
BARKER! GIVE YOURSELF UP!
HE WON'T LISTEN! HE'S GONNA SHOOT IT OUT WITH US!
CLOSE IN, MEN!
KEEP LOW!
YOU'RE SURROUNDED, BARKER! YOU HAVEN'T GOT A CHANCE!
THROW OUT YORE GUN! COME OUT WITH YORE HANDS BEHIND YORE HEAD!
MA'S BOYS DON'T PLAY THAT WAY! RUSH HIM, MEN!
BAM
A SHOT-- INSIDE THE HOUSE!
I DON'T LIKE THAT!
IT WAS ALL OVER WHEN THE POLICE BROKE IN! THEY STARED MOODILY AT THE END PRODUCT OF MA BARKER'S DREAM!
HOLD IT!
DAWGONE!

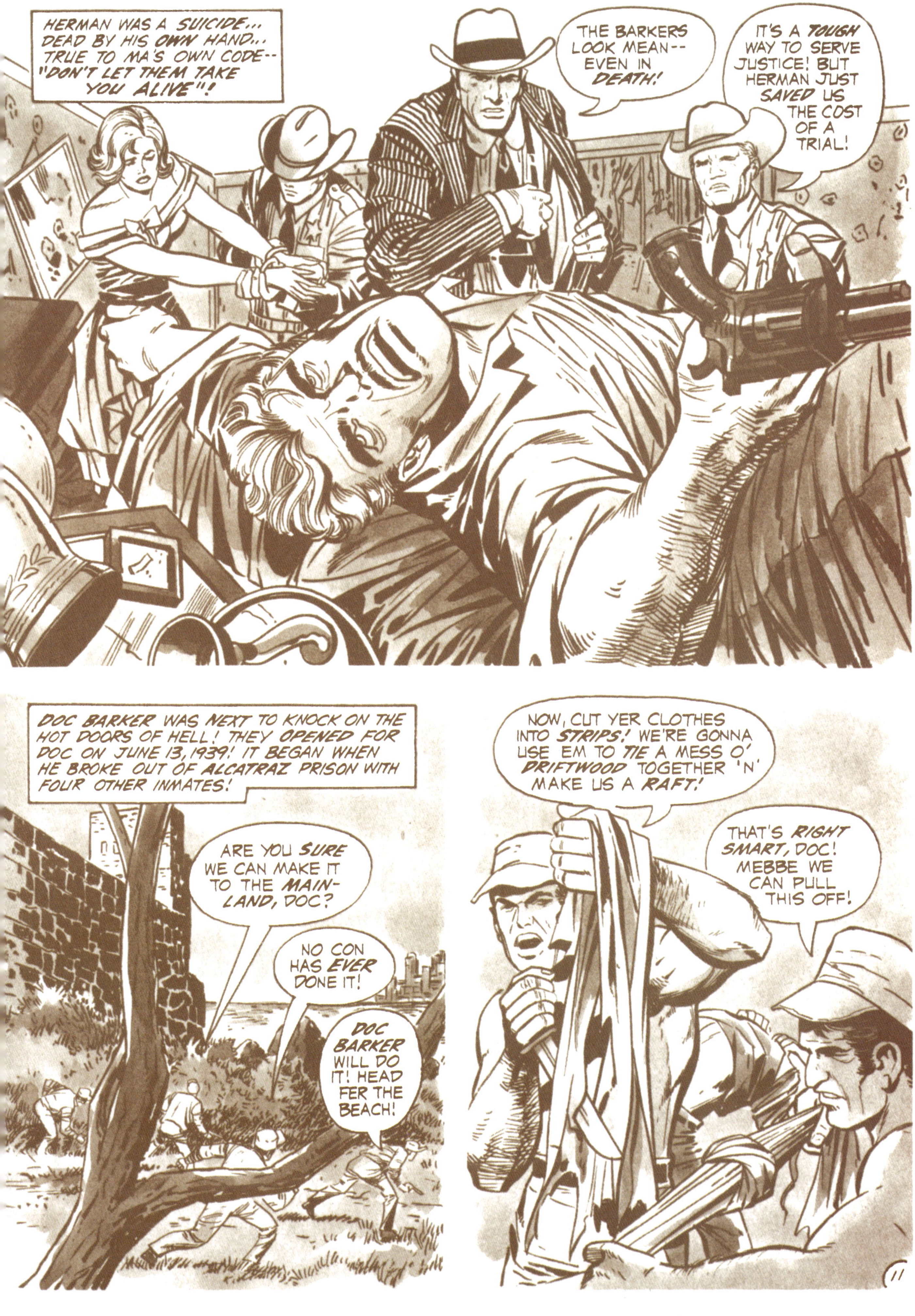

HERMAN WAS A SUICIDE... DEAD BY HIS OWN HAND... TRUE TO MA'S OWN CODE-- "DON'T LET THEM TAKE YOU ALIVE"!
THE BARKERS LOOK MEAN-- EVEN IN DEATH!
IT'S A TOUGH WAY TO SERVE JUSTICE! BUT HERMAN JUST SAVED US THE COST OF A TRIAL!
DOC BARKER WAS NEXT TO KNOCK ON THE HOT DOORS OF HELL! THEY OPENED FOR DOC ON JUNE 13, 1939! IT BEGAN WHEN HE BROKE OUT OF ALCATRAZ PRISON WITH FOUR OTHER INMATES!
ARE YOU SURE WE CAN MAKE IT TO THE MAINLAND, DOC?
NO CON HAS EVER DONE IT!
DOC BARKER WILL DO IT! HEAD FER THE BEACH!
NOW, CUT YER CLOTHES INTO STRIPS! WE'RE GONNA USE EM TO TIE A MESS O' DRIFTWOOD TOGETHER 'N' MAKE US A RAFT!
THAT'S RIGHT SMART, DOC! MEBBE WE CAN PULL THIS OFF!
11

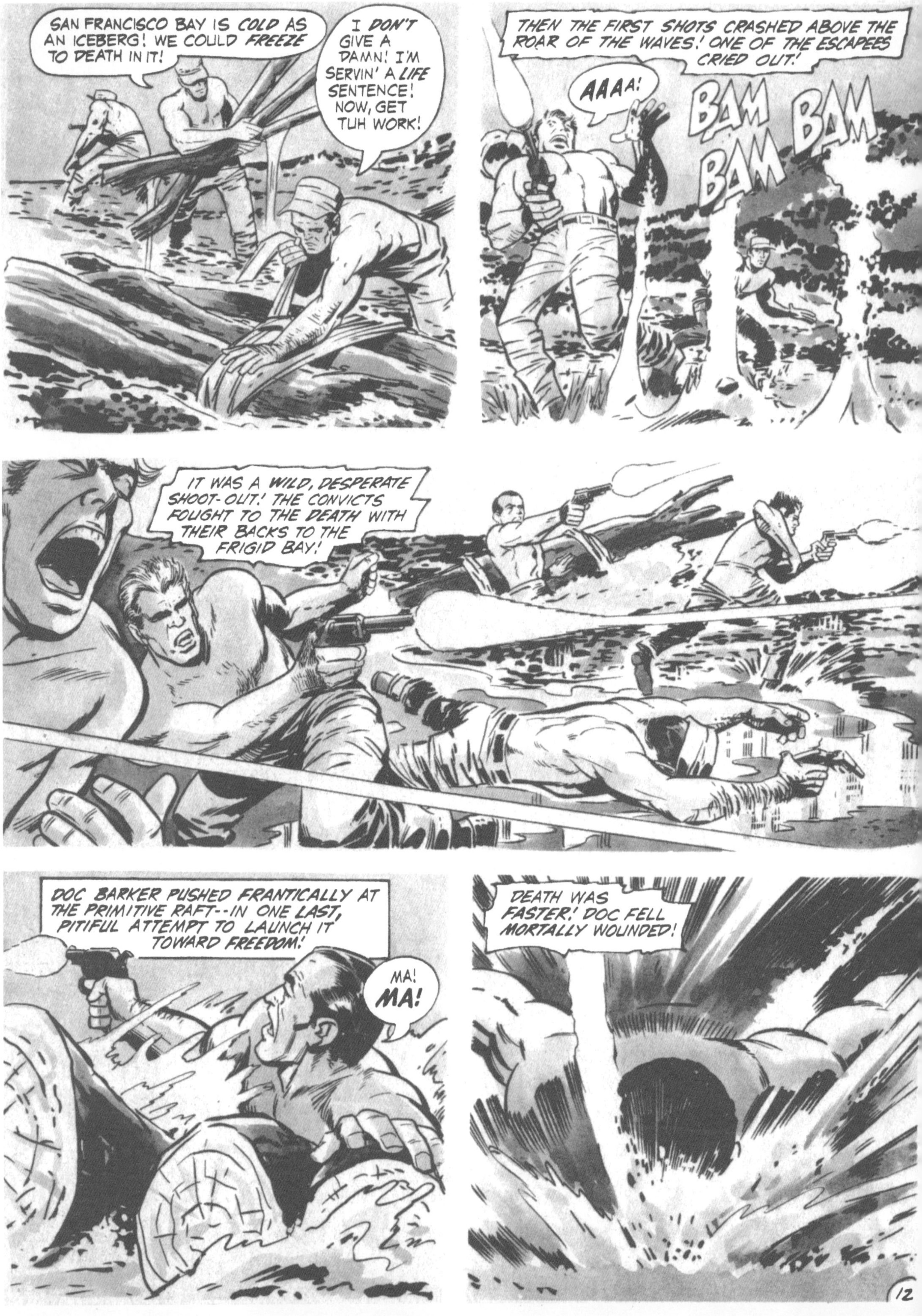
SAN FRANCISCO BAY IS COLD AS AN ICEBERG! WE COULD FREEZE TO DEATH IN IT!
I DON'T GIVE A DAMN! I'M SERVIN' A LIFE SENTENCE! NOW, GET TUH WORK!
THEN THE FIRST SHOTS CRASHED ABOVE THE ROAR OF THE WAVES! ONE OF THE ESCAPEES CRIED OUT!
AAAA!
BAM BAM BAM BAM
IT WAS A WILD, DESPERATE SHOOT-OUT! THE CONVICTS FOUGHT TO THE DEATH WITH THEIR BACKS TO THE FRIGID BAY!
DOC BARKER PUSHED FRANTICALLY AT THE PRIMITIVE RAFT--IN ONE LAST, PITIFUL ATTEMPT TO LAUNCH IT TOWARD FREEDOM!
MA! MA!
DEATH WAS FASTER! DOC FELL MORTALLY WOUNDED!

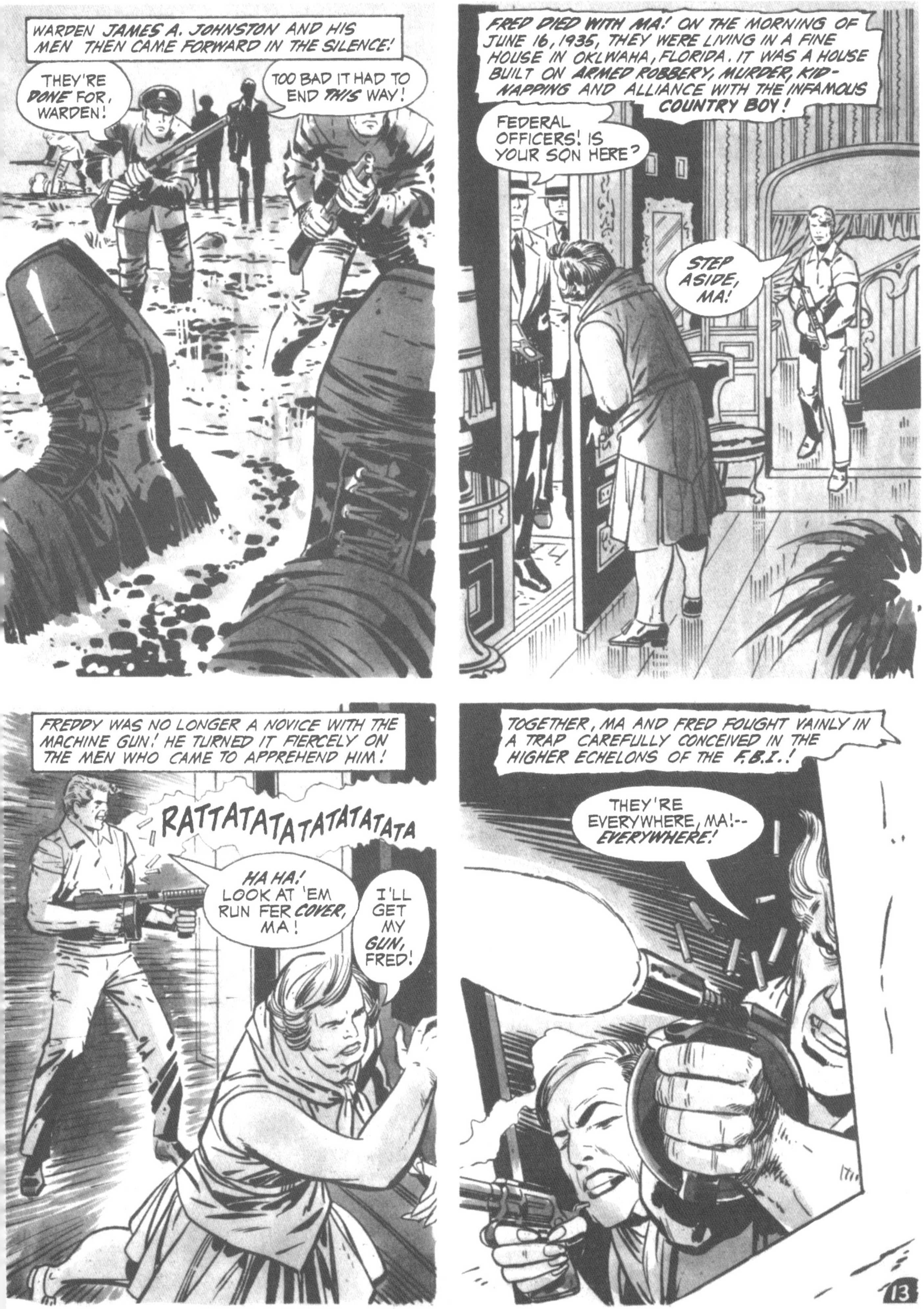
WARDEN JAMES A. JOHNSTON AND HIS MEN THEN CAME FORWARD IN THE SILENCE!
THEY'RE DONE FOR, WARDEN!
TOO BAD IT HAD TO END THIS WAY!
FRED DIED WITH MA! ON THE MORNING OF JUNE 16, 1935, THEY WERE LIVING IN A FINE HOUSE IN OKLWAHA, FLORIDA. IT WAS A HOUSE BUILT ON ARMED ROBBERY, MURDER, KID-NAPPING AND ALLIANCE WITH THE INFAMOUS COUNTRY BOY!
FEDERAL OFFICERS! IS YOUR SON HERE?
STEP ASIDE, MA!
FREDDY WAS NO LONGER A NOVICE WITH THE MACHINE GUN! HE TURNED IT FIERCELY ON THE MEN WHO CAME TO APPREHEND HIM!
RATTATATATATATATATATA
HA HA! LOOK AT 'EM RUN FER COVER, MA!
I'LL GET MY GUN, FRED!
TOGETHER, MA AND FRED FOUGHT VAINLY IN A TRAP CAREFULLY CONCEIVED IN THE HIGHER ECHELONS OF THE F.B.I.!
THEY'RE EVERYWHERE, MA!-- EVERYWHERE!
13

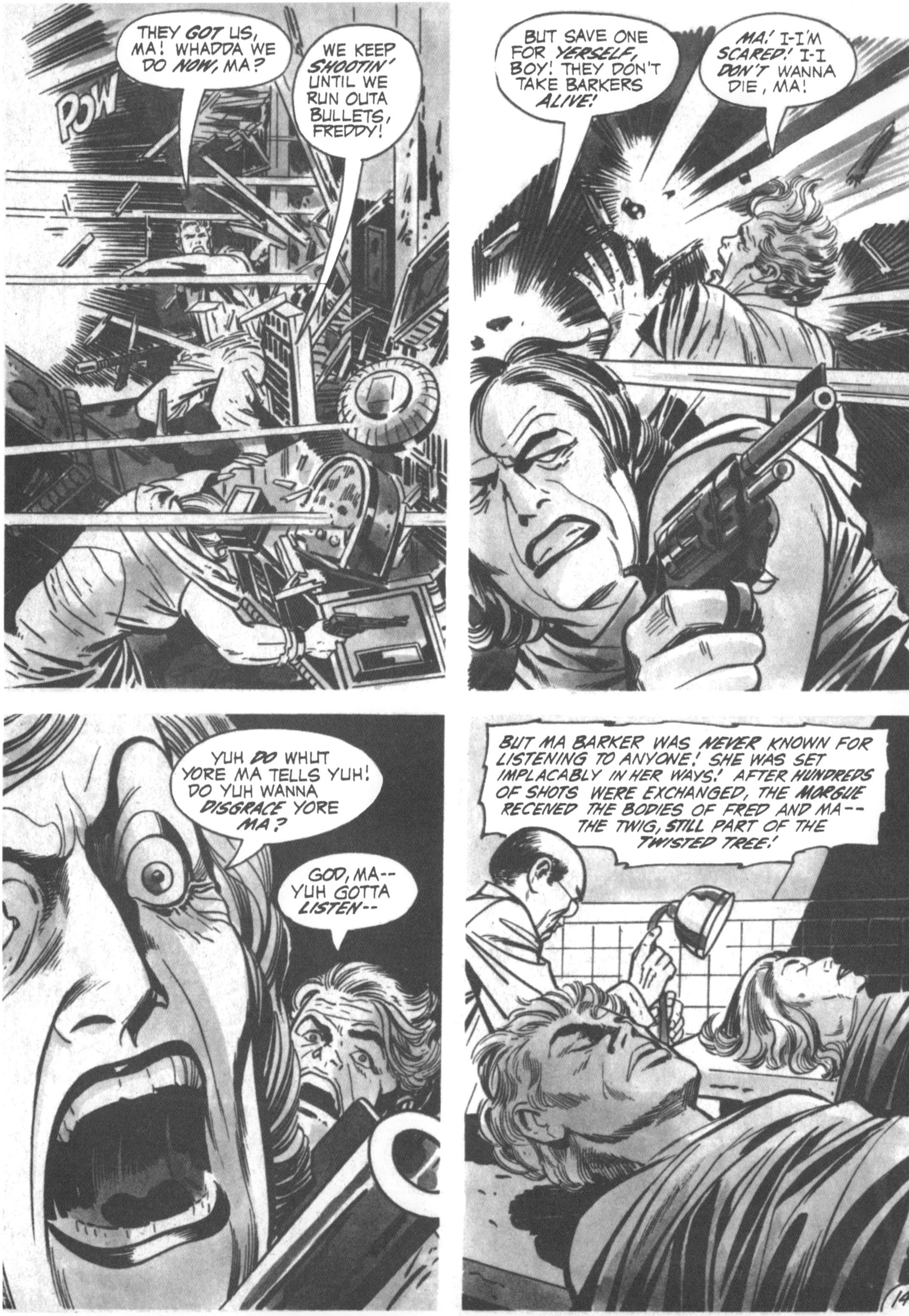
POW
THEY GOT US, MA! WHADDA WE DO NOW, MA?
WE KEEP SHOOTIN' UNTIL WE RUN OUTA BULLETS, FREDDY!
BUT SAVE ONE FOR YERSELF, BOY! THEY DON'T TAKE BARKERS ALIVE!
MA! I-I'M SCARED! I-I DON'T WANNA DIE, MA!
YUH DO WHUT YORE MA TELLS YUH! DO YUH WANNA DISGRACE YORE MA?
GOD, MA-- YUH GOTTA LISTEN--
BUT MA BARKER WAS NEVER KNOWN FOR LISTENING TO ANYONE! SHE WAS SET IMPLACABLY IN HER WAYS! AFTER HUNDREDS OF SHOTS WERE EXCHANGED, THE MORGUE RECEIVED THE BODIES OF FRED AND MA-- THE TWIG, STILL PART OF THE TWISTED TREE!

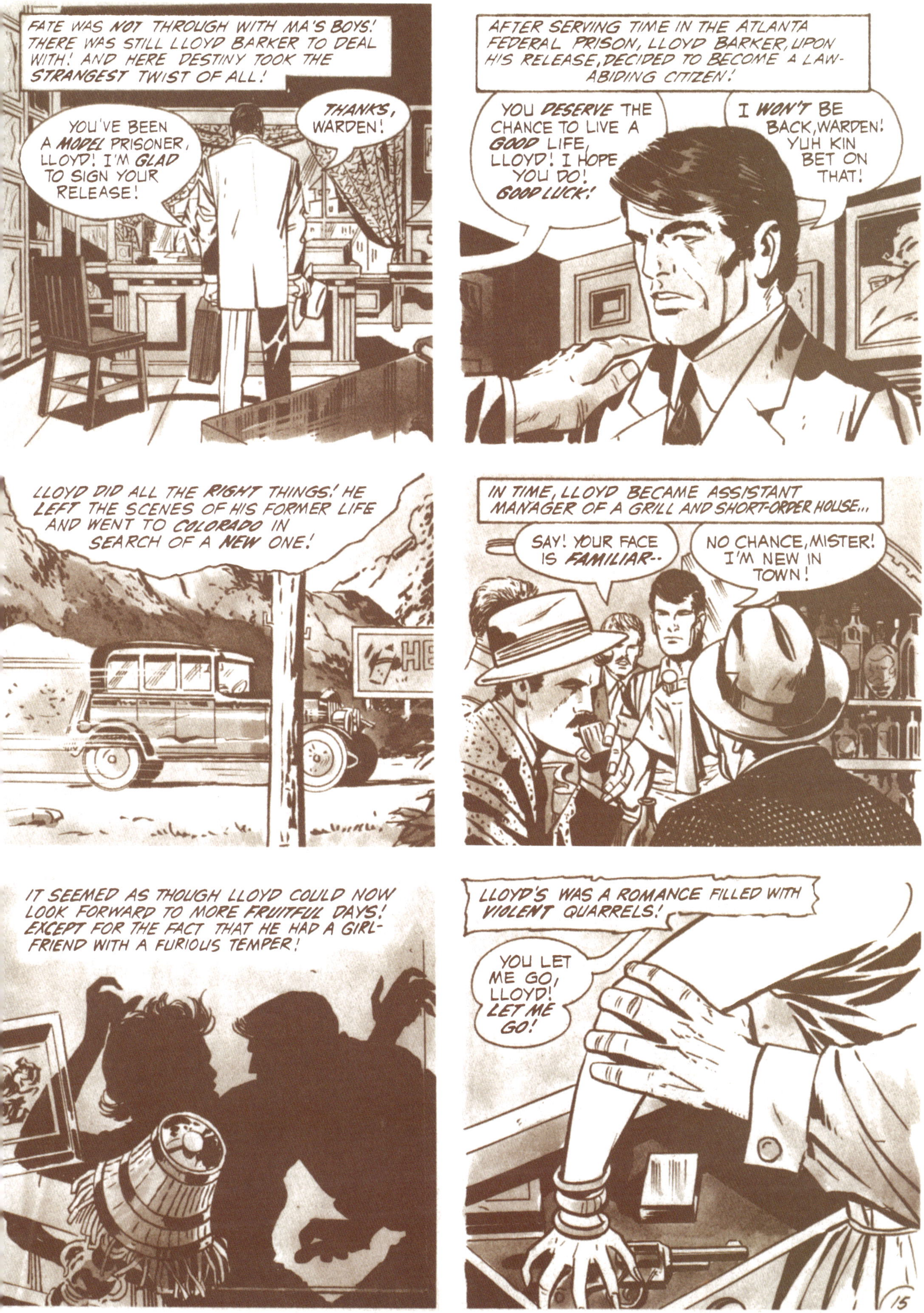
FATE WAS NOT THROUGH WITH MA'S BOYS! THERE WAS STILL LLOYD BARKER TO DEAL WITH! AND HERE DESTINY TOOK THE STRANGEST TWIST OF ALL!
YOU'VE BEEN A MODEL PRISONER, LLOYD! I'M GLAD TO SIGN YOUR RELEASE!
THANKS, WARDEN!
AFTER SERVING TIME IN THE ATLANTA FEDERAL PRISON, LLOYD BARKER, UPON HIS RELEASE, DECIDED TO BECOME A LAW-ABIDING CITIZEN!
YOU DESERVE THE CHANCE TO LIVE A GOOD LIFE, LLOYD! I HOPE YOU DO! GOOD LUCK!
I WON'T BE BACK, WARDEN! YUH KIN BET ON THAT!
LLOYD DID ALL THE RIGHT THINGS! HE LEFT THE SCENES OF HIS FORMER LIFE AND WENT TO COLORADO IN SEARCH OF A NEW ONE!
IN TIME, LLOYD BECAME ASSISTANT MANAGER OF A GRILL AND SHORT-ORDER HOUSE...
SAY! YOUR FACE IS FAMILIAR--
NO CHANCE, MISTER! I'M NEW IN TOWN!
IT SEEMED AS THOUGH LLOYD COULD NOW LOOK FORWARD TO MORE FRUITFUL DAYS! EXCEPT FOR THE FACT THAT HE HAD A GIRL-FRIEND WITH A FURIOUS TEMPER!
LLOYD'S WAS A ROMANCE FILLED WITH VIOLENT QUARRELS!
YOU LET ME GO, LLOYD! LET ME GO!

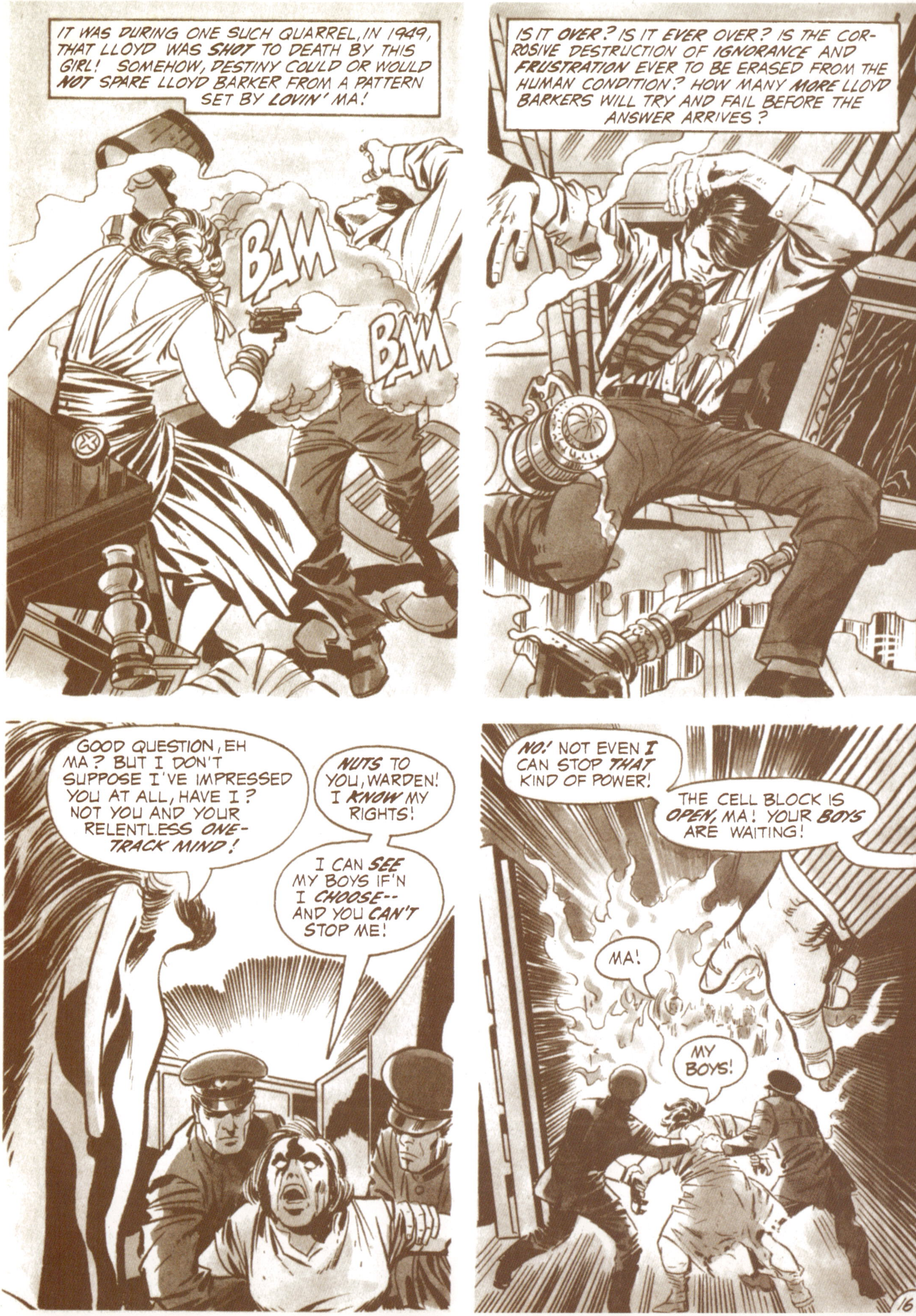
IT WAS DURING ONE SUCH QUARREL, IN 1949, THAT LLOYD WAS SHOT TO DEATH BY THIS GIRL! SOMEHOW, DESTINY COULD OR WOULD NOT SPARE LLOYD BARKER FROM A PATTERN SET BY LOVIN' MA!
BAM
BAM
IS IT OVER? IS IT EVER OVER? IS THE CORROSIVE DESTRUCTION OF IGNORANCE AND FRUSTRATION EVER TO BE ERASED FROM THE HUMAN CONDITION? HOW MANY MORE LLOYD BARKERS WILL TRY AND FAIL BEFORE THE ANSWER ARRIVES?
GOOD QUESTION, EH MA? BUT I DON'T SUPPOSE I'VE IMPRESSED YOU AT ALL, HAVE I? NOT YOU AND YOUR RELENTLESS ONE-TRACK MIND!
NUTS TO YOU, WARDEN! I KNOW MY RIGHTS!
I CAN SEE MY BOYS IF'N I CHOOSE-- AND YOU CAN'T STOP ME!
NO! NOT EVEN I CAN STOP THAT KIND OF POWER!
THE CELL BLOCK IS OPEN, MA! YOUR BOYS ARE WAITING!
MA!
MY BOYS!

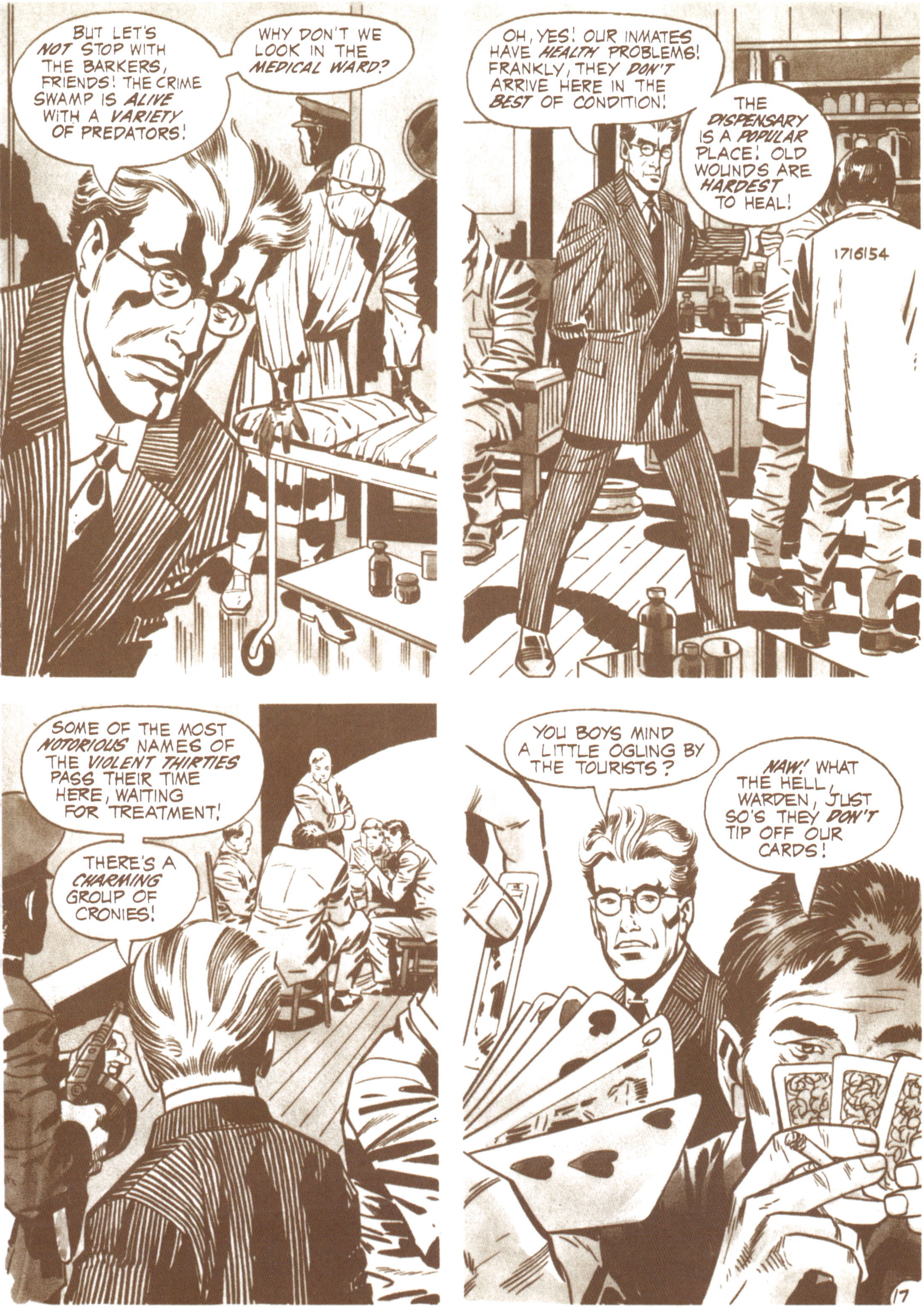
BUT LET'S NOT STOP WITH THE BARKERS, FRIENDS! THE CRIME SWAMP IS ALIVE WITH A VARIETY OF PREDATORS!
WHY DON'T WE LOOK IN THE MEDICAL WARD?
OH, YES! OUR INMATES HAVE HEALTH PROBLEMS! FRANKLY, THEY DON'T ARRIVE HERE IN THE BEST OF CONDITION!
THE DISPENSARY IS A POPULAR PLACE! OLD WOUNDS ARE HARDEST TO HEAL!
1716154
SOME OF THE MOST NOTORIOUS NAMES OF THE VIOLENT THIRTIES PASS THEIR TIME HERE, WAITING FOR TREATMENT!
THERE'S A CHARMING GROUP OF CRONIES!
YOU BOYS MIND A LITTLE OGLING BY THE TOURISTS?
NAW! WHAT THE HELL, WARDEN, JUST SO'S THEY DON'T TIP OFF OUR CARDS!

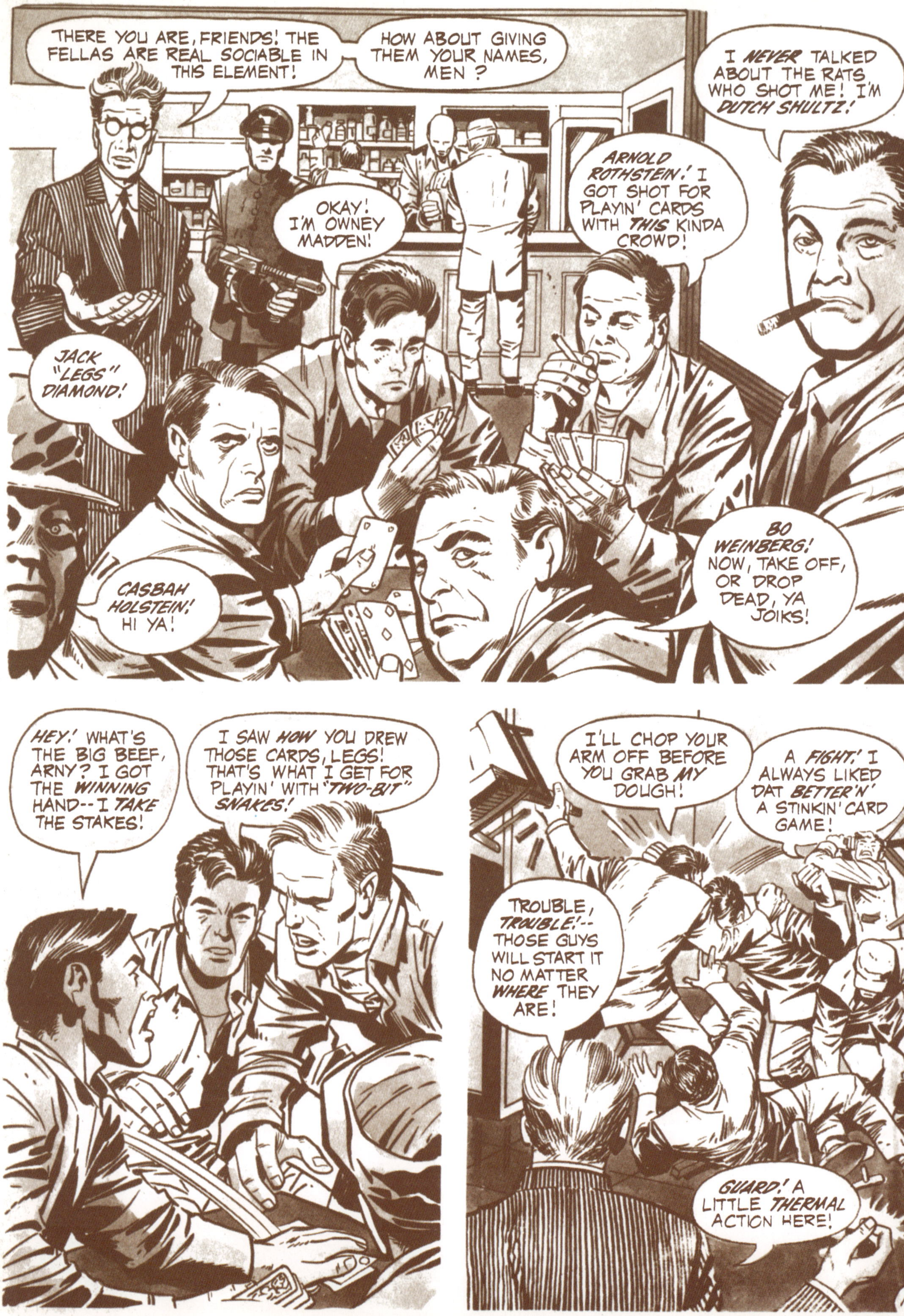
THERE YOU ARE, FRIENDS! THE FELLAS ARE REAL SOCIABLE IN THIS ELEMENT!
HOW ABOUT GIVING THEM YOUR NAMES, MEN ?
I *NEVER* TALKED ABOUT THE RATS WHO SHOT ME! I'M *DUTCH SHULTZ!*
OKAY! I'M OWNEY MADDEN!
*ARNOLD ROTHSTEIN!* I GOT SHOT FOR PLAYIN' CARDS WITH *THIS* KINDA CROWD!
*JACK "LEGS" DIAMOND!*
*CASBAH HOLSTEIN!* HI YA!
*BO WEINBERG!* NOW, TAKE OFF, OR DROP DEAD, YA JOIKS!
*HEY!* WHAT'S THE BIG BEEF, ARNY? I GOT THE *WINNING* HAND--I *TAKE* THE STAKES!
I SAW *HOW* YOU DREW THOSE CARDS, LEGS! THAT'S WHAT I GET FOR PLAYIN' WITH *"TWO-BIT" SNAKES!*
I'LL CHOP YOUR ARM OFF BEFORE YOU GRAB *MY* DOUGH!
A *FIGHT!* I ALWAYS LIKED DAT *BETTER'N'* A STINKIN' CARD GAME!
TROUBLE, *TROUBLE!*-- THOSE GUYS WILL START IT NO MATTER *WHERE* THEY ARE!
*GUARD!* A LITTLE *THERMAL* ACTION HERE!

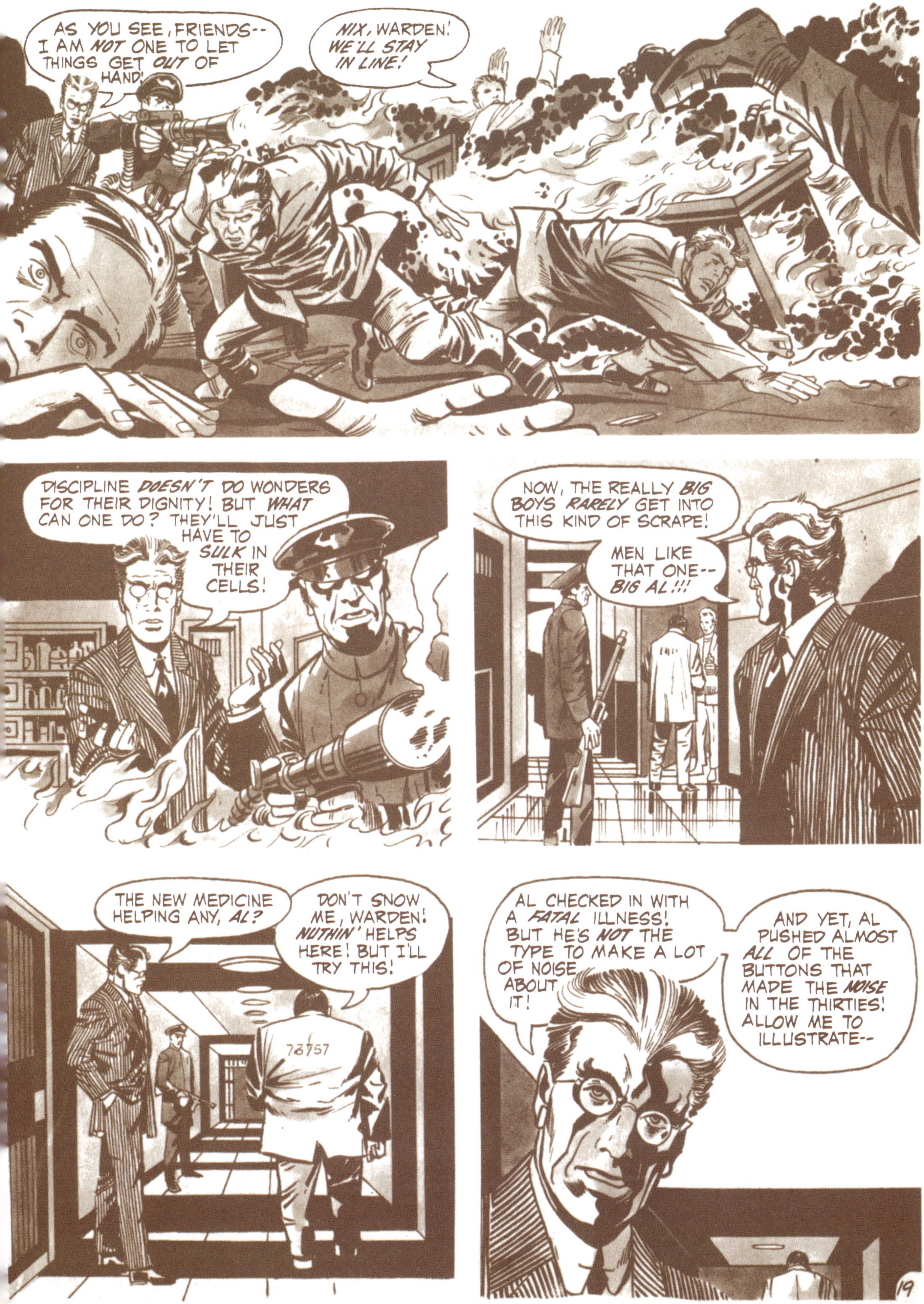
AS YOU SEE, FRIENDS-- I AM NOT ONE TO LET THINGS GET OUT OF HAND!
NIX, WARDEN! WE'LL STAY IN LINE!
DISCIPLINE DOESN'T DO WONDERS FOR THEIR DIGNITY! BUT WHAT CAN ONE DO? THEY'LL JUST HAVE TO SULK IN THEIR CELLS!
NOW, THE REALLY BIG BOYS RARELY GET INTO THIS KIND OF SCRAPE!
MEN LIKE THAT ONE-- BIG AL!!!
THE NEW MEDICINE HELPING ANY, AL?
DON'T SNOW ME, WARDEN! NUTHIN' HELPS HERE! BUT I'LL TRY THIS!
73757
AL CHECKED IN WITH A FATAL ILLNESS! BUT HE'S NOT THE TYPE TO MAKE A LOT OF NOISE ABOUT IT!
AND YET, AL PUSHED ALMOST ALL OF THE BUTTONS THAT MADE THE NOISE IN THE THIRTIES! ALLOW ME TO ILLUSTRATE--
19

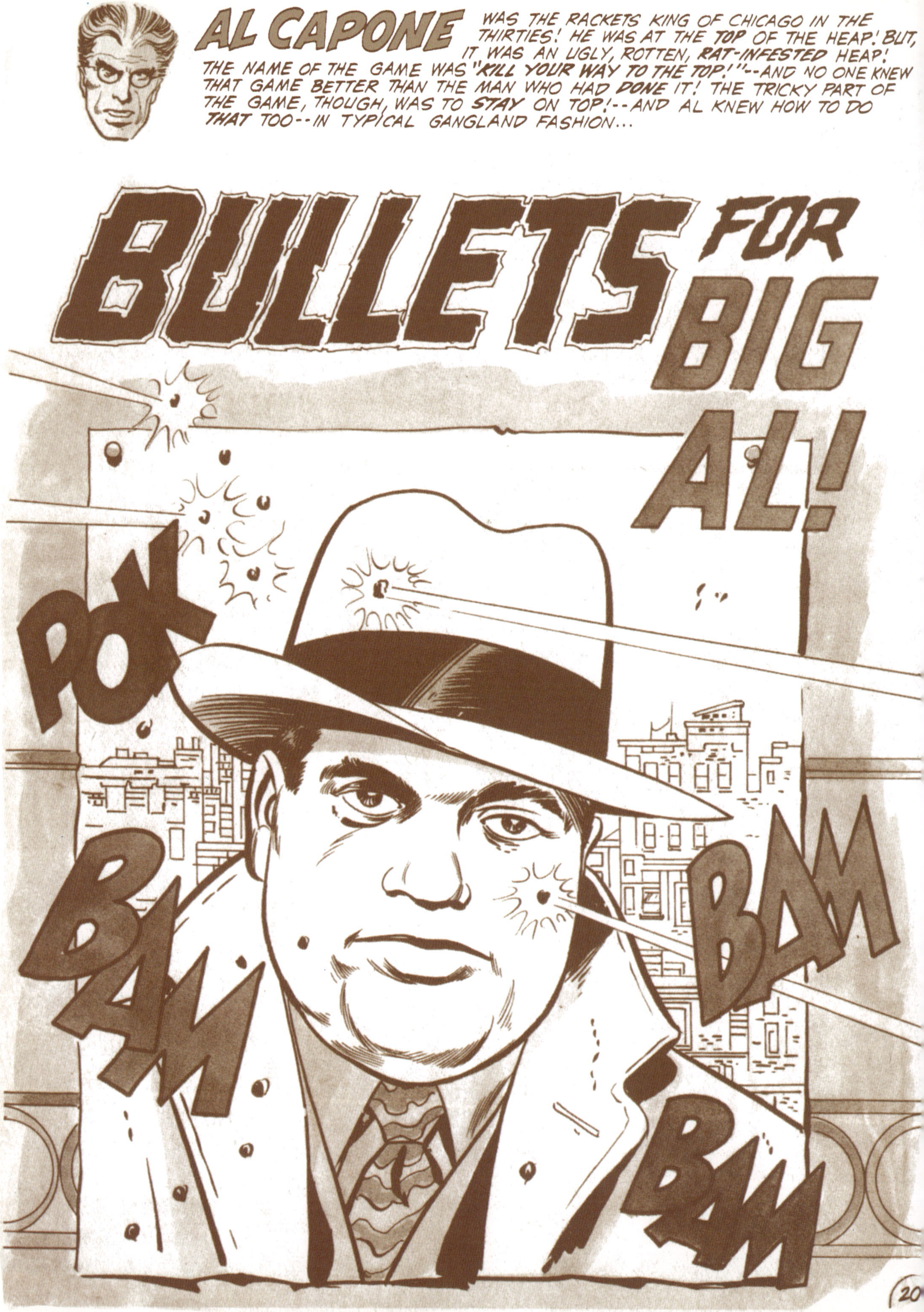
AL CAPONE WAS THE RACKETS KING OF CHICAGO IN THE THIRTIES! HE WAS AT THE TOP OF THE HEAP! BUT, IT WAS AN UGLY, ROTTEN, RAT-INFESTED HEAP! THE NAME OF THE GAME WAS "KILL YOUR WAY TO THE TOP!"--AND NO ONE KNEW THAT GAME BETTER THAN THE MAN WHO HAD DONE IT! THE TRICKY PART OF THE GAME, THOUGH, WAS TO STAY ON TOP!--AND AL KNEW HOW TO DO THAT TOO--IN TYPICAL GANGLAND FASHION...
BULLETS FOR BIG AL!
POK
BAM
BAM
BAM
BAM
BAM

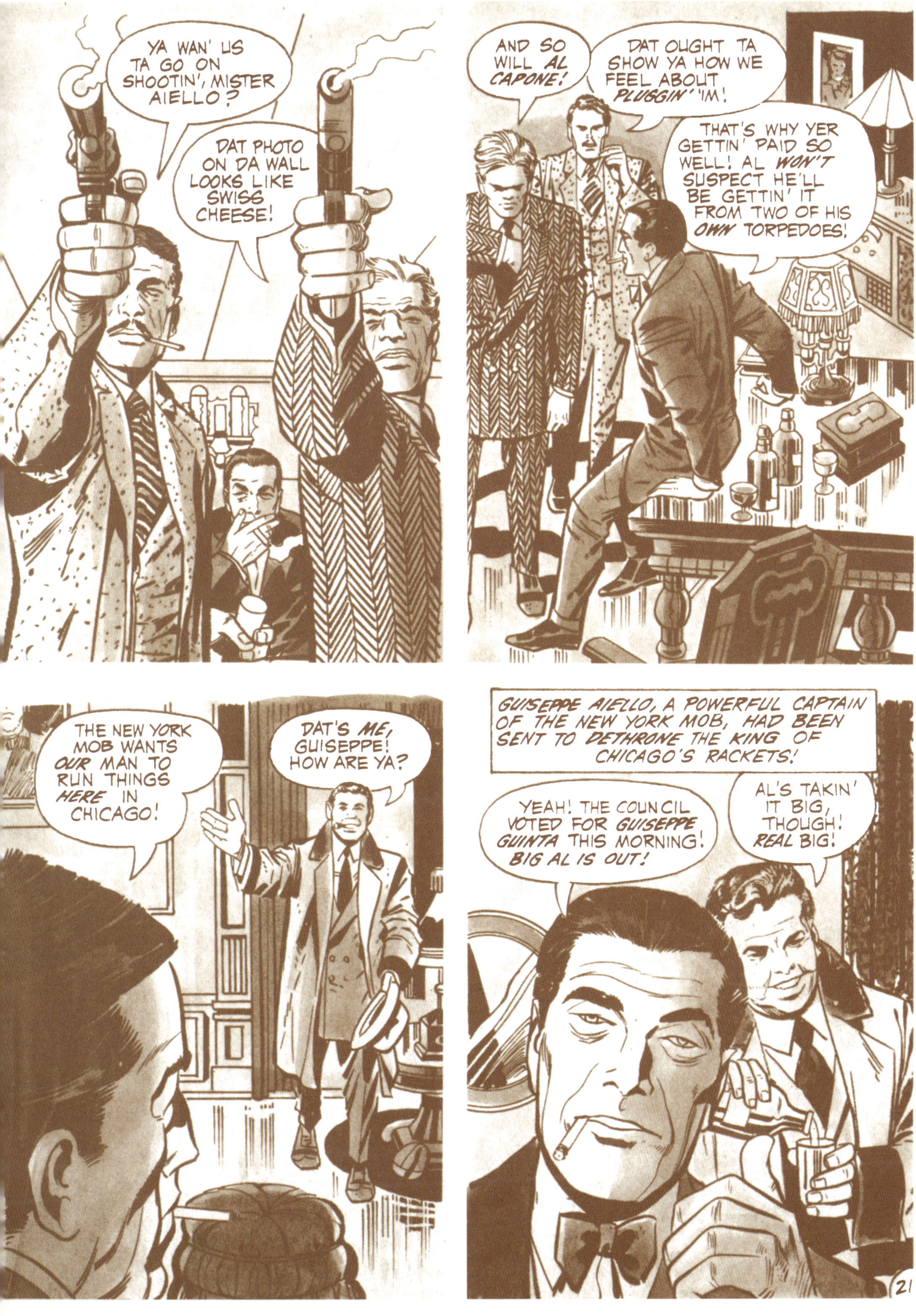
YA WAN' US TA GO ON SHOOTIN', MISTER AIELLO?
DAT PHOTO ON DA WALL LOOKS LIKE SWISS CHEESE!
AND SO WILL AL CAPONE!
DAT OUGHT TA SHOW YA HOW WE FEEL ABOUT PLUGGIN' 'IM!
THAT'S WHY YER GETTIN' PAID SO WELL! AL WON'T SUSPECT HE'LL BE GETTIN' IT FROM TWO OF HIS OWN TORPEDOES!
THE NEW YORK MOB WANTS OUR MAN TO RUN THINGS HERE IN CHICAGO!
DAT'S ME, GUISEPPE! HOW ARE YA?
GUISEPPE AIELLO, A POWERFUL CAPTAIN OF THE NEW YORK MOB, HAD BEEN SENT TO DETHRONE THE KING OF CHICAGO'S RACKETS!
YEAH! THE COUNCIL VOTED FOR GUISEPPE GUINTA THIS MORNING! BIG AL IS OUT!
AL'S TAKIN' IT BIG, THOUGH! REAL BIG!

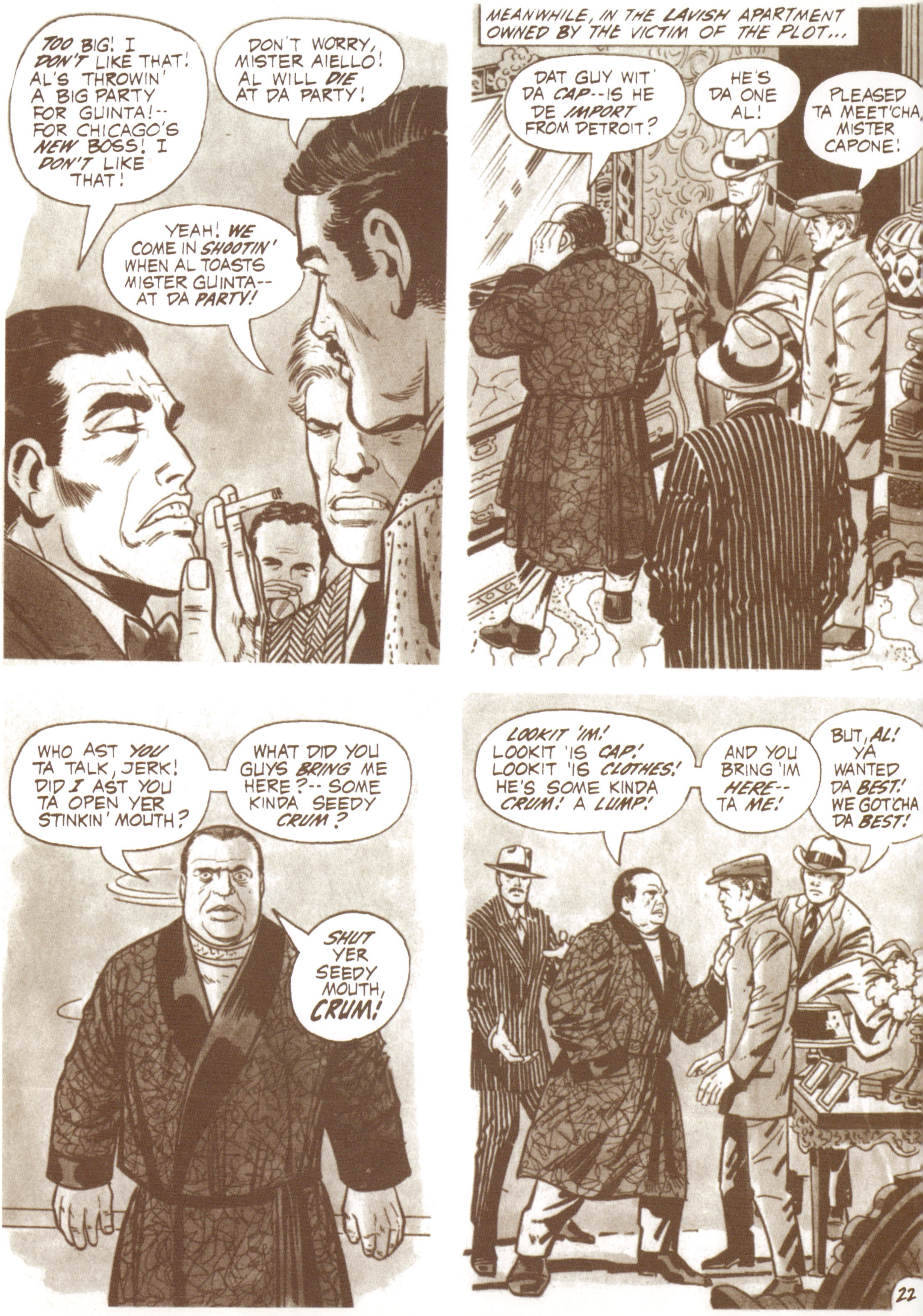
TOO BIG! I DON'T LIKE THAT! AL'S THROWIN' A BIG PARTY FOR GUINTA!-- FOR CHICAGO'S NEW BOSS! I DON'T LIKE THAT!
DON'T WORRY, MISTER AIELLO! AL WILL DIE AT DA PARTY!
YEAH! WE COME IN SHOOTIN' WHEN AL TOASTS MISTER GUINTA-- AT DA PARTY!
MEANWHILE, IN THE LAVISH APARTMENT OWNED BY THE VICTIM OF THE PLOT...
DAT GUY WIT' DA CAP--IS HE DE IMPORT FROM DETROIT?
HE'S DA ONE AL!
PLEASED TA MEET'CHA MISTER CAPONE!
WHO AST YOU TA TALK, JERK! DID I AST YOU TA OPEN YER STINKIN' MOUTH?
WHAT DID YOU GUYS BRING ME HERE?-- SOME KINDA SEEDY CRUM?
SHUT YER SEEDY MOUTH, CRUM!
LOOKIT 'IM! LOOKIT 'IS CAP! LOOKIT 'IS CLOTHES! HE'S SOME KINDA CRUM! A LUMP!
AND YOU BRING 'IM HERE-- TA ME!
BUT, AL! YA WANTED DA BEST! WE GOT'CHA DA BEST!

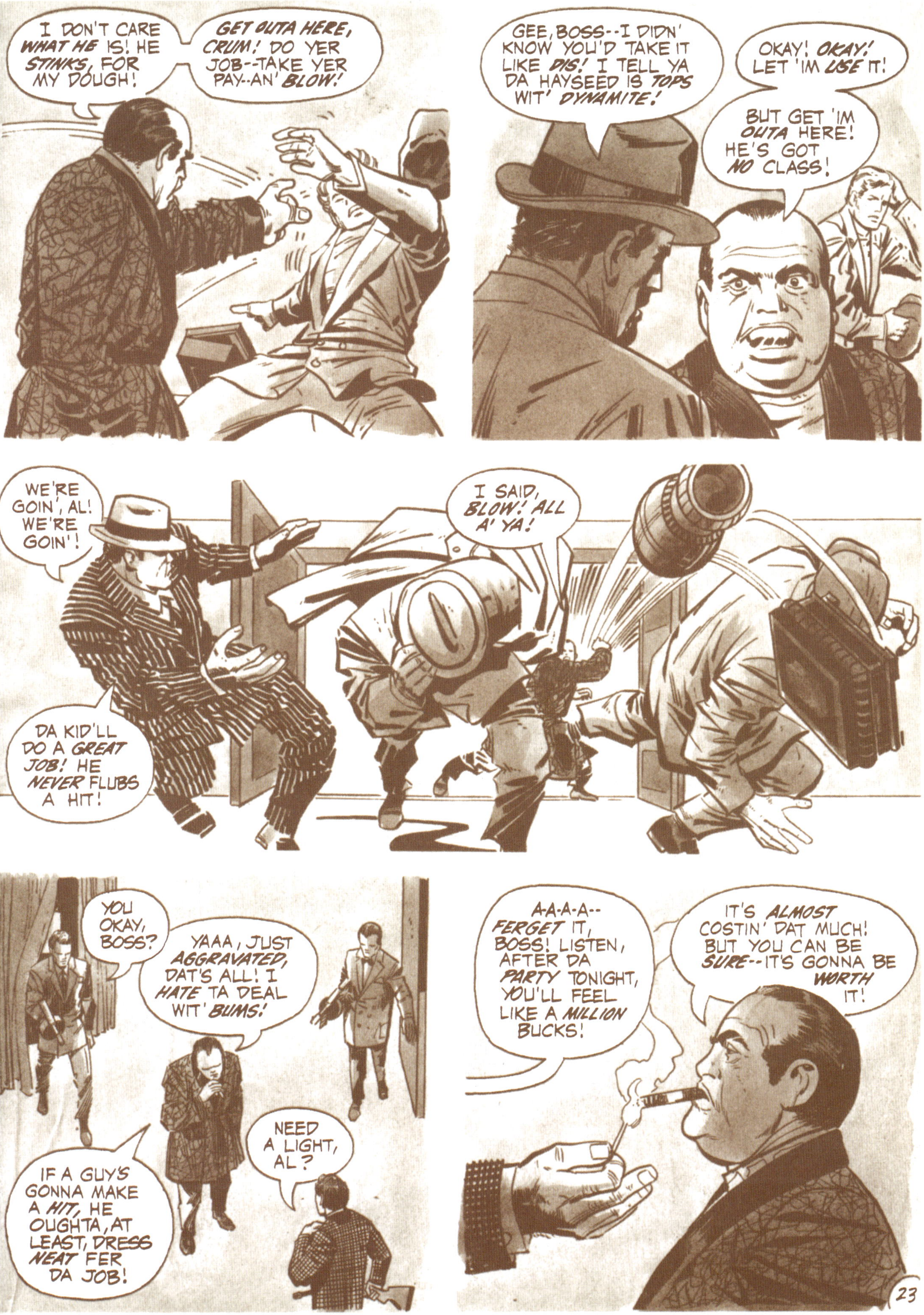
I DON'T CARE WHAT HE IS! HE STINKS, FOR MY DOUGH!
GET OUTA HERE, CRUM! DO YER JOB--TAKE YER PAY--AN' BLOW!
GEE, BOSS--I DIDN' KNOW YOU'D TAKE IT LIKE DIS! I TELL YA DA HAYSEED IS TOPS WIT' DYNAMITE!
OKAY! OKAY! LET 'IM USE IT!
BUT GET 'IM OUTA HERE! HE'S GOT NO CLASS!
WE'RE GOIN', AL! WE'RE GOIN'!
DA KID'LL DO A GREAT JOB! HE NEVER FLUBS A HIT!
I SAID, BLOW! ALL A' YA!
YOU OKAY, BOSS?
YAAA, JUST AGGRAVATED, DAT'S ALL! I HATE TA DEAL WIT' BUMS!
IF A GUY'S GONNA MAKE A HIT, HE OUGHTA, AT LEAST, DRESS NEAT FER DA JOB!
NEED A LIGHT, AL?
A-A-A-A-- FERGET IT, BOSS! LISTEN, AFTER DA PARTY TONIGHT, YOU'LL FEEL LIKE A MILLION BUCKS!
IT'S ALMOST COSTIN' DAT MUCH! BUT YOU CAN BE SURE--IT'S GONNA BE WORTH IT!

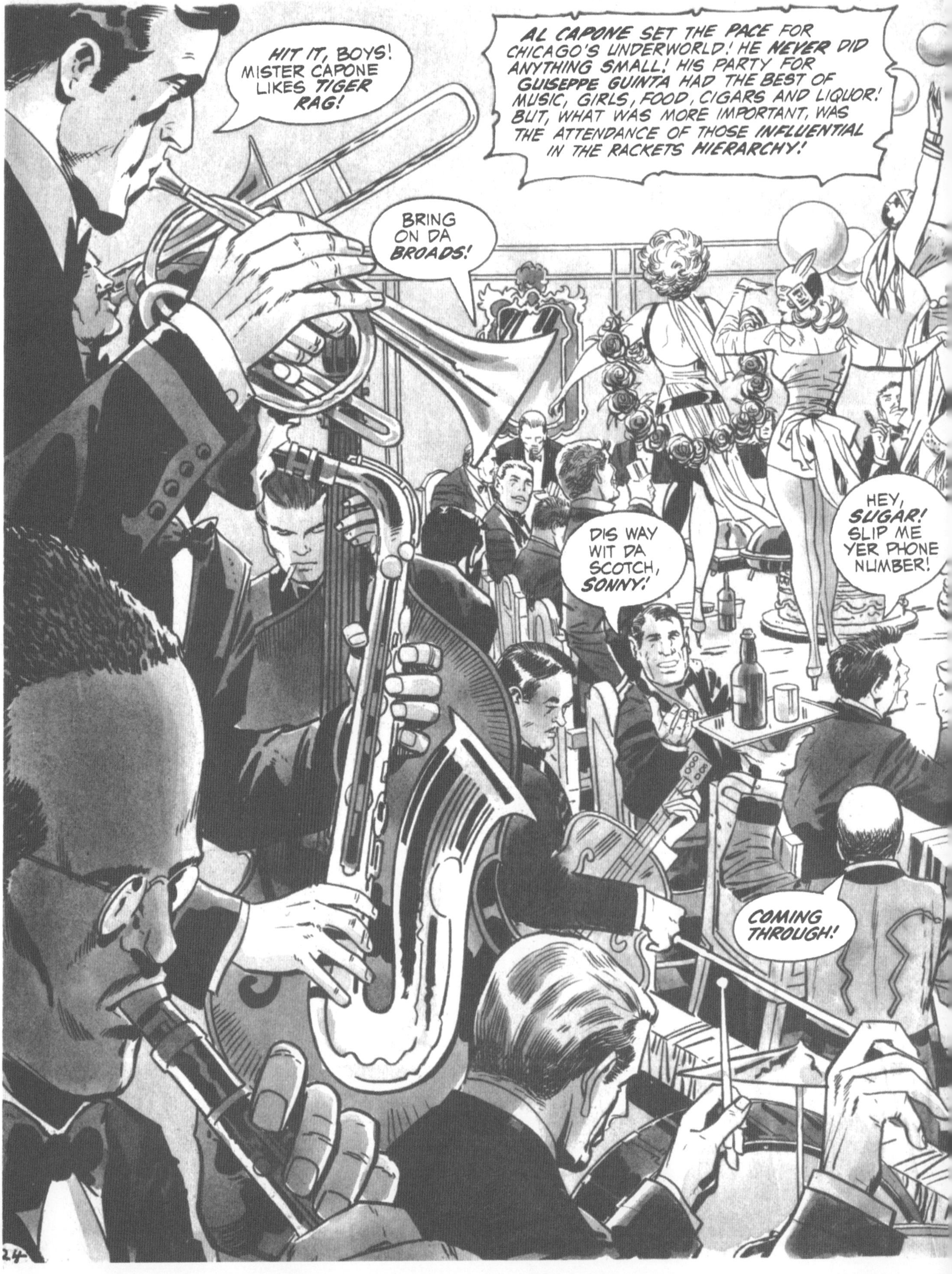
HIT IT, BOYS! MISTER CAPONE LIKES TIGER RAG!
AL CAPONE SET THE PACE FOR CHICAGO'S UNDERWORLD! HE NEVER DID ANYTHING SMALL! HIS PARTY FOR GUISEPPE GUINTA HAD THE BEST OF MUSIC, GIRLS, FOOD, CIGARS AND LIQUOR! BUT, WHAT WAS MORE IMPORTANT, WAS THE ATTENDANCE OF THOSE INFLUENTIAL IN THE RACKETS HIERARCHY!
BRING ON DA BROADS!
DIS WAY WIT DA SCOTCH, SONNY!
HEY, SUGAR! SLIP ME YER PHONE NUMBER!
COMING THROUGH!

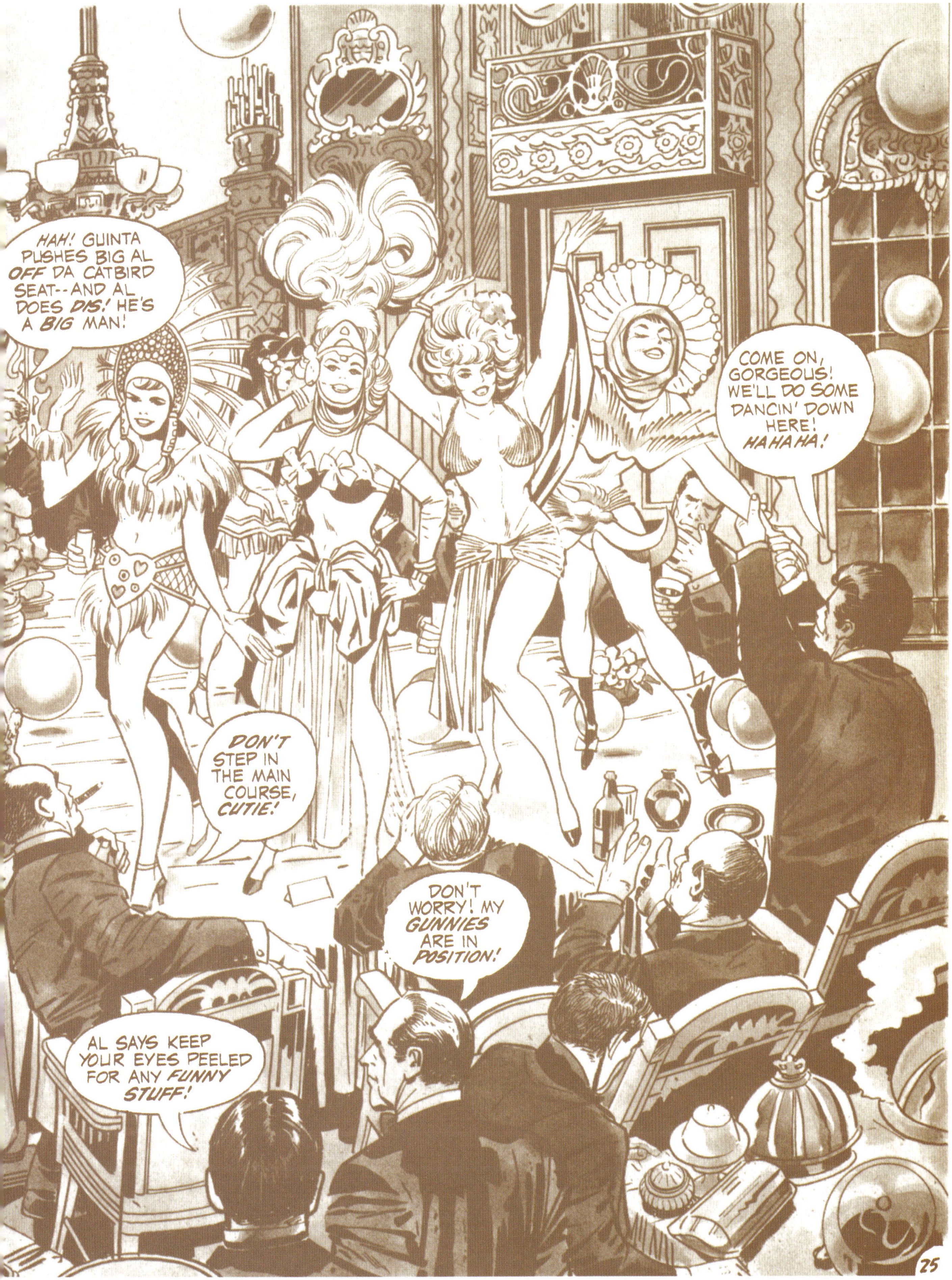
HAH! GUINTA PUSHES BIG AL OFF DA CATBIRD SEAT--AND AL DOES DIS! HE'S A BIG MAN!
COME ON, GORGEOUS! WE'LL DO SOME DANCIN' DOWN HERE! HAHAHA!
DON'T STEP IN THE MAIN COURSE, CUTIE!
DON'T WORRY! MY GUNNIES ARE IN POSITION!
AL SAYS KEEP YOUR EYES PEELED FOR ANY FUNNY STUFF!

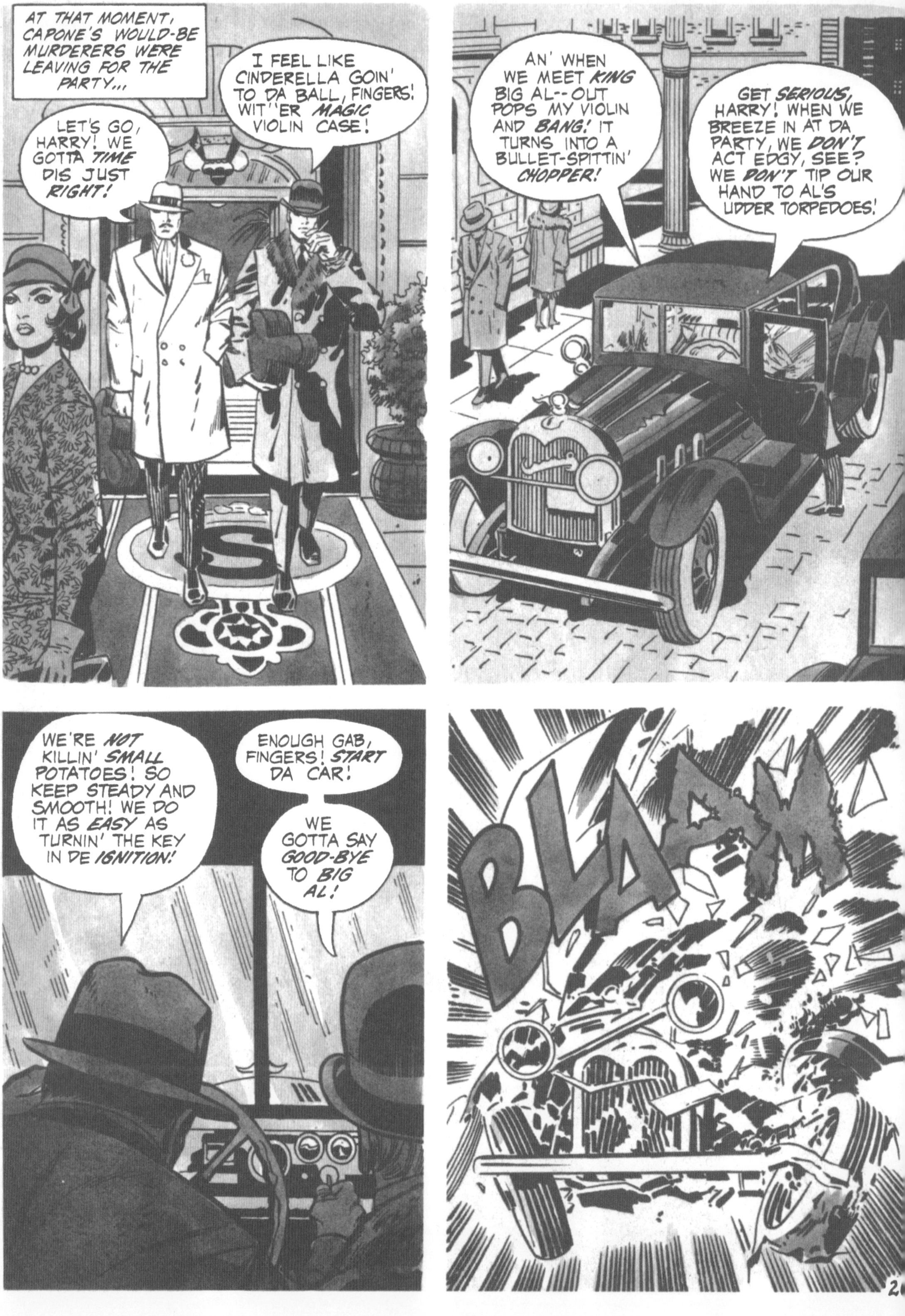

AT THAT MOMENT, CAPONE'S WOULD-BE MURDERERS WERE LEAVING FOR THE PARTY...
I FEEL LIKE CINDERELLA GOIN' TO DA BALL, FINGERS! WIT''ER MAGIC VIOLIN CASE!
LET'S GO, HARRY! WE GOTTA TIME DIS JUST RIGHT!
AN' WHEN WE MEET KING BIG AL--OUT POPS MY VIOLIN AND BANG! IT TURNS INTO A BULLET-SPITTIN' CHOPPER!
GET SERIOUS, HARRY! WHEN WE BREEZE IN AT DA PARTY, WE DON'T ACT EDGY, SEE? WE DON'T TIP OUR HAND TO AL'S UDDER TORPEDOES!
WE'RE NOT KILLIN' SMALL POTATOES! SO KEEP STEADY AND SMOOTH! WE DO IT AS EASY AS TURNIN' THE KEY IN DE IGNITION!
ENOUGH GAB, FINGERS! START DA CAR!
WE GOTTA SAY GOOD-BYE TO BIG AL!
BLAM

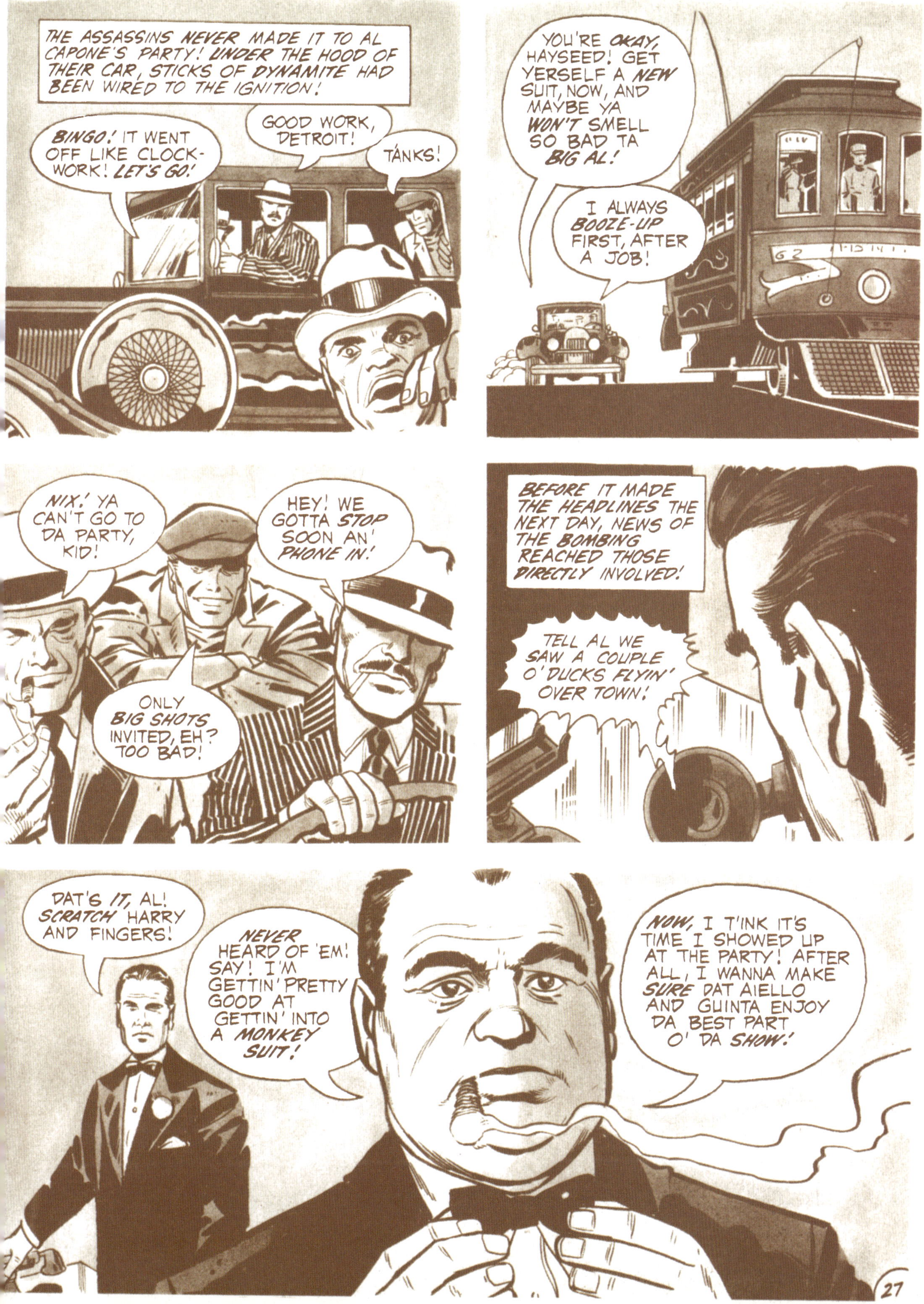
THE ASSASSINS NEVER MADE IT TO AL CAPONE'S PARTY! UNDER THE HOOD OF THEIR CAR, STICKS OF DYNAMITE HAD BEEN WIRED TO THE IGNITION!
BINGO! IT WENT OFF LIKE CLOCK-WORK! LET'S GO!
GOOD WORK, DETROIT!
TANKS!
YOU'RE OKAY, HAYSEED! GET YERSELF A NEW SUIT, NOW, AND MAYBE YA WON'T SMELL SO BAD TA BIG AL!
I ALWAYS BOOZE-UP FIRST, AFTER A JOB!
NIX! YA CAN'T GO TO DA PARTY, KID!
HEY! WE GOTTA STOP SOON AN' PHONE IN!
ONLY BIG SHOTS INVITED, EH? TOO BAD!
BEFORE IT MADE THE HEADLINES THE NEXT DAY, NEWS OF THE BOMBING REACHED THOSE DIRECTLY INVOLVED!
TELL AL WE SAW A COUPLE O' DUCKS FLYIN' OVER TOWN!
DAT'S IT, AL! SCRATCH HARRY AND FINGERS!
NEVER HEARD OF 'EM! SAY! I'M GETTIN' PRETTY GOOD AT GETTIN' INTO A MONKEY SUIT!
NOW, I T'INK IT'S TIME I SHOWED UP AT THE PARTY! AFTER ALL, I WANNA MAKE SURE DAT AIELLO AND GUINTA ENJOY DA BEST PART O' DA SHOW!

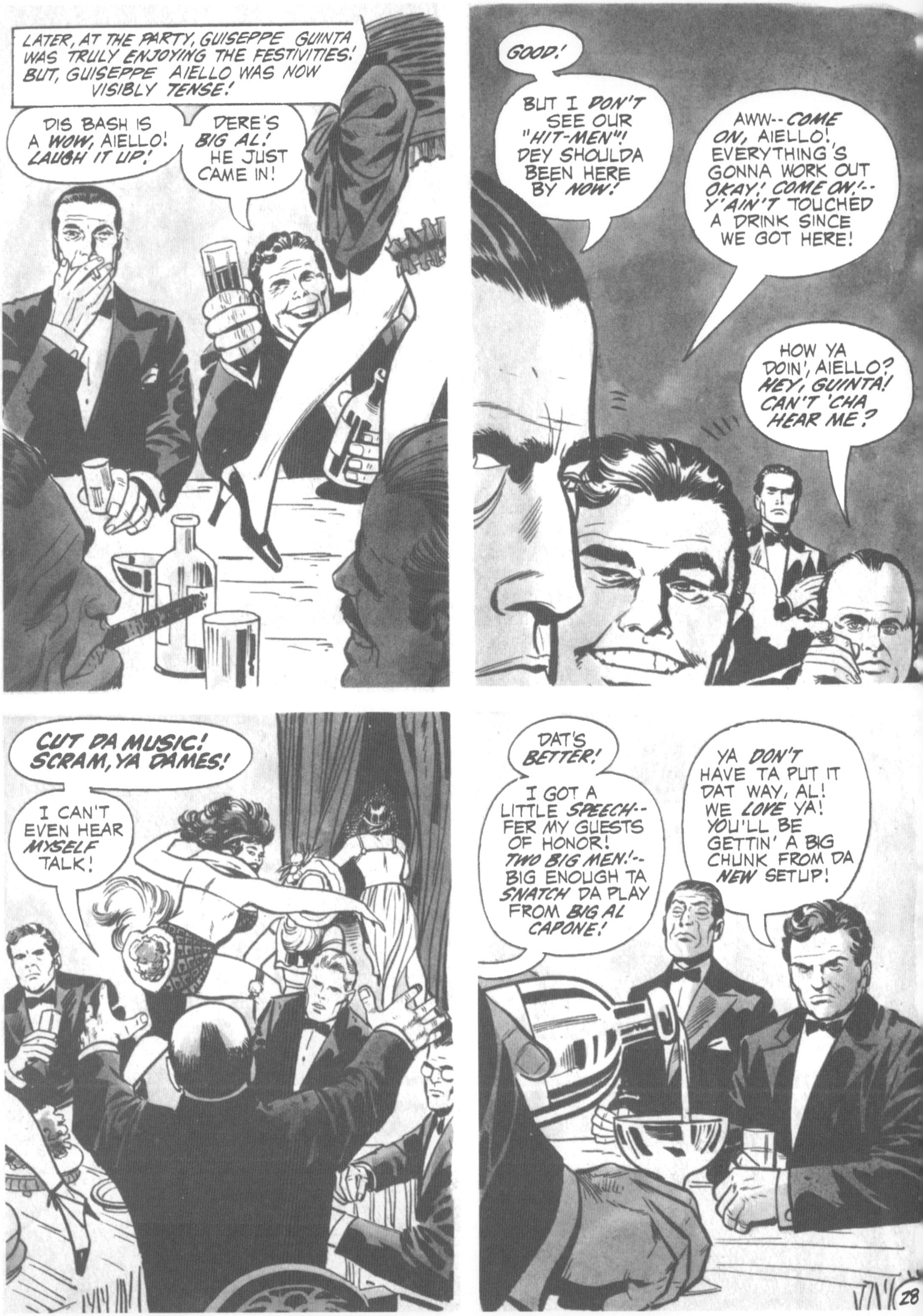
LATER, AT THE PARTY, GUISEPPE GUINTA WAS TRULY ENJOYING THE FESTIVITIES! BUT, GUISEPPE AIELLO WAS NOW VISIBLY TENSE!
DIS BASH IS A WOW, AIELLO! LAUGH IT UP!
DERE'S BIG AL! HE JUST CAME IN!
GOOD!
BUT I DON'T SEE OUR "HIT-MEN"! DEY SHOULDA BEEN HERE BY NOW!
AWW--COME ON, AIELLO! EVERYTHING'S GONNA WORK OUT OKAY! COME ON!--Y'AIN'T TOUCHED A DRINK SINCE WE GOT HERE!
HOW YA DOIN', AIELLO? HEY, GUINTA! CAN'T 'CHA HEAR ME?
CUT DA MUSIC! SCRAM, YA DAMES!
I CAN'T EVEN HEAR MYSELF TALK!
DAT'S BETTER!
I GOT A LITTLE SPEECH--FER MY GUESTS OF HONOR! TWO BIG MEN!--BIG ENOUGH TA SNATCH DA PLAY FROM BIG AL CAPONE!
YA DON'T HAVE TA PUT IT DAT WAY, AL! WE LOVE YA! YOU'LL BE GETTIN' A BIG CHUNK FROM DA NEW SETUP!

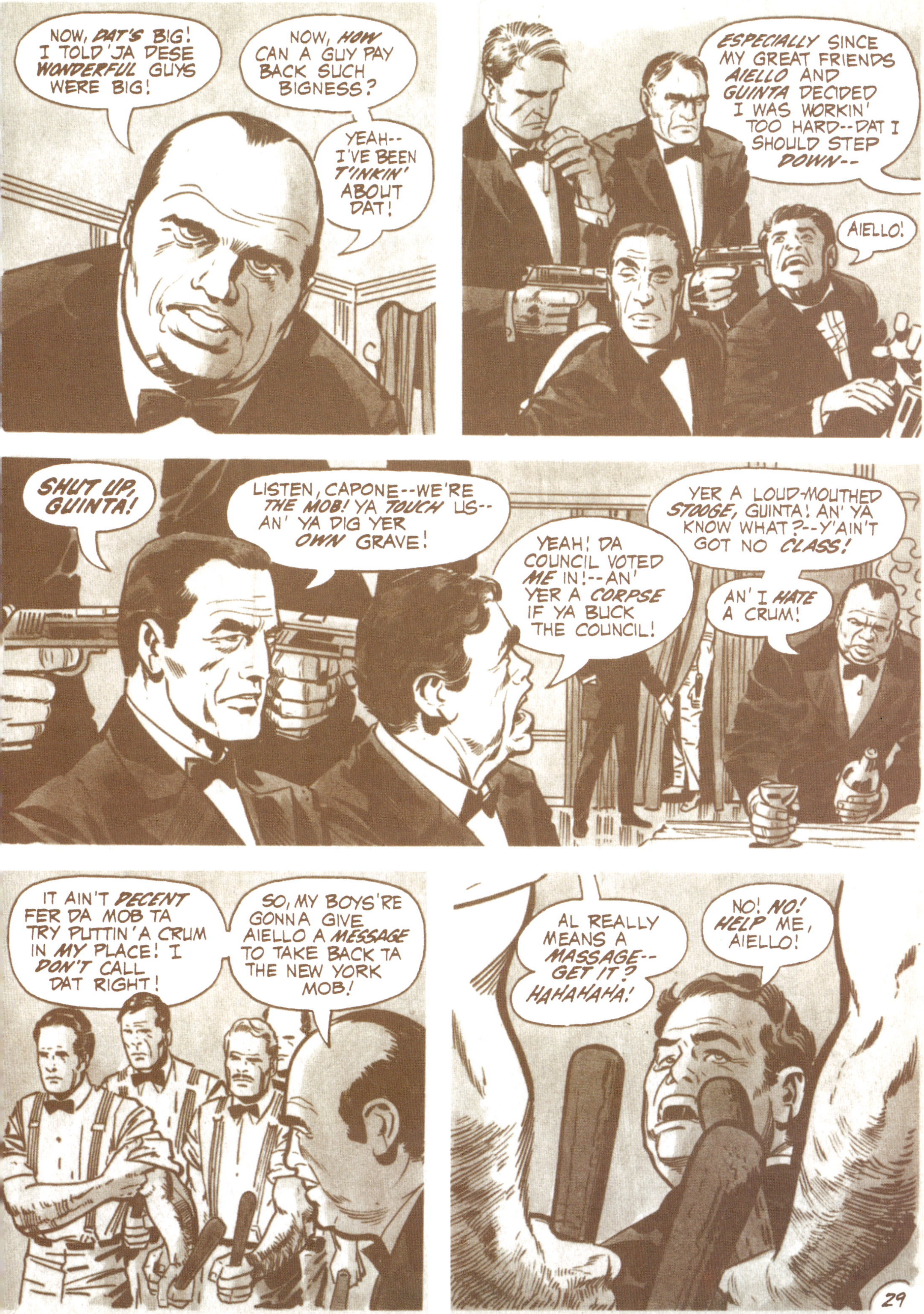
NOW, DAT'S BIG! I TOLD'JA DESE WONDERFUL GUYS WERE BIG!
NOW, HOW CAN A GUY PAY BACK SUCH BIGNESS?
YEAH-- I'VE BEEN T'INKIN' ABOUT DAT!
ESPECIALLY SINCE MY GREAT FRIENDS AIELLO AND GUINTA DECIDED I WAS WORKIN' TOO HARD--DAT I SHOULD STEP DOWN--
AIELLO!
SHUT UP, GUINTA!
LISTEN, CAPONE--WE'RE THE MOB! YA TOUCH US-- AN' YA DIG YER OWN GRAVE!
YEAH! DA COUNCIL VOTED ME IN!--AN' YER A CORPSE IF YA BUCK THE COUNCIL!
YER A LOUD-MOUTHED STOOGE, GUINTA! AN' YA KNOW WHAT?--Y'AIN'T GOT NO CLASS!
AN' I HATE A CRUM!
IT AIN'T DECENT FER DA MOB TA TRY PUTTIN' A CRUM IN MY PLACE! I DON'T CALL DAT RIGHT!
SO, MY BOYS'RE GONNA GIVE AIELLO A MESSAGE TO TAKE BACK TA THE NEW YORK MOB!
AL REALLY MEANS A MASSAGE-- GET IT? HAHAHAHA!
NO! NO! HELP ME, AIELLO!

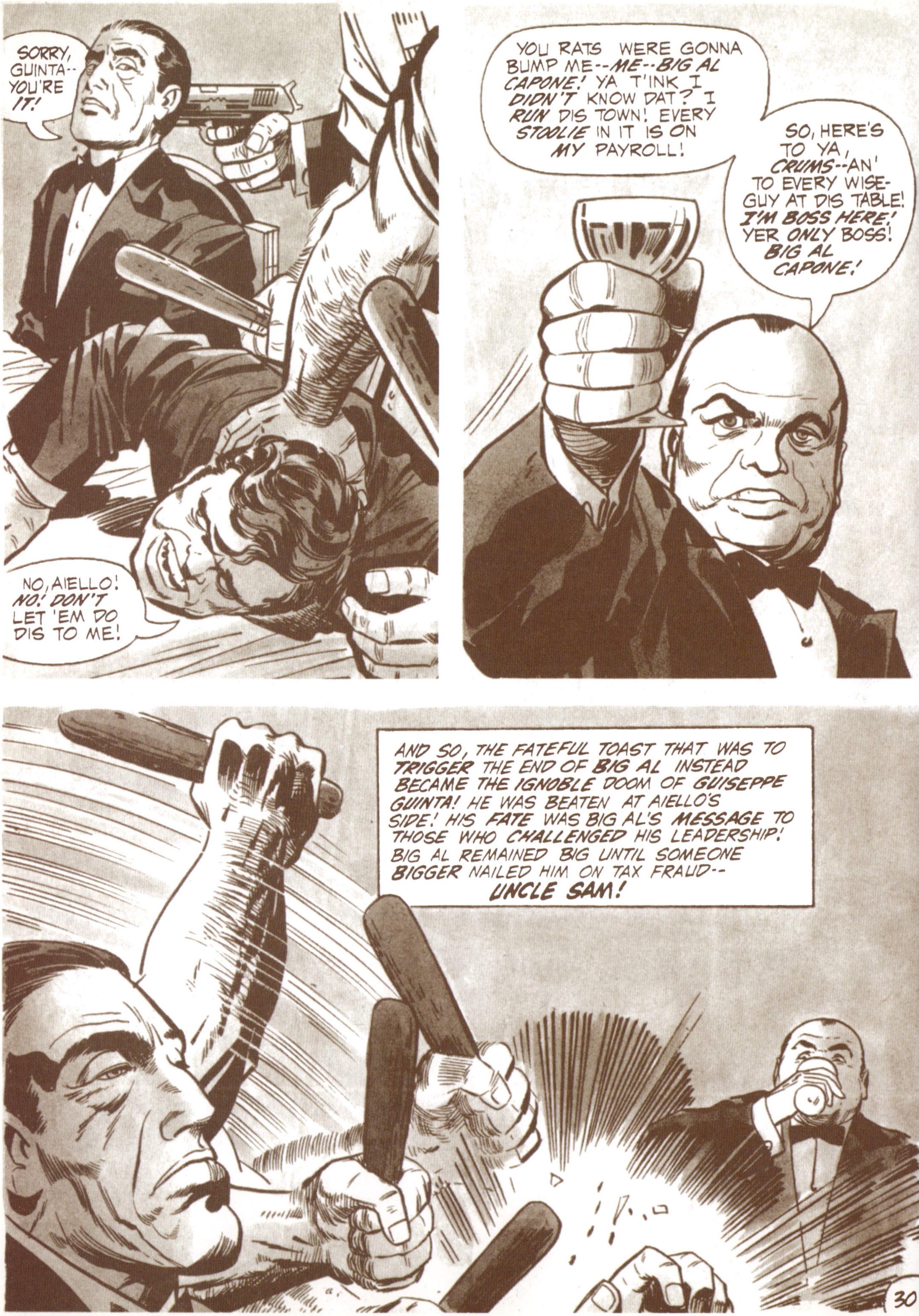

SORRY, GUINTA-- YOU'RE IT!
NO, AIELLO! NO! DON'T LET 'EM DO DIS TO ME!
YOU RATS WERE GONNA BUMP ME--ME--BIG AL CAPONE! YA T'INK I DIDN'T KNOW DAT? I RUN DIS TOWN! EVERY STOOLIE IN IT IS ON MY PAYROLL!
SO, HERE'S TO YA, CRUMS--AN' TO EVERY WISE-GUY AT DIS TABLE! I'M BOSS HERE! YER ONLY BOSS! BIG AL CAPONE!
AND SO, THE FATEFUL TOAST THAT WAS TO TRIGGER THE END OF BIG AL INSTEAD BECAME THE IGNOBLE DOOM OF GUISEPPE GUINTA! HE WAS BEATEN AT AIELLO'S SIDE! HIS FATE WAS BIG AL'S MESSAGE TO THOSE WHO CHALLENGED HIS LEADERSHIP! BIG AL REMAINED BIG UNTIL SOMEONE BIGGER NAILED HIM ON TAX FRAUD-- UNCLE SAM!

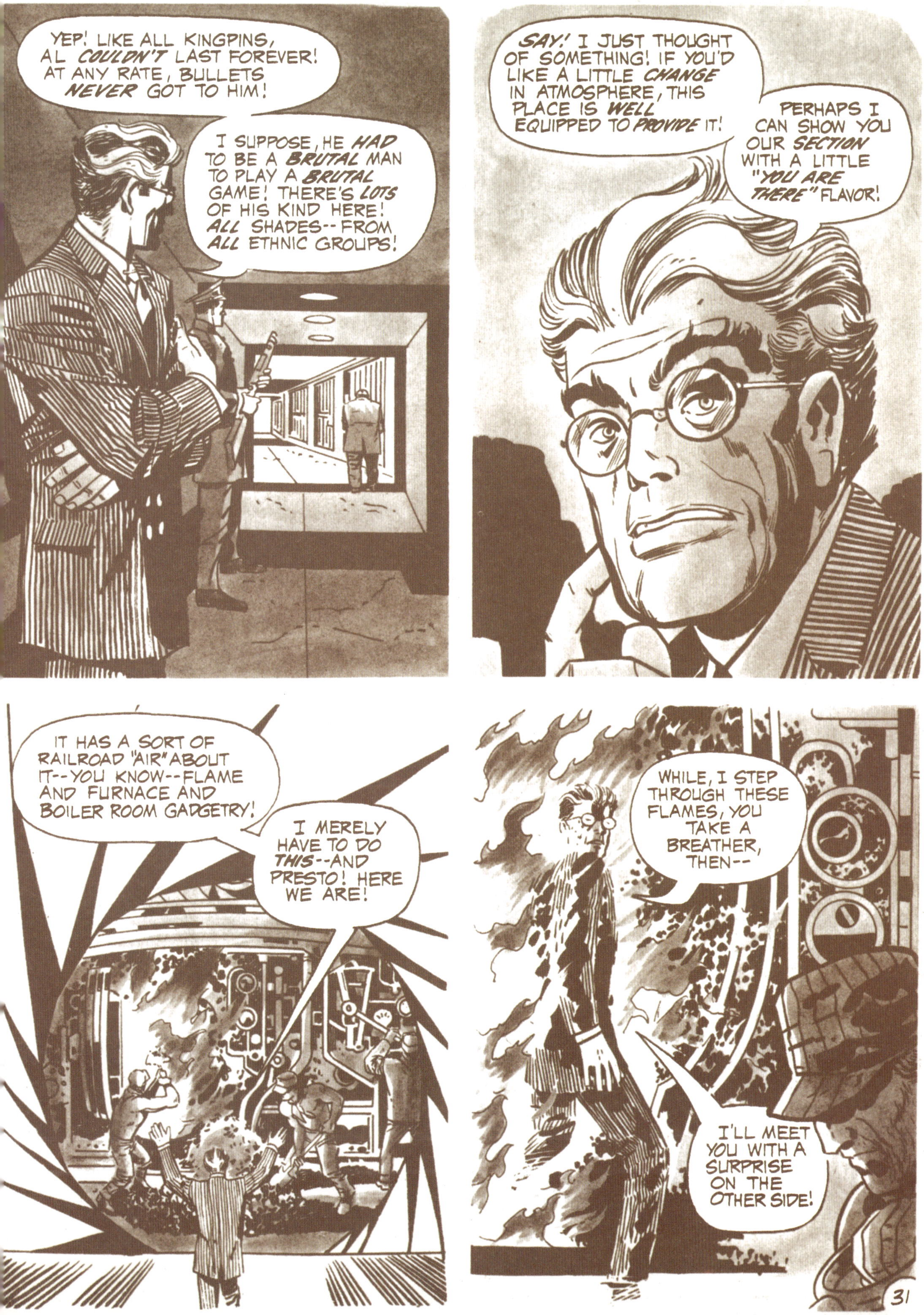
YEP! LIKE ALL KINGPINS, AL COULDN'T LAST FOREVER! AT ANY RATE, BULLETS NEVER GOT TO HIM!
I SUPPOSE, HE HAD TO BE A BRUTAL MAN TO PLAY A BRUTAL GAME! THERE'S LOTS OF HIS KIND HERE! ALL SHADES--FROM ALL ETHNIC GROUPS!
SAY! I JUST THOUGHT OF SOMETHING! IF YOU'D LIKE A LITTLE CHANGE IN ATMOSPHERE, THIS PLACE IS WELL EQUIPPED TO PROVIDE IT!
PERHAPS I CAN SHOW YOU OUR SECTION WITH A LITTLE "YOU ARE THERE" FLAVOR!
IT HAS A SORT OF RAILROAD "AIR" ABOUT IT--YOU KNOW--FLAME AND FURNACE AND BOILER ROOM GADGETRY!
I MERELY HAVE TO DO THIS--AND PRESTO! HERE WE ARE!
WHILE, I STEP THROUGH THESE FLAMES, YOU TAKE A BREATHER, THEN--
I'LL MEET YOU WITH A SURPRISE ON THE OTHER SIDE!
31

FEATURETTE

# THE BREEDING GROUND!

*America, in the days of the Mob, was broke, sick and white.* The blacks of that day were no more visible in the national *Crime* picture than they were in the prevailing *social* order of that era.

In the crowded, seething slums of the nation, man was at war with his environment, depressed by his insecure status, and buffeted by the turbulence within his own family!

Hopelessness, hunger and hostility plagued the young! They had to break free of it! Of the many who made it with honor, there were others who turned ugly in pursuit of money, power and—escape!

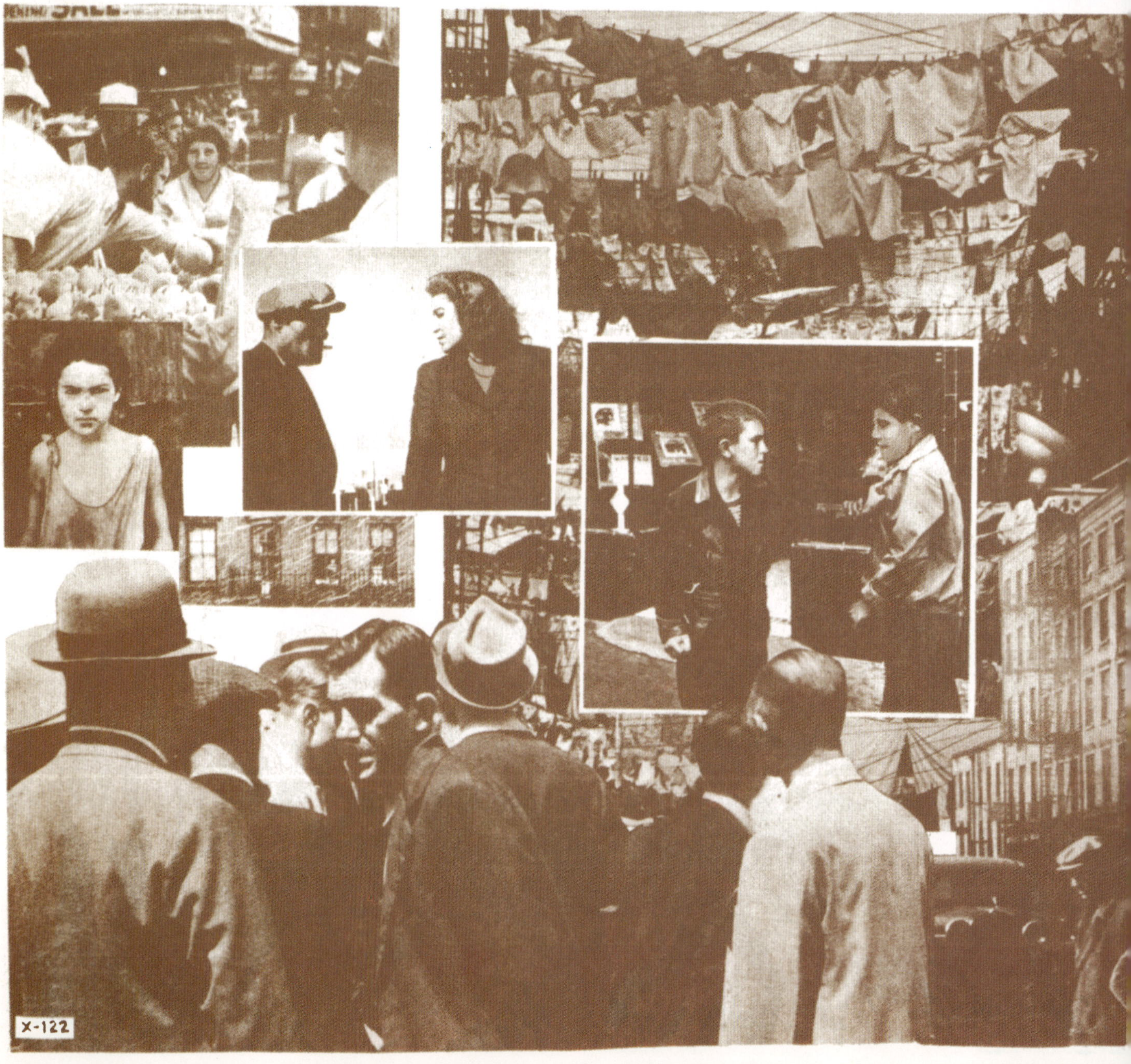

Rural America was faces — with hard, wrinkled lines like the shriveled earth which offered nothing but dust to the blowing winds.

To the Bible-reader, God was nowhere to be seen! Instead, there were foreclosures of farms—layoffs at the mines and the creation of migrant wanderers in rickety automobiles who bore the label "Oakies!"

Look at these faces! —Both old and young—reflecting the crunch of hard times—from what was behind these faces came the *Bonnie Parkers, Clyde Barrows* and *"Pretty Boy" Floyds!*

From this segment of America came *Baby Face Nelson,* The Bloody *Barkers* and *Dillinger!*

The banks and railroads smelled of gunpowder and the nation's presses raced madly to follow their infamous careers!

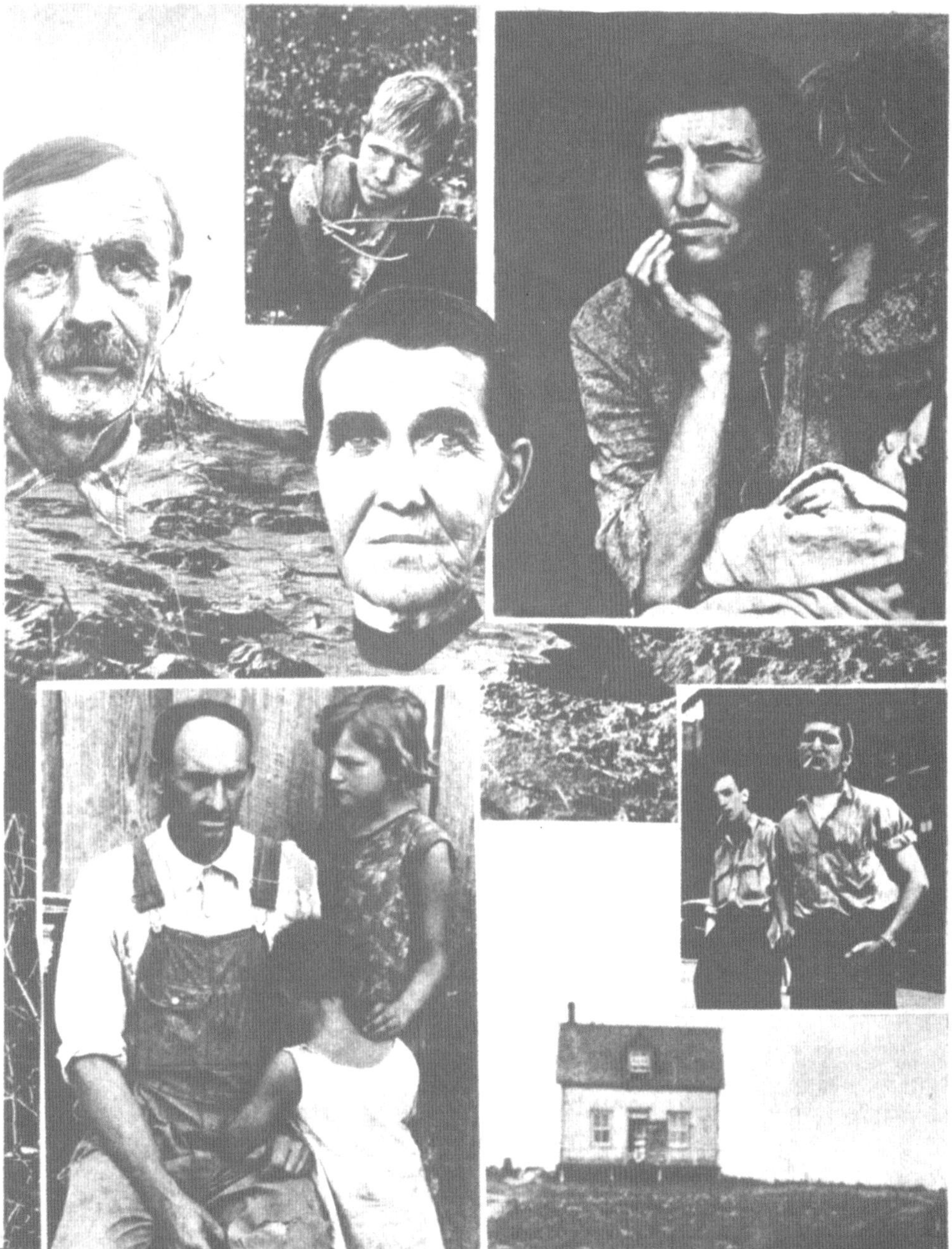

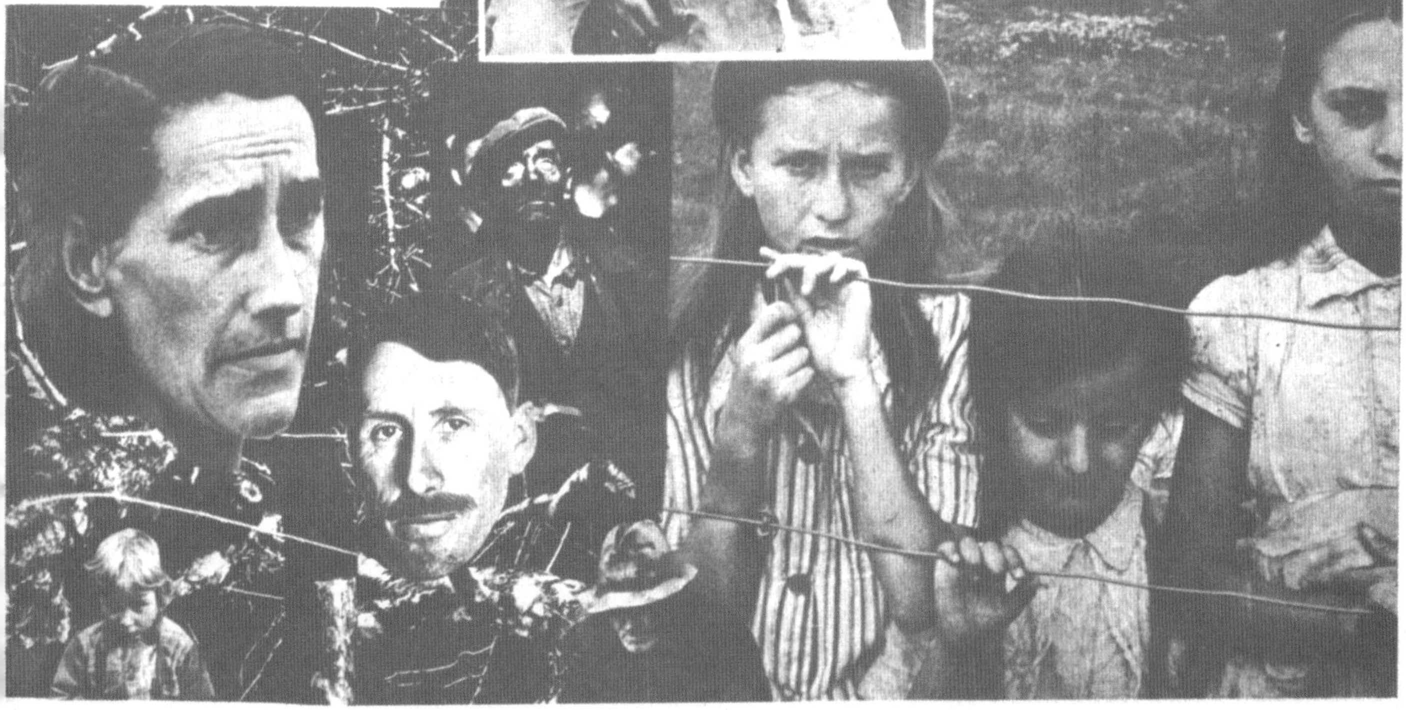

Across the land, the available media *rejected* the reality—reshaped it into an assortment of *salable* products which an *escape-hungry* public consumed both mentally and physically!!

Films and newspapers burgeoned with *sensation* and fantasy! Joy was *distilled* in night clubs and dance palaces in which freakish marathons provided circuses of degradation in the form of entertainment! Jazz became legitimate and rose as a true art form!

But *gambling, vice* and *drink* were the *big* money makers—the true channel of escape for the *aggressive!* They swarmed into the dirty water, singly and in groups!—*Goons! Hoods! Punks! Torpedoes!* They fought for control of the rackets—lived quickly—died suddenly! And those left branched out—enveloped the cities—became the evil entity called—*THE MOB!*

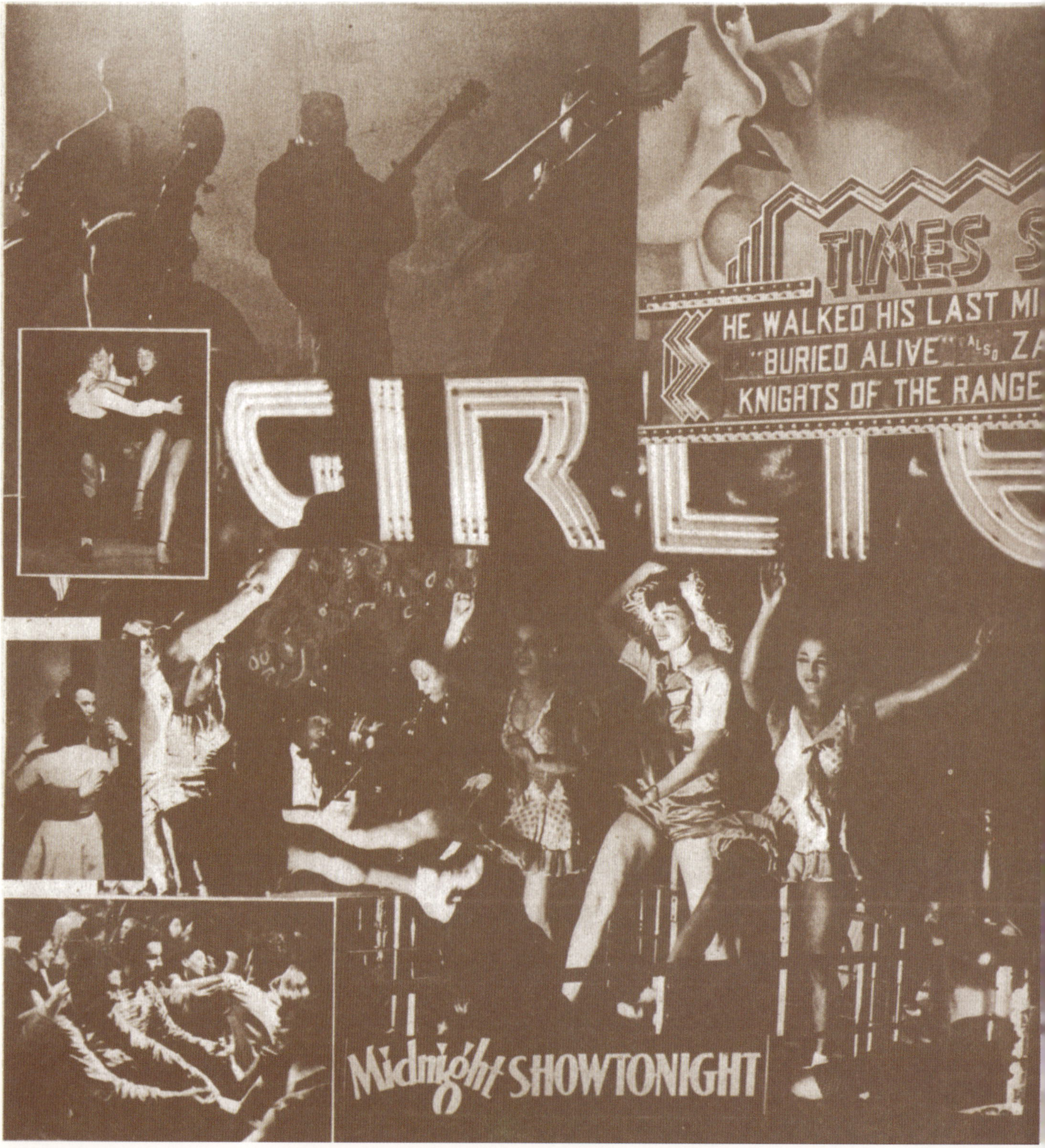
TIMES S
HE WALKED HIS LAST MI
"BURIED ALIVE" ALSO ZA
KNIGHTS OF THE RANGE
Midnight SHOWTONIGHT

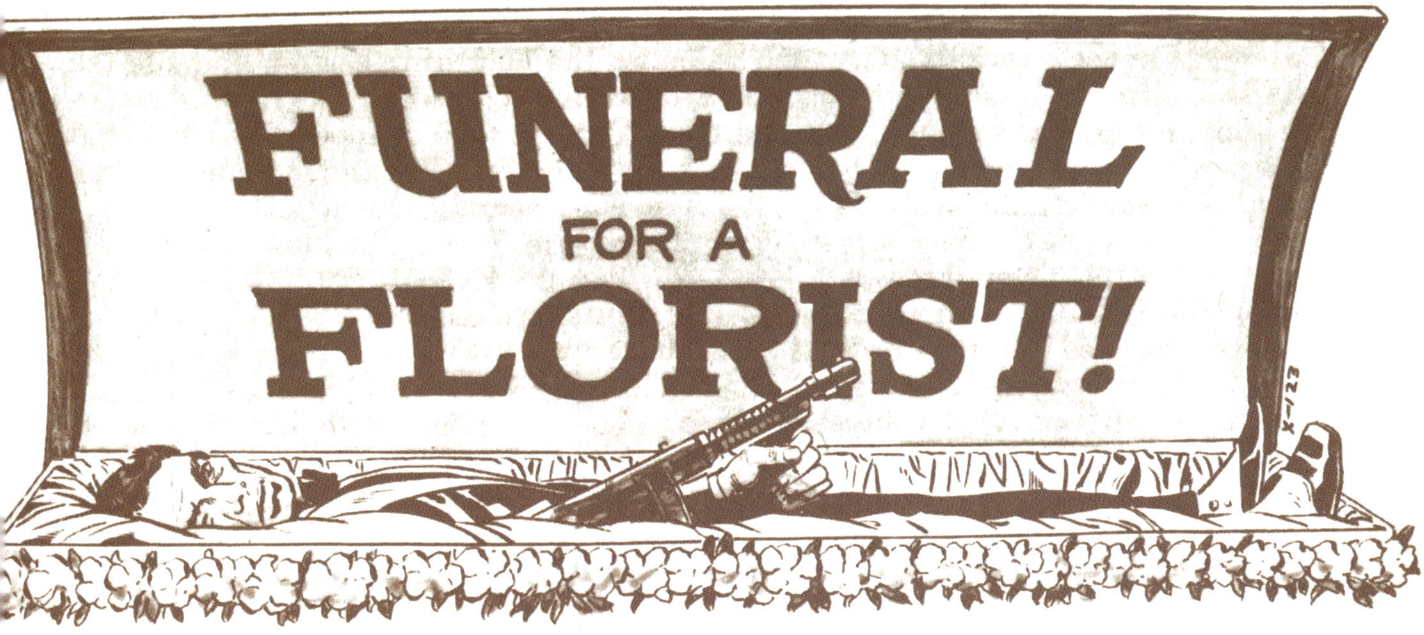
FUNERAL
FOR A
FLORIST!

***A FACTUAL ACCOUNT IN THE TRADITION OF ACE REPORTERS OF THE THIRTIES!***

***BY MARK EVANIER AND STEVE SHERMAN***

Chicago, during prohibition, was in the grip of bootleggers. Al Capone and Johnny Torrio had divided up the city and were extracting goodly sums from all kinds of people for liquor produced in secret breweries. The traffic was heavy and when someone went too far, his body might well be found, face down, in a gutter somewhere. When this happened, however, the deceased's gangland buddies would throw him a full-scale gangland funeral, complete with thousands of dollars' worth of flowers and a parade of hoodlums and so-called "respectable" citizens.

Most of these flowers came from a little flower shop on North State Street run by a certain Dion O'Banion. Al Capone bought all his flowers there, as did Johnny Torrio. What made this matter curious was that O'Banion was the number three man in Chicago bootlegging and would frequently find himself filling orders for flowers to be sent to some "dearly departed" he had ordered "bumped off". O'Banion had bought half-interest in the florist business as a front for his other operations and had taken such a liking to it that he assumed personal management and personally arranged most of the floral bouquets. Henchmen, wishing to discuss plans for hijackings or safe-robberies, had to come to the shop and talk to the boss while he arranged chrysanthemums for a wedding. Despite the fact that Capone and Torrio hated O'Banion deeply, he *was* gangland's "official" florist and buying flowers anywhere else would have seemed somehow disrespectful.

O'Banion once explained why his flower shop did such good business all the time. When someone in the underworld was bumped off, O'Banion supplied the flowers for the funeral and then the deceased's buddies would go out and shoot the guy who had killed their friend, thus creating the need for *another* funeral and flowers.

The death of one of O'Banion's henchmen was, however, a violation of this principle. "Nails" Morton, who had been a First Lieutenant in World War I and was instrumental in O'Banion's control of brewery traffic in parts of Chicago, was killed when a horse he was riding in Lincoln Park threw him and kicked him to death. After the funeral, a delegation from O'Banion's gang went out to the park, found the horse, dragged it to the scene of the accident, and killed it.

Johnny Torrio, above all others, hated O'Banion. Torrio, in one of his schemes to take over Capone's rackets, had tried to enlist the help of O'Banion and the many votes he controlled in an upcoming Chicago election. O'Banion was not interested in expanding his criminal empire, being perfectly content with his operations, which netted him a million a year in addition to a large gross from his florist shop. O'Banion threw his support to Capone's men and Torrio got a sound trouncing.

But that was not the only reason Torrio hated him. One of the most important elements in O'Banion's empire was a brewery which produced, illegally, most of the liquor in Chicago. O'Banion, through his informants, learned that a raid of the premises was being planned and that Federal authorities intended to close him up. He went to Torrio, who already owned a small interest in the brewery, and said he was retiring and would sell the whole operation cheap. Torrio agreed, with the provisio that O'Banion accompany him to oversee an upcoming shipment. That's how O'Banion happened to be at the brewery when the police broke in. But O'Banion had covered himself well. All the evidence had been planted so that *Torrio* was the one who was arrested and convicted.

Torrio pulled strings to stay out of prison and managed to remain out on bail. Certain now that O'Banion had double-crossed him, he vowed to kill the man who had led him into that trap. But Mike Merlo, boss of some of the smaller rackets, put pressure on him to leave O'Banion unharmed. As long as Merlo had anything to do with it, O'Banion would stay alive.

Two days later, Merlo was found dead in his living room.

The underworld had never seen quite as lavish a funeral as was given Merlo. Although he dealt with petty rackets, he influenced most of Chicago and they all turned out to say goodbye to him. O'Banion filled a $10,000 floral order from Torrio and a slightly smaller one from Capone. As part of Merlo's funeral procession, a twelve-foot floral statue of him was erected and driven in front of the hearse. O'Banion and his staff worked all night preparing the flowers. The next morning, however, there was one funeral wreath which had not been picked up.

Worried that the wreath might not be called for, O'Banion started to take it out to his car to deliver personally, when they walked in, three men abreast. O'Banion spoke up: "Hello, boys—you want Merlo's flowers?"

They looked at each other, then at him. O'Banion, who had a habit of keeping his right hand in his pistol pocket, that morning had a pair of garden shears in the pocket. The three men grabbed him and fired five bullets into his body. As they turned to run out, one spun around and fired a sixth shot into the head of the dead crime boss.

Officially, the murder of Dion O'Banion is unsolved. But word had it that Torrio and Capone had planned it together and that the three men who had fired the death shots were members of Merlo's gang who each received $10,000 and a $3,000 diamond ring. They had come in earlier to buy flowers for their boss and to familiarize themselves with the layout of the shop.

The little flower shop closed up the next day. For O'Banion's funeral, then, flowers had to be brought from miles around and, in fact, more than twenty-five trucks carried the masses of floral tributes to O'Banion's home where they filled the house, the lawn, and even a neighbor's empty swimming pool. O'Banion's boys chipped in and bought a special casket for $10,000 and the funeral had to be delayed while it was shipped from Philadelphia. The funeral procession was a mile long and included a police procession, three bands, and more than ten thousand people, most of whom had been involved in one or another of O'Banion's rackets.

That Dion O'Banion had robbed, smuggled illegal liquor, and ordered men killed reminds us that he was another gangland boss. But one of his associates was heard to remark at the funeral: "O'Banion was a kind man. The last couple of years of his life, all he talked about was how he wanted to get out of the rackets and run his flower shop in peace. Well, he's out of them now!"

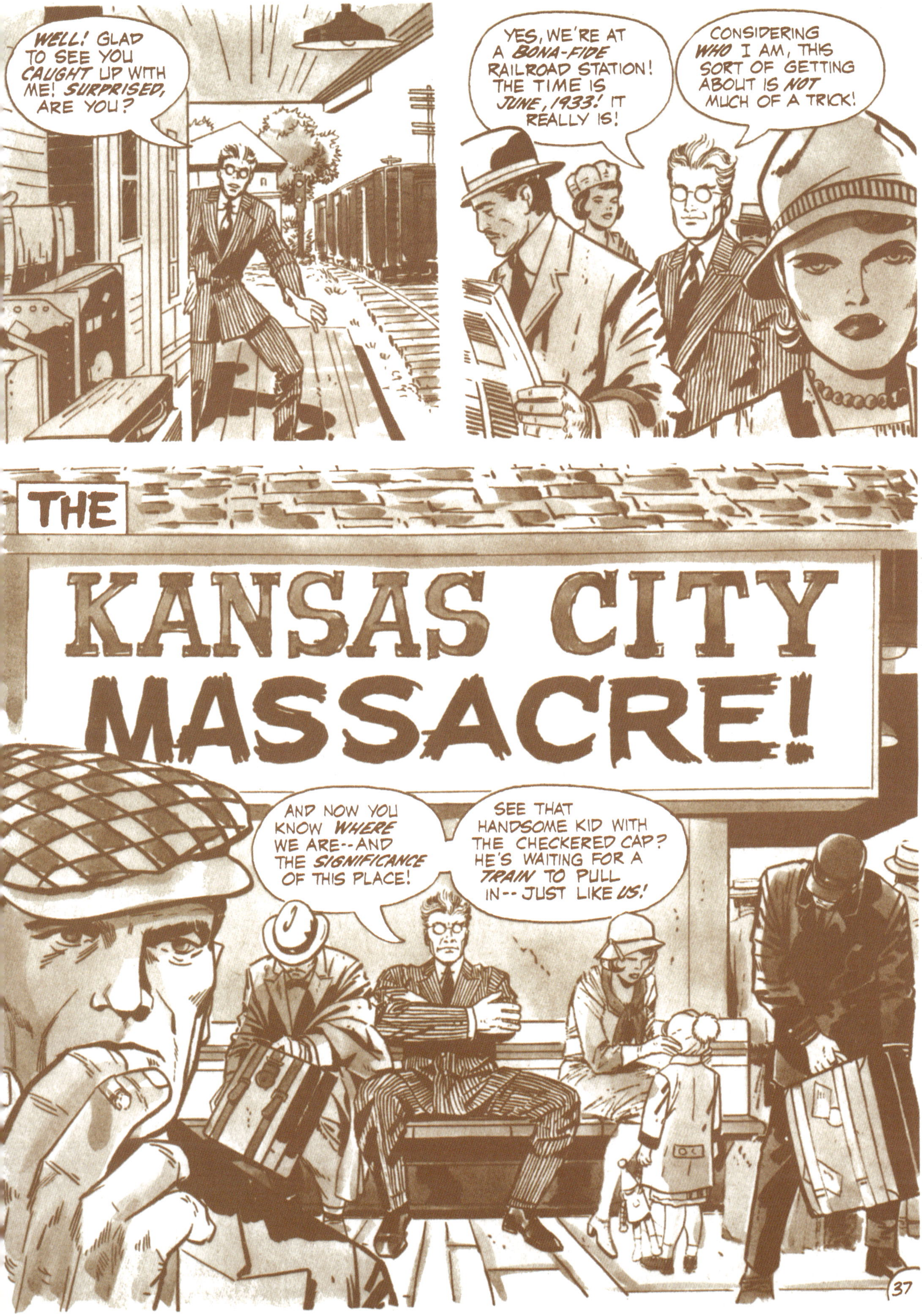
WELL! GLAD TO SEE YOU CAUGHT UP WITH ME! SURPRISED, ARE YOU?
YES, WE'RE AT A BONA-FIDE RAILROAD STATION! THE TIME IS JUNE, 1933! IT REALLY IS!
CONSIDERING WHO I AM, THIS SORT OF GETTING ABOUT IS NOT MUCH OF A TRICK!
THE
KANSAS CITY
MASSACRE!
AND NOW YOU KNOW WHERE WE ARE--AND THE SIGNIFICANCE OF THIS PLACE!
SEE THAT HANDSOME KID WITH THE CHECKERED CAP? HE'S WAITING FOR A TRAIN TO PULL IN-- JUST LIKE US!

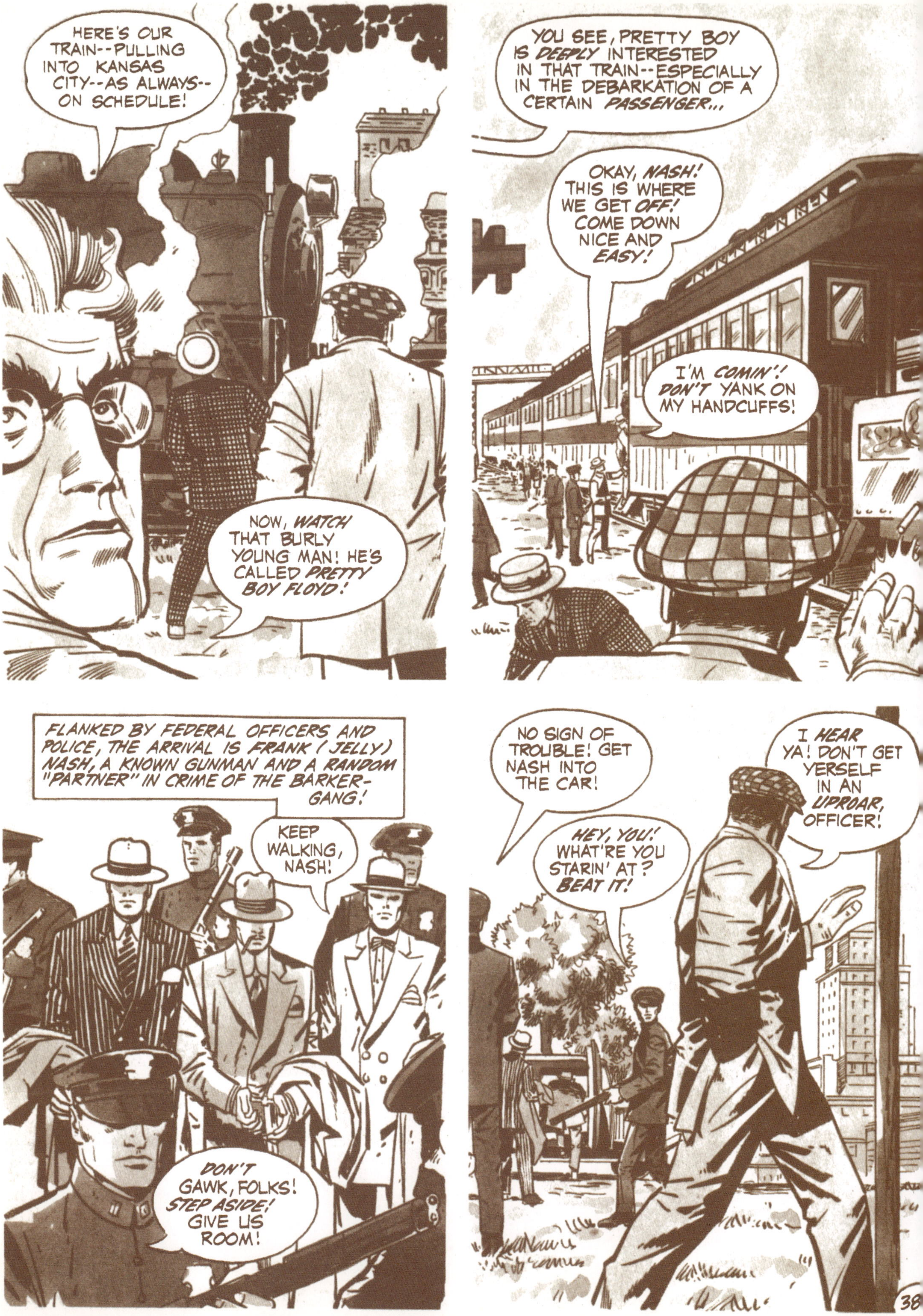
HERE'S OUR TRAIN--PULLING INTO KANSAS CITY--AS ALWAYS--ON SCHEDULE!
NOW, WATCH THAT BURLY YOUNG MAN! HE'S CALLED PRETTY BOY FLOYD!
YOU SEE, PRETTY BOY IS DEEPLY INTERESTED IN THAT TRAIN--ESPECIALLY IN THE DEBARKATION OF A CERTAIN PASSENGER...
OKAY, NASH! THIS IS WHERE WE GET OFF! COME DOWN NICE AND EASY!
I'M COMIN'! DON'T YANK ON MY HANDCUFFS!
FLANKED BY FEDERAL OFFICERS AND POLICE, THE ARRIVAL IS FRANK (JELLY) NASH, A KNOWN GUNMAN AND A RANDOM "PARTNER" IN CRIME OF THE BARKER-GANG!
KEEP WALKING, NASH!
DON'T GAWK, FOLKS! STEP ASIDE! GIVE US ROOM!
NO SIGN OF TROUBLE! GET NASH INTO THE CAR!
HEY, YOU! WHAT'RE YOU STARIN' AT? BEAT IT!
I HEAR YA! DON'T GET YERSELF IN AN UPROAR, OFFICER!

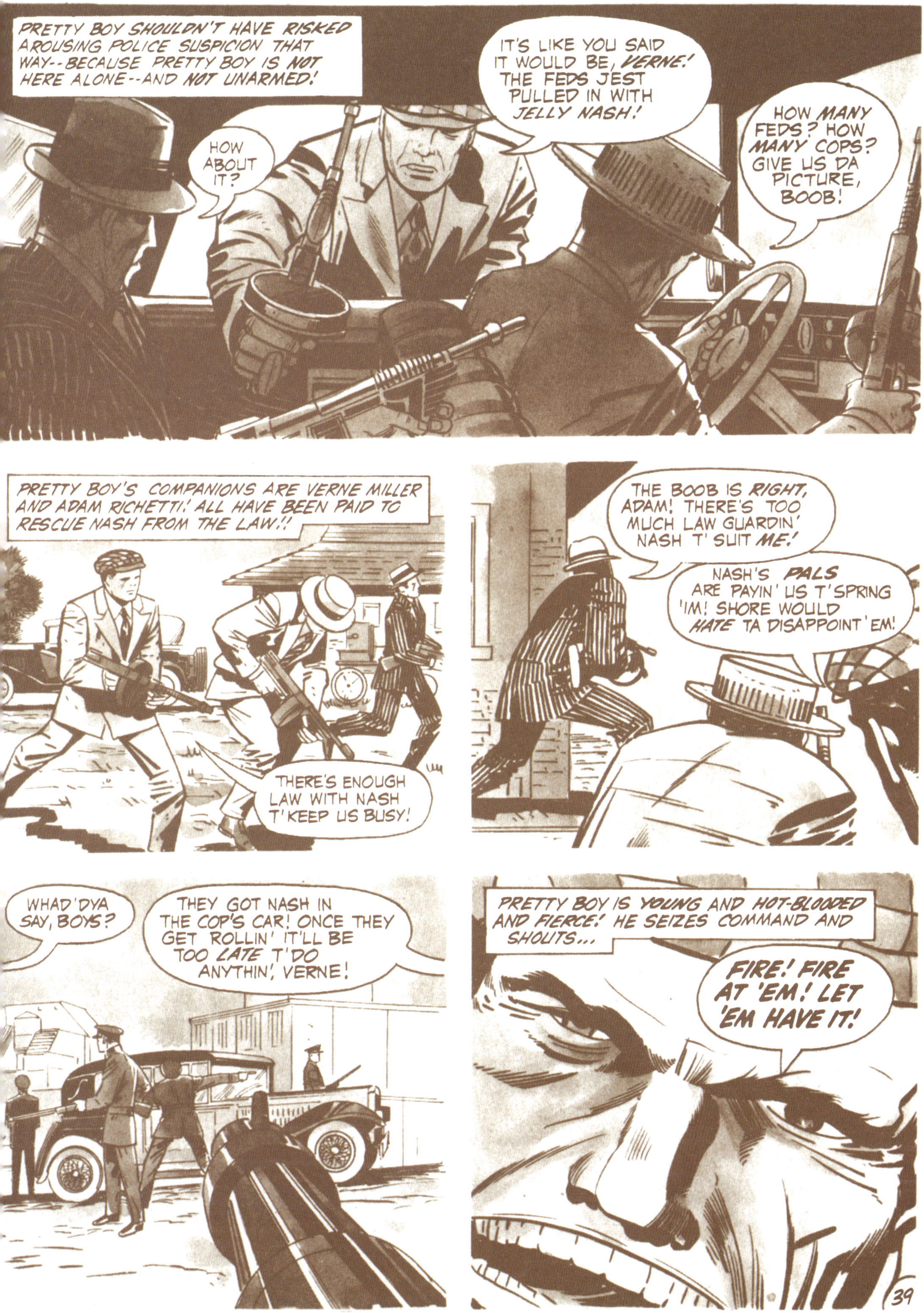
PRETTY BOY SHOULDN'T HAVE RISKED AROUSING POLICE SUSPICION THAT WAY--BECAUSE PRETTY BOY IS NOT HERE ALONE--AND NOT UNARMED!
HOW ABOUT IT?
IT'S LIKE YOU SAID IT WOULD BE, VERNE! THE FEDS JEST PULLED IN WITH JELLY NASH!
HOW MANY FEDS? HOW MANY COPS? GIVE US DA PICTURE, BOOB!
PRETTY BOY'S COMPANIONS ARE VERNE MILLER AND ADAM RICHETTI! ALL HAVE BEEN PAID TO RESCUE NASH FROM THE LAW!!
THERE'S ENOUGH LAW WITH NASH T'KEEP US BUSY!
THE BOOB IS RIGHT, ADAM! THERE'S TOO MUCH LAW GUARDIN' NASH T' SUIT ME!
NASH'S PALS ARE PAYIN' US T'SPRING 'IM! SHORE WOULD HATE TA DISAPPOINT 'EM!
WHAD'DYA SAY, BOYS?
THEY GOT NASH IN THE COP'S CAR! ONCE THEY GET ROLLIN' IT'LL BE TOO LATE T'DO ANYTHIN', VERNE!
PRETTY BOY IS YOUNG AND HOT-BLOODED AND FIERCE! HE SEIZES COMMAND AND SHOUTS...
FIRE! FIRE AT 'EM! LET 'EM HAVE IT!

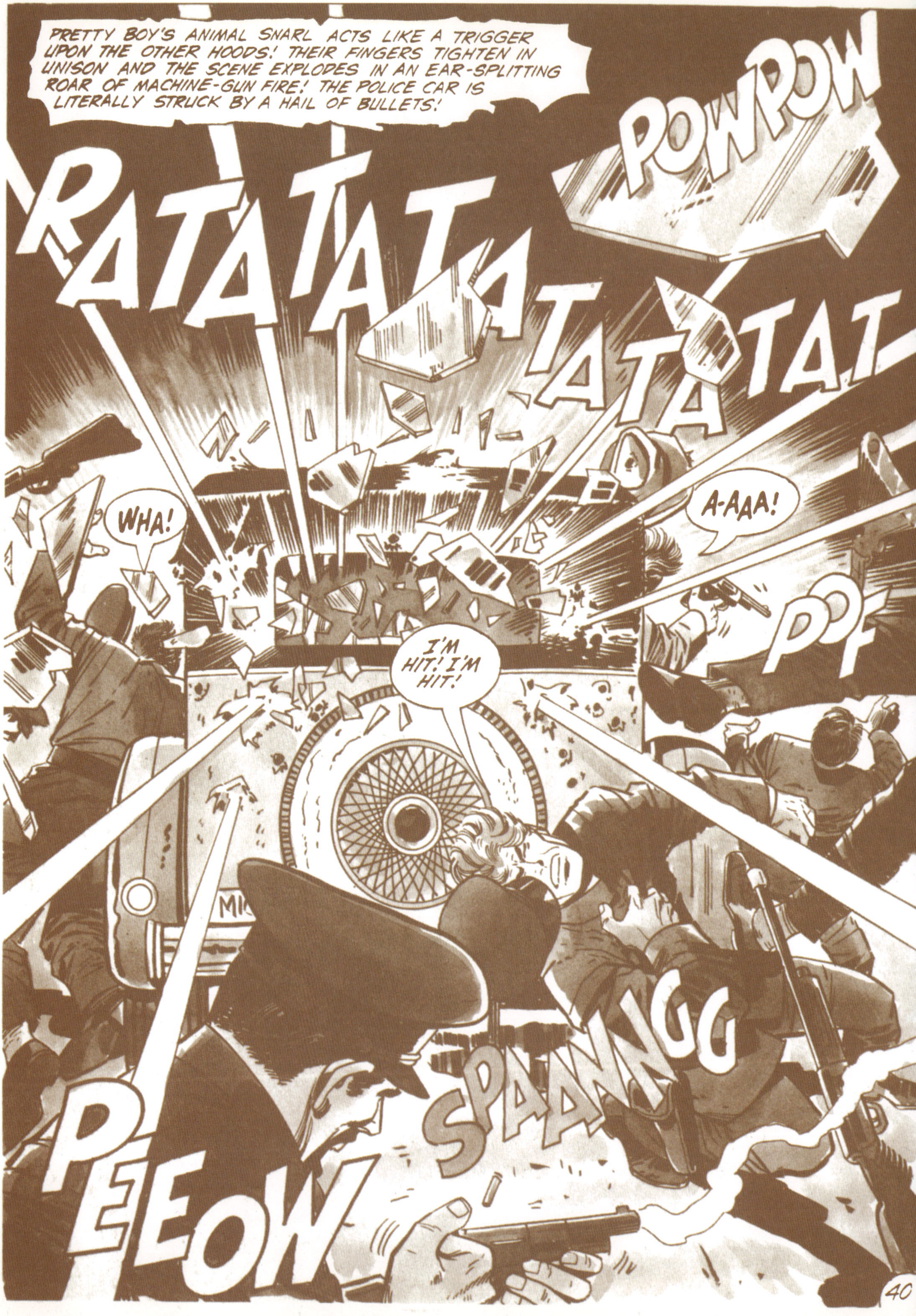
PRETTY BOY'S ANIMAL SNARL ACTS LIKE A TRIGGER UPON THE OTHER HOODS! THEIR FINGERS TIGHTEN IN UNISON AND THE SCENE EXPLODES IN AN EAR-SPLITTING ROAR OF MACHINE-GUN FIRE! THE POLICE CAR IS LITERALLY STRUCK BY A HAIL OF BULLETS!
POWPOW
RATATATATATATATAT
WHA!
A-AAA!
I'M HIT! I'M HIT!
POF
SPAANGG
PEEOW

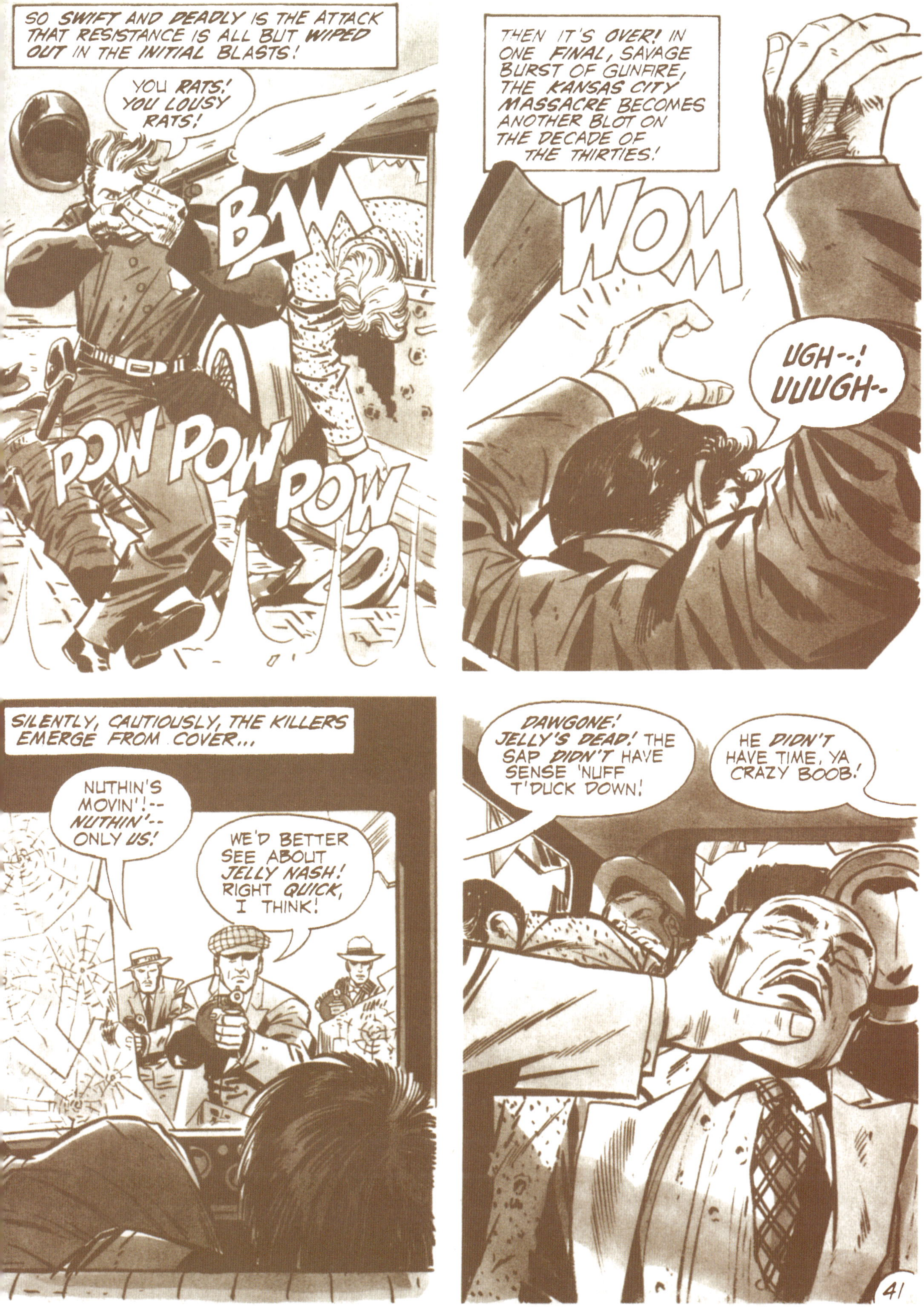
SO SWIFT AND DEADLY IS THE ATTACK THAT RESISTANCE IS ALL BUT WIPED OUT IN THE INITIAL BLASTS!
YOU RATS! YOU LOUSY RATS!
BAM
POW POW POW
THEN IT'S OVER! IN ONE FINAL, SAVAGE BURST OF GUNFIRE, THE KANSAS CITY MASSACRE BECOMES ANOTHER BLOT ON THE DECADE OF THE THIRTIES!
WOM
UGH--! UUUGH--
SILENTLY, CAUTIOUSLY, THE KILLERS EMERGE FROM COVER...
NUTHIN'S MOVIN'!-- NUTHIN'-- ONLY US!
WE'D BETTER SEE ABOUT JELLY NASH! RIGHT QUICK, I THINK!
DAWGONE! JELLY'S DEAD! THE SAP DIDN'T HAVE SENSE 'NUFF T'DUCK DOWN!
HE DIDN'T HAVE TIME, YA CRAZY BOOB!

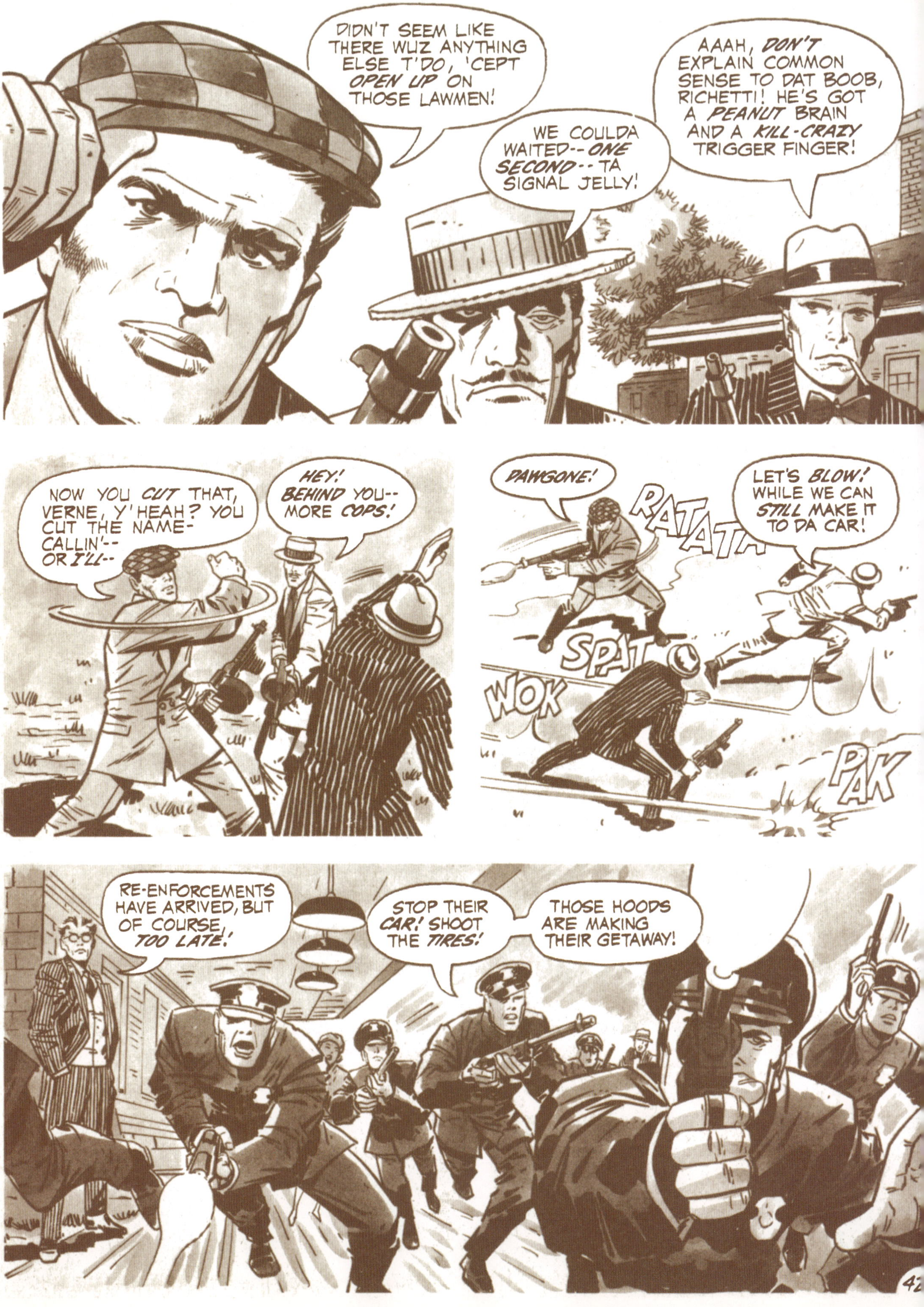
DIDN'T SEEM LIKE THERE WUZ ANYTHING ELSE T'DO, 'CEPT OPEN UP ON THOSE LAWMEN!
WE COULDA WAITED-- ONE SECOND-- TA SIGNAL JELLY!
AAAH, DON'T EXPLAIN COMMON SENSE TO DAT BOOB, RICHETTI! HE'S GOT A PEANUT BRAIN AND A KILL-CRAZY TRIGGER FINGER!
NOW YOU CUT THAT, VERNE, Y'HEAH? YOU CUT THE NAME-CALLIN'-- OR I'LL--
HEY! BEHIND YOU-- MORE COPS!
DAWGONE!
RATATATA
LET'S BLOW! WHILE WE CAN STILL MAKE IT TO DA CAR!
SPAT
WOK
PAK
RE-ENFORCEMENTS HAVE ARRIVED, BUT OF COURSE, TOO LATE!
STOP THEIR CAR! SHOOT THE TIRES!
THOSE HOODS ARE MAKING THEIR GETAWAY!

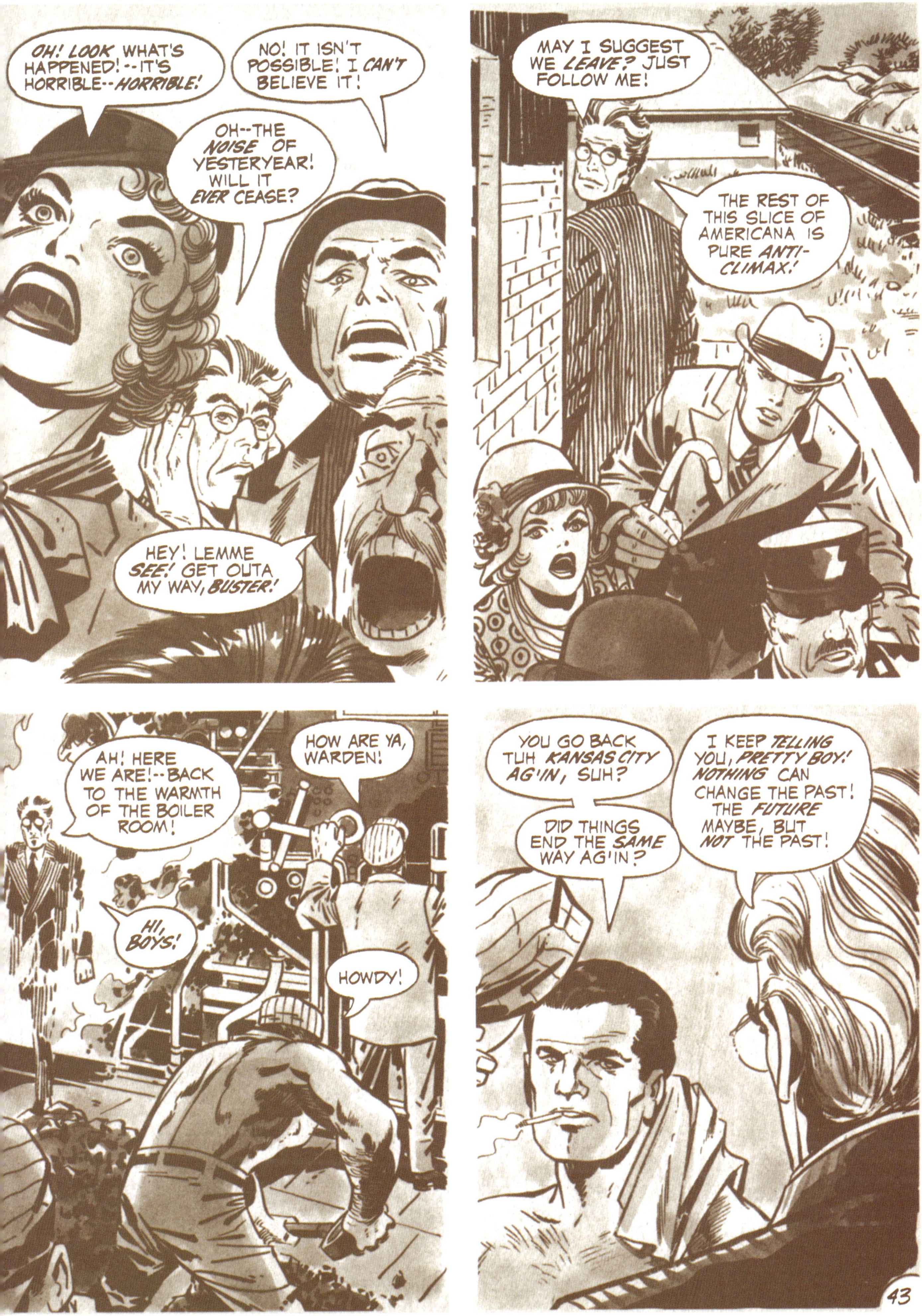
OH! LOOK WHAT'S HAPPENED! --IT'S HORRIBLE--HORRIBLE!
NO! IT ISN'T POSSIBLE! I CAN'T BELIEVE IT!
OH--THE NOISE OF YESTERYEAR! WILL IT EVER CEASE?
HEY! LEMME SEE! GET OUTA MY WAY, BUSTER!
MAY I SUGGEST WE LEAVE? JUST FOLLOW ME!
THE REST OF THIS SLICE OF AMERICANA IS PURE ANTI-CLIMAX!
AH! HERE WE ARE!--BACK TO THE WARMTH OF THE BOILER ROOM!
HOW ARE YA, WARDEN!
HI, BOYS!
HOWDY!
YOU GO BACK TUH KANSAS CITY AG'IN, SUH?
DID THINGS END THE SAME WAY AG'IN?
I KEEP TELLING YOU, PRETTY BOY! NOTHING CAN CHANGE THE PAST! THE FUTURE MAYBE, BUT NOT THE PAST!

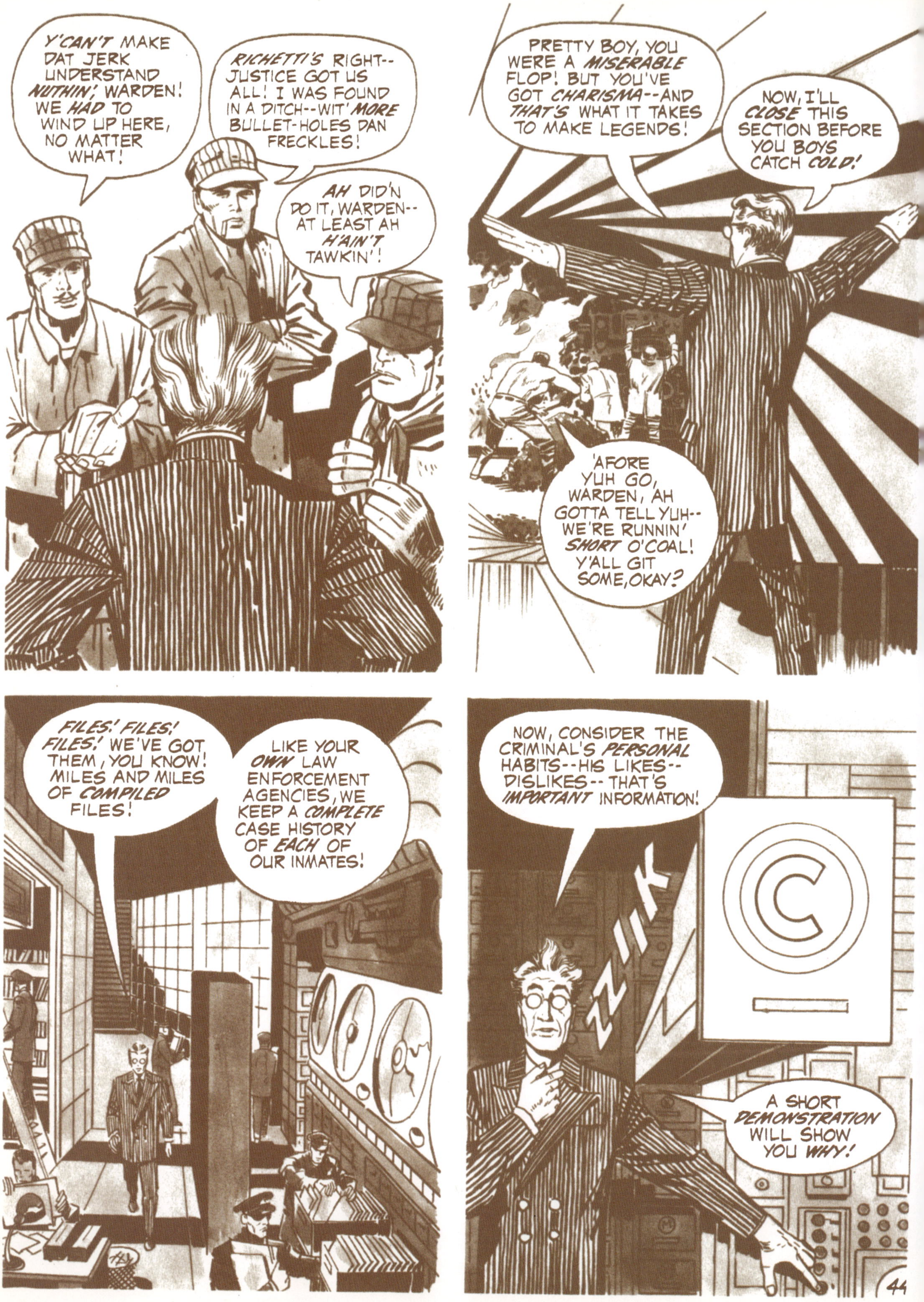
Y'CAN'T MAKE DAT JERK UNDERSTAND NUTHIN'; WARDEN! WE HAD TO WIND UP HERE, NO MATTER WHAT!
RICHETTI'S RIGHT-- JUSTICE GOT US ALL! I WAS FOUND IN A DITCH--WIT' MORE BULLET-HOLES DAN FRECKLES!
AH DID'N DO IT, WARDEN-- AT LEAST AH H'AIN'T TAWKIN'!
PRETTY BOY, YOU WERE A MISERABLE FLOP! BUT YOU'VE GOT CHARISMA--AND THAT'S WHAT IT TAKES TO MAKE LEGENDS!
NOW, I'LL CLOSE THIS SECTION BEFORE YOU BOYS CATCH COLD!
'AFORE YUH GO, WARDEN, AH GOTTA TELL YUH-- WE'RE RUNNIN' SHORT O'COAL! Y'ALL GIT SOME, OKAY?
FILES! FILES! FILES! WE'VE GOT THEM, YOU KNOW! MILES AND MILES OF COMPILED FILES!
LIKE YOUR OWN LAW ENFORCEMENT AGENCIES, WE KEEP A COMPLETE CASE HISTORY OF EACH OF OUR INMATES!
NOW, CONSIDER THE CRIMINAL'S PERSONAL HABITS--HIS LIKES-- DISLIKES-- THAT'S IMPORTANT INFORMATION!
ZZIIK
A SHORT DEMONSTRATION WILL SHOW YOU WHY!

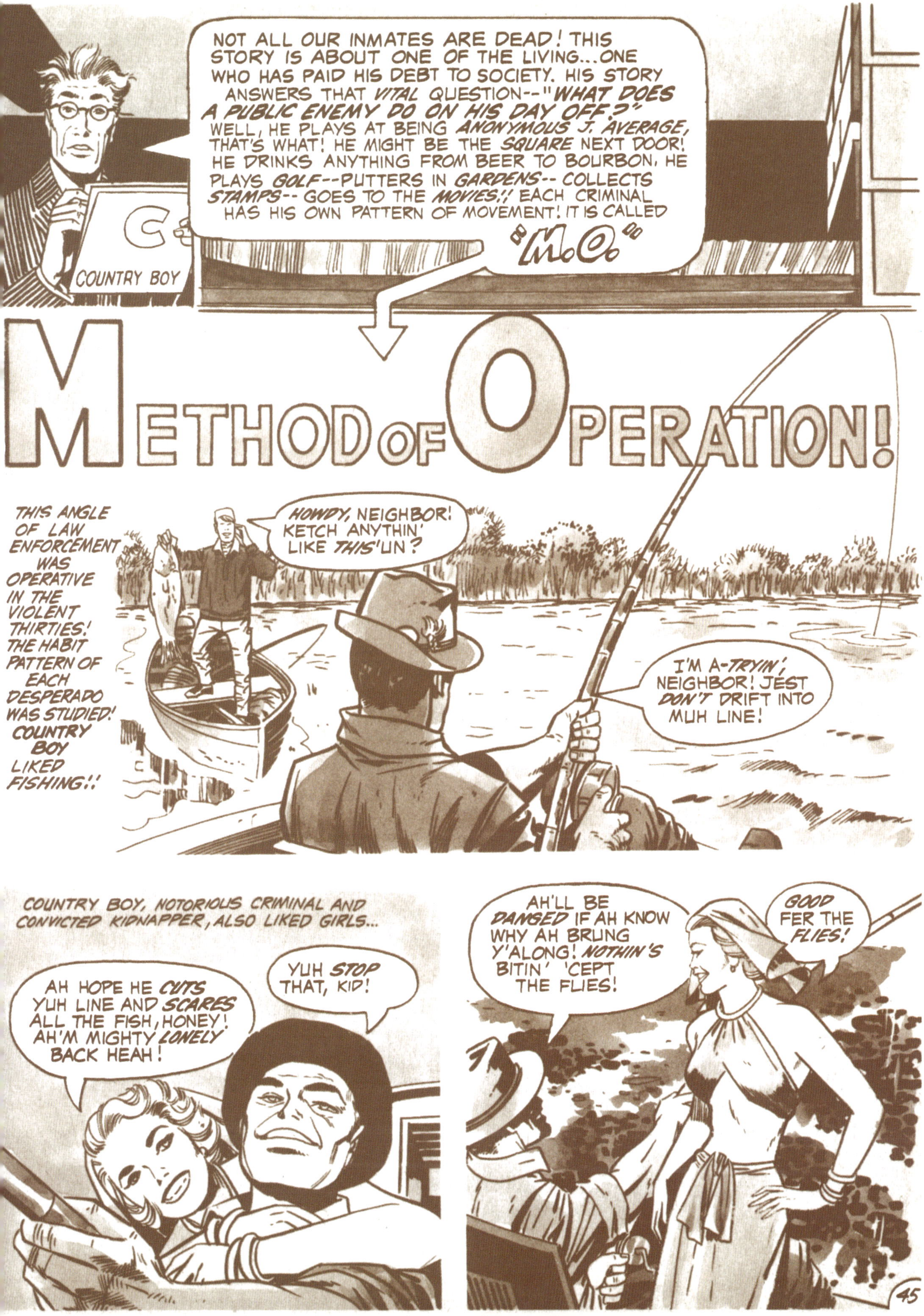

NOT ALL OUR INMATES ARE DEAD! THIS STORY IS ABOUT ONE OF THE LIVING...ONE WHO HAS PAID HIS DEBT TO SOCIETY. HIS STORY ANSWERS THAT VITAL QUESTION--"WHAT DOES A PUBLIC ENEMY DO ON HIS DAY OFF?" WELL, HE PLAYS AT BEING ANONYMOUS J. AVERAGE, THAT'S WHAT! HE MIGHT BE THE SQUARE NEXT DOOR! HE DRINKS ANYTHING FROM BEER TO BOURBON. HE PLAYS GOLF--PUTTERS IN GARDENS-- COLLECTS STAMPS-- GOES TO THE MOVIES!! EACH CRIMINAL HAS HIS OWN PATTERN OF MOVEMENT! IT IS CALLED "M.O."
COUNTRY BOY
METHOD OF OPERATION!
THIS ANGLE OF LAW ENFORCEMENT WAS OPERATIVE IN THE VIOLENT THIRTIES! THE HABIT PATTERN OF EACH DESPERADO WAS STUDIED! COUNTRY BOY LIKED FISHING!!
HOWDY, NEIGHBOR! KETCH ANYTHIN' LIKE THIS'UN?
I'M A-TRYIN', NEIGHBOR! JEST DON'T DRIFT INTO MUH LINE!
COUNTRY BOY, NOTORIOUS CRIMINAL AND CONVICTED KIDNAPPER, ALSO LIKED GIRLS...
AH HOPE HE CUTS YUH LINE AND SCARES ALL THE FISH, HONEY! AH'M MIGHTY LONELY BACK HEAH!
YUH STOP THAT, KID!
AH'LL BE DANGED IF AH KNOW WHY AH BRUNG Y'ALONG! NOTHIN'S BITIN' 'CEPT THE FLIES!
GOOD FER THE FLIES!

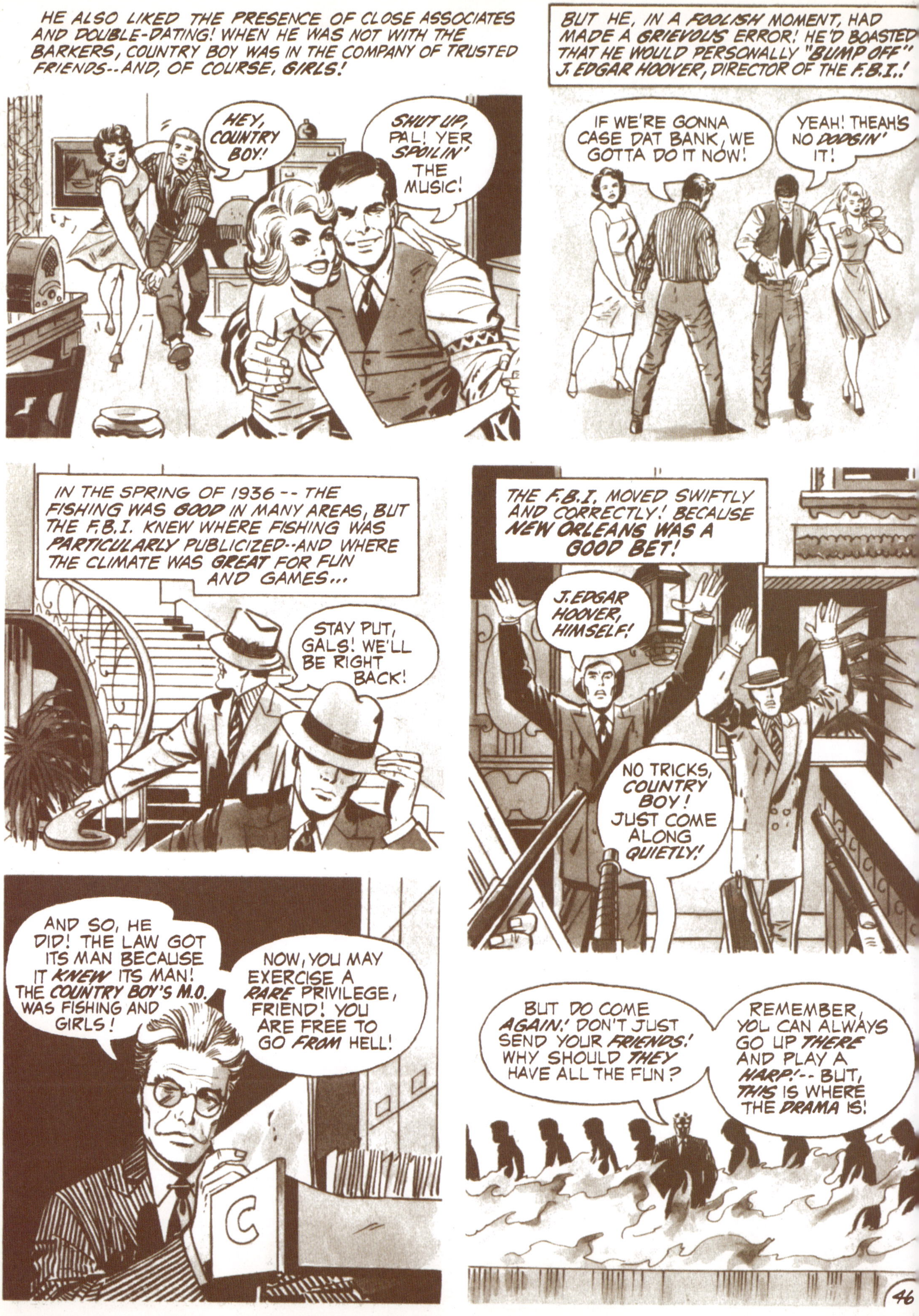
HE ALSO LIKED THE PRESENCE OF CLOSE ASSOCIATES AND DOUBLE-DATING! WHEN HE WAS NOT WITH THE BARKERS, COUNTRY BOY WAS IN THE COMPANY OF TRUSTED FRIENDS--AND, OF COURSE, GIRLS!
HEY, COUNTRY BOY!
SHUT UP, PAL! YER SPOILIN' THE MUSIC!
BUT HE, IN A FOOLISH MOMENT, HAD MADE A GRIEVOUS ERROR! HE'D BOASTED THAT HE WOULD PERSONALLY "BUMP OFF" J. EDGAR HOOVER, DIRECTOR OF THE F.B.I.!
IF WE'RE GONNA CASE DAT BANK, WE GOTTA DO IT NOW!
YEAH! THEAH'S NO DODGIN' IT!
IN THE SPRING OF 1936 -- THE FISHING WAS GOOD IN MANY AREAS, BUT THE F.B.I. KNEW WHERE FISHING WAS PARTICULARLY PUBLICIZED--AND WHERE THE CLIMATE WAS GREAT FOR FUN AND GAMES...
STAY PUT, GALS! WE'LL BE RIGHT BACK!
THE F.B.I. MOVED SWIFTLY AND CORRECTLY! BECAUSE NEW ORLEANS WAS A GOOD BET!
J. EDGAR HOOVER, HIMSELF!
NO TRICKS, COUNTRY BOY! JUST COME ALONG QUIETLY!
AND SO, HE DID! THE LAW GOT ITS MAN BECAUSE IT KNEW ITS MAN! THE COUNTRY BOY'S M.O. WAS FISHING AND GIRLS!
NOW, YOU MAY EXERCISE A RARE PRIVILEGE, FRIEND! YOU ARE FREE TO GO FROM HELL!
C
BUT DO COME AGAIN! DON'T JUST SEND YOUR FRIENDS! WHY SHOULD THEY HAVE ALL THE FUN?
REMEMBER, YOU CAN ALWAYS GO UP THERE AND PLAY A HARP!-- BUT, THIS IS WHERE THE DRAMA IS!

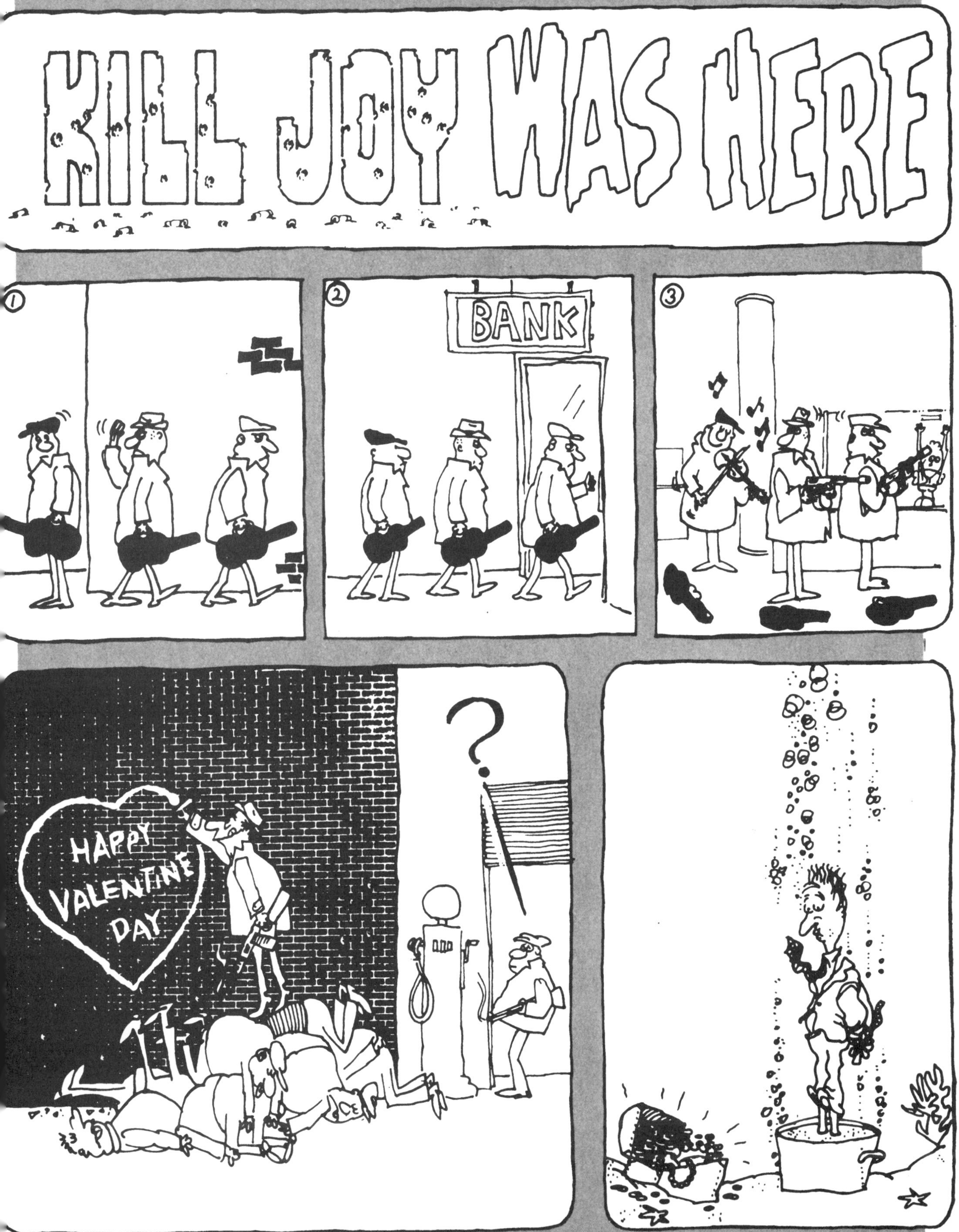
KILL JOY WAS HERE
①
②
BANK
③
HAPPY VALENTINE DAY
?

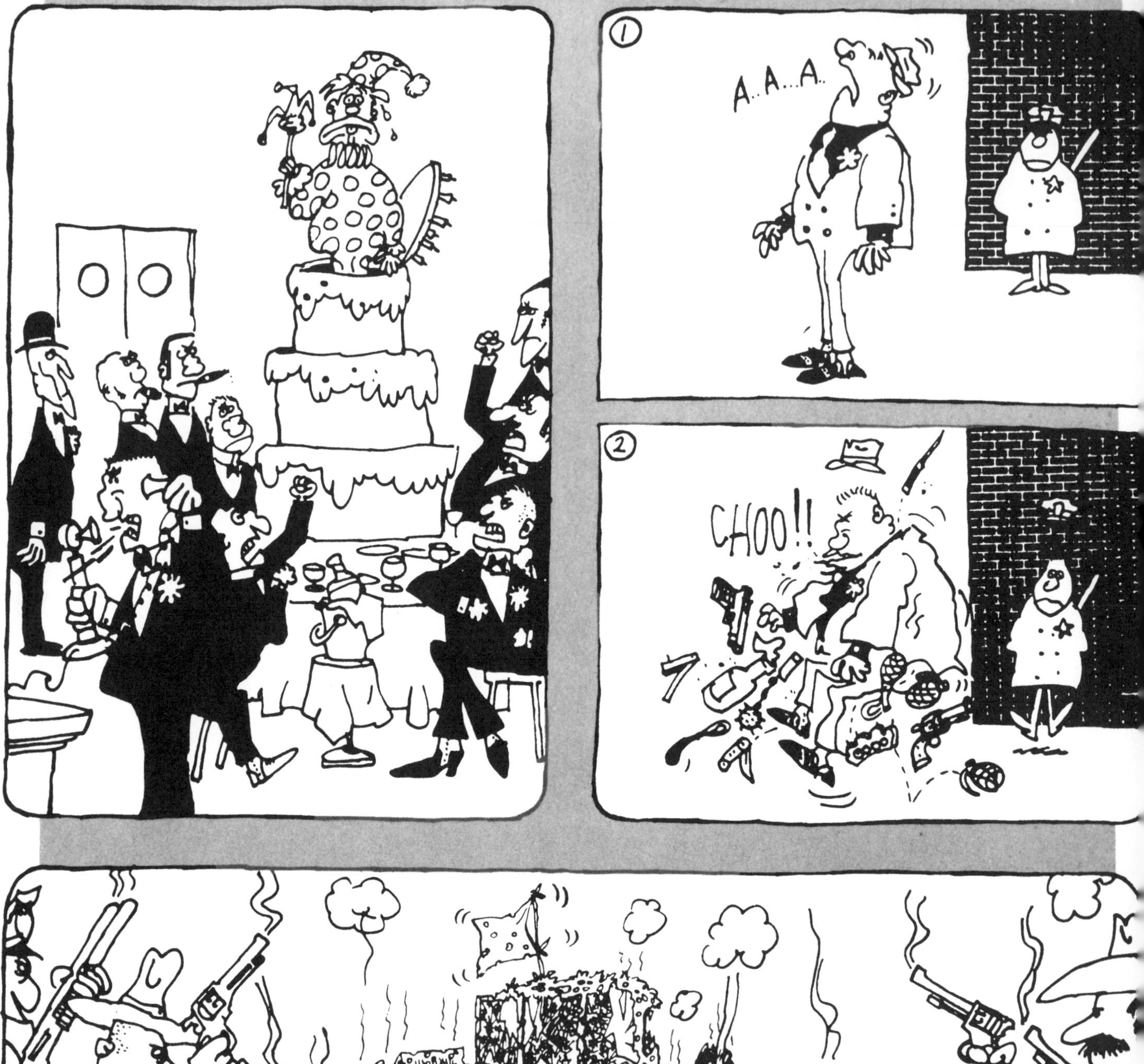
1
A..A..A..
2
CHOO!!
ARAGONÉS

# WANTED

## IN 5 STATES

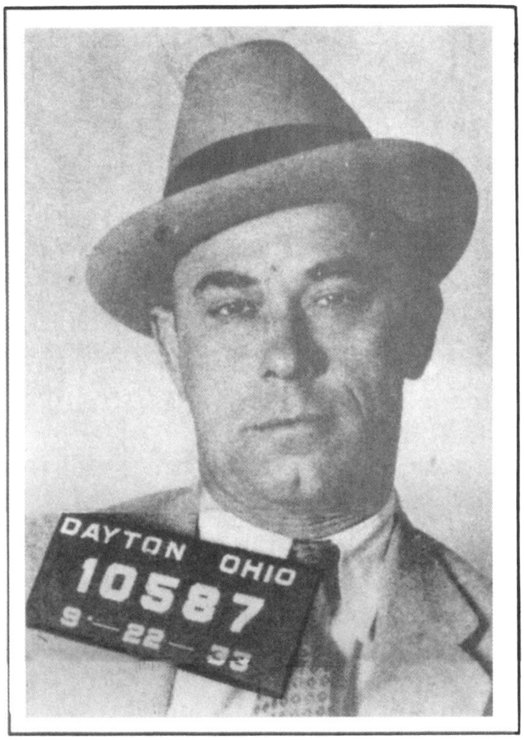
DAYTON OHIO
10587
9-22-33

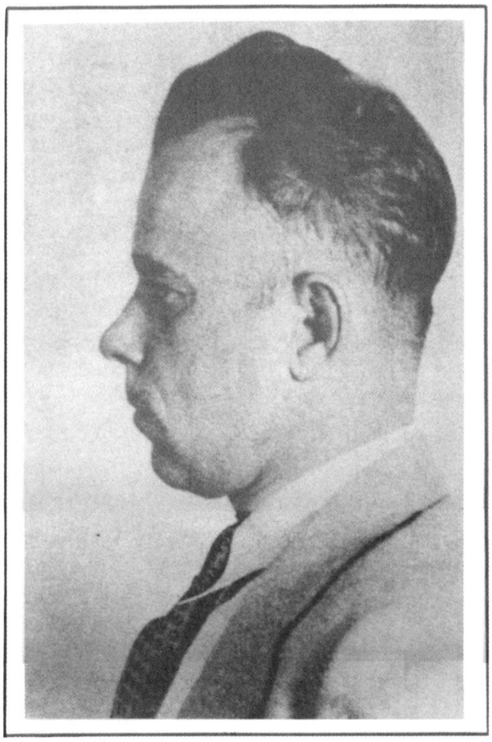

## JOHN DILLINGER

# PUBLIC ENEMY NUMBER ONE!

The Attorney General of the U.S. has authorized a

# $20,000 REWARD!

for information leading to the arrest of John Dillinger.

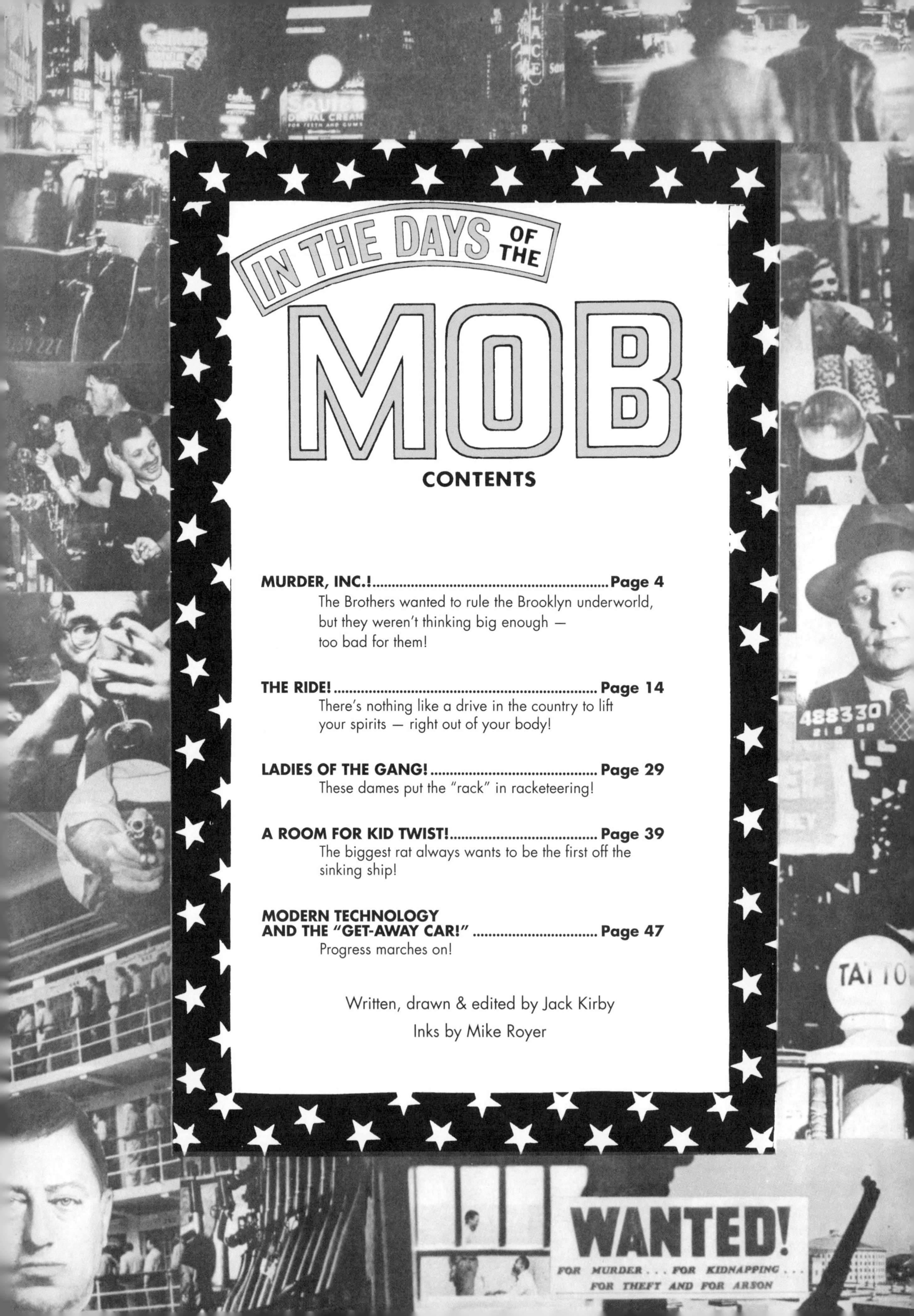

# IN THE DAYS OF THE MOB

## CONTENTS

**MURDER, INC.!** ............................................................. Page 4
  The Brothers wanted to rule the Brooklyn underworld,
  but they weren't thinking big enough —
  too bad for them!

**THE RIDE!** ..................................................................... Page 14
  There's nothing like a drive in the country to lift
  your spirits — right out of your body!

**LADIES OF THE GANG!** ............................................ Page 29
  These dames put the "rack" in racketeering!

**A ROOM FOR KID TWIST!** ....................................... Page 39
  The biggest rat always wants to be the first off the
  sinking ship!

**MODERN TECHNOLOGY
AND THE "GET-AWAY CAR!"** ................................. Page 47
  Progress marches on!

Written, drawn & edited by Jack Kirby

Inks by Mike Royer

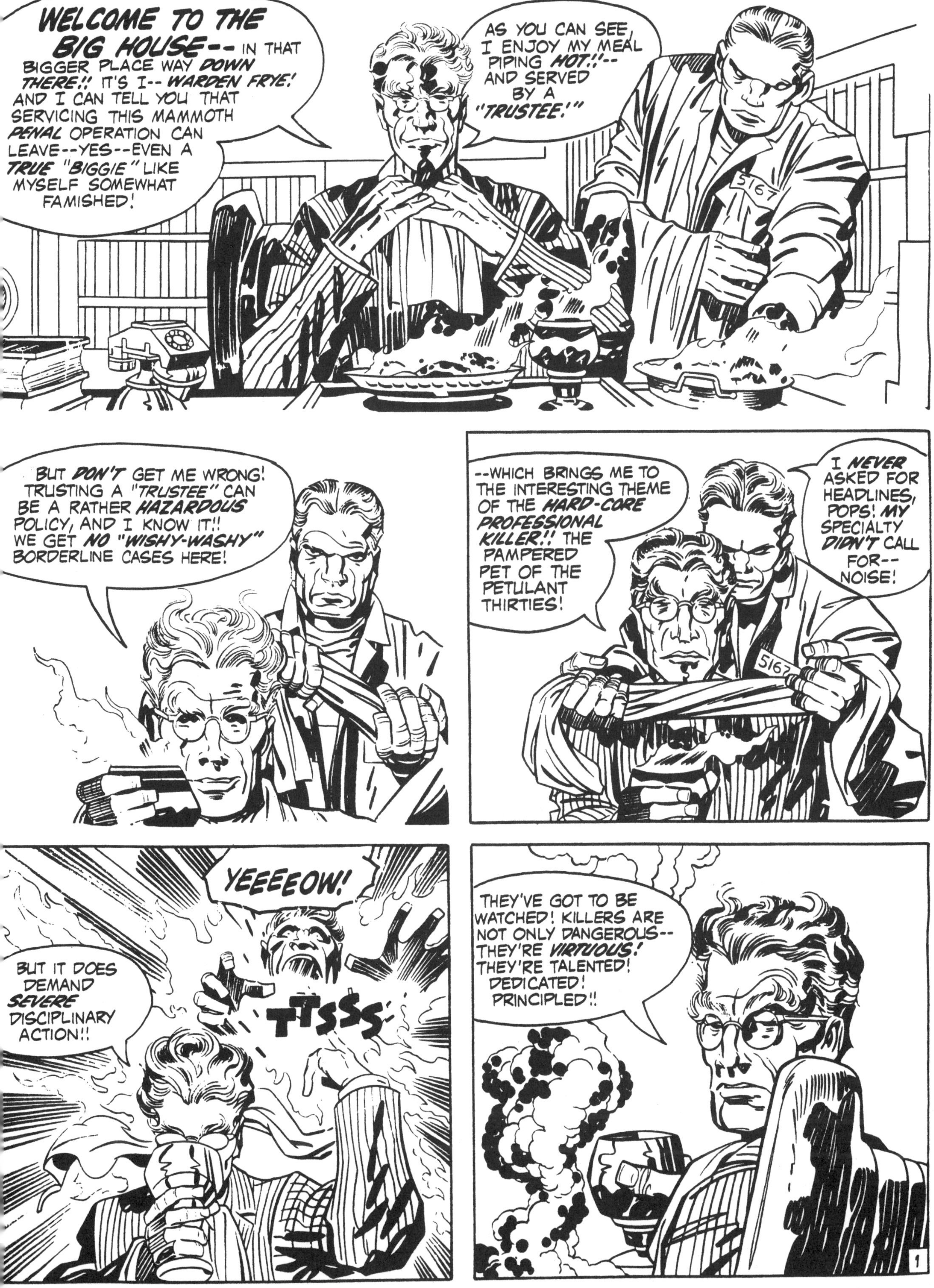
WELCOME TO THE BIG HOUSE-- IN THAT BIGGER PLACE WAY DOWN THERE!! IT'S I-- WARDEN FRYE! AND I CAN TELL YOU THAT SERVICING THIS MAMMOTH PENAL OPERATION CAN LEAVE--YES--EVEN A TRUE "BIGGIE" LIKE MYSELF SOMEWHAT FAMISHED!
AS YOU CAN SEE, I ENJOY MY MEAL PIPING HOT!'-- AND SERVED BY A "TRUSTEE!"
5167
BUT DON'T GET ME WRONG! TRUSTING A "TRUSTEE" CAN BE A RATHER HAZARDOUS POLICY, AND I KNOW IT!! WE GET NO "WISHY-WASHY" BORDERLINE CASES HERE!
--WHICH BRINGS ME TO THE INTERESTING THEME OF THE HARD-CORE PROFESSIONAL KILLER!! THE PAMPERED PET OF THE PETULANT THIRTIES!
I NEVER ASKED FOR HEADLINES, POPS! MY SPECIALTY DIDN'T CALL FOR-- NOISE!
5167
YEEEEOW!
BUT IT DOES DEMAND SEVERE DISCIPLINARY ACTION!!
TTSSS
THEY'VE GOT TO BE WATCHED! KILLERS ARE NOT ONLY DANGEROUS-- THEY'RE VIRTUOUS! THEY'RE TALENTED! DEDICATED! PRINCIPLED!!

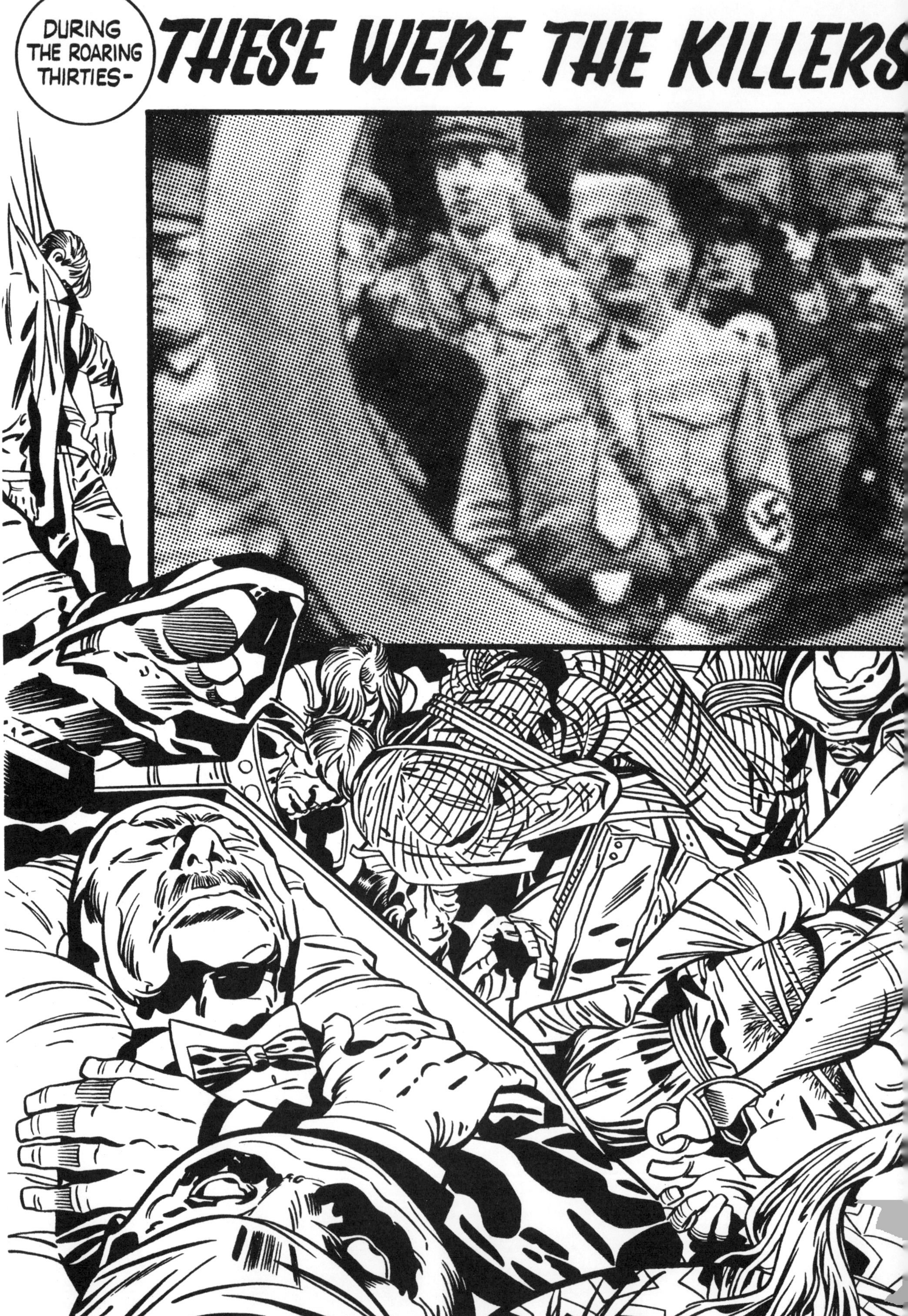
DURING THE ROARING THIRTIES-
THESE WERE THE KILLERS

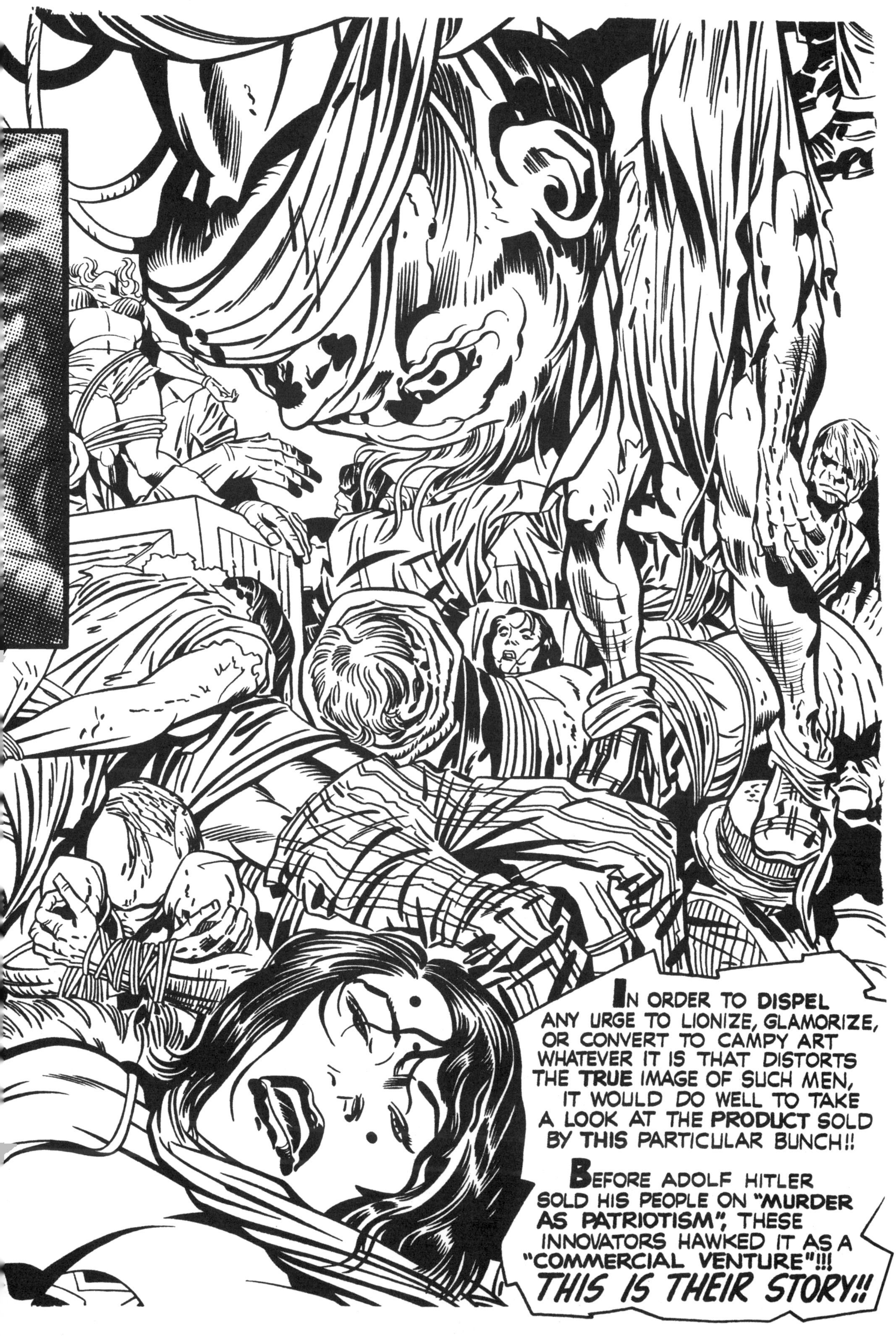
IN ORDER TO DISPEL ANY URGE TO LIONIZE, GLAMORIZE, OR CONVERT TO CAMPY ART WHATEVER IT IS THAT DISTORTS THE TRUE IMAGE OF SUCH MEN, IT WOULD DO WELL TO TAKE A LOOK AT THE PRODUCT SOLD BY THIS PARTICULAR BUNCH!!
BEFORE ADOLF HITLER SOLD HIS PEOPLE ON "MURDER AS PATRIOTISM", THESE INNOVATORS HAWKED IT AS A "COMMERCIAL VENTURE"!!!
THIS IS THEIR STORY!!

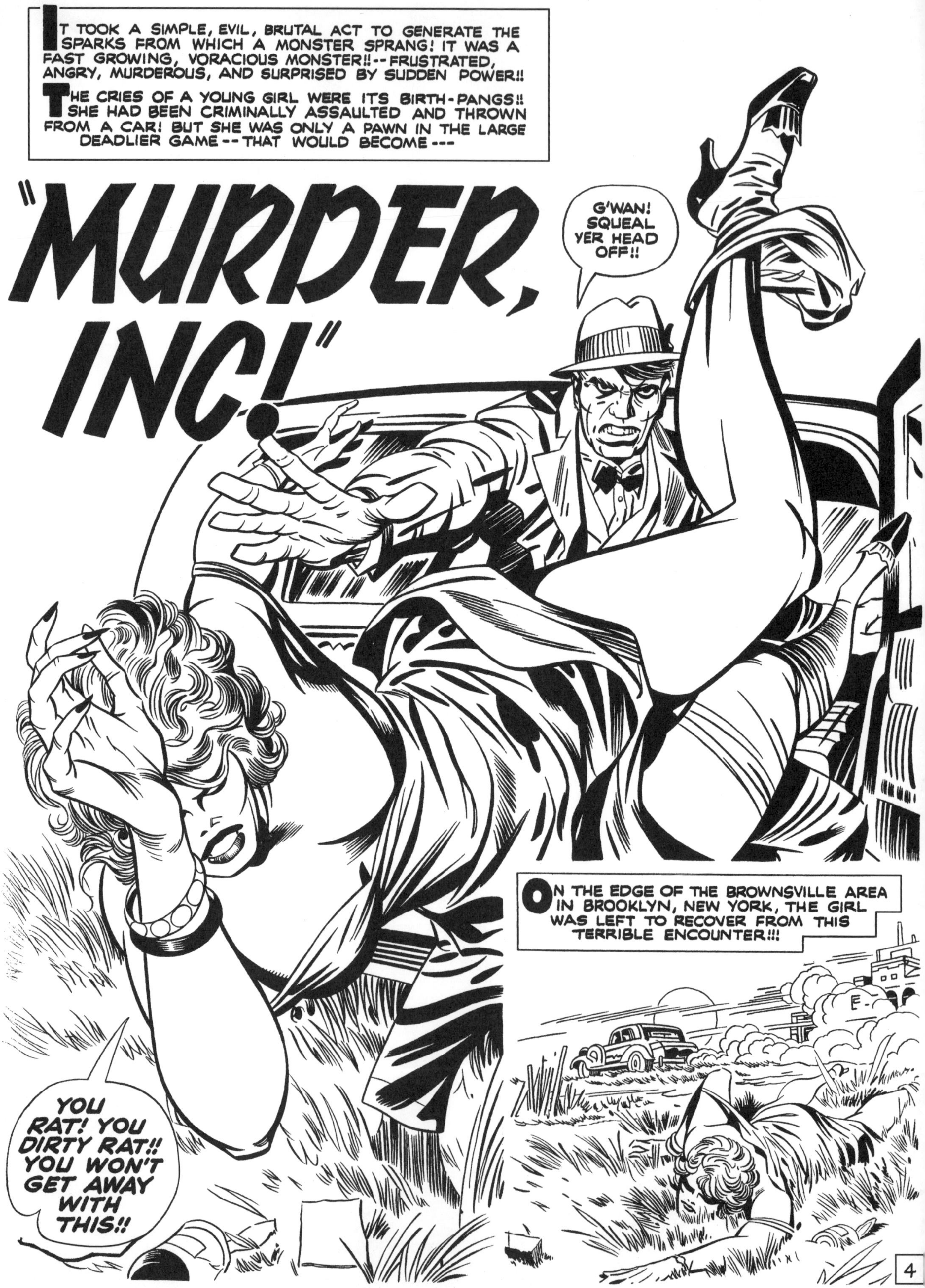
IT TOOK A SIMPLE, EVIL, BRUTAL ACT TO GENERATE THE SPARKS FROM WHICH A MONSTER SPRANG! IT WAS A FAST GROWING, VORACIOUS MONSTER!!--FRUSTRATED, ANGRY, MURDEROUS, AND SURPRISED BY SUDDEN POWER!!
THE CRIES OF A YOUNG GIRL WERE ITS BIRTH-PANGS!! SHE HAD BEEN CRIMINALLY ASSAULTED AND THROWN FROM A CAR! BUT SHE WAS ONLY A PAWN IN THE LARGE DEADLIER GAME--THAT WOULD BECOME---
"MURDER, INC!"
G'WAN! SQUEAL YER HEAD OFF!!
YOU RAT! YOU DIRTY RAT!! YOU WON'T GET AWAY WITH THIS!!
ON THE EDGE OF THE BROWNSVILLE AREA IN BROOKLYN, NEW YORK, THE GIRL WAS LEFT TO RECOVER FROM THIS TERRIBLE ENCOUNTER!!!

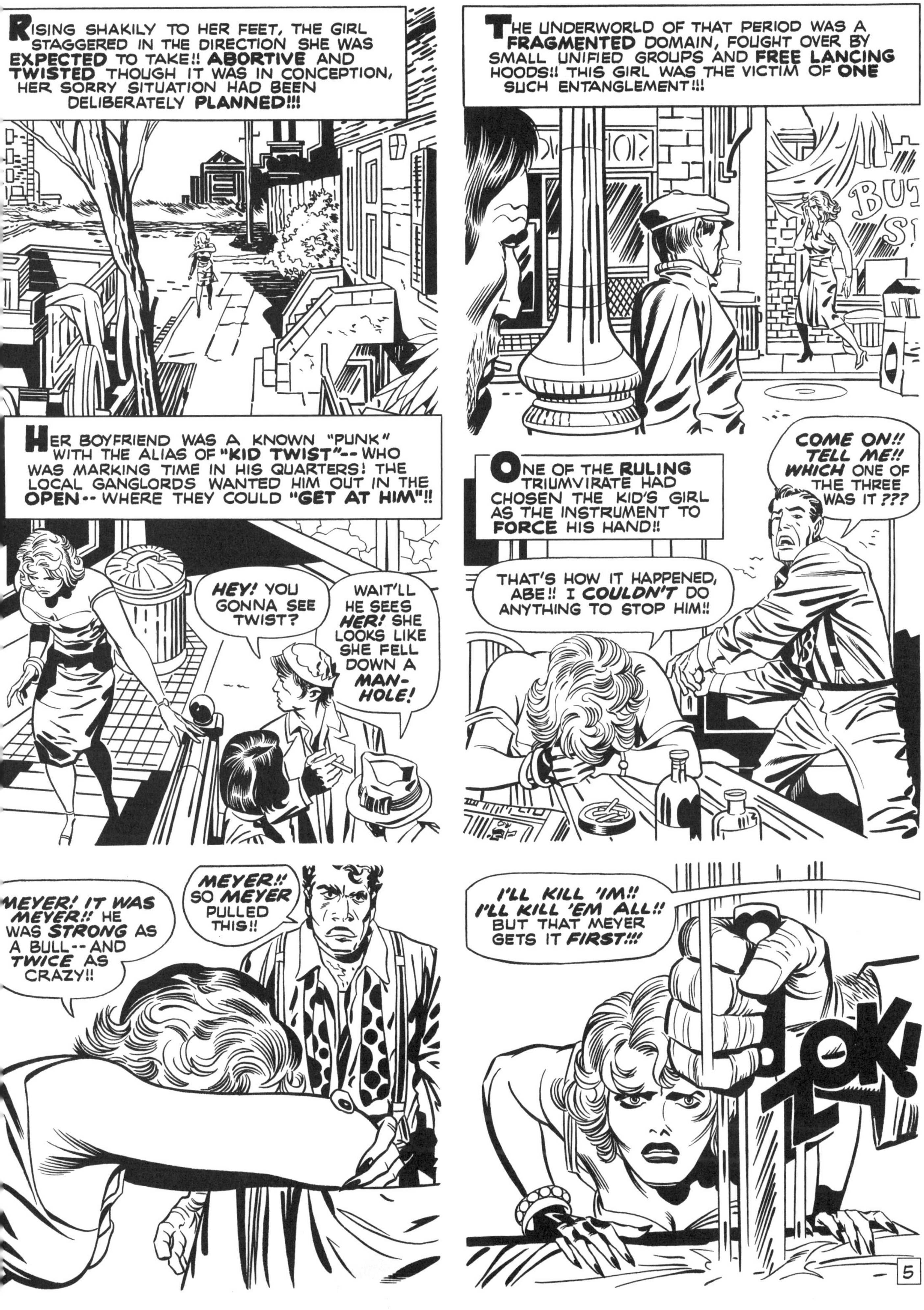
RISING SHAKILY TO HER FEET, THE GIRL STAGGERED IN THE DIRECTION SHE WAS EXPECTED TO TAKE!! ABORTIVE AND TWISTED THOUGH IT WAS IN CONCEPTION, HER SORRY SITUATION HAD BEEN DELIBERATELY PLANNED!!!
THE UNDERWORLD OF THAT PERIOD WAS A FRAGMENTED DOMAIN, FOUGHT OVER BY SMALL UNIFIED GROUPS AND FREE LANCING HOODS!! THIS GIRL WAS THE VICTIM OF ONE SUCH ENTANGLEMENT!!!
HER BOYFRIEND WAS A KNOWN "PUNK" WITH THE ALIAS OF "KID TWIST"-- WHO WAS MARKING TIME IN HIS QUARTERS! THE LOCAL GANGLORDS WANTED HIM OUT IN THE OPEN-- WHERE THEY COULD "GET AT HIM"!!
HEY! YOU GONNA SEE TWIST?
WAIT'LL HE SEES HER! SHE LOOKS LIKE SHE FELL DOWN A MAN-HOLE!
ONE OF THE RULING TRIUMVIRATE HAD CHOSEN THE KID'S GIRL AS THE INSTRUMENT TO FORCE HIS HAND!!
COME ON!! TELL ME!! WHICH ONE OF THE THREE WAS IT???
THAT'S HOW IT HAPPENED, ABE!! I COULDN'T DO ANYTHING TO STOP HIM!!
MEYER! IT WAS MEYER!! HE WAS STRONG AS A BULL-- AND TWICE AS CRAZY!!
MEYER!! SO MEYER PULLED THIS!!
I'LL KILL 'IM!! I'LL KILL 'EM ALL!! BUT THAT MEYER GETS IT FIRST!!!
TOK!

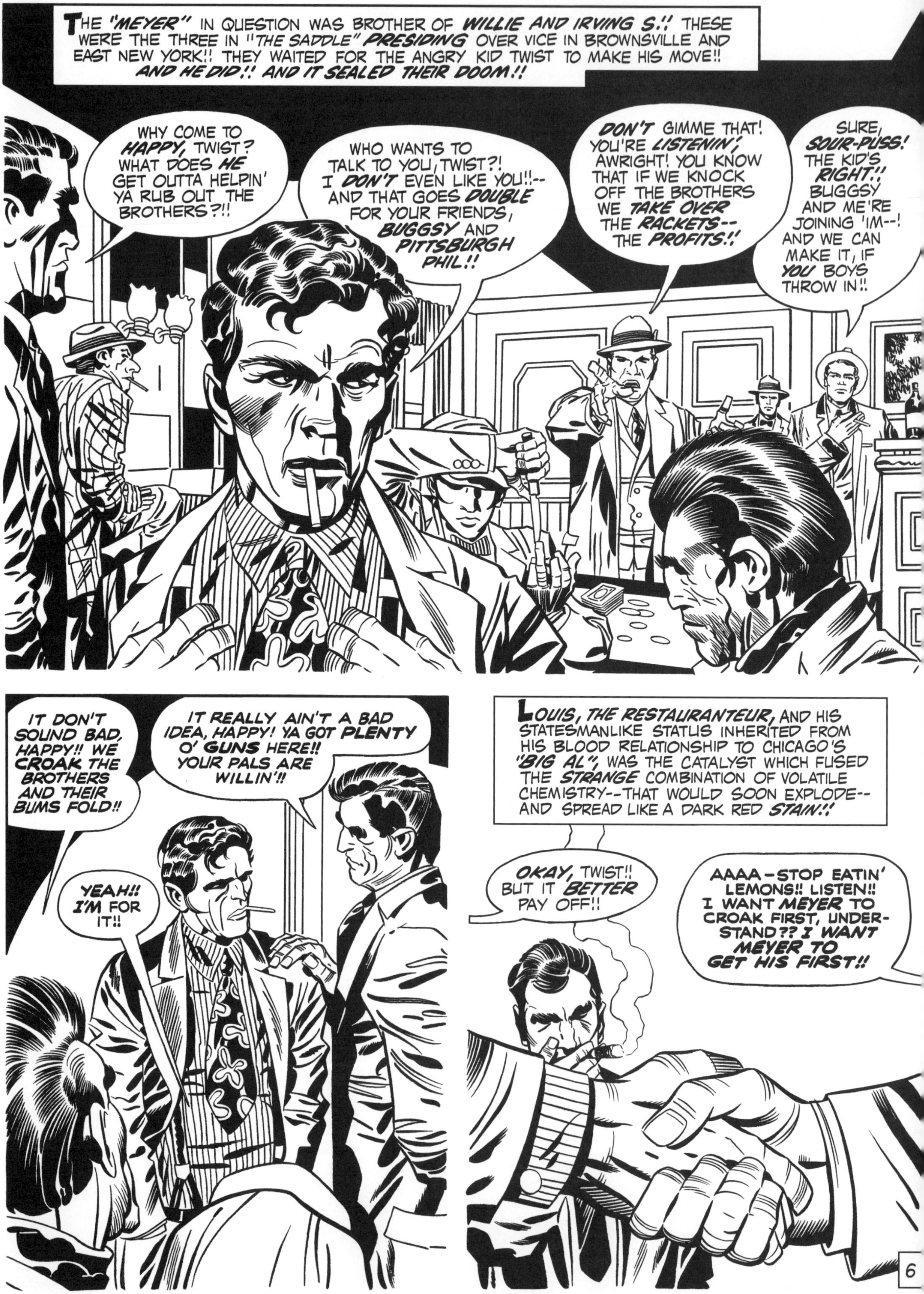
THE "MEYER" IN QUESTION WAS BROTHER OF WILLIE AND IRVING S.!! THESE WERE THE THREE IN "THE SADDLE" PRESIDING OVER VICE IN BROWNSVILLE AND EAST NEW YORK!! THEY WAITED FOR THE ANGRY KID TWIST TO MAKE HIS MOVE!! AND HE DID!! AND IT SEALED THEIR DOOM!!
WHY COME TO HAPPY, TWIST? WHAT DOES HE GET OUTTA HELPIN' YA RUB OUT THE BROTHERS?!!
WHO WANTS TO TALK TO YOU, TWIST?! I DON'T EVEN LIKE YOU!!-- AND THAT GOES DOUBLE FOR YOUR FRIENDS, BUGGSY AND PITTSBURGH PHIL!!
DON'T GIMME THAT! YOU'RE LISTENIN'! AWRIGHT! YOU KNOW THAT IF WE KNOCK OFF THE BROTHERS WE TAKE OVER THE RACKETS-- THE PROFITS!!
SURE, SOUR-PUSS! THE KID'S RIGHT!! BUGGSY AND ME'RE JOINING 'IM--! AND WE CAN MAKE IT, IF YOU BOYS THROW IN!!
IT DON'T SOUND BAD, HAPPY!! WE CROAK THE BROTHERS AND THEIR BUMS FOLD!!
IT REALLY AIN'T A BAD IDEA, HAPPY! YA GOT PLENTY O' GUNS HERE!! YOUR PALS ARE WILLIN'!!
YEAH!! I'M FOR IT!!
LOUIS, THE RESTAURANTEUR, AND HIS STATESMANLIKE STATUS INHERITED FROM HIS BLOOD RELATIONSHIP TO CHICAGO'S "BIG AL", WAS THE CATALYST WHICH FUSED THE STRANGE COMBINATION OF VOLATILE CHEMISTRY--THAT WOULD SOON EXPLODE-- AND SPREAD LIKE A DARK RED STAIN!!
OKAY, TWIST!! BUT IT BETTER PAY OFF!!
AAAA-STOP EATIN' LEMONS!! LISTEN!! I WANT MEYER TO CROAK FIRST, UNDER-STAND?? I WANT MEYER TO GET HIS FIRST!!
6

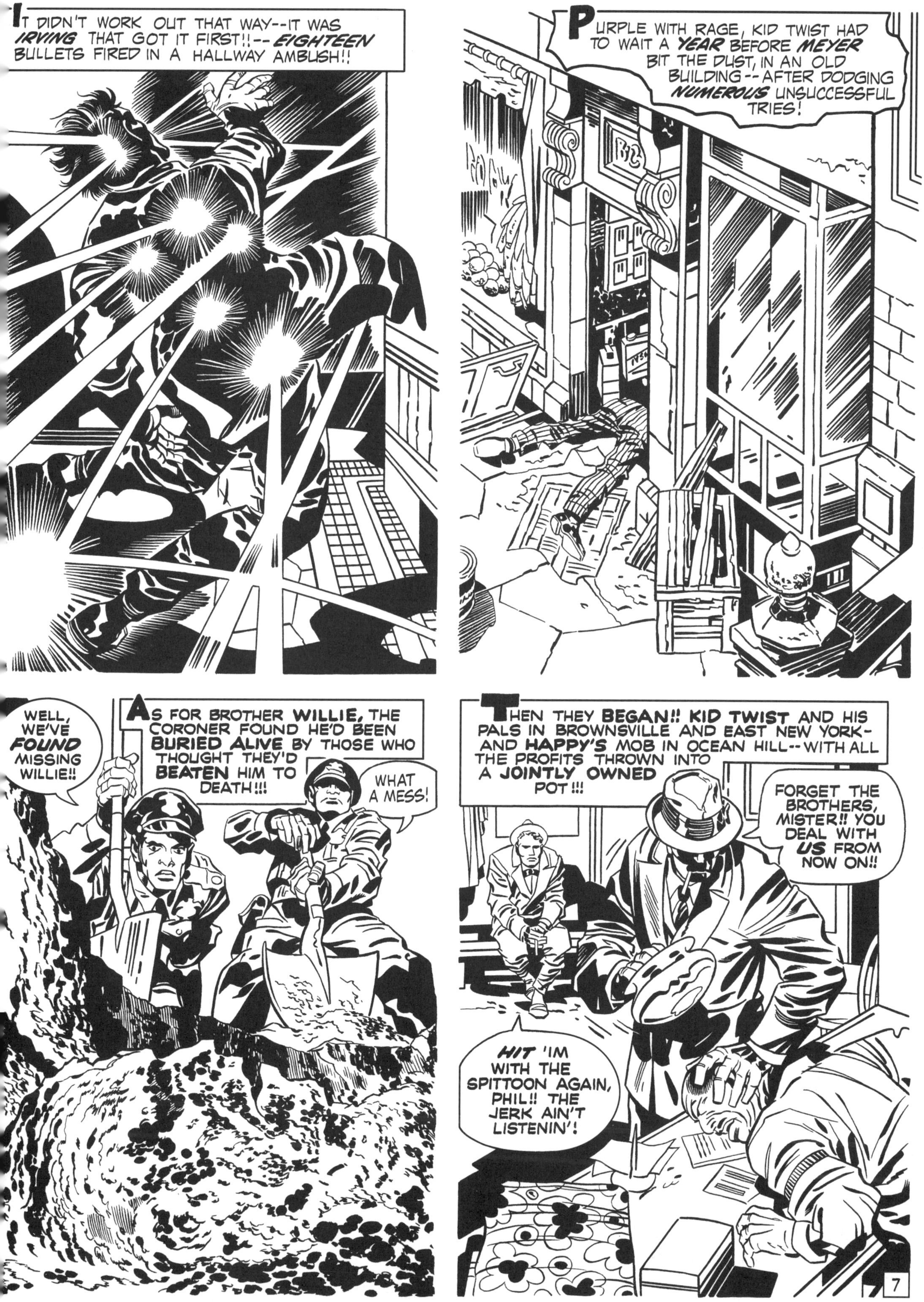
IT DIDN'T WORK OUT THAT WAY--IT WAS IRVING THAT GOT IT FIRST!!--EIGHTEEN BULLETS FIRED IN A HALLWAY AMBUSH!!
PURPLE WITH RAGE, KID TWIST HAD TO WAIT A YEAR BEFORE MEYER BIT THE DUST, IN AN OLD BUILDING--AFTER DODGING NUMEROUS UNSUCCESSFUL TRIES!
WELL, WE'VE FOUND MISSING WILLIE!!
AS FOR BROTHER WILLIE, THE CORONER FOUND HE'D BEEN BURIED ALIVE BY THOSE WHO THOUGHT THEY'D BEATEN HIM TO DEATH!!!
WHAT A MESS!
THEN THEY BEGAN!! KID TWIST AND HIS PALS IN BROWNSVILLE AND EAST NEW YORK-AND HAPPY'S MOB IN OCEAN HILL--WITH ALL THE PROFITS THROWN INTO A JOINTLY OWNED POT!!!
FORGET THE BROTHERS, MISTER!! YOU DEAL WITH US FROM NOW ON!!
HIT 'IM WITH THE SPITTOON AGAIN, PHIL!! THE JERK AIN'T LISTENIN'!

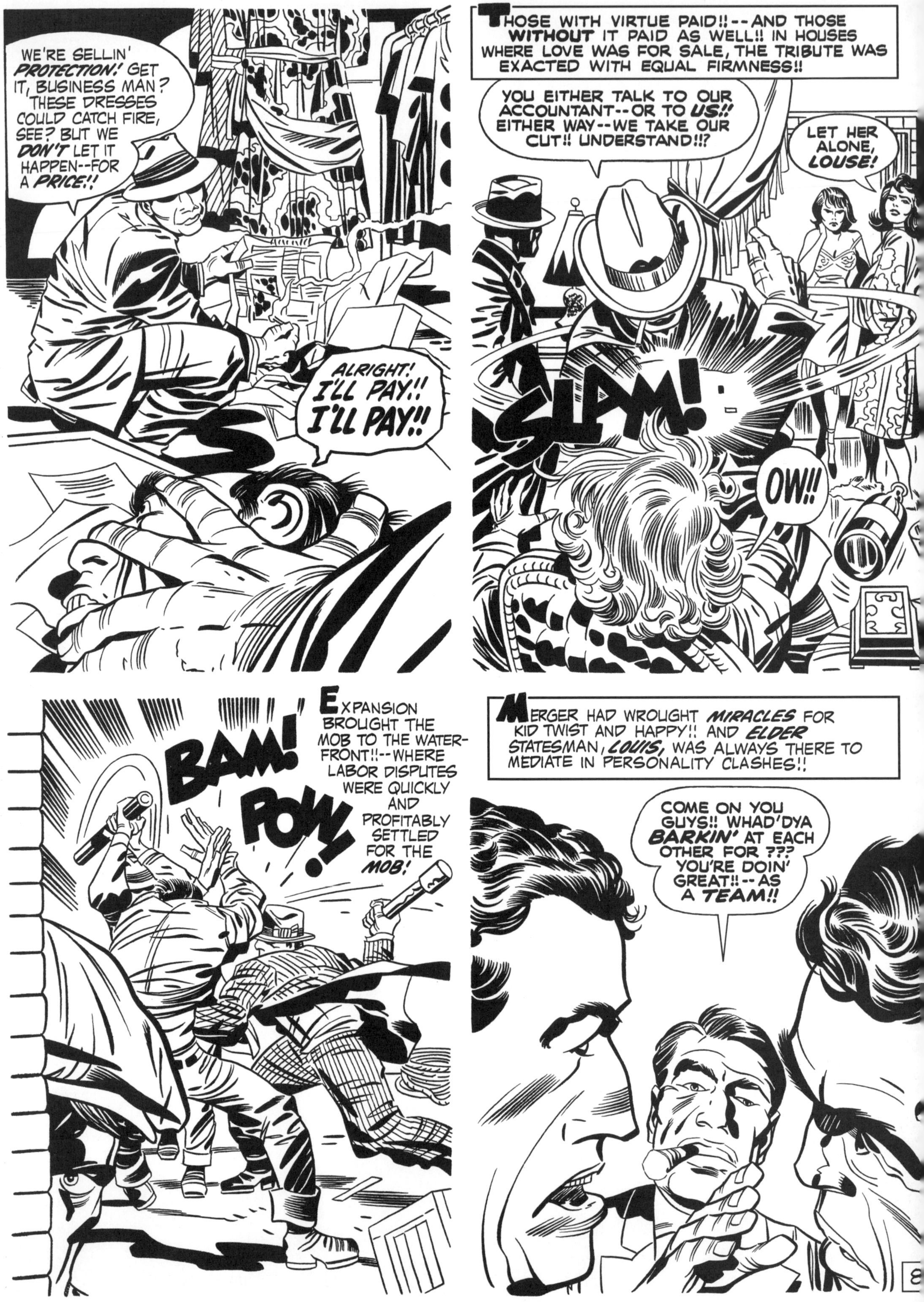
WE'RE SELLIN' PROTECTION! GET IT, BUSINESS MAN? THESE DRESSES COULD CATCH FIRE, SEE? BUT WE DON'T LET IT HAPPEN--FOR A PRICE!!
ALRIGHT! I'LL PAY!! I'LL PAY!!
THOSE WITH VIRTUE PAID!!--AND THOSE WITHOUT IT PAID AS WELL!! IN HOUSES WHERE LOVE WAS FOR SALE, THE TRIBUTE WAS EXACTED WITH EQUAL FIRMNESS!!
YOU EITHER TALK TO OUR ACCOUNTANT--OR TO US!! EITHER WAY--WE TAKE OUR CUT!! UNDERSTAND!!?
LET HER ALONE, LOUSE!
SLAM!
OW!!
EXPANSION BROUGHT THE MOB TO THE WATER-FRONT!!--WHERE LABOR DISPUTES WERE QUICKLY AND PROFITABLY SETTLED FOR THE MOB!
BAM!
POW!!
MERGER HAD WROUGHT MIRACLES FOR KID TWIST AND HAPPY!! AND ELDER STATESMAN, LOUIS, WAS ALWAYS THERE TO MEDIATE IN PERSONALITY CLASHES!!
COME ON YOU GUYS!! WHAD'DYA BARKIN' AT EACH OTHER FOR ??? YOU'RE DOIN' GREAT!!--AS A TEAM!!

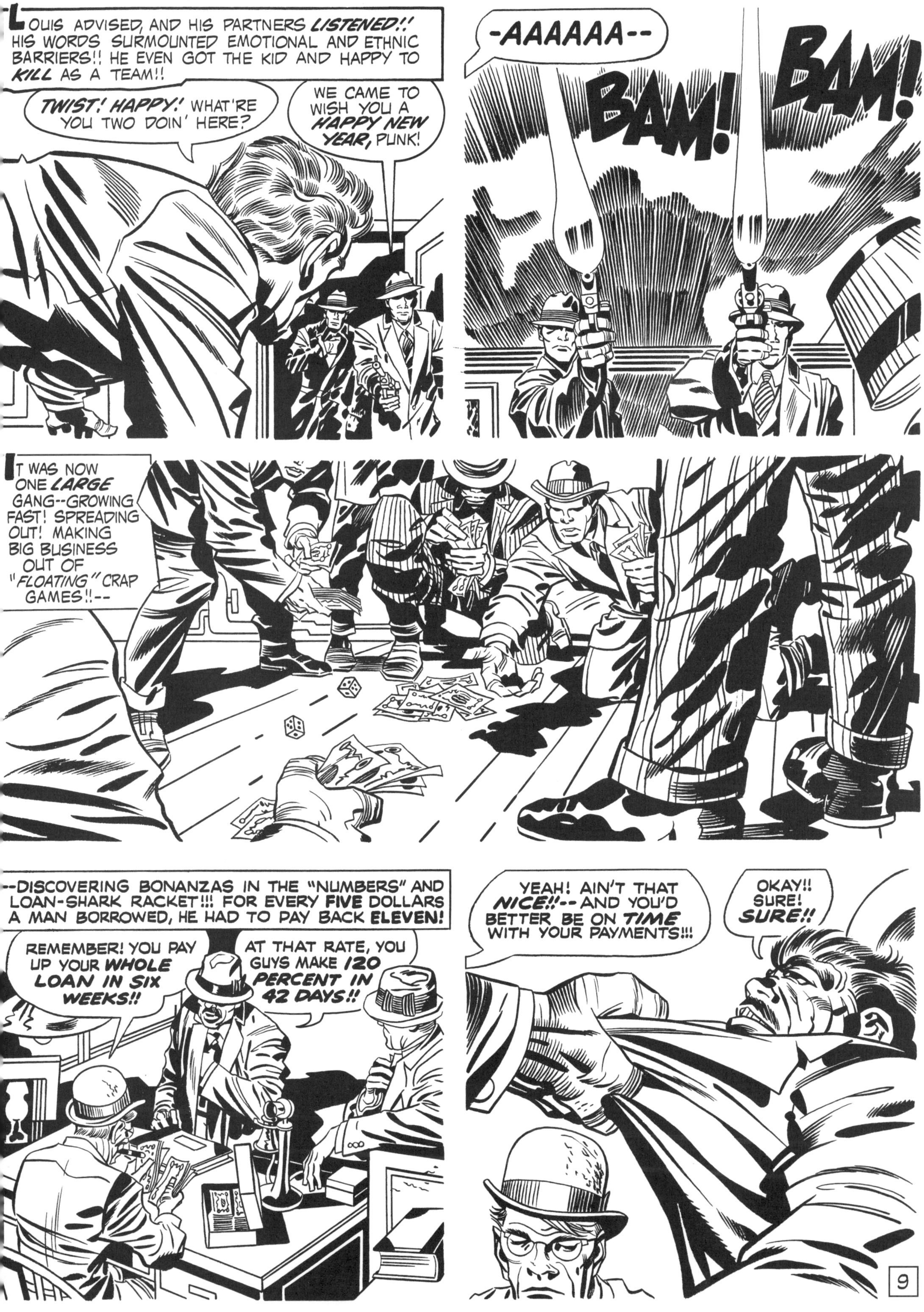
LOUIS ADVISED, AND HIS PARTNERS LISTENED!! HIS WORDS SURMOUNTED EMOTIONAL AND ETHNIC BARRIERS!! HE EVEN GOT THE KID AND HAPPY TO KILL AS A TEAM!!
TWIST! HAPPY! WHAT'RE YOU TWO DOIN' HERE?
WE CAME TO WISH YOU A HAPPY NEW YEAR, PUNK!
-AAAAAA--
BAM! BAM!
IT WAS NOW ONE LARGE GANG--GROWING FAST! SPREADING OUT! MAKING BIG BUSINESS OUT OF "FLOATING" CRAP GAMES!!--
--DISCOVERING BONANZAS IN THE "NUMBERS" AND LOAN-SHARK RACKET!!! FOR EVERY FIVE DOLLARS A MAN BORROWED, HE HAD TO PAY BACK ELEVEN!
REMEMBER! YOU PAY UP YOUR WHOLE LOAN IN SIX WEEKS!!
AT THAT RATE, YOU GUYS MAKE 120 PERCENT IN 42 DAYS!!
YEAH! AIN'T THAT NICE!!--AND YOU'D BETTER BE ON TIME WITH YOUR PAYMENTS!!!
OKAY!! SURE! SURE!!

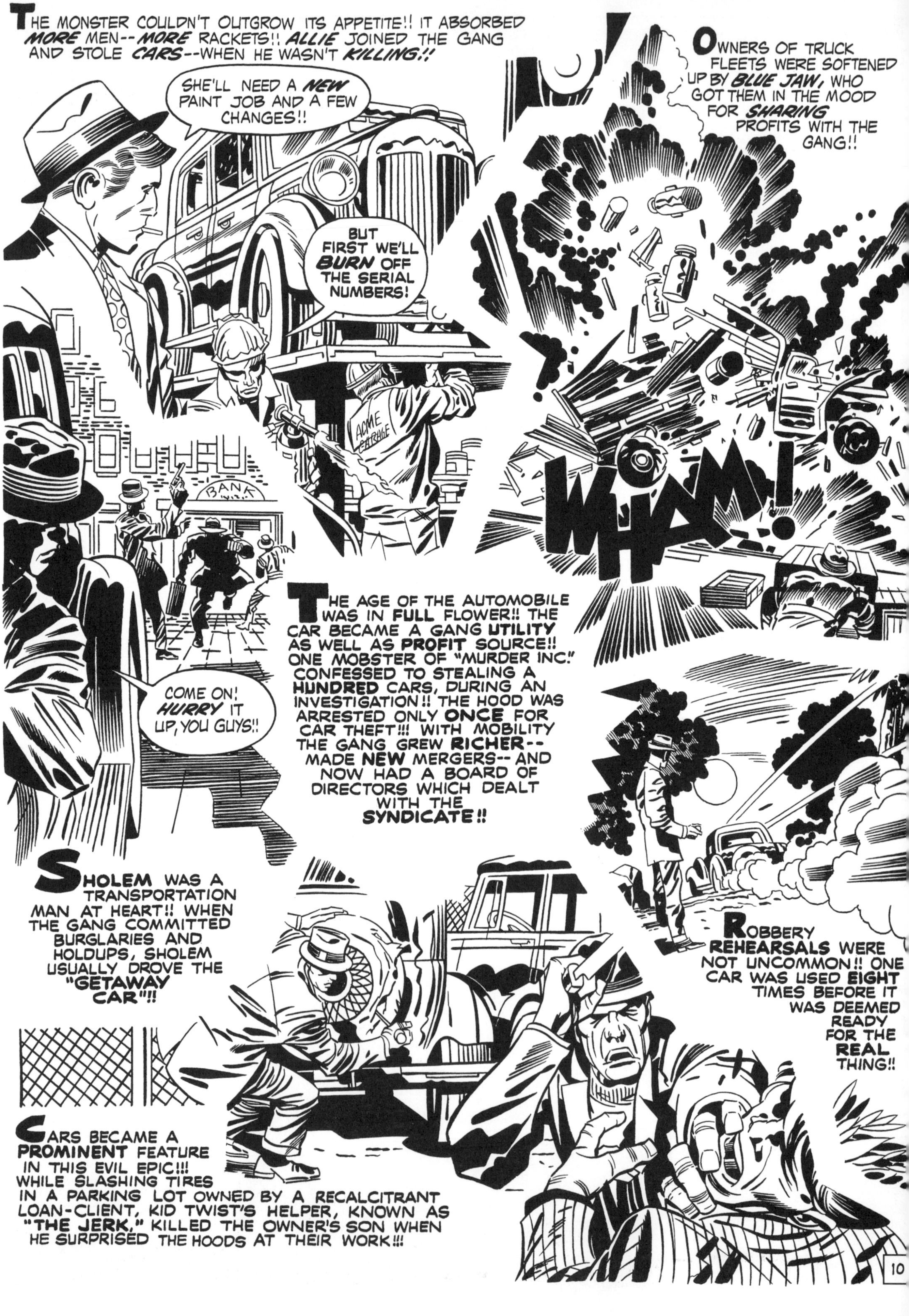

THE MONSTER COULDN'T OUTGROW ITS APPETITE!! IT ABSORBED MORE MEN--MORE RACKETS!! ALLIE JOINED THE GANG AND STOLE CARS--WHEN HE WASN'T KILLING!!
SHE'LL NEED A NEW PAINT JOB AND A FEW CHANGES!!
BUT FIRST WE'LL BURN OFF THE SERIAL NUMBERS!
ACME GARAGE
BANK
COME ON! HURRY IT UP, YOU GUYS!!
OWNERS OF TRUCK FLEETS WERE SOFTENED UP BY BLUE JAW, WHO GOT THEM IN THE MOOD FOR SHARING PROFITS WITH THE GANG!!
WHAM!
THE AGE OF THE AUTOMOBILE WAS IN FULL FLOWER!! THE CAR BECAME A GANG UTILITY AS WELL AS PROFIT SOURCE!! ONE MOBSTER OF "MURDER INC." CONFESSED TO STEALING A HUNDRED CARS, DURING AN INVESTIGATION!! THE HOOD WAS ARRESTED ONLY ONCE FOR CAR THEFT!!! WITH MOBILITY THE GANG GREW RICHER--MADE NEW MERGERS-- AND NOW HAD A BOARD OF DIRECTORS WHICH DEALT WITH THE SYNDICATE!!
SHOLEM WAS A TRANSPORTATION MAN AT HEART!! WHEN THE GANG COMMITTED BURGLARIES AND HOLDUPS, SHOLEM USUALLY DROVE THE "GETAWAY CAR"!!
ROBBERY REHEARSALS WERE NOT UNCOMMON!! ONE CAR WAS USED EIGHT TIMES BEFORE IT WAS DEEMED READY FOR THE REAL THING!!
CARS BECAME A PROMINENT FEATURE IN THIS EVIL EPIC!!! WHILE SLASHING TIRES IN A PARKING LOT OWNED BY A RECALCITRANT LOAN-CLIENT, KID TWIST'S HELPER, KNOWN AS "THE JERK," KILLED THE OWNER'S SON WHEN HE SURPRISED THE HOODS AT THEIR WORK!!!

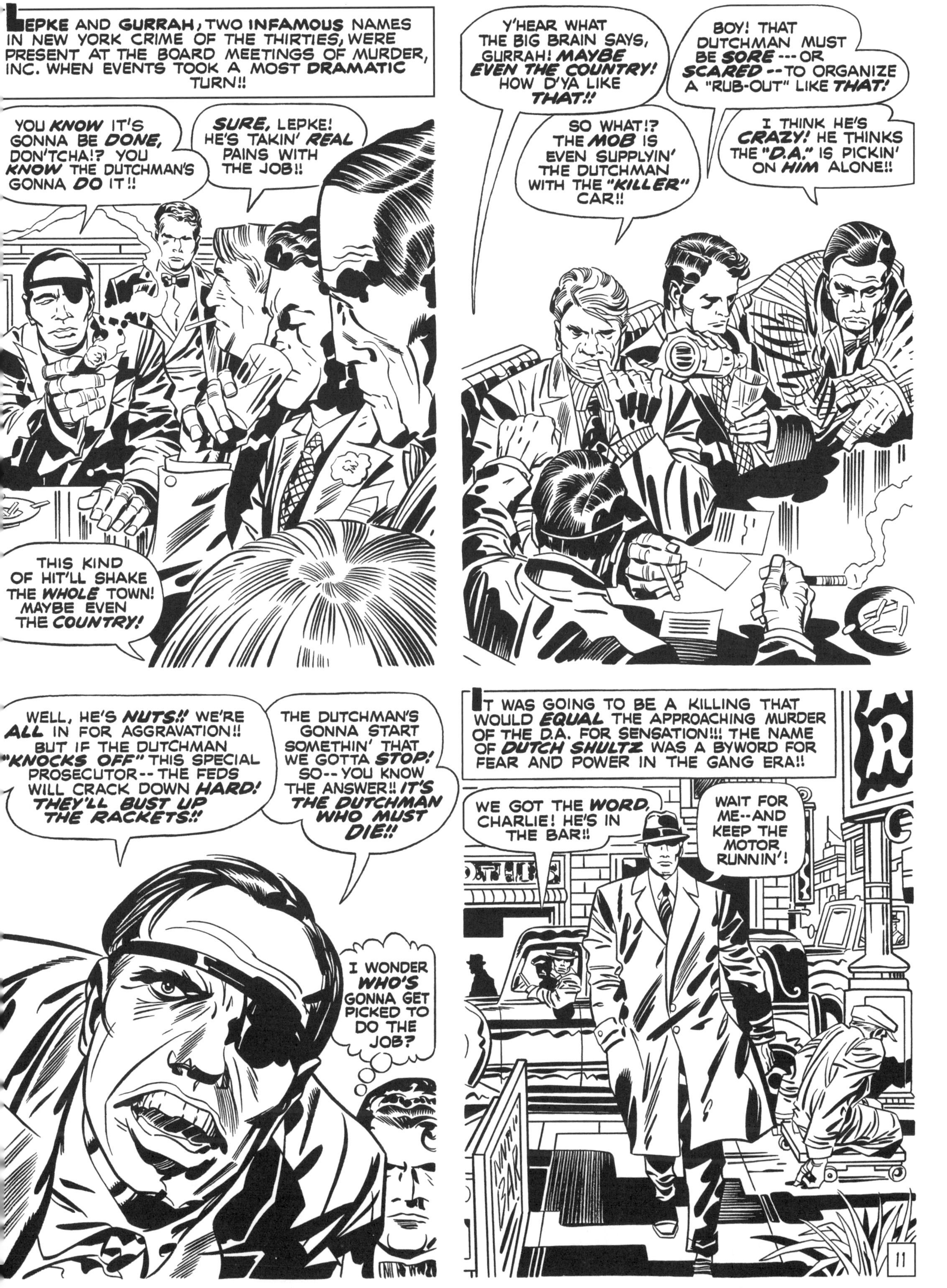
LEPKE AND GURRAH, TWO INFAMOUS NAMES IN NEW YORK CRIME OF THE THIRTIES, WERE PRESENT AT THE BOARD MEETINGS OF MURDER, INC. WHEN EVENTS TOOK A MOST DRAMATIC TURN!!
YOU KNOW IT'S GONNA BE DONE, DON'TCHA!? YOU KNOW THE DUTCHMAN'S GONNA DO IT!!
SURE, LEPKE! HE'S TAKIN' REAL PAINS WITH THE JOB!!
THIS KIND OF HIT'LL SHAKE THE WHOLE TOWN! MAYBE EVEN THE COUNTRY!
Y'HEAR WHAT THE BIG BRAIN SAYS, GURRAH! MAYBE EVEN THE COUNTRY! HOW D'YA LIKE THAT!!
SO WHAT!? THE MOB IS EVEN SUPPLYIN' THE DUTCHMAN WITH THE "KILLER" CAR!!
BOY! THAT DUTCHMAN MUST BE SORE --- OR SCARED -- TO ORGANIZE A "RUB-OUT" LIKE THAT!
I THINK HE'S CRAZY! HE THINKS THE "D.A." IS PICKIN' ON HIM ALONE!!
WELL, HE'S NUTS!! WE'RE ALL IN FOR AGGRAVATION!! BUT IF THE DUTCHMAN "KNOCKS OFF" THIS SPECIAL PROSECUTOR-- THE FEDS WILL CRACK DOWN HARD! THEY'LL BUST UP THE RACKETS!!
THE DUTCHMAN'S GONNA START SOMETHIN' THAT WE GOTTA STOP! SO-- YOU KNOW THE ANSWER!! IT'S THE DUTCHMAN WHO MUST DIE!!
I WONDER WHO'S GONNA GET PICKED TO DO THE JOB?
IT WAS GOING TO BE A KILLING THAT WOULD EQUAL THE APPROACHING MURDER OF THE D.A. FOR SENSATION!!! THE NAME OF DUTCH SHULTZ WAS A BYWORD FOR FEAR AND POWER IN THE GANG ERA!!
WE GOT THE WORD, CHARLIE! HE'S IN THE BAR!!
WAIT FOR ME--AND KEEP THE MOTOR RUNNIN'!
BAR

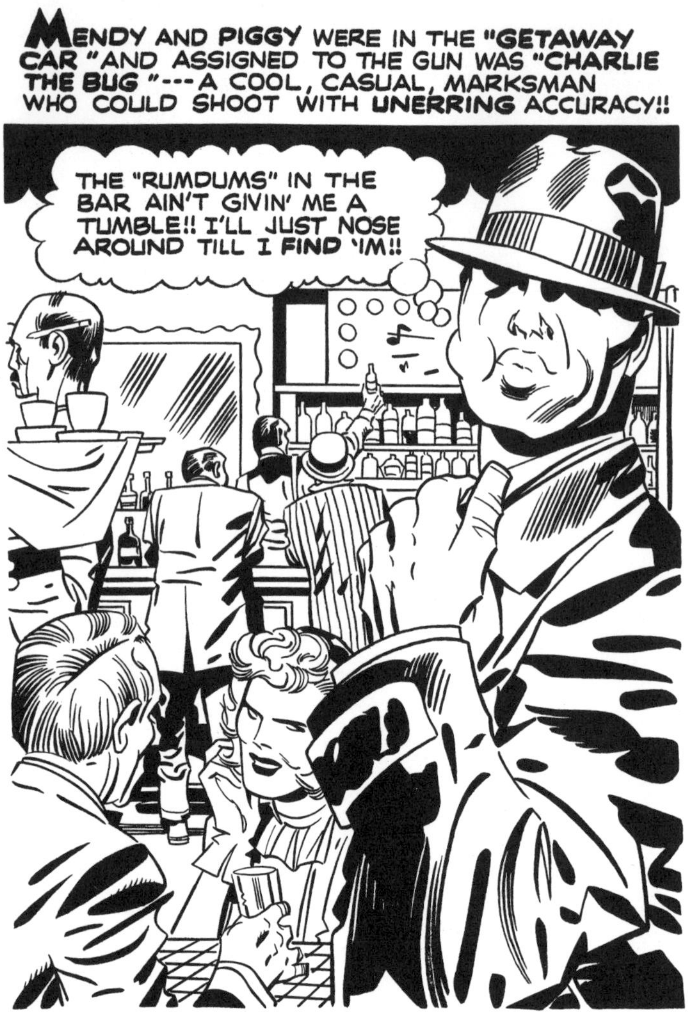
MENDY AND PIGGY WERE IN THE "GETAWAY CAR" AND ASSIGNED TO THE GUN WAS "CHARLIE THE BUG"---A COOL, CASUAL, MARKSMAN WHO COULD SHOOT WITH UNERRING ACCURACY!!
THE "RUMDUMS" IN THE BAR AIN'T GIVIN' ME A TUMBLE!! I'LL JUST NOSE AROUND TILL I FIND 'IM!!

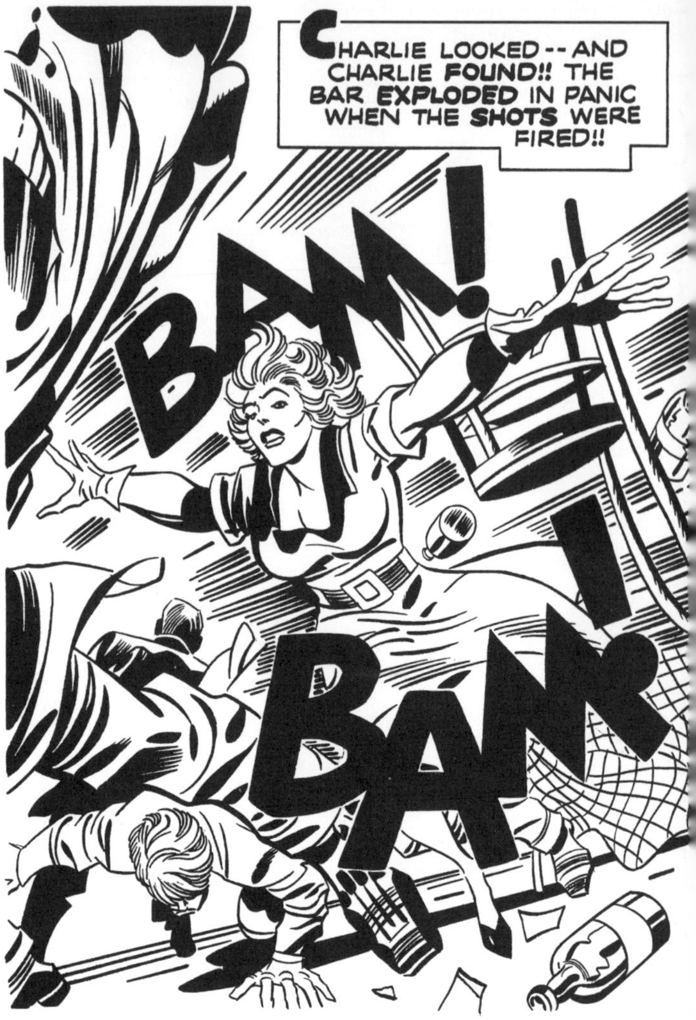
CHARLIE LOOKED--AND CHARLIE FOUND!! THE BAR EXPLODED IN PANIC WHEN THE SHOTS WERE FIRED!!
BAM!
BAM!

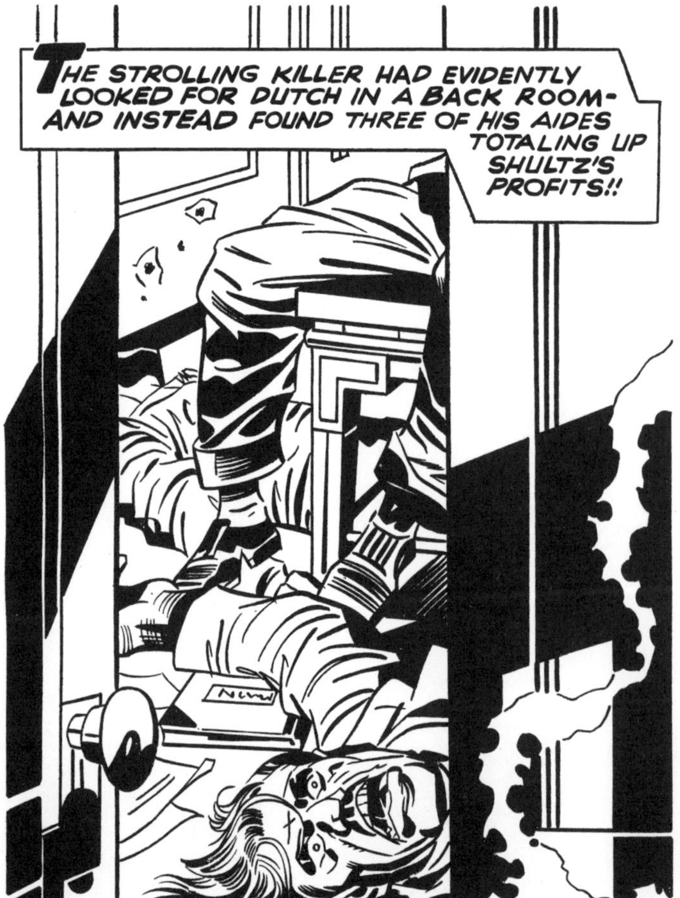
THE STROLLING KILLER HAD EVIDENTLY LOOKED FOR DUTCH IN A BACK ROOM-AND INSTEAD FOUND THREE OF HIS AIDES TOTALING UP SHULTZ'S PROFITS!!

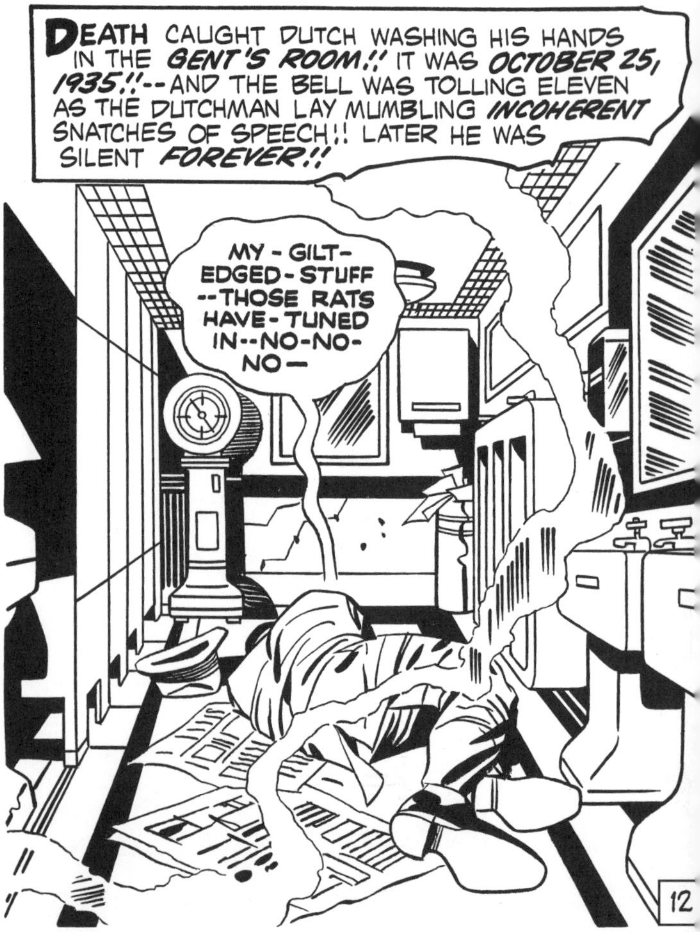
DEATH CAUGHT DUTCH WASHING HIS HANDS IN THE GENT'S ROOM!! IT WAS OCTOBER 25, 1935!!--AND THE BELL WAS TOLLING ELEVEN AS THE DUTCHMAN LAY MUMBLING INCOHERENT SNATCHES OF SPEECH!! LATER HE WAS SILENT FOREVER!!
MY-GILT-EDGED-STUFF --THOSE RATS HAVE-TUNED IN--NO-NO-NO—

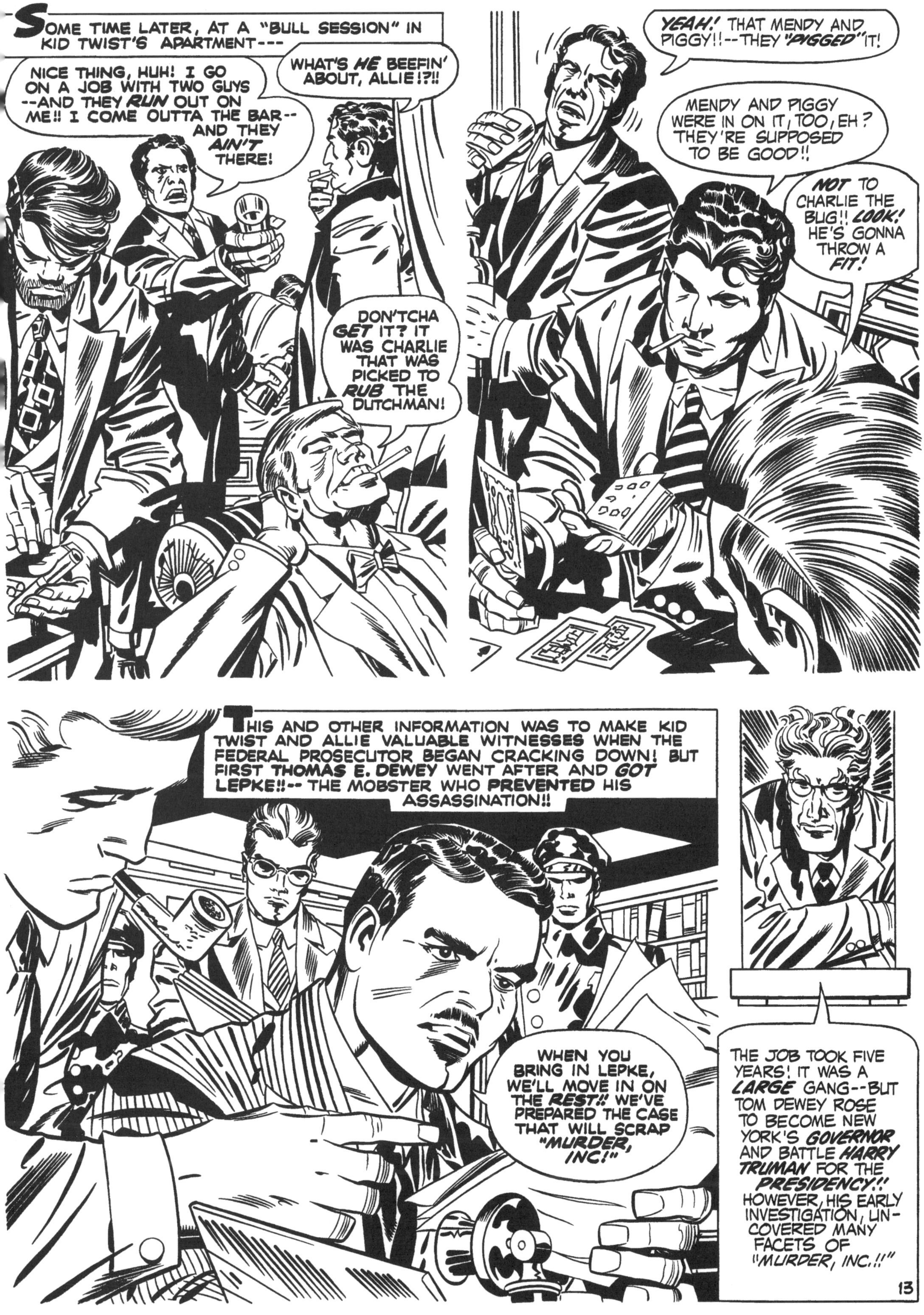
SOME TIME LATER, AT A "BULL SESSION" IN KID TWIST'S APARTMENT---
NICE THING, HUH! I GO ON A JOB WITH TWO GUYS --AND THEY RUN OUT ON ME!! I COME OUTTA THE BAR-- AND THEY AIN'T THERE!
WHAT'S HE BEEFIN' ABOUT, ALLIE!?!!
DON'TCHA GET IT? IT WAS CHARLIE THAT WAS PICKED TO RUB THE DUTCHMAN!
YEAH! THAT MENDY AND PIGGY!!--THEY "PIGGED" IT!
MENDY AND PIGGY WERE IN ON IT, TOO, EH? THEY'RE SUPPOSED TO BE GOOD!!
NOT TO CHARLIE THE BUG!! LOOK! HE'S GONNA THROW A FIT!
THIS AND OTHER INFORMATION WAS TO MAKE KID TWIST AND ALLIE VALUABLE WITNESSES WHEN THE FEDERAL PROSECUTOR BEGAN CRACKING DOWN! BUT FIRST THOMAS E. DEWEY WENT AFTER AND GOT LEPKE!!-- THE MOBSTER WHO PREVENTED HIS ASSASSINATION!!
WHEN YOU BRING IN LEPKE, WE'LL MOVE IN ON THE REST!! WE'VE PREPARED THE CASE THAT WILL SCRAP "MURDER, INC!"
THE JOB TOOK FIVE YEARS! IT WAS A LARGE GANG--BUT TOM DEWEY ROSE TO BECOME NEW YORK'S GOVERNOR AND BATTLE HARRY TRUMAN FOR THE PRESIDENCY!! HOWEVER, HIS EARLY INVESTIGATION, UNCOVERED MANY FACETS OF "MURDER, INC.!!"
13

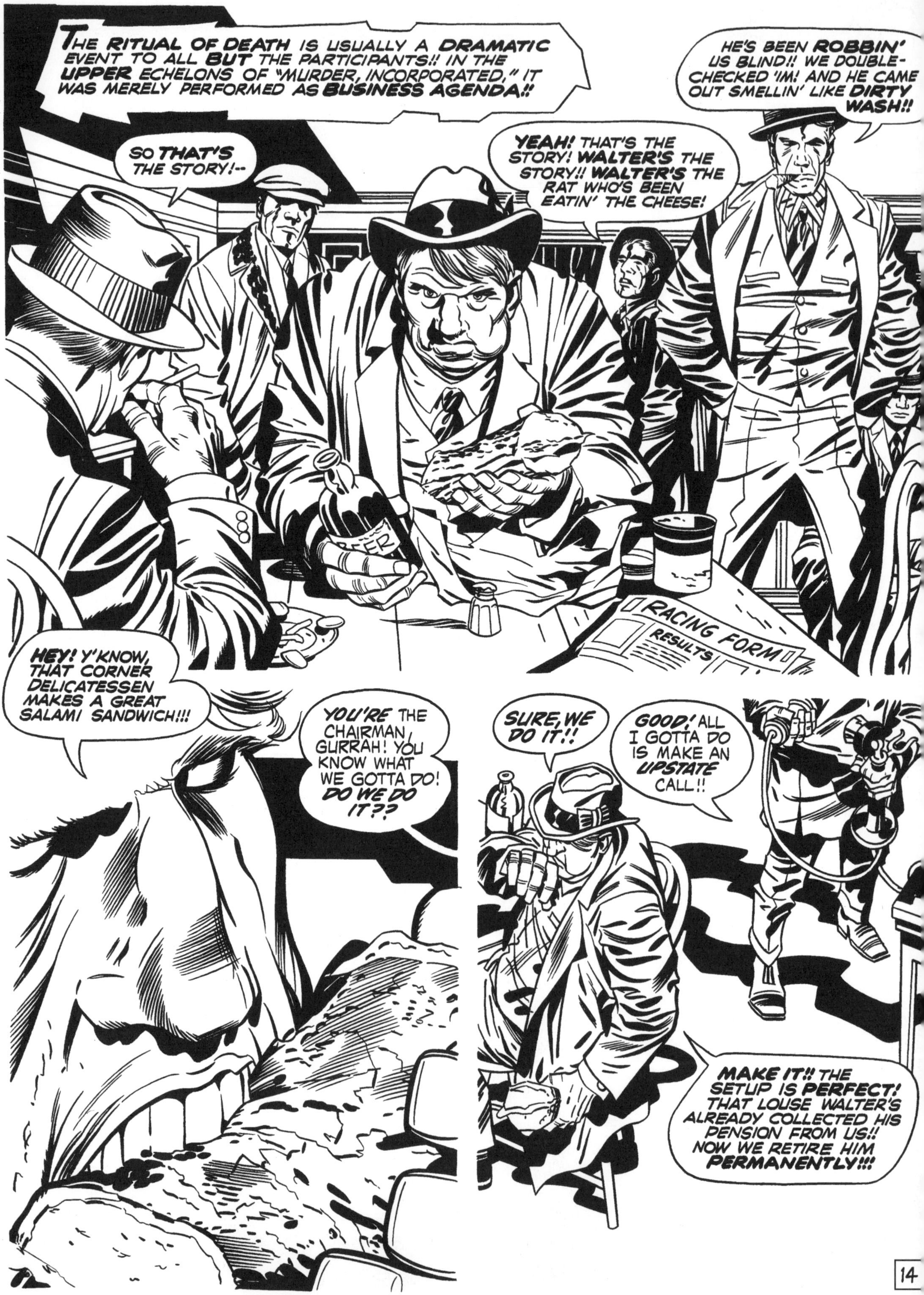
THE RITUAL OF DEATH IS USUALLY A DRAMATIC EVENT TO ALL BUT THE PARTICIPANTS!! IN THE UPPER ECHELONS OF "MURDER, INCORPORATED," IT WAS MERELY PERFORMED AS BUSINESS AGENDA!!
SO THAT'S THE STORY!--
YEAH! THAT'S THE STORY! WALTER'S THE STORY!! WALTER'S THE RAT WHO'S BEEN EATIN' THE CHEESE!
HE'S BEEN ROBBIN' US BLIND!! WE DOUBLE-CHECKED 'IM! AND HE CAME OUT SMELLIN' LIKE DIRTY WASH!!
RACING FORM
RESULTS
HEY! Y'KNOW, THAT CORNER DELICATESSEN MAKES A GREAT SALAMI SANDWICH!!!
YOU'RE THE CHAIRMAN, GURRAH! YOU KNOW WHAT WE GOTTA DO! DO WE DO IT??
SURE, WE DO IT!!
GOOD! ALL I GOTTA DO IS MAKE AN UPSTATE CALL!!
MAKE IT!! THE SETUP IS PERFECT! THAT LOUSE WALTER'S ALREADY COLLECTED HIS PENSION FROM US!! NOW WE RETIRE HIM PERMANENTLY!!!

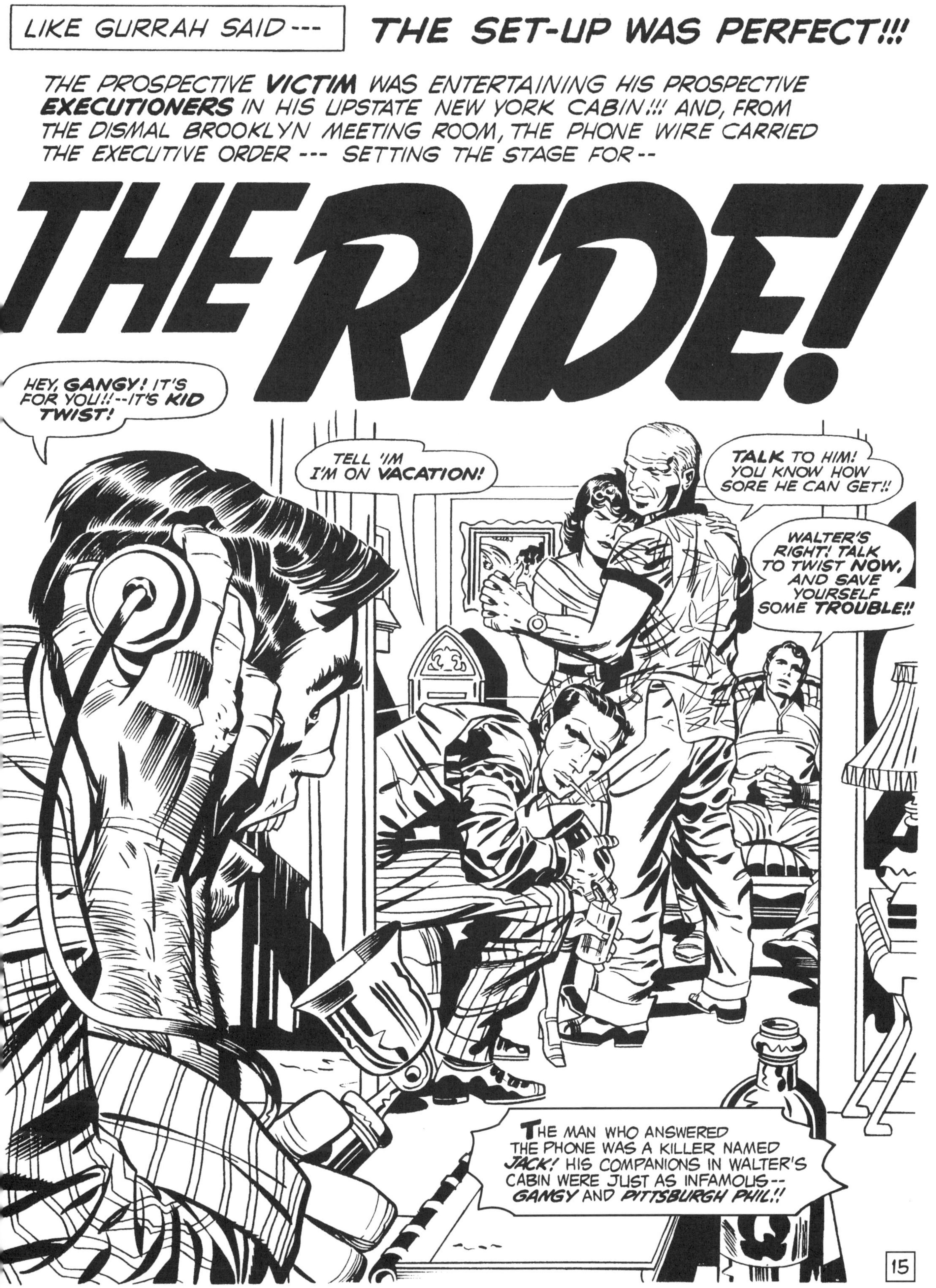
LIKE GURRAH SAID---
THE SET-UP WAS PERFECT!!!
THE PROSPECTIVE VICTIM WAS ENTERTAINING HIS PROSPECTIVE EXECUTIONERS IN HIS UPSTATE NEW YORK CABIN!!! AND, FROM THE DISMAL BROOKLYN MEETING ROOM, THE PHONE WIRE CARRIED THE EXECUTIVE ORDER --- SETTING THE STAGE FOR--
THE RIDE!
HEY, GANGY! IT'S FOR YOU!!--IT'S KID TWIST!
TELL 'IM I'M ON VACATION!
TALK TO HIM! YOU KNOW HOW SORE HE CAN GET!!
WALTER'S RIGHT! TALK TO TWIST NOW, AND SAVE YOURSELF SOME TROUBLE!!
THE MAN WHO ANSWERED THE PHONE WAS A KILLER NAMED JACK! HIS COMPANIONS IN WALTER'S CABIN WERE JUST AS INFAMOUS-- GANGY AND PITTSBURGH PHIL!!

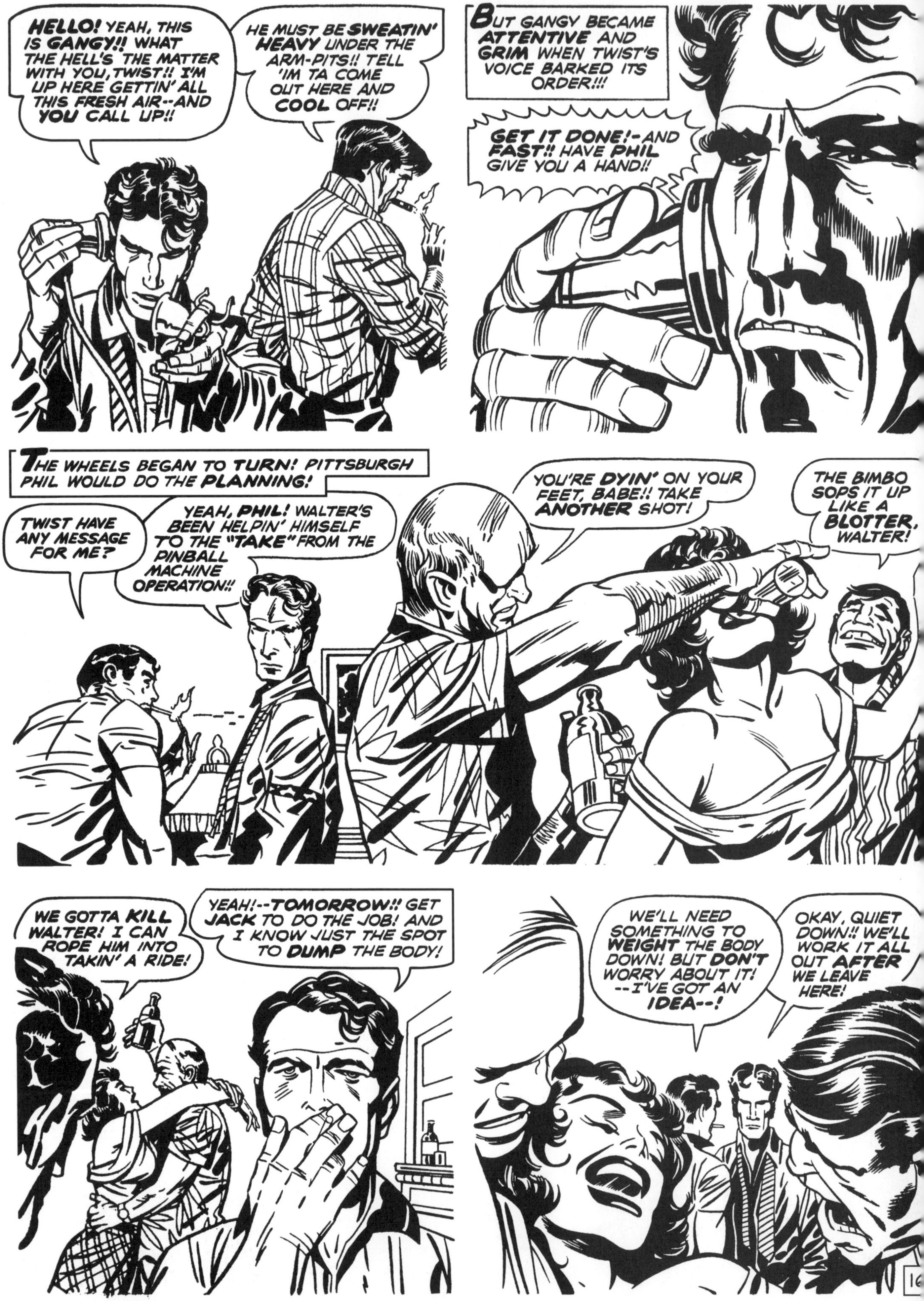
HELLO! YEAH, THIS IS GANGY!! WHAT THE HELL'S THE MATTER WITH YOU, TWIST!! I'M UP HERE GETTIN' ALL THIS FRESH AIR--AND YOU CALL UP!!
HE MUST BE SWEATIN' HEAVY UNDER THE ARM-PITS!! TELL 'IM TA COME OUT HERE AND COOL OFF!!
BUT GANGY BECAME ATTENTIVE AND GRIM WHEN TWIST'S VOICE BARKED ITS ORDER!!!
GET IT DONE!-AND FAST!! HAVE PHIL GIVE YOU A HAND!!
THE WHEELS BEGAN TO TURN! PITTSBURGH PHIL WOULD DO THE PLANNING!
TWIST HAVE ANY MESSAGE FOR ME?
YEAH, PHIL! WALTER'S BEEN HELPIN' HIMSELF TO THE "TAKE" FROM THE PINBALL MACHINE OPERATION!!
YOU'RE DYIN' ON YOUR FEET, BABE!! TAKE ANOTHER SHOT!
THE BIMBO SOPS IT UP LIKE A BLOTTER, WALTER!
WE GOTTA KILL WALTER! I CAN ROPE HIM INTO TAKIN' A RIDE!
YEAH!--TOMORROW!! GET JACK TO DO THE JOB! AND I KNOW JUST THE SPOT TO DUMP THE BODY!
WE'LL NEED SOMETHING TO WEIGHT THE BODY DOWN! BUT DON'T WORRY ABOUT IT! --I'VE GOT AN IDEA--!
OKAY, QUIET DOWN!! WE'LL WORK IT ALL OUT AFTER WE LEAVE HERE!

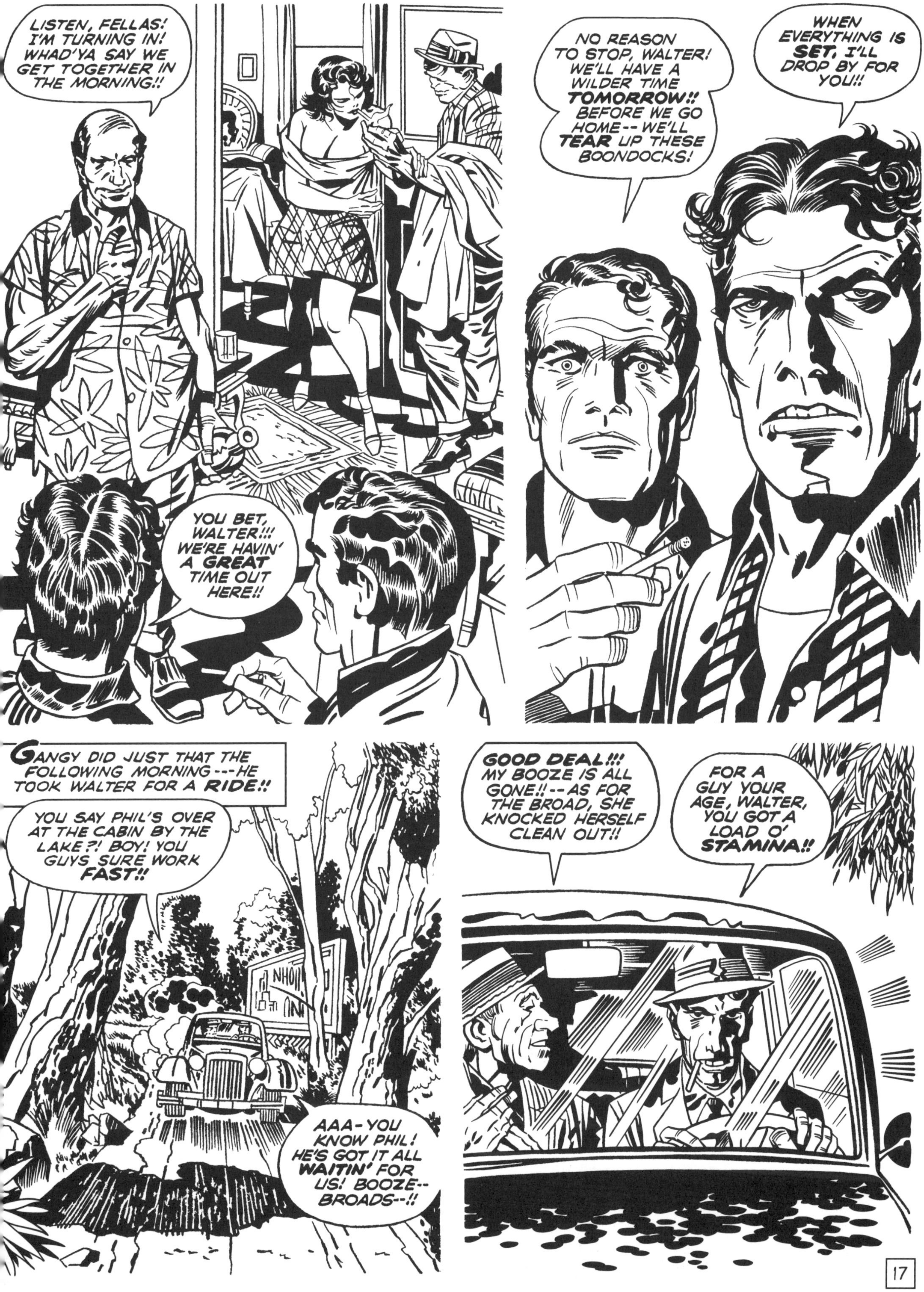

LISTEN, FELLAS! I'M TURNING IN! WHAD'YA SAY WE GET TOGETHER IN THE MORNING!!
YOU BET, WALTER!!! WE'RE HAVIN' A GREAT TIME OUT HERE!!
NO REASON TO STOP, WALTER! WE'LL HAVE A WILDER TIME TOMORROW!! BEFORE WE GO HOME--WE'LL TEAR UP THESE BOONDOCKS!
WHEN EVERYTHING IS SET, I'LL DROP BY FOR YOU!!
GANGY DID JUST THAT THE FOLLOWING MORNING---HE TOOK WALTER FOR A RIDE!!
YOU SAY PHIL'S OVER AT THE CABIN BY THE LAKE?! BOY! YOU GUYS SURE WORK FAST!!
AAA-YOU KNOW PHIL! HE'S GOT IT ALL WAITIN' FOR US! BOOZE--BROADS--!!
GOOD DEAL!!! MY BOOZE IS ALL GONE!!--AS FOR THE BROAD, SHE KNOCKED HERSELF CLEAN OUT!!
FOR A GUY YOUR AGE, WALTER, YOU GOT A LOAD O' STAMINA!!

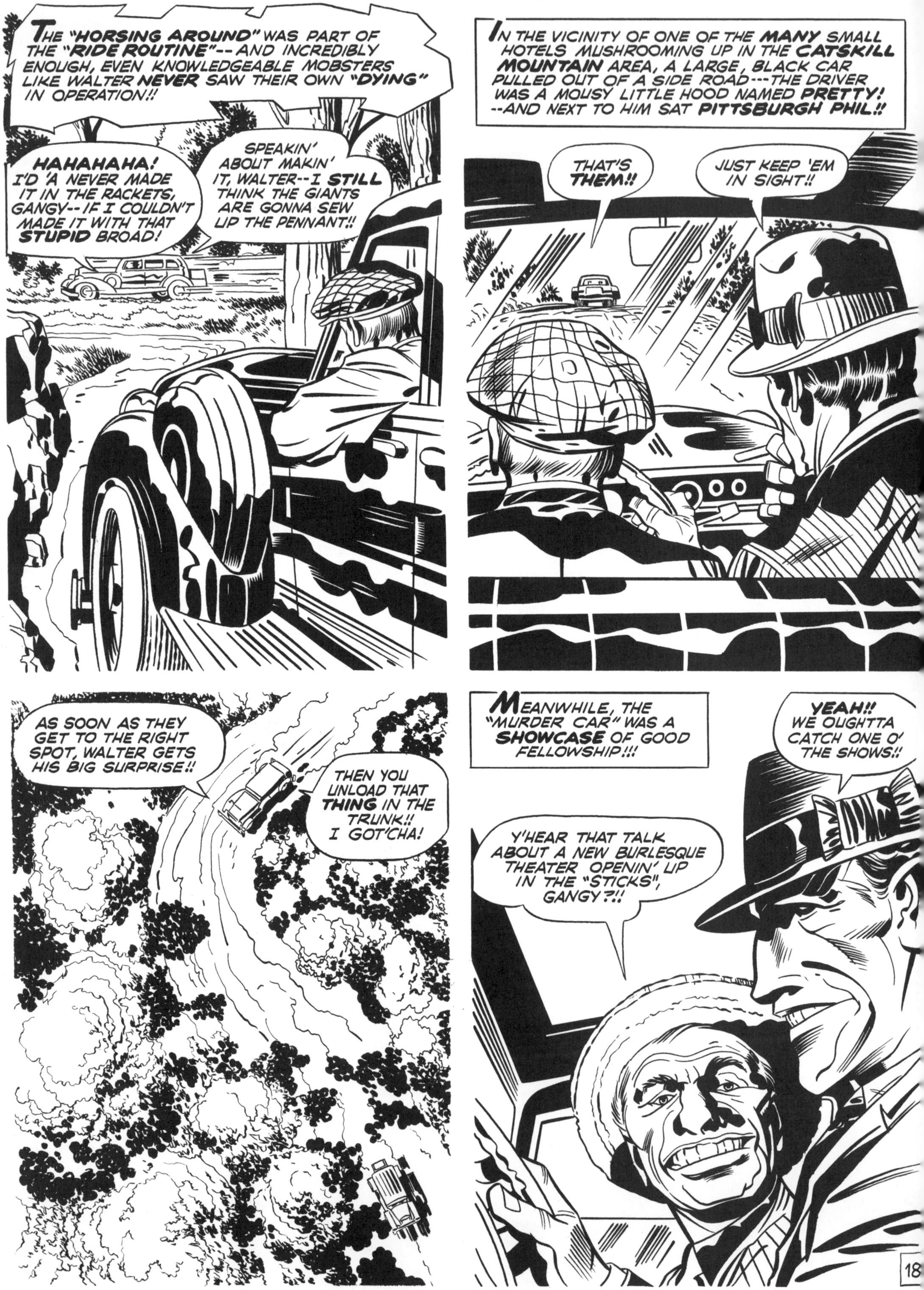
THE "HORSING AROUND" WAS PART OF THE "RIDE ROUTINE"-- AND INCREDIBLY ENOUGH, EVEN KNOWLEDGEABLE MOBSTERS LIKE WALTER NEVER SAW THEIR OWN "DYING" IN OPERATION!!
HAHAHAHA! I'D 'A NEVER MADE IT IN THE RACKETS, GANGY--IF I COULDN'T MADE IT WITH THAT STUPID BROAD!
SPEAKIN' ABOUT MAKIN' IT, WALTER--I STILL THINK THE GIANTS ARE GONNA SEW UP THE PENNANT!!
IN THE VICINITY OF ONE OF THE MANY SMALL HOTELS MUSHROOMING UP IN THE CATSKILL MOUNTAIN AREA, A LARGE, BLACK CAR PULLED OUT OF A SIDE ROAD---THE DRIVER WAS A MOUSY LITTLE HOOD NAMED PRETTY! --AND NEXT TO HIM SAT PITTSBURGH PHIL!!
THAT'S THEM!!
JUST KEEP 'EM IN SIGHT!!
AS SOON AS THEY GET TO THE RIGHT SPOT, WALTER GETS HIS BIG SURPRISE!!
THEN YOU UNLOAD THAT THING IN THE TRUNK!! I GOT'CHA!
MEANWHILE, THE "MURDER CAR" WAS A SHOWCASE OF GOOD FELLOWSHIP!!!
YEAH!! WE OUGHTTA CATCH ONE O' THE SHOWS!!
Y'HEAR THAT TALK ABOUT A NEW BURLESQUE THEATER OPENIN' UP IN THE "STICKS", GANGY?!!
18

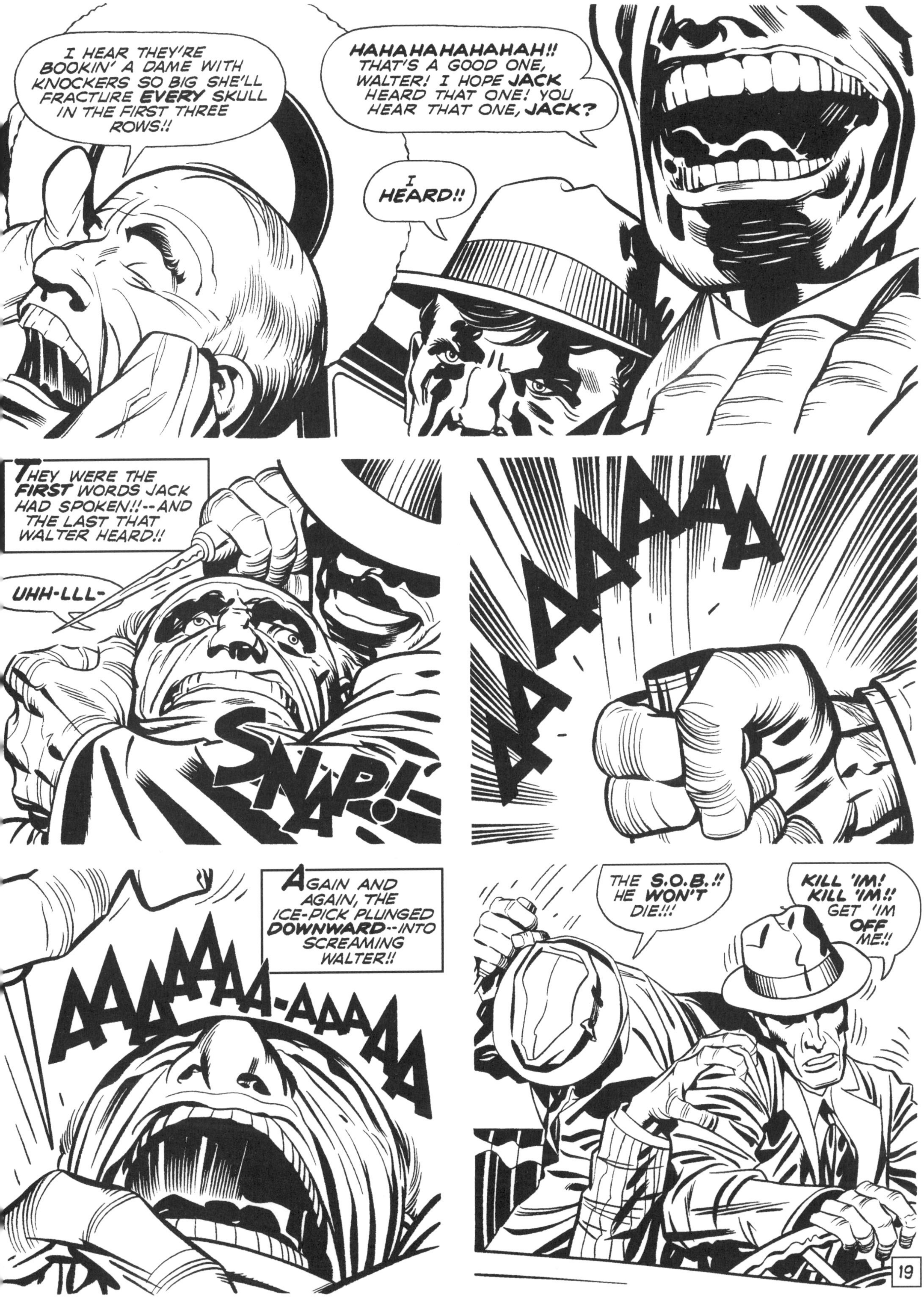

I HEAR THEY'RE BOOKIN' A DAME WITH KNOCKERS SO BIG SHE'LL FRACTURE EVERY SKULL IN THE FIRST THREE ROWS!!
HAHAHAHAHAHAH!! THAT'S A GOOD ONE, WALTER! I HOPE JACK HEARD THAT ONE! YOU HEAR THAT ONE, JACK?
I HEARD!!
THEY WERE THE FIRST WORDS JACK HAD SPOKEN!!--AND THE LAST THAT WALTER HEARD!!
UHH-LLL-
SNAP!
AAAAAAA
AGAIN AND AGAIN, THE ICE-PICK PLUNGED DOWNWARD--INTO SCREAMING WALTER!!
AAAAAAA-AAAAAA
THE S.O.B.!! HE WON'T DIE!!!
KILL 'IM! KILL 'IM!! GET 'IM OFF ME!!

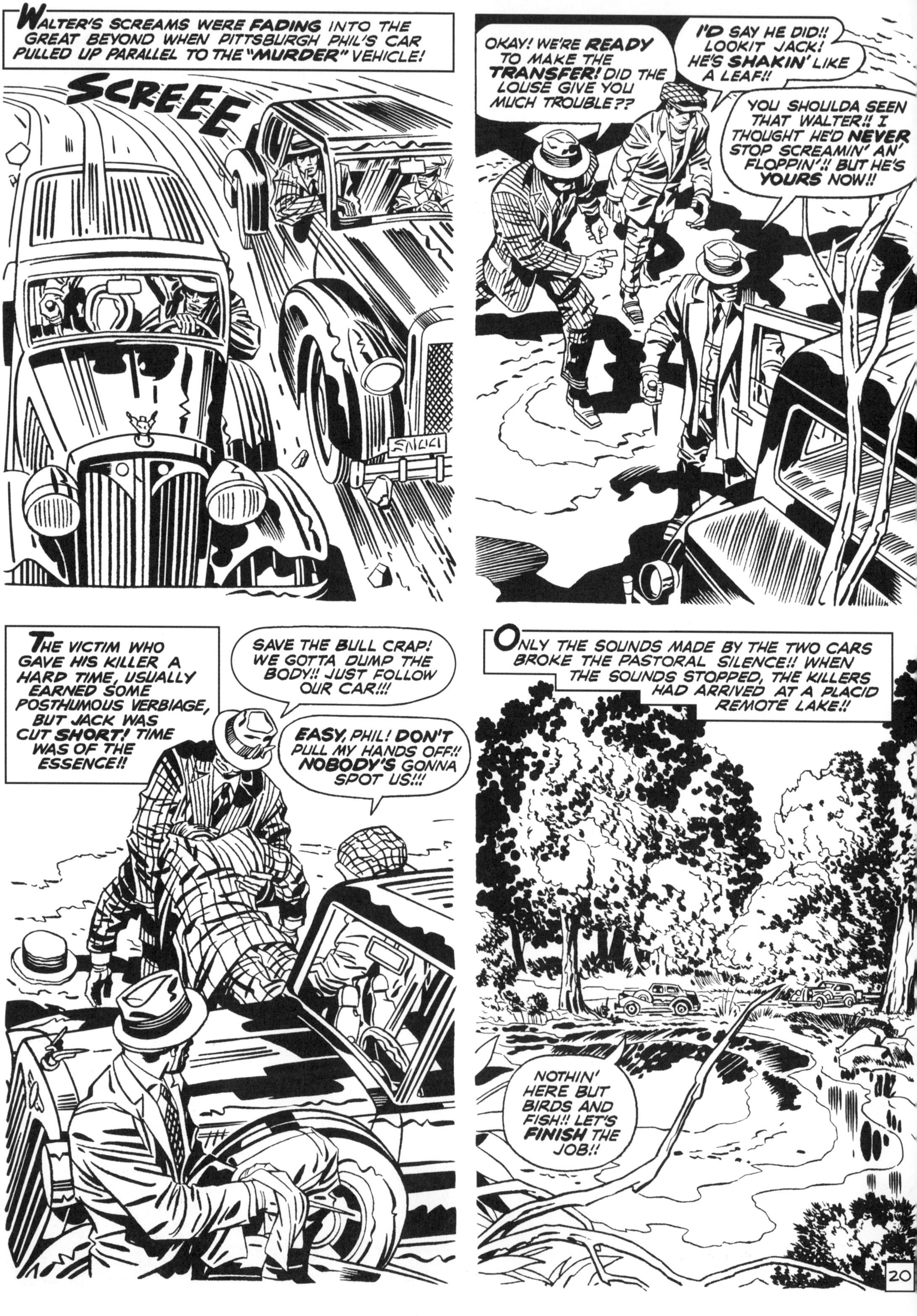
WALTER'S SCREAMS WERE FADING INTO THE GREAT BEYOND WHEN PITTSBURGH PHIL'S CAR PULLED UP PARALLEL TO THE "MURDER" VEHICLE!
SCREEE
OKAY! WE'RE READY TO MAKE THE TRANSFER! DID THE LOUSE GIVE YOU MUCH TROUBLE??
I'D SAY HE DID!! LOOKIT JACK! HE'S SHAKIN' LIKE A LEAF!!
YOU SHOULDA SEEN THAT WALTER!! I THOUGHT HE'D NEVER STOP SCREAMIN' AN' FLOPPIN'!! BUT HE'S YOURS NOW!!
THE VICTIM WHO GAVE HIS KILLER A HARD TIME, USUALLY EARNED SOME POSTHUMOUS VERBIAGE, BUT JACK WAS CUT SHORT! TIME WAS OF THE ESSENCE!!
SAVE THE BULL CRAP! WE GOTTA DUMP THE BODY!! JUST FOLLOW OUR CAR!!!
EASY, PHIL! DON'T PULL MY HANDS OFF!! NOBODY'S GONNA SPOT US!!!
ONLY THE SOUNDS MADE BY THE TWO CARS BROKE THE PASTORAL SILENCE!! WHEN THE SOUNDS STOPPED, THE KILLERS HAD ARRIVED AT A PLACID REMOTE LAKE!!
NOTHIN' HERE BUT BIRDS AND FISH!! LET'S FINISH THE JOB!!

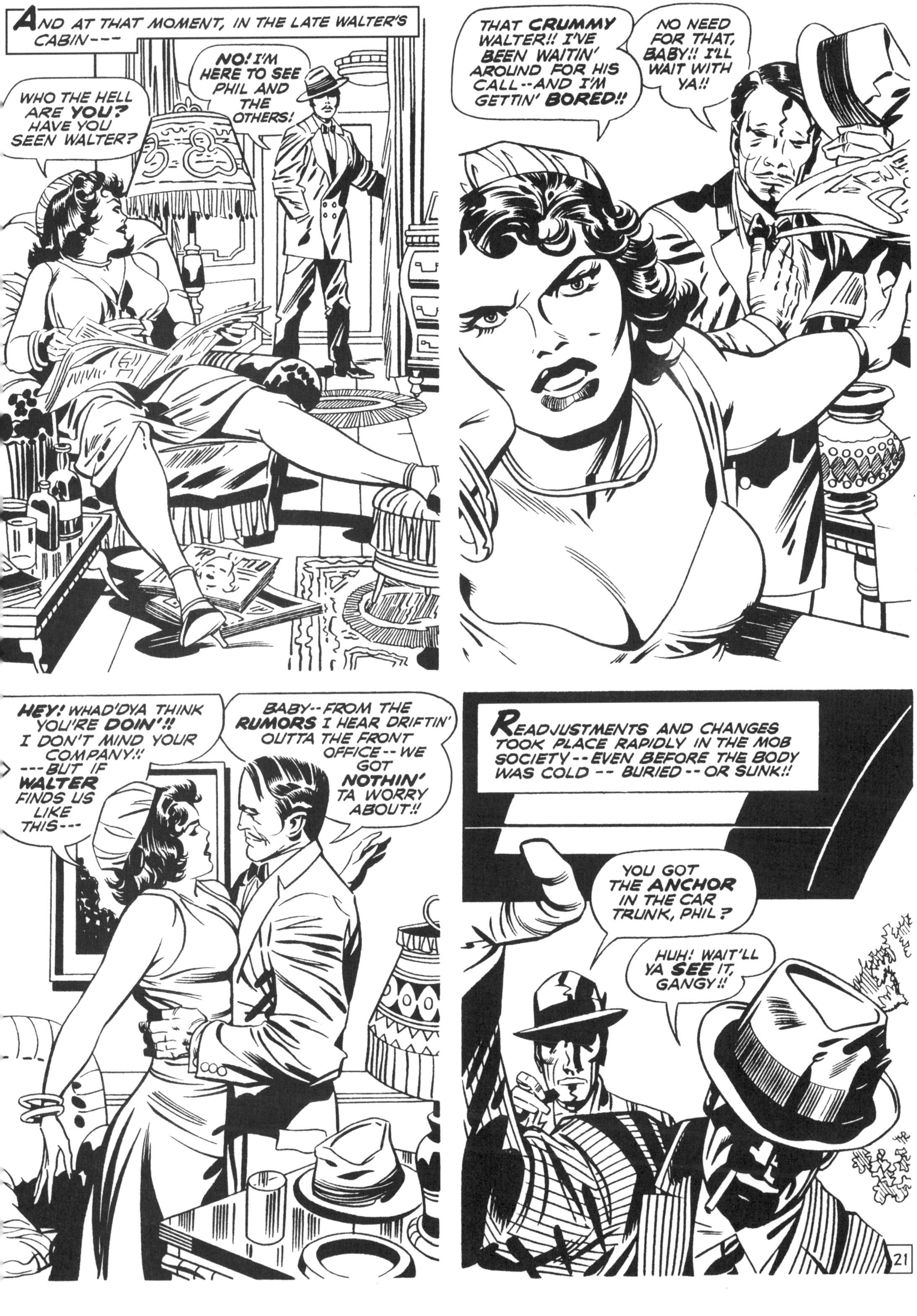

AND AT THAT MOMENT, IN THE LATE WALTER'S CABIN---
WHO THE HELL ARE YOU? HAVE YOU SEEN WALTER?
NO! I'M HERE TO SEE PHIL AND THE OTHERS!
THAT CRUMMY WALTER!! I'VE BEEN WAITIN' AROUND FOR HIS CALL--AND I'M GETTIN' BORED!!
NO NEED FOR THAT, BABY!! I'LL WAIT WITH YA!!
HEY! WHAD'DYA THINK YOU'RE DOIN'!! I DON'T MIND YOUR COMPANY!! ---BUT IF WALTER FINDS US LIKE THIS---
BABY--FROM THE RUMORS I HEAR DRIFTIN' OUTTA THE FRONT OFFICE--WE GOT NOTHIN' TA WORRY ABOUT!!
READJUSTMENTS AND CHANGES TOOK PLACE RAPIDLY IN THE MOB SOCIETY--EVEN BEFORE THE BODY WAS COLD -- BURIED -- OR SUNK!!
YOU GOT THE ANCHOR IN THE CAR TRUNK, PHIL?
HUH! WAIT'LL YA SEE IT, GANGY!!

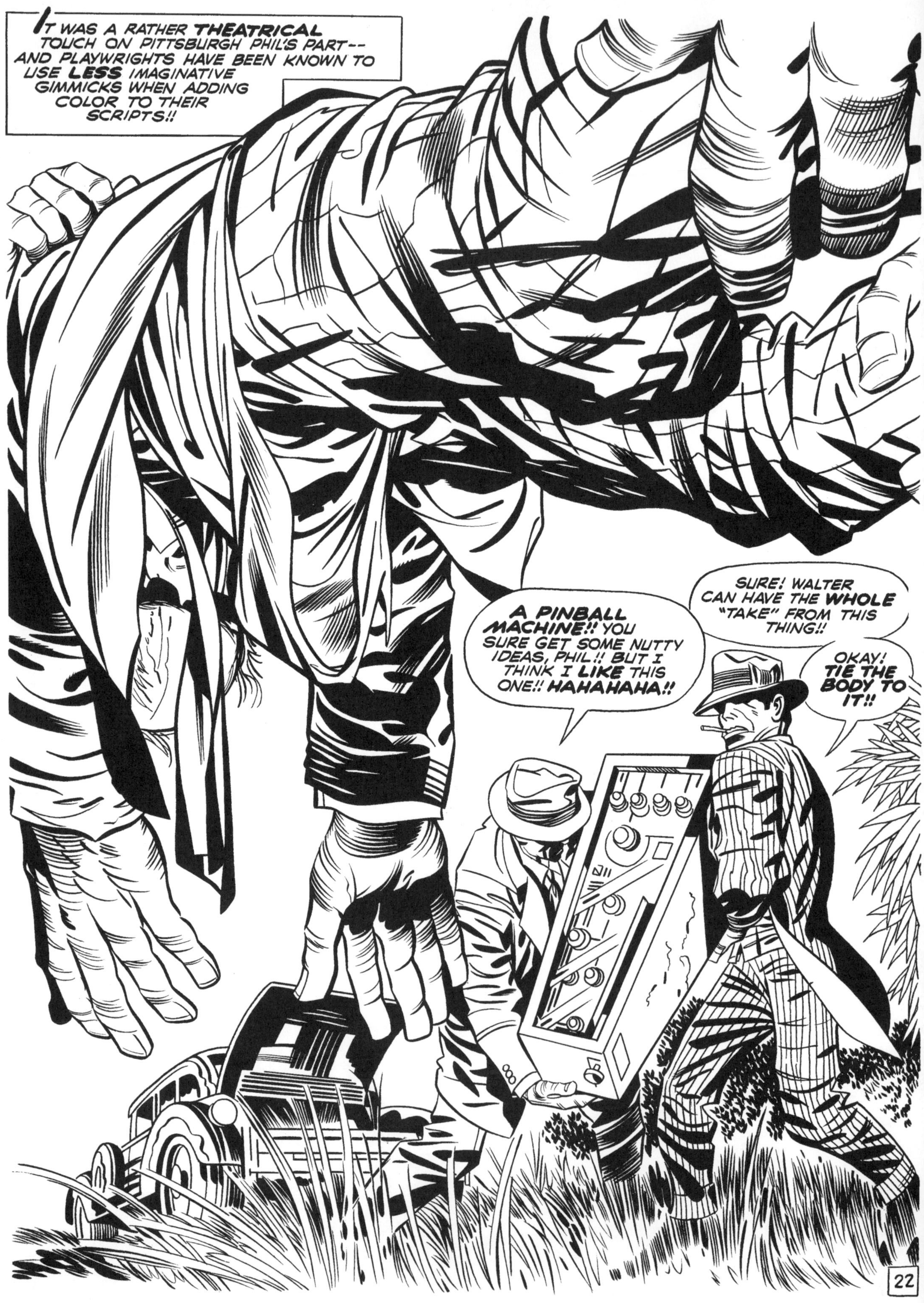
IT WAS A RATHER THEATRICAL TOUCH ON PITTSBURGH PHIL'S PART-- AND PLAYWRIGHTS HAVE BEEN KNOWN TO USE LESS IMAGINATIVE GIMMICKS WHEN ADDING COLOR TO THEIR SCRIPTS!!
A PINBALL MACHINE!! YOU SURE GET SOME NUTTY IDEAS, PHIL!! BUT I THINK I LIKE THIS ONE!! HAHAHAHA!!
SURE! WALTER CAN HAVE THE WHOLE "TAKE" FROM THIS THING!!
OKAY! TIE THE BODY TO IT!!

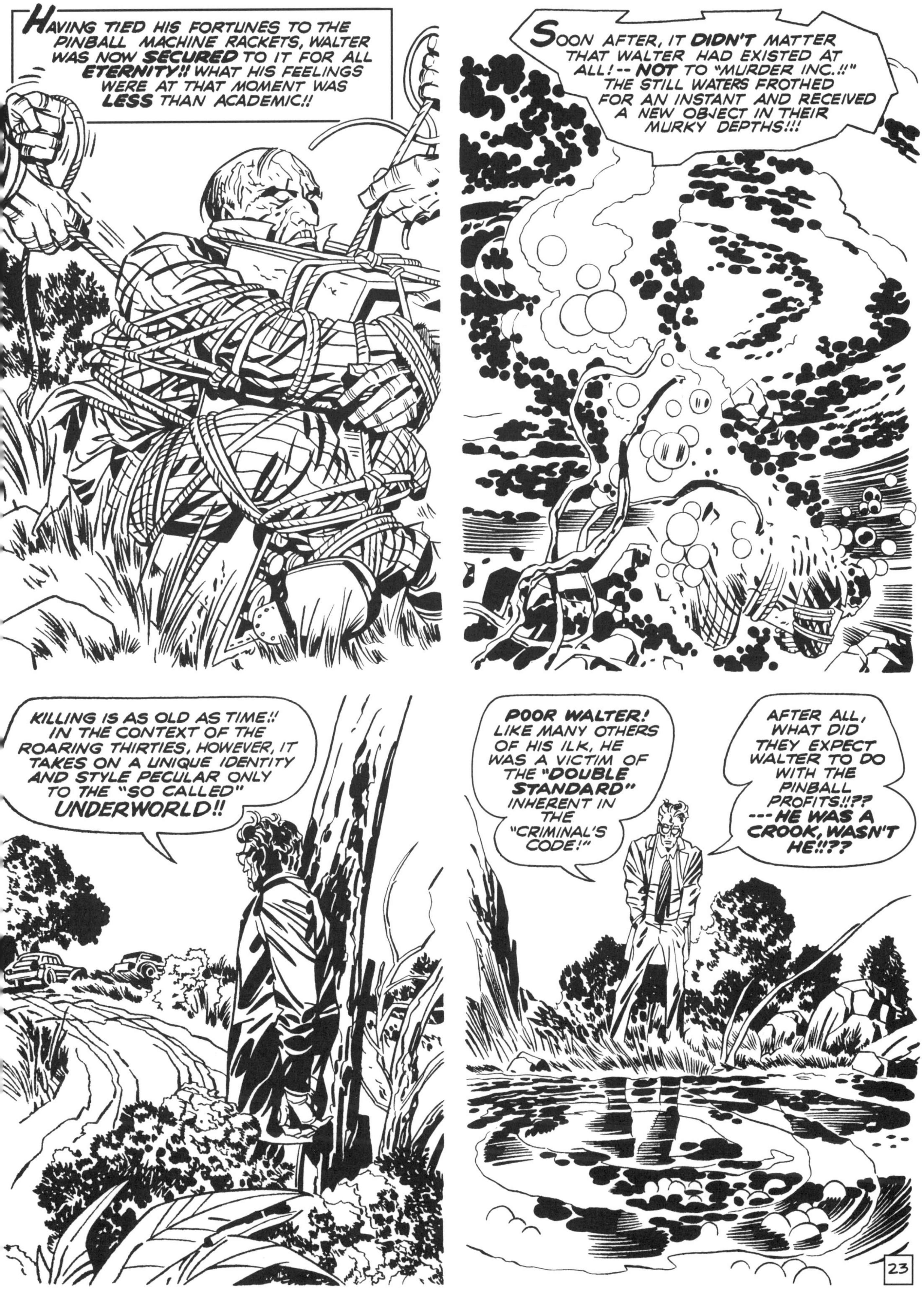
HAVING TIED HIS FORTUNES TO THE PINBALL MACHINE RACKETS, WALTER WAS NOW SECURED TO IT FOR ALL ETERNITY!! WHAT HIS FEELINGS WERE AT THAT MOMENT WAS LESS THAN ACADEMIC!!
SOON AFTER, IT DIDN'T MATTER THAT WALTER HAD EXISTED AT ALL! -- NOT TO "MURDER INC.!!" THE STILL WATERS FROTHED FOR AN INSTANT AND RECEIVED A NEW OBJECT IN THEIR MURKY DEPTHS!!!
KILLING IS AS OLD AS TIME!! IN THE CONTEXT OF THE ROARING THIRTIES, HOWEVER, IT TAKES ON A UNIQUE IDENTITY AND STYLE PECULAR ONLY TO THE "SO CALLED" UNDERWORLD!!
POOR WALTER! LIKE MANY OTHERS OF HIS ILK, HE WAS A VICTIM OF THE "DOUBLE STANDARD" INHERENT IN THE "CRIMINAL'S CODE!"
AFTER ALL, WHAT DID THEY EXPECT WALTER TO DO WITH THE PINBALL PROFITS!!?? --- HE WAS A CROOK, WASN'T HE!!??
23

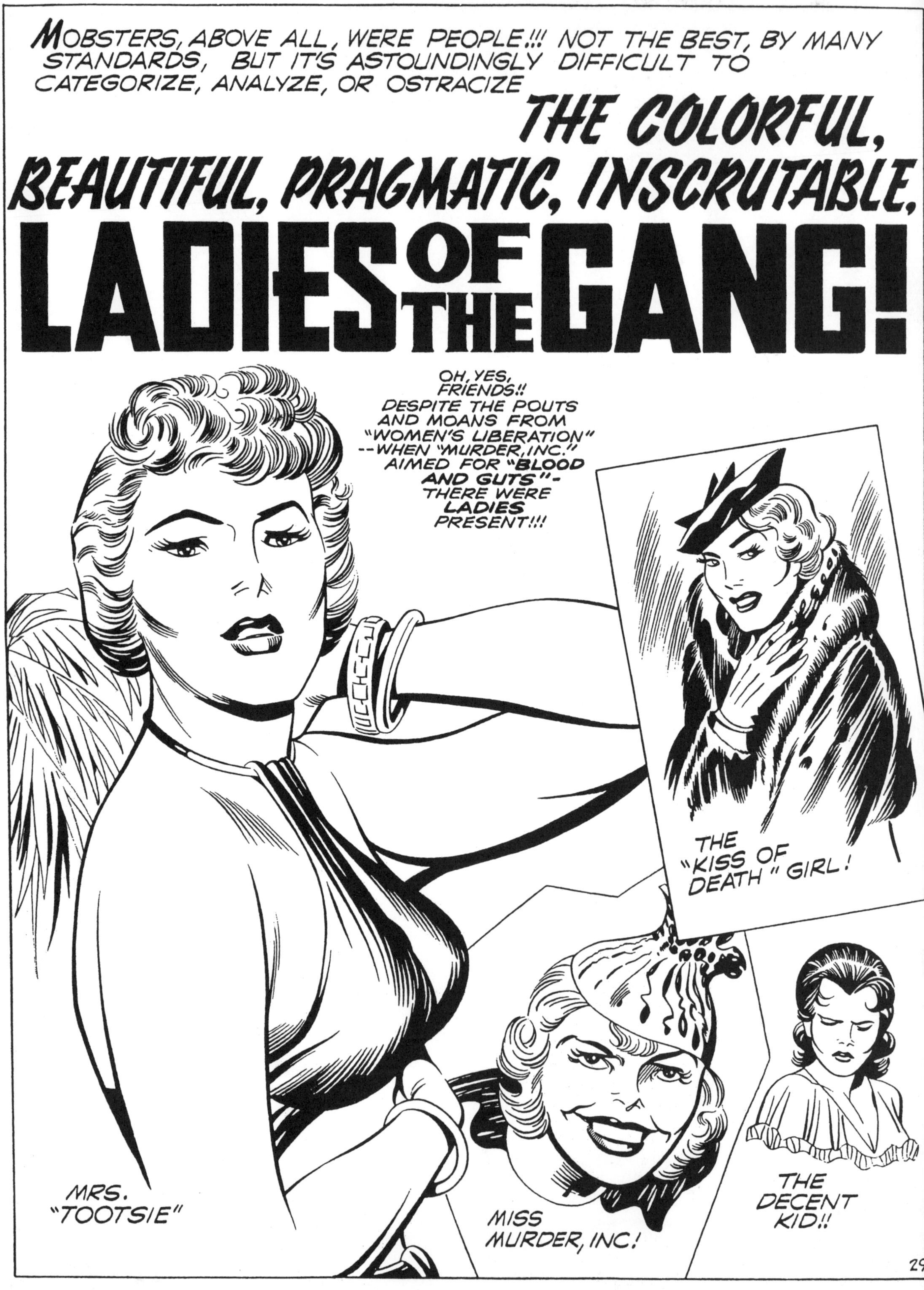
MOBSTERS, ABOVE ALL, WERE PEOPLE!!! NOT THE BEST, BY MANY STANDARDS, BUT IT'S ASTOUNDINGLY DIFFICULT TO CATEGORIZE, ANALYZE, OR OSTRACIZE
THE COLORFUL, BEAUTIFUL, PRAGMATIC, INSCRUTABLE, LADIES OF THE GANG!
OH, YES, FRIENDS!! DESPITE THE POUTS AND MOANS FROM "WOMEN'S LIBERATION" --WHEN "MURDER, INC." AIMED FOR "BLOOD AND GUTS"- THERE WERE LADIES PRESENT!!!
THE "KISS OF DEATH" GIRL!
MRS. "TOOTSIE"
MISS MURDER, INC!
THE DECENT KID!!

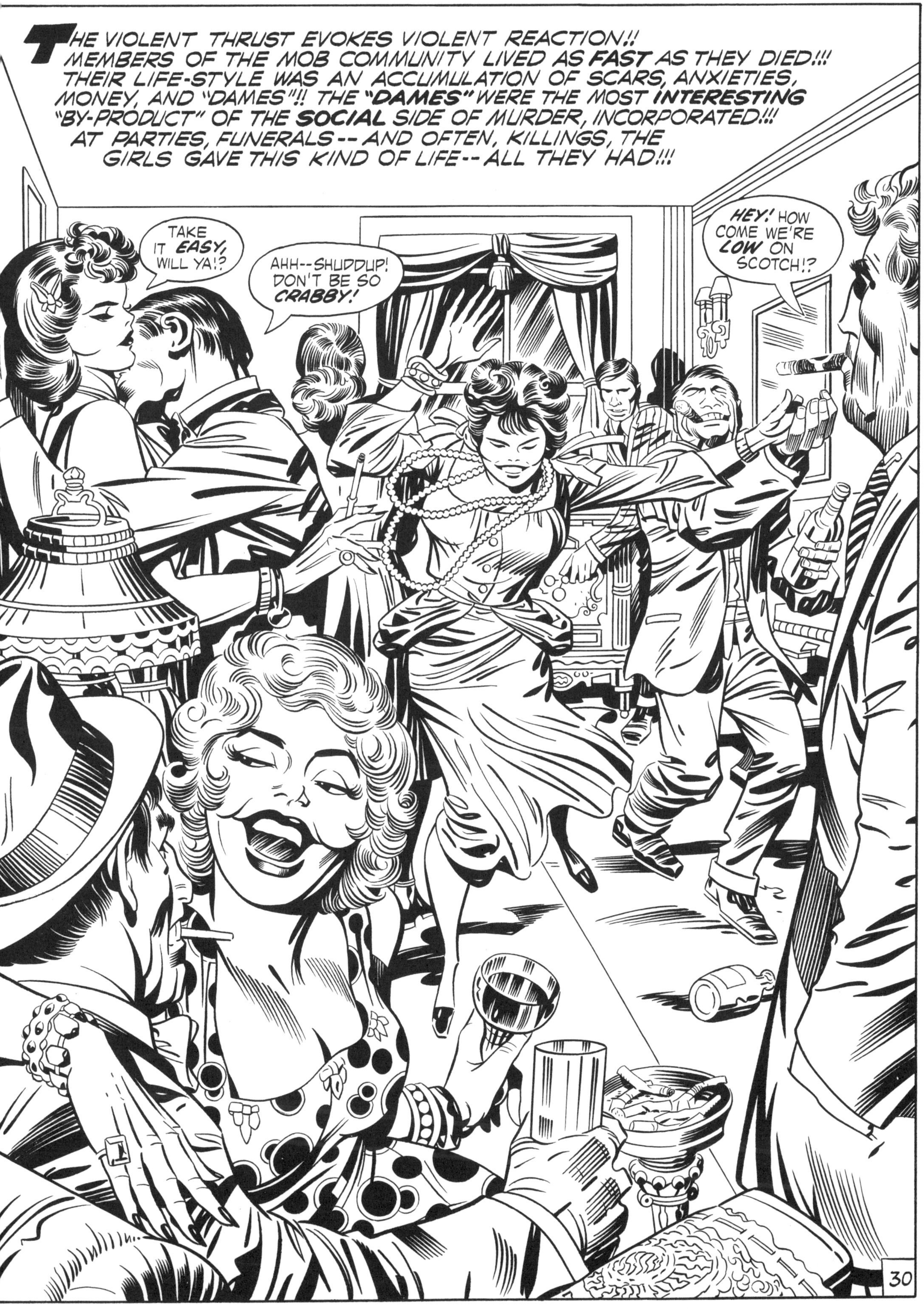
THE VIOLENT THRUST EVOKES VIOLENT REACTION!! MEMBERS OF THE MOB COMMUNITY LIVED AS FAST AS THEY DIED!!! THEIR LIFE-STYLE WAS AN ACCUMULATION OF SCARS, ANXIETIES, MONEY, AND "DAMES"!! THE "DAMES" WERE THE MOST INTERESTING "BY-PRODUCT" OF THE SOCIAL SIDE OF MURDER, INCORPORATED!!! AT PARTIES, FUNERALS-- AND OFTEN, KILLINGS, THE GIRLS GAVE THIS KIND OF LIFE-- ALL THEY HAD!!!
TAKE IT EASY, WILL YA!?
AHH--SHUDDUP! DON'T BE SO CRABBY!
HEY! HOW COME WE'RE LOW ON SCOTCH!?
30

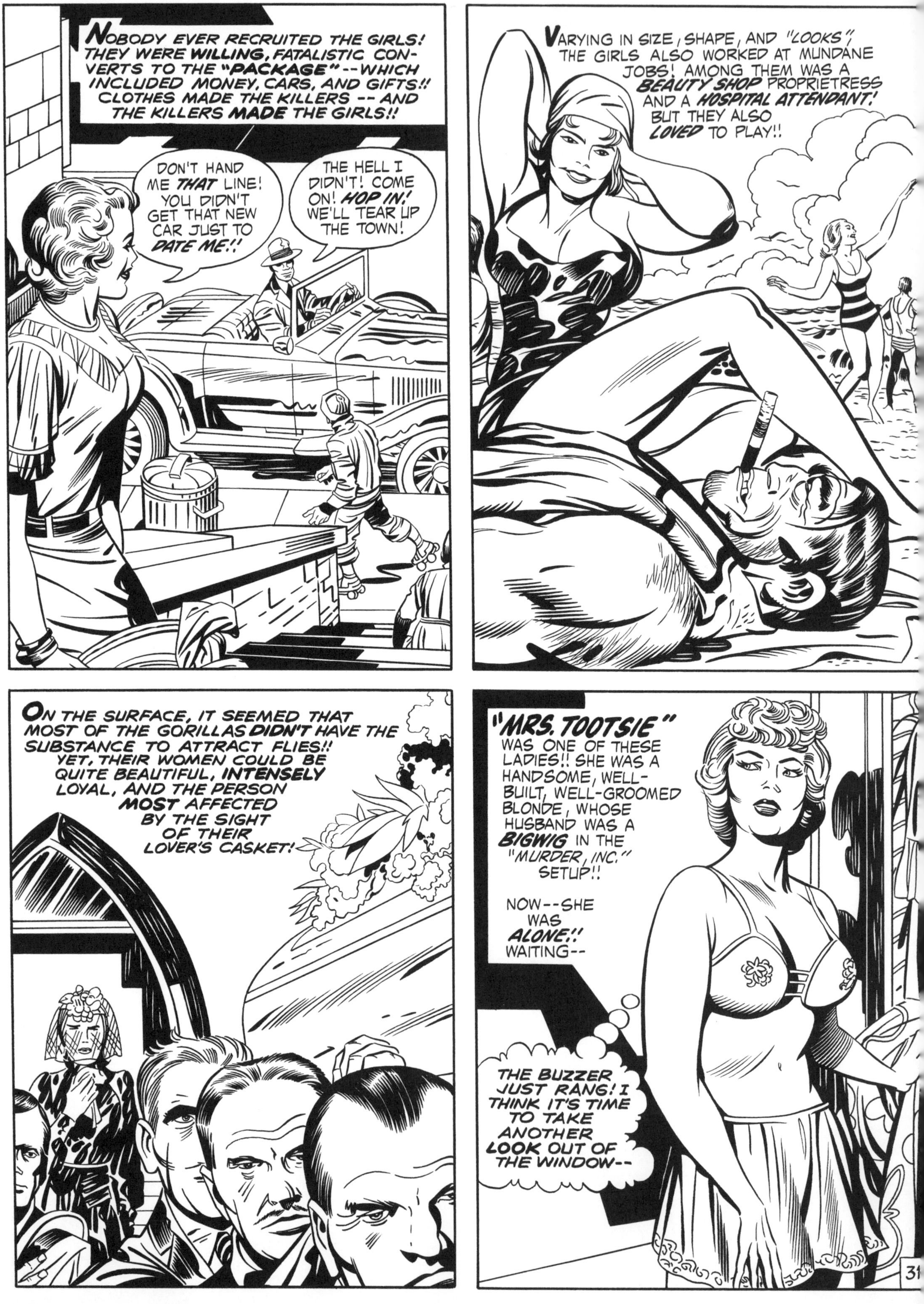
NOBODY EVER RECRUITED THE GIRLS! THEY WERE WILLING, FATALISTIC CONVERTS TO THE "PACKAGE" --WHICH INCLUDED MONEY, CARS, AND GIFTS!! CLOTHES MADE THE KILLERS -- AND THE KILLERS MADE THE GIRLS!!
DON'T HAND ME THAT LINE! YOU DIDN'T GET THAT NEW CAR JUST TO DATE ME!!
THE HELL I DIDN'T! COME ON! HOP IN! WE'LL TEAR UP THE TOWN!
VARYING IN SIZE, SHAPE, AND "LOOKS", THE GIRLS ALSO WORKED AT MUNDANE JOBS! AMONG THEM WAS A BEAUTY SHOP PROPRIETRESS AND A HOSPITAL ATTENDANT! BUT THEY ALSO LOVED TO PLAY!!
ON THE SURFACE, IT SEEMED THAT MOST OF THE GORILLAS DIDN'T HAVE THE SUBSTANCE TO ATTRACT FLIES!! YET, THEIR WOMEN COULD BE QUITE BEAUTIFUL, INTENSELY LOYAL, AND THE PERSON MOST AFFECTED BY THE SIGHT OF THEIR LOVER'S CASKET!
"MRS. TOOTSIE" WAS ONE OF THESE LADIES!! SHE WAS A HANDSOME, WELL-BUILT, WELL-GROOMED BLONDE, WHOSE HUSBAND WAS A BIGWIG IN THE "MURDER, INC." SETUP!!
NOW--SHE WAS ALONE!! WAITING--
THE BUZZER JUST RANG! I THINK IT'S TIME TO TAKE ANOTHER LOOK OUT OF THE WINDOW--
31

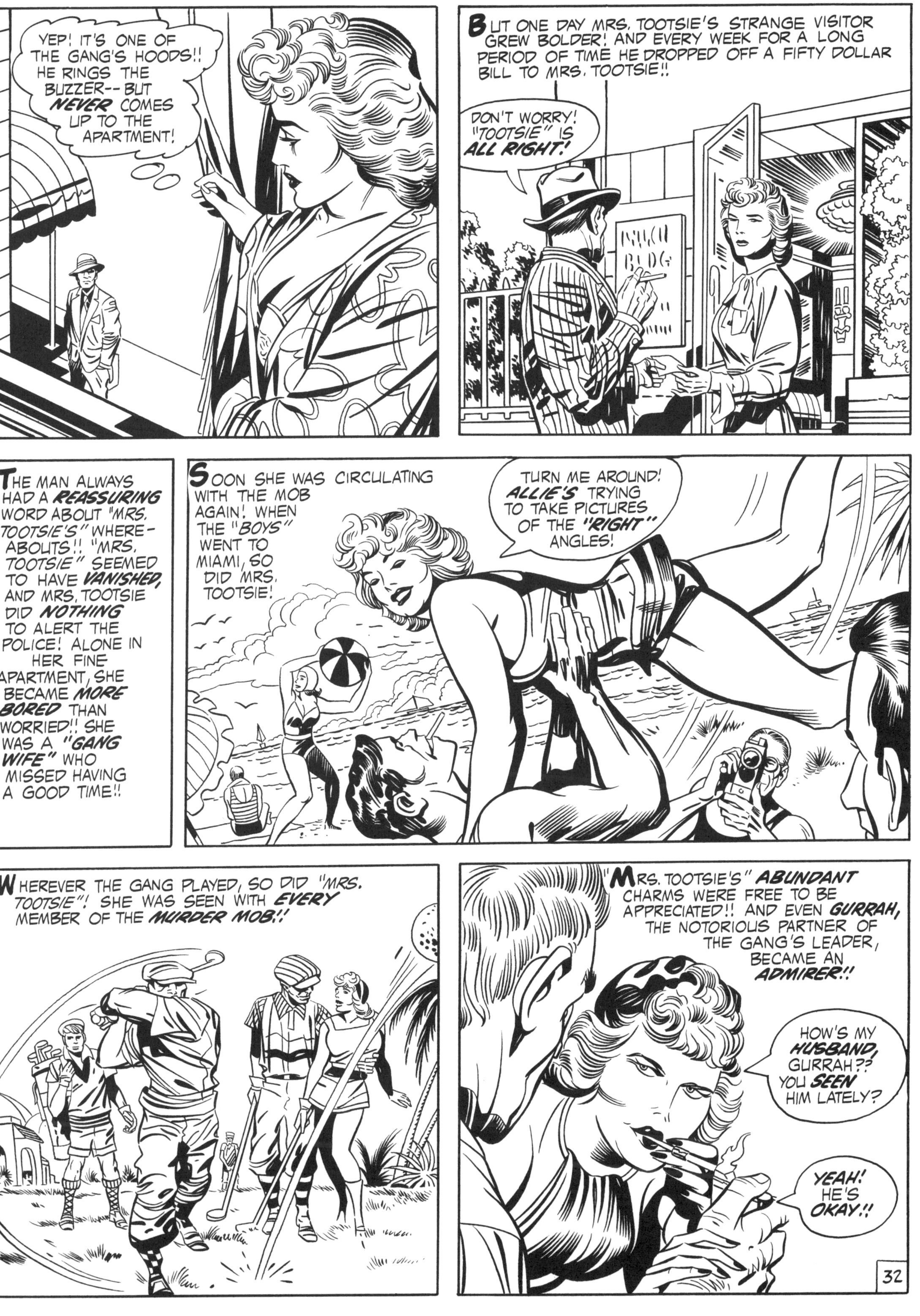
YEP! IT'S ONE OF THE GANG'S HOODS!! HE RINGS THE BUZZER-- BUT NEVER COMES UP TO THE APARTMENT!
BUT ONE DAY MRS. TOOTSIE'S STRANGE VISITOR GREW BOLDER! AND EVERY WEEK FOR A LONG PERIOD OF TIME HE DROPPED OFF A FIFTY DOLLAR BILL TO MRS. TOOTSIE!!
DON'T WORRY! "TOOTSIE" IS ALL RIGHT!
THE MAN ALWAYS HAD A REASSURING WORD ABOUT "MRS. TOOTSIE'S" WHEREABOUTS!! "MRS. TOOTSIE" SEEMED TO HAVE VANISHED, AND MRS. TOOTSIE DID NOTHING TO ALERT THE POLICE! ALONE IN HER FINE APARTMENT, SHE BECAME MORE BORED THAN WORRIED!! SHE WAS A "GANG WIFE" WHO MISSED HAVING A GOOD TIME!!
SOON SHE WAS CIRCULATING WITH THE MOB AGAIN! WHEN THE "BOYS" WENT TO MIAMI, SO DID MRS. TOOTSIE!
TURN ME AROUND! ALLIE'S TRYING TO TAKE PICTURES OF THE "RIGHT" ANGLES!
WHEREVER THE GANG PLAYED, SO DID "MRS. TOOTSIE"! SHE WAS SEEN WITH EVERY MEMBER OF THE MURDER MOB!!
"MRS. TOOTSIE'S" ABUNDANT CHARMS WERE FREE TO BE APPRECIATED!! AND EVEN GURRAH, THE NOTORIOUS PARTNER OF THE GANG'S LEADER, BECAME AN ADMIRER!!
HOW'S MY HUSBAND, GURRAH?? YOU SEEN HIM LATELY?
YEAH! HE'S OKAY!!
32

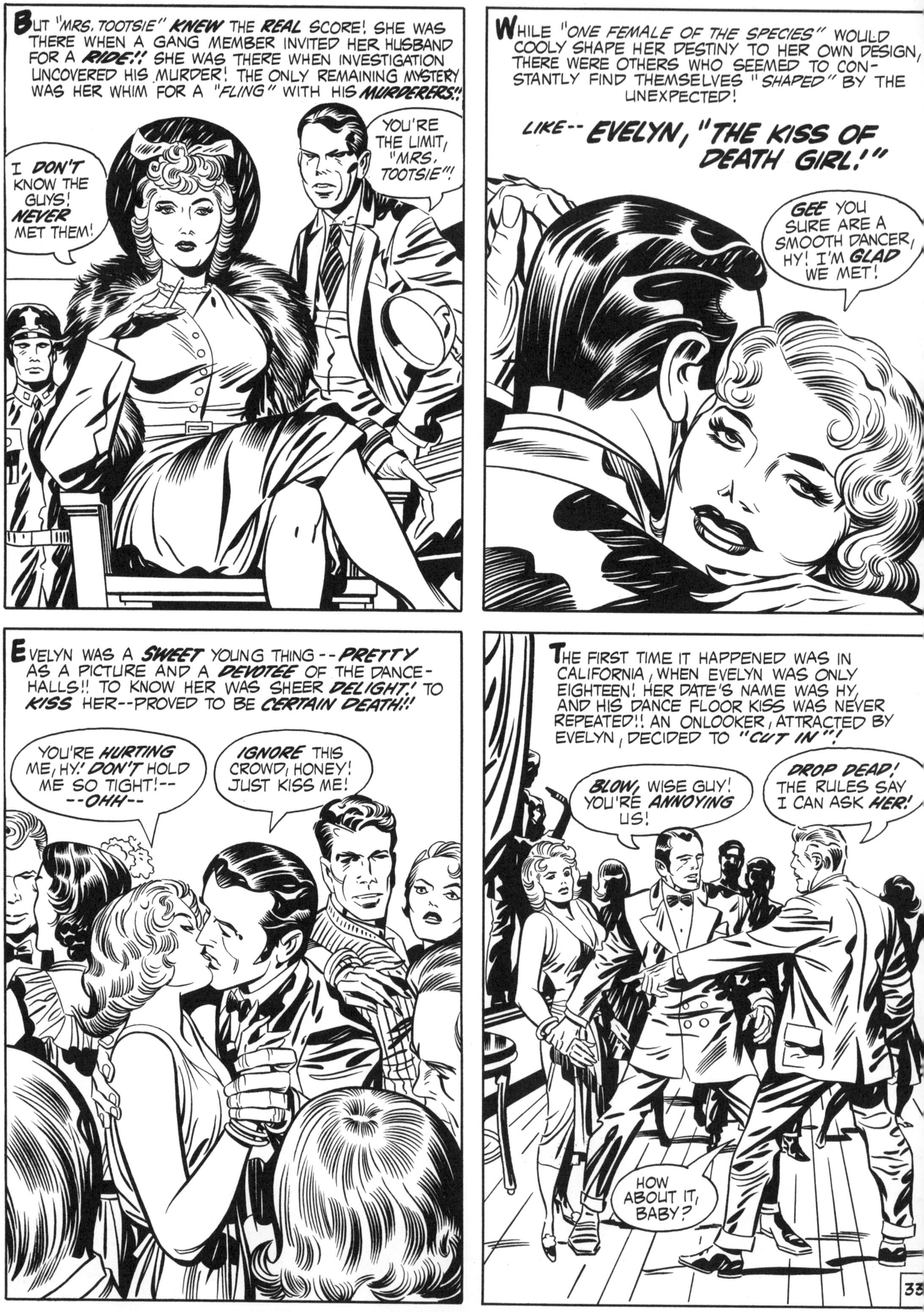
BUT "MRS. TOOTSIE" KNEW THE REAL SCORE! SHE WAS THERE WHEN A GANG MEMBER INVITED HER HUSBAND FOR A RIDE!! SHE WAS THERE WHEN INVESTIGATION UNCOVERED HIS MURDER! THE ONLY REMAINING MYSTERY WAS HER WHIM FOR A "FLING" WITH HIS MURDERERS!!
I DON'T KNOW THE GUYS! NEVER MET THEM!
YOU'RE THE LIMIT, "MRS. TOOTSIE"!!
WHILE "ONE FEMALE OF THE SPECIES" WOULD COOLY SHAPE HER DESTINY TO HER OWN DESIGN, THERE WERE OTHERS WHO SEEMED TO CONSTANTLY FIND THEMSELVES "SHAPED" BY THE UNEXPECTED!
LIKE-- EVELYN, "THE KISS OF DEATH GIRL!"
GEE YOU SURE ARE A SMOOTH DANCER, HY! I'M GLAD WE MET!
EVELYN WAS A SWEET YOUNG THING--PRETTY AS A PICTURE AND A DEVOTEE OF THE DANCE-HALLS!! TO KNOW HER WAS SHEER DELIGHT! TO KISS HER--PROVED TO BE CERTAIN DEATH!!
YOU'RE HURTING ME, HY! DON'T HOLD ME SO TIGHT!-- --OHH--
IGNORE THIS CROWD, HONEY! JUST KISS ME!
THE FIRST TIME IT HAPPENED WAS IN CALIFORNIA, WHEN EVELYN WAS ONLY EIGHTEEN! HER DATE'S NAME WAS HY, AND HIS DANCE FLOOR KISS WAS NEVER REPEATED!! AN ONLOOKER, ATTRACTED BY EVELYN, DECIDED TO "CUT IN"!
BLOW, WISE GUY! YOU'RE ANNOYING US!
DROP DEAD! THE RULES SAY I CAN ASK HER!
HOW ABOUT IT, BABY?

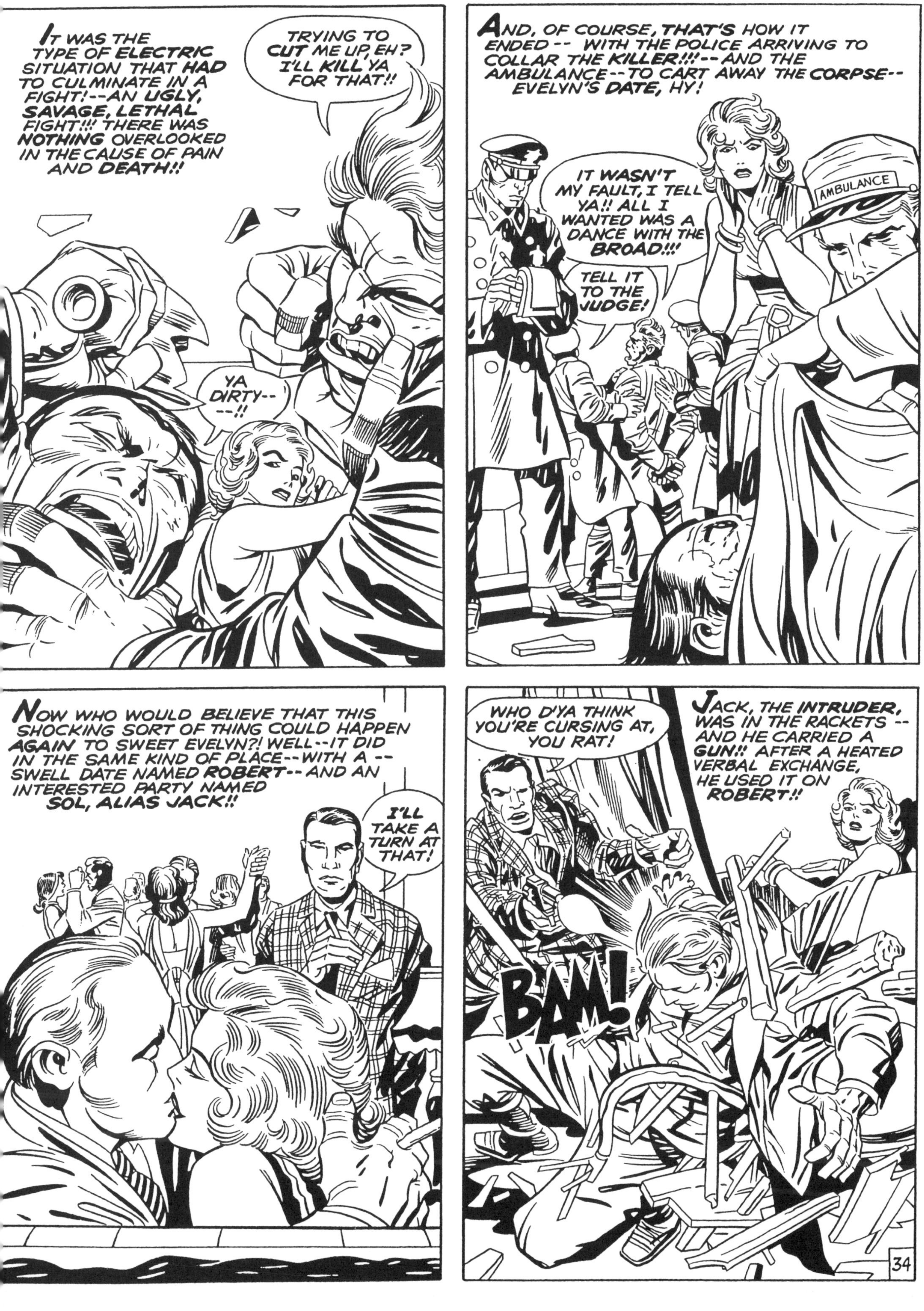
IT WAS THE TYPE OF ELECTRIC SITUATION THAT HAD TO CULMINATE IN A FIGHT!--AN UGLY, SAVAGE, LETHAL FIGHT!!! THERE WAS NOTHING OVERLOOKED IN THE CAUSE OF PAIN AND DEATH!!
TRYING TO CUT ME UP, EH? I'LL KILL YA FOR THAT!!
YA DIRTY-- --!!
AND, OF COURSE, THAT'S HOW IT ENDED -- WITH THE POLICE ARRIVING TO COLLAR THE KILLER!!!--AND THE AMBULANCE--TO CART AWAY THE CORPSE-- EVELYN'S DATE, HY!
IT WASN'T MY FAULT, I TELL YA!! ALL I WANTED WAS A DANCE WITH THE BROAD!!!
TELL IT TO THE JUDGE!
AMBULANCE
NOW WHO WOULD BELIEVE THAT THIS SHOCKING SORT OF THING COULD HAPPEN AGAIN TO SWEET EVELYN?! WELL--IT DID IN THE SAME KIND OF PLACE--WITH A -- SWELL DATE NAMED ROBERT-- AND AN INTERESTED PARTY NAMED SOL, ALIAS JACK!!
I'LL TAKE A TURN AT THAT!
WHO D'YA THINK YOU'RE CURSING AT, YOU RAT!
JACK, THE INTRUDER, WAS IN THE RACKETS -- AND HE CARRIED A GUN!! AFTER A HEATED VERBAL EXCHANGE, HE USED IT ON ROBERT!!
BAM!

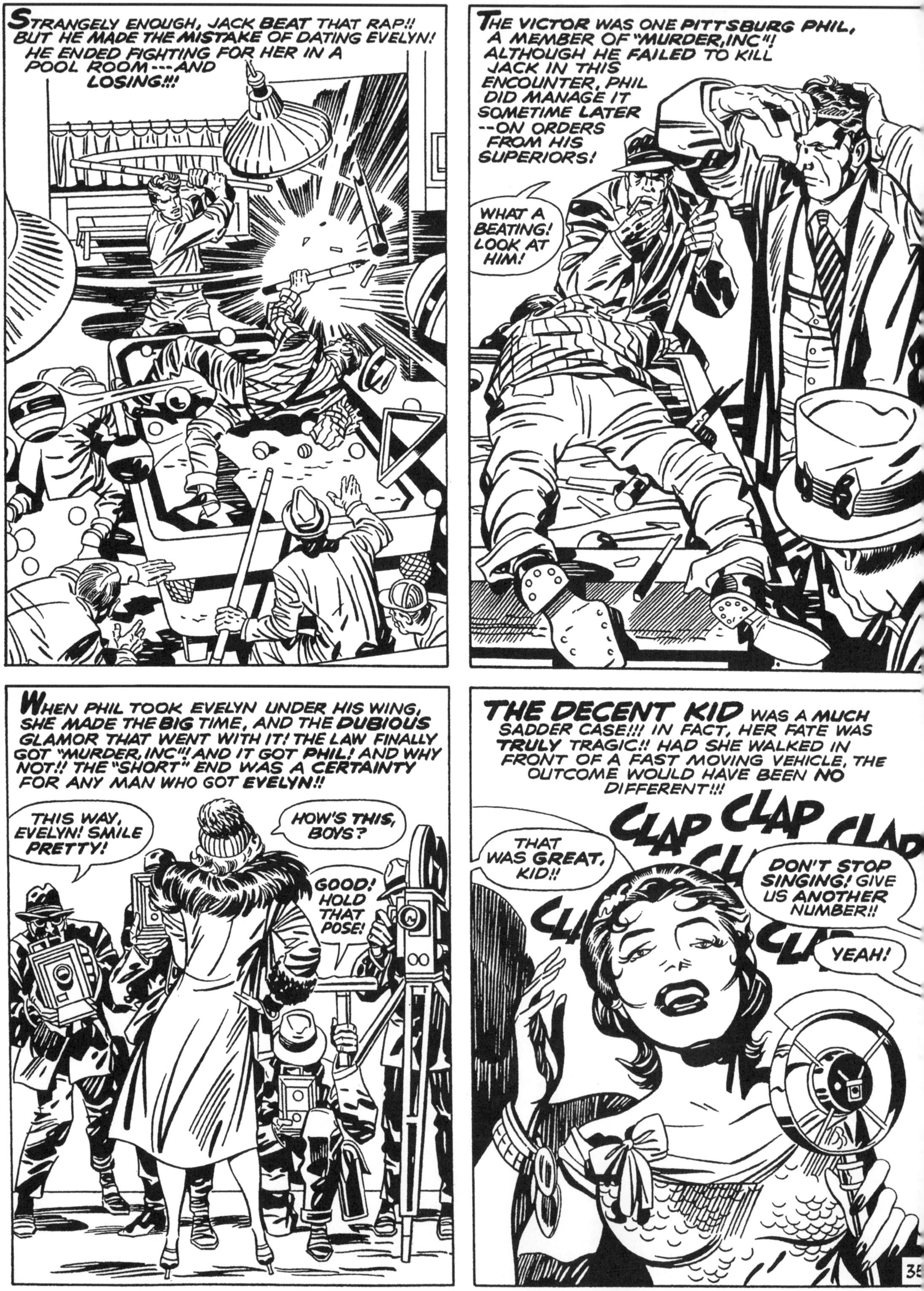
STRANGELY ENOUGH, JACK BEAT THAT RAP!! BUT HE MADE THE MISTAKE OF DATING EVELYN! HE ENDED FIGHTING FOR HER IN A POOL ROOM---AND LOSING!!!
THE VICTOR WAS ONE PITTSBURG PHIL, A MEMBER OF "MURDER,INC"! ALTHOUGH HE FAILED TO KILL JACK IN THIS ENCOUNTER, PHIL DID MANAGE IT SOMETIME LATER --ON ORDERS FROM HIS SUPERIORS!
WHAT A BEATING! LOOK AT HIM!
WHEN PHIL TOOK EVELYN UNDER HIS WING, SHE MADE THE BIG TIME, AND THE DUBIOUS GLAMOR THAT WENT WITH IT! THE LAW FINALLY GOT "MURDER,INC"!! AND IT GOT PHIL! AND WHY NOT!! THE "SHORT" END WAS A CERTAINTY FOR ANY MAN WHO GOT EVELYN!!
THIS WAY, EVELYN! SMILE PRETTY!
HOW'S THIS, BOYS?
GOOD! HOLD THAT POSE!
THE DECENT KID WAS A MUCH SADDER CASE!!! IN FACT, HER FATE WAS TRULY TRAGIC!! HAD SHE WALKED IN FRONT OF A FAST MOVING VEHICLE, THE OUTCOME WOULD HAVE BEEN NO DIFFERENT!!!
CLAP CLAP
THAT WAS GREAT, KID!!
DON'T STOP SINGING! GIVE US ANOTHER NUMBER!!
YEAH!

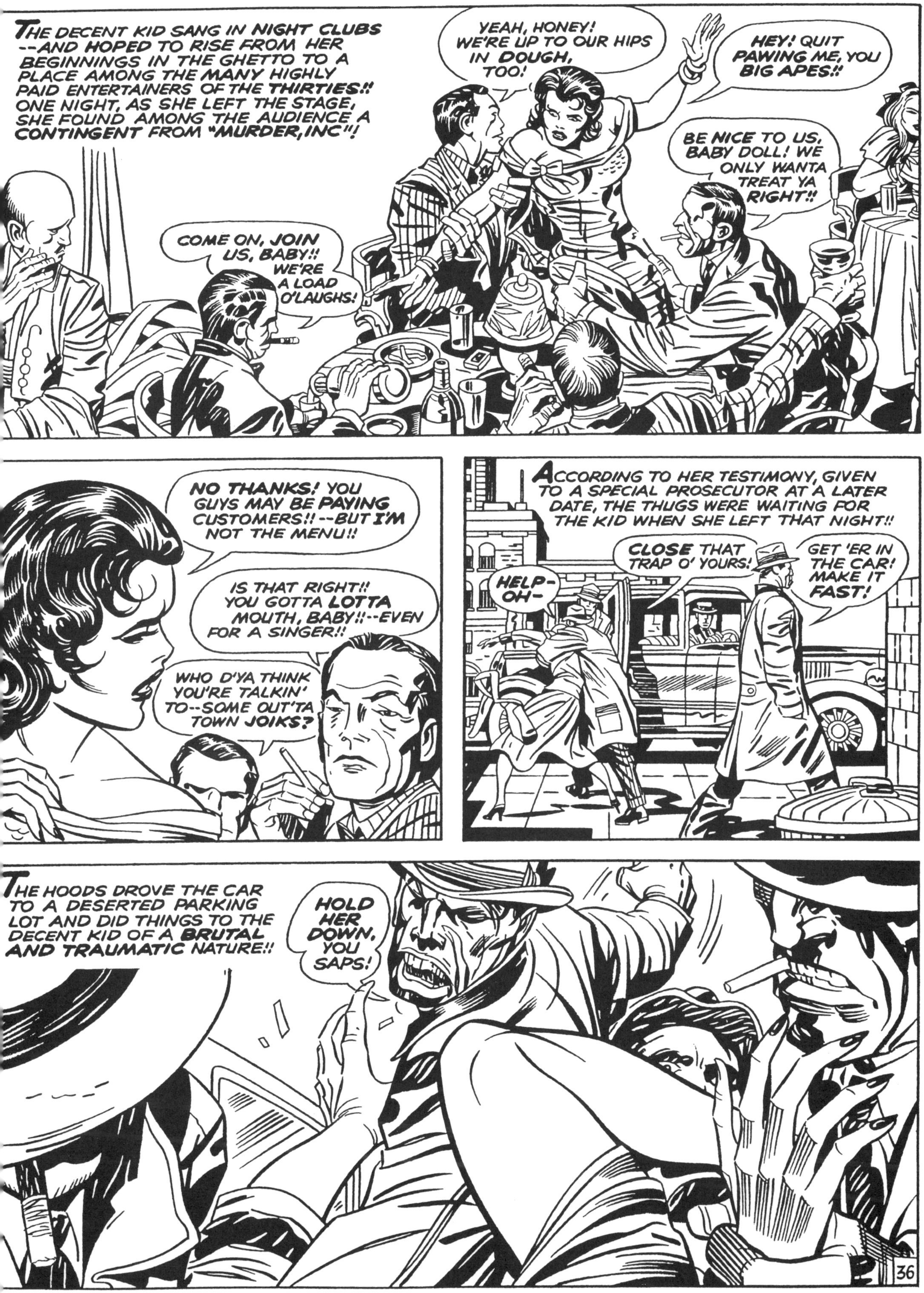
THE DECENT KID SANG IN NIGHT CLUBS --AND HOPED TO RISE FROM HER BEGINNINGS IN THE GHETTO TO A PLACE AMONG THE MANY HIGHLY PAID ENTERTAINERS OF THE THIRTIES!! ONE NIGHT, AS SHE LEFT THE STAGE, SHE FOUND AMONG THE AUDIENCE A CONTINGENT FROM "MURDER, INC"!
YEAH, HONEY! WE'RE UP TO OUR HIPS IN DOUGH, TOO!
HEY! QUIT PAWING ME, YOU BIG APES!!
BE NICE TO US, BABY DOLL! WE ONLY WANTA TREAT YA RIGHT!!
COME ON, JOIN US, BABY!! WE'RE A LOAD O'LAUGHS!
NO THANKS! YOU GUYS MAY BE PAYING CUSTOMERS!! --BUT I'M NOT THE MENU!!
IS THAT RIGHT!! YOU GOTTA LOTTA MOUTH, BABY!!--EVEN FOR A SINGER!!
WHO D'YA THINK YOU'RE TALKIN' TO--SOME OUT'TA TOWN JOIKS?
ACCORDING TO HER TESTIMONY, GIVEN TO A SPECIAL PROSECUTOR AT A LATER DATE, THE THUGS WERE WAITING FOR THE KID WHEN SHE LEFT THAT NIGHT!!
HELP-OH-
CLOSE THAT TRAP O' YOURS!
GET 'ER IN THE CAR! MAKE IT FAST!
THE HOODS DROVE THE CAR TO A DESERTED PARKING LOT AND DID THINGS TO THE DECENT KID OF A BRUTAL AND TRAUMATIC NATURE!!
HOLD HER DOWN, YOU SAPS!

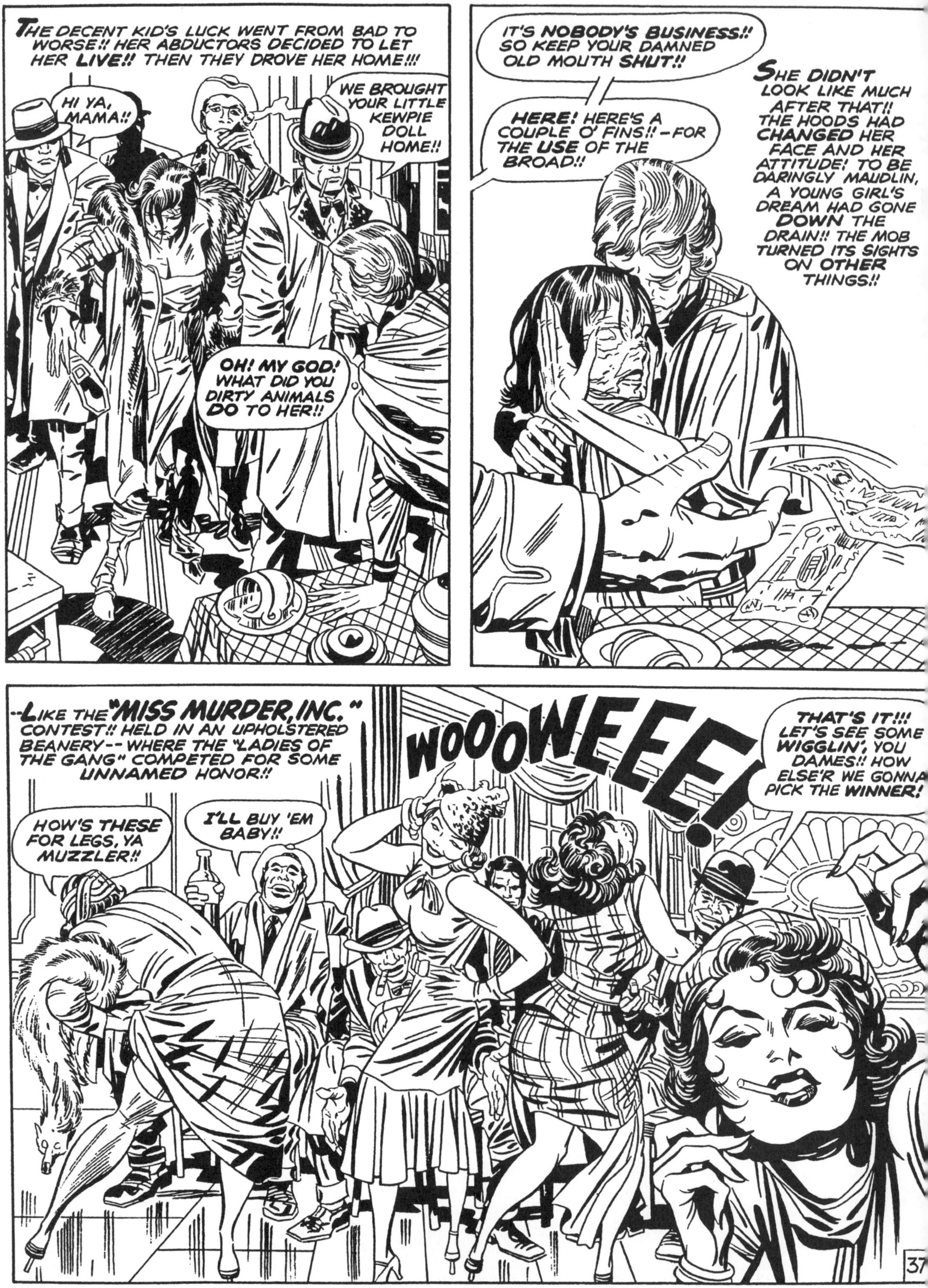
THE DECENT KID'S LUCK WENT FROM BAD TO WORSE!! HER ABDUCTORS DECIDED TO LET HER LIVE!! THEN THEY DROVE HER HOME!!!
HI YA, MAMA!!
WE BROUGHT YOUR LITTLE KEWPIE DOLL HOME!!
OH! MY GOD! WHAT DID YOU DIRTY ANIMALS DO TO HER!!
IT'S NOBODY'S BUSINESS!! SO KEEP YOUR DAMNED OLD MOUTH SHUT!!
HERE! HERE'S A COUPLE O' FINS!! --FOR THE USE OF THE BROAD!!
SHE DIDN'T LOOK LIKE MUCH AFTER THAT!! THE HOODS HAD CHANGED HER FACE AND HER ATTITUDE! TO BE DARINGLY MAUDLIN, A YOUNG GIRL'S DREAM HAD GONE DOWN THE DRAIN!! THE MOB TURNED ITS SIGHTS ON OTHER THINGS!!
--LIKE THE "MISS MURDER, INC." CONTEST!! HELD IN AN UPHOLSTERED BEANERY-- WHERE THE "LADIES OF THE GANG" COMPETED FOR SOME UNNAMED HONOR!!
WOOOWEEE!
THAT'S IT!!! LET'S SEE SOME WIGGLIN', YOU DAMES!! HOW ELSE'R WE GONNA PICK THE WINNER!
HOW'S THESE FOR LEGS, YA MUZZLER!!
I'LL BUY 'EM BABY!!

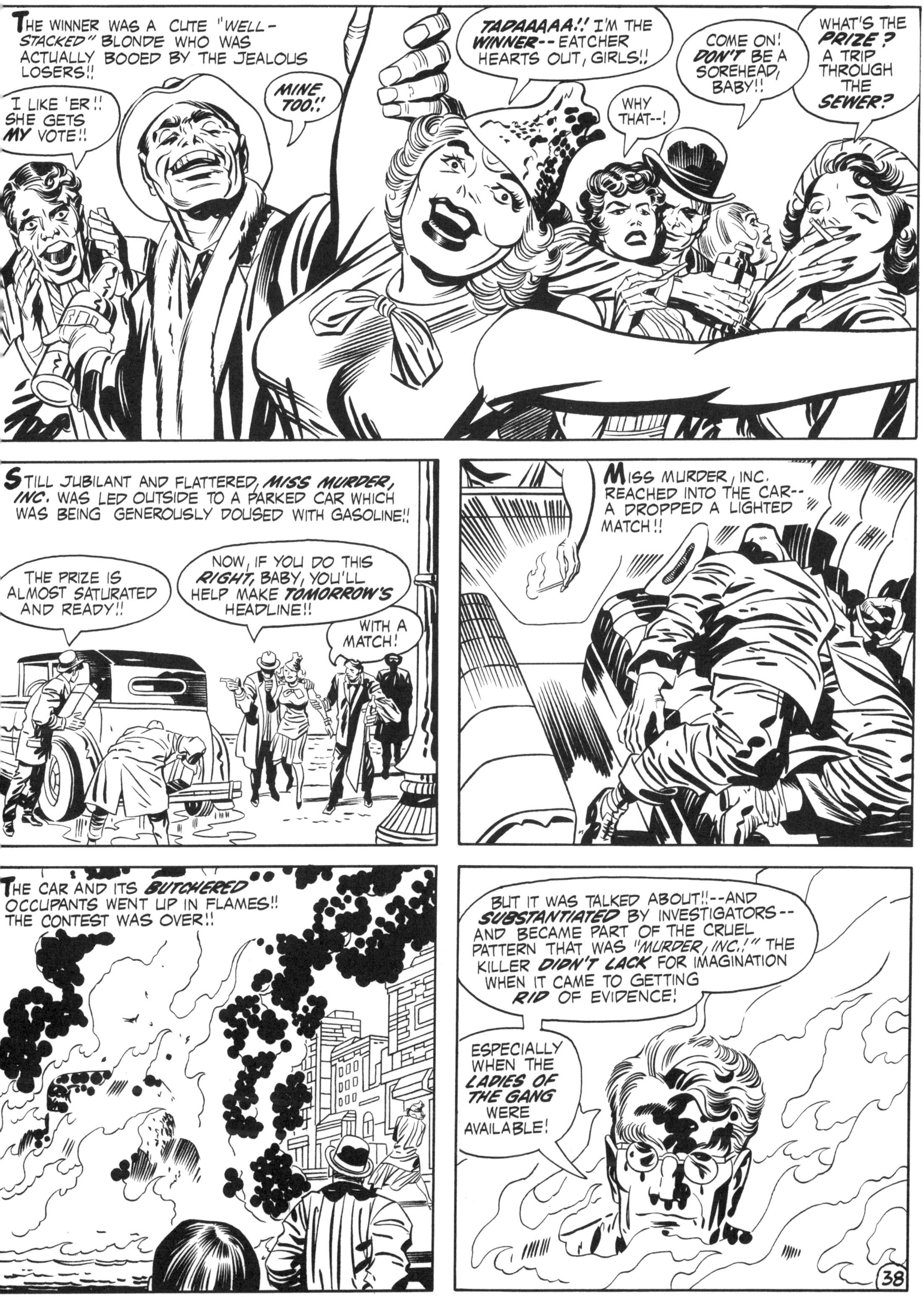
THE WINNER WAS A CUTE "WELL-STACKED" BLONDE WHO WAS ACTUALLY BOOED BY THE JEALOUS LOSERS!!
I LIKE 'ER!! SHE GETS MY VOTE!!
MINE TOO!!
TADAAAAAA!! I'M THE WINNER-- EATCHER HEARTS OUT, GIRLS!!
WHY THAT--!
COME ON! DON'T BE A SOREHEAD, BABY!!
WHAT'S THE PRIZE? A TRIP THROUGH THE SEWER?
STILL JUBILANT AND FLATTERED, MISS MURDER, INC. WAS LED OUTSIDE TO A PARKED CAR WHICH WAS BEING GENEROUSLY DOUSED WITH GASOLINE!!
THE PRIZE IS ALMOST SATURATED AND READY!!
NOW, IF YOU DO THIS RIGHT, BABY, YOU'LL HELP MAKE TOMORROW'S HEADLINE!!
WITH A MATCH!
MISS MURDER, INC. REACHED INTO THE CAR-- A DROPPED A LIGHTED MATCH!!
THE CAR AND ITS BUTCHERED OCCUPANTS WENT UP IN FLAMES!! THE CONTEST WAS OVER!!
BUT IT WAS TALKED ABOUT!!--AND SUBSTANTIATED BY INVESTIGATORS-- AND BECAME PART OF THE CRUEL PATTERN THAT WAS "MURDER, INC.!" THE KILLER DIDN'T LACK FOR IMAGINATION WHEN IT CAME TO GETTING RID OF EVIDENCE!
ESPECIALLY WHEN THE LADIES OF THE GANG WERE AVAILABLE!
38

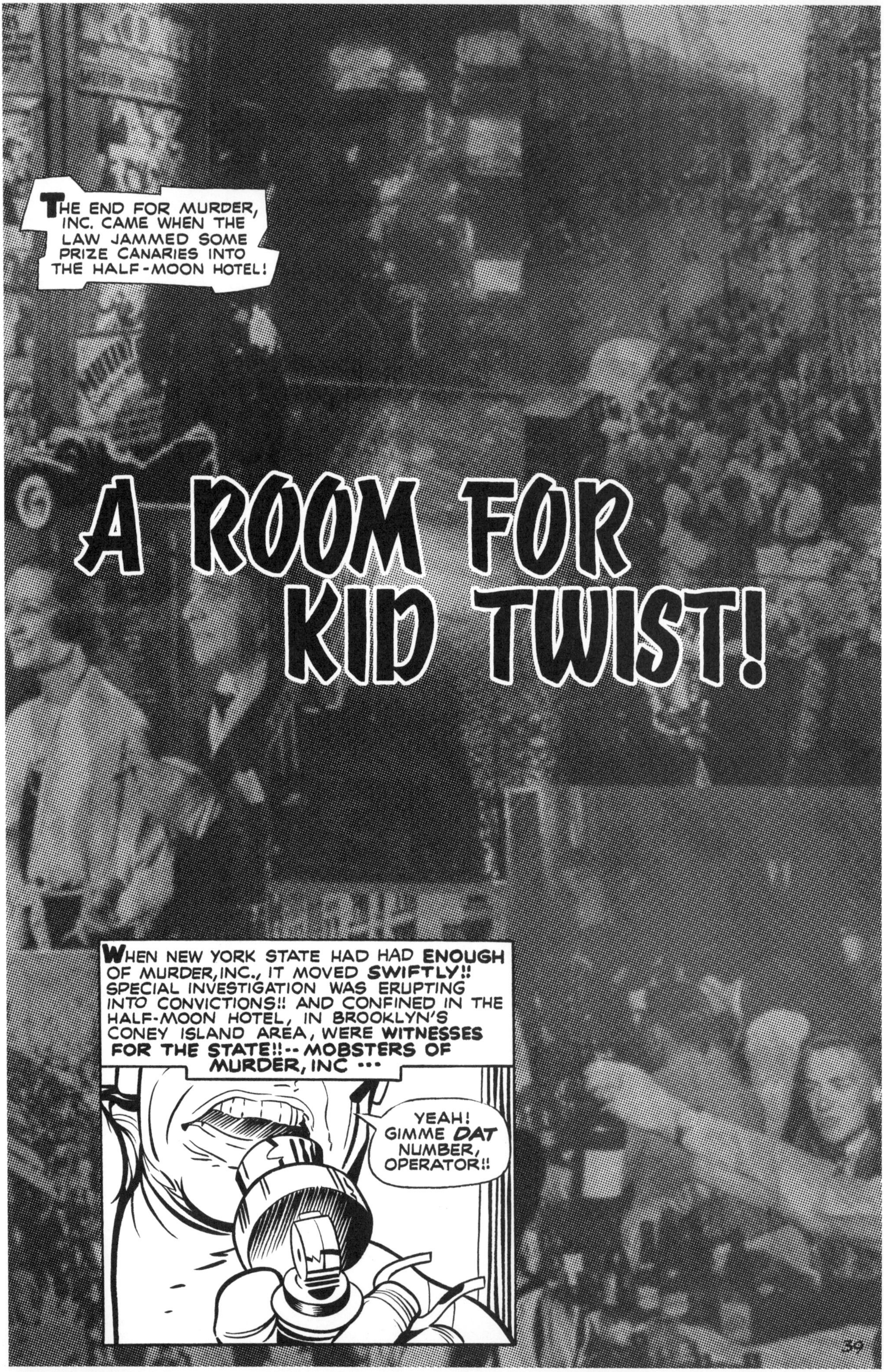
THE END FOR MURDER, INC. CAME WHEN THE LAW JAMMED SOME PRIZE CANARIES INTO THE HALF-MOON HOTEL!
A ROOM FOR KID TWIST!
WHEN NEW YORK STATE HAD HAD ENOUGH OF MURDER, INC., IT MOVED SWIFTLY!! SPECIAL INVESTIGATION WAS ERUPTING INTO CONVICTIONS!! AND CONFINED IN THE HALF-MOON HOTEL, IN BROOKLYN'S CONEY ISLAND AREA, WERE WITNESSES FOR THE STATE!!-- MOBSTERS OF MURDER, INC ···
YEAH! GIMME DAT NUMBER, OPERATOR!!

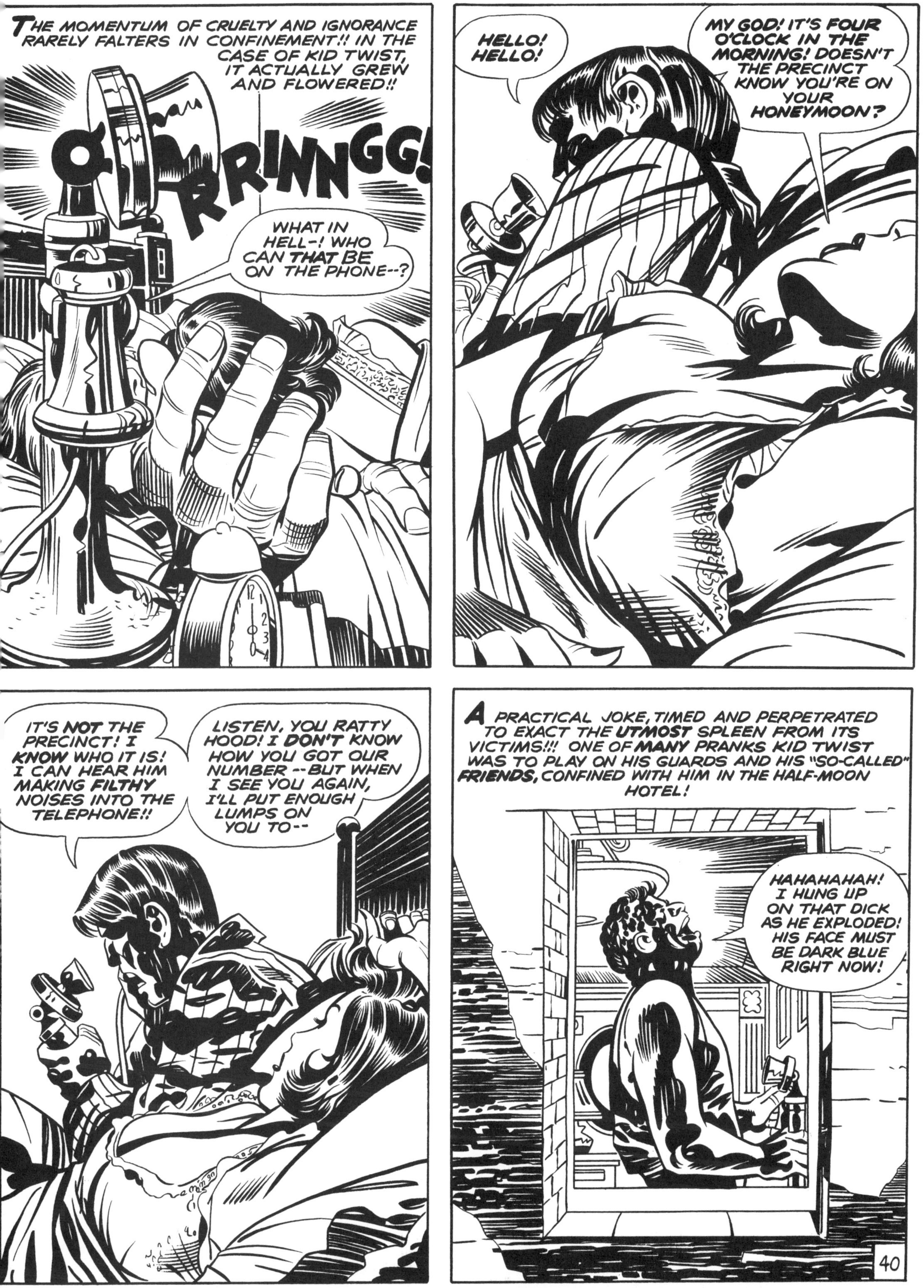
THE MOMENTUM OF CRUELTY AND IGNORANCE RARELY FALTERS IN CONFINEMENT!! IN THE CASE OF KID TWIST, IT ACTUALLY GREW AND FLOWERED!!
RRINNGG!
WHAT IN HELL-! WHO CAN THAT BE ON THE PHONE--?
HELLO! HELLO!
MY GOD! IT'S FOUR O'CLOCK IN THE MORNING! DOESN'T THE PRECINCT KNOW YOU'RE ON YOUR HONEYMOON?
IT'S NOT THE PRECINCT! I KNOW WHO IT IS! I CAN HEAR HIM MAKING FILTHY NOISES INTO THE TELEPHONE!!
LISTEN, YOU RATTY HOOD! I DON'T KNOW HOW YOU GOT OUR NUMBER --BUT WHEN I SEE YOU AGAIN, I'LL PUT ENOUGH LUMPS ON YOU TO--
A PRACTICAL JOKE, TIMED AND PERPETRATED TO EXACT THE UTMOST SPLEEN FROM ITS VICTIMS!!! ONE OF MANY PRANKS KID TWIST WAS TO PLAY ON HIS GUARDS AND HIS "SO-CALLED" FRIENDS, CONFINED WITH HIM IN THE HALF-MOON HOTEL!
HAHAHAHAH! I HUNG UP ON THAT DICK AS HE EXPLODED! HIS FACE MUST BE DARK BLUE RIGHT NOW!

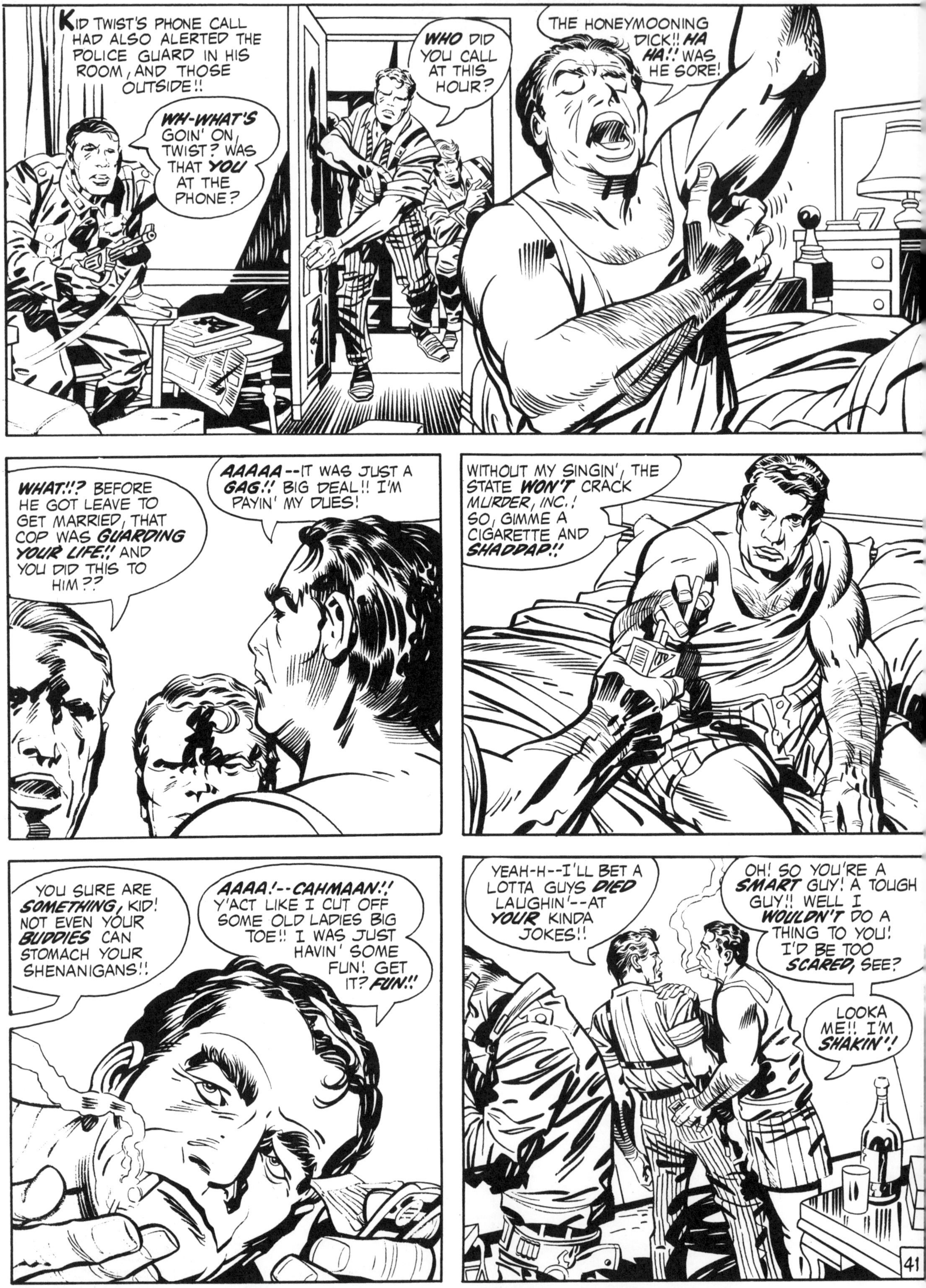

KID TWIST'S PHONE CALL HAD ALSO ALERTED THE POLICE GUARD IN HIS ROOM, AND THOSE OUTSIDE!!
WH-WHAT'S GOIN' ON, TWIST? WAS THAT YOU AT THE PHONE?
WHO DID YOU CALL AT THIS HOUR?
THE HONEYMOONING DICK!! HA HA!! WAS HE SORE!
WHAT!!? BEFORE HE GOT LEAVE TO GET MARRIED, THAT COP WAS GUARDING YOUR LIFE!! AND YOU DID THIS TO HIM??
AAAAA--IT WAS JUST A GAG!! BIG DEAL!! I'M PAYIN' MY DUES!
WITHOUT MY SINGIN', THE STATE WON'T CRACK MURDER, INC.! SO, GIMME A CIGARETTE AND SHADDAP!!
YOU SURE ARE SOMETHING, KID! NOT EVEN YOUR BUDDIES CAN STOMACH YOUR SHENANIGANS!!
AAAA!--CAHMAAN!! Y'ACT LIKE I CUT OFF SOME OLD LADIES BIG TOE!! I WAS JUST HAVIN' SOME FUN! GET IT? FUN!!
YEAH-H--I'LL BET A LOTTA GUYS DIED LAUGHIN'--AT YOUR KINDA JOKES!!
OH! SO YOU'RE A SMART GUY! A TOUGH GUY!! WELL I WOULDN'T DO A THING TO YOU! I'D BE TOO SCARED, SEE?
LOOKA ME!! I'M SHAKIN'!

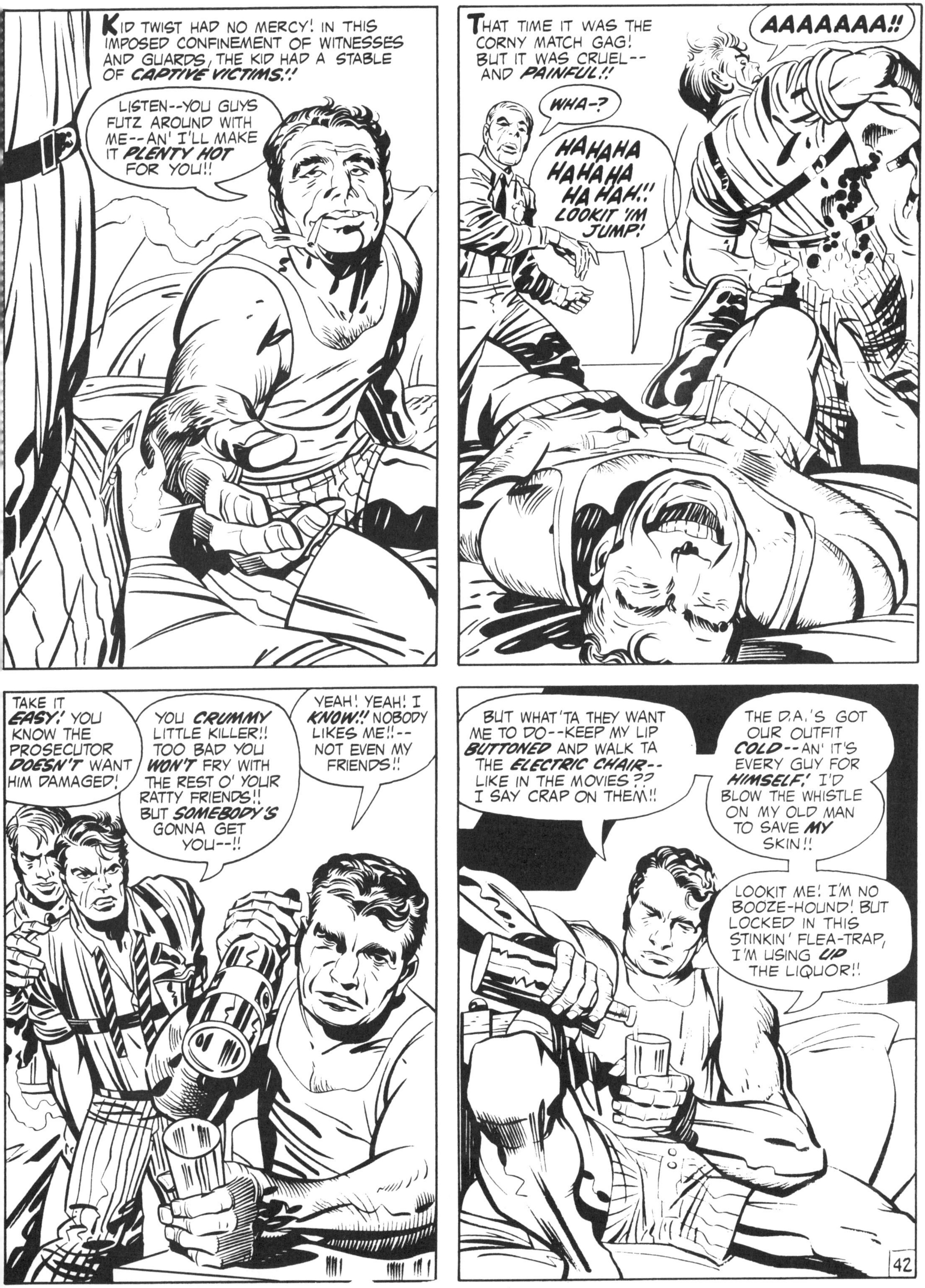
KID TWIST HAD NO MERCY! IN THIS IMPOSED CONFINEMENT OF WITNESSES AND GUARDS, THE KID HAD A STABLE OF CAPTIVE VICTIMS!!
LISTEN--YOU GUYS FUTZ AROUND WITH ME--AN' I'LL MAKE IT PLENTY HOT FOR YOU!!
THAT TIME IT WAS THE CORNY MATCH GAG! BUT IT WAS CRUEL--AND PAINFUL!!
AAAAAAA!!
WHA-?
HAHAHA HAHAHA HA HAH!! LOOKIT 'IM JUMP!
TAKE IT EASY! YOU KNOW THE PROSECUTOR DOESN'T WANT HIM DAMAGED!
YOU CRUMMY LITTLE KILLER!! TOO BAD YOU WON'T FRY WITH THE REST O' YOUR RATTY FRIENDS!! BUT SOMEBODY'S GONNA GET YOU--!!
YEAH! YEAH! I KNOW!! NOBODY LIKES ME!!--NOT EVEN MY FRIENDS!!
BUT WHAT'TA THEY WANT ME TO DO--KEEP MY LIP BUTTONED AND WALK TA THE ELECTRIC CHAIR--LIKE IN THE MOVIES?? I SAY CRAP ON THEM!!
THE D.A.'S GOT OUR OUTFIT COLD--AN' IT'S EVERY GUY FOR HIMSELF! I'D BLOW THE WHISTLE ON MY OLD MAN TO SAVE MY SKIN!!
LOOKIT ME! I'M NO BOOZE-HOUND! BUT LOCKED IN THIS STINKIN' FLEA-TRAP, I'M USING UP THE LIQUOR!!
42

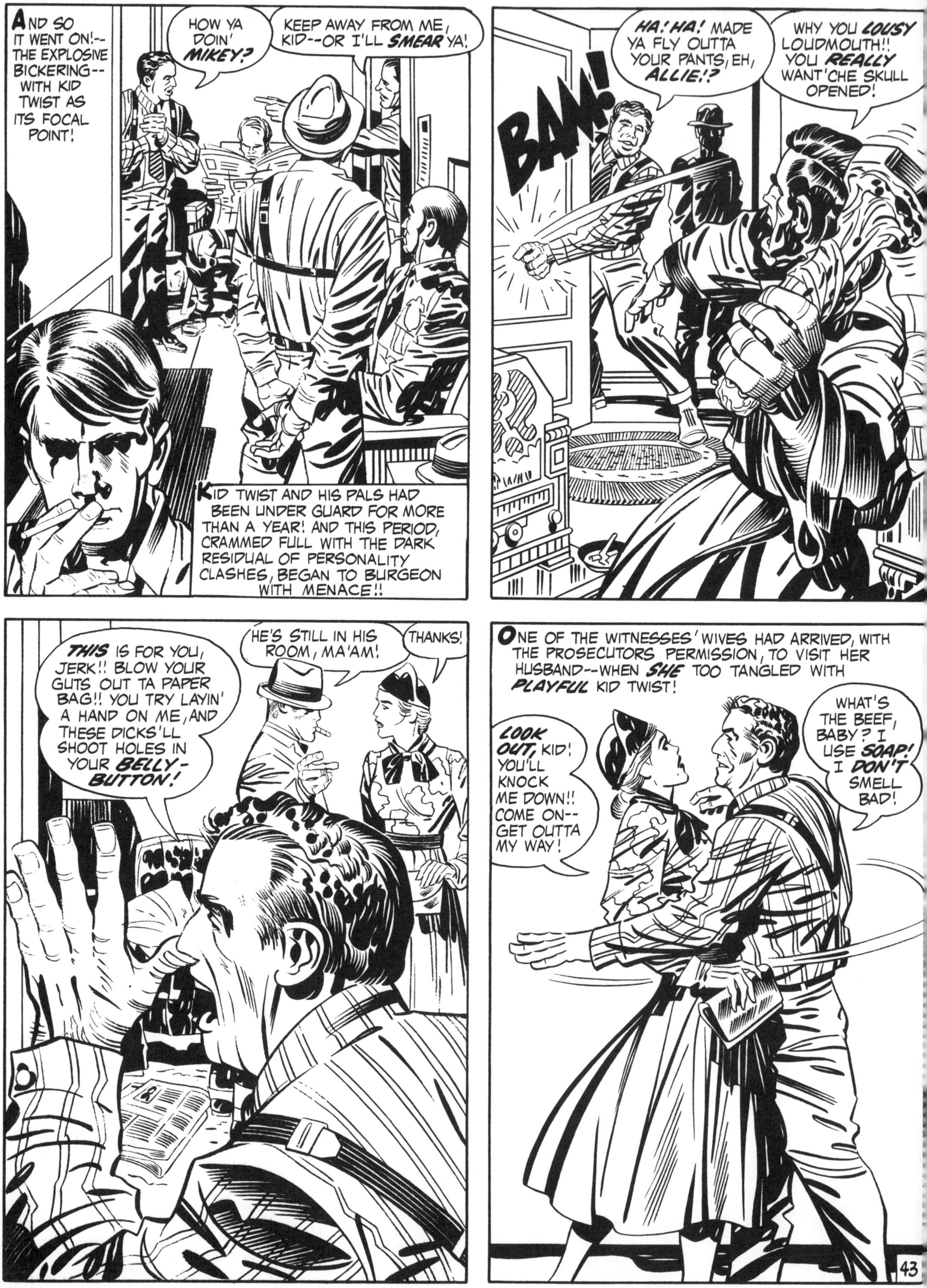
AND SO IT WENT ON!-- THE EXPLOSIVE BICKERING-- WITH KID TWIST AS ITS FOCAL POINT!
HOW YA DOIN' MIKEY?
KEEP AWAY FROM ME, KID--OR I'LL SMEAR YA!
KID TWIST AND HIS PALS HAD BEEN UNDER GUARD FOR MORE THAN A YEAR! AND THIS PERIOD, CRAMMED FULL WITH THE DARK RESIDUAL OF PERSONALITY CLASHES, BEGAN TO BURGEON WITH MENACE!!
BAM!
HA! HA! MADE YA FLY OUTTA YOUR PANTS, EH, ALLIE!?
WHY YOU LOUSY LOUDMOUTH!! YOU REALLY WANT'CHE SKULL OPENED!
THIS IS FOR YOU, JERK!! BLOW YOUR GUTS OUT TA PAPER BAG!! YOU TRY LAYIN' A HAND ON ME, AND THESE DICKS'LL SHOOT HOLES IN YOUR BELLY-BUTTON!
HE'S STILL IN HIS ROOM, MA'AM!
THANKS!
ONE OF THE WITNESSES' WIVES HAD ARRIVED, WITH THE PROSECUTORS PERMISSION, TO VISIT HER HUSBAND--WHEN SHE TOO TANGLED WITH PLAYFUL KID TWIST!
LOOK OUT, KID! YOU'LL KNOCK ME DOWN!! COME ON-- GET OUTTA MY WAY!
WHAT'S THE BEEF, BABY? I USE SOAP! I DON'T SMELL BAD!

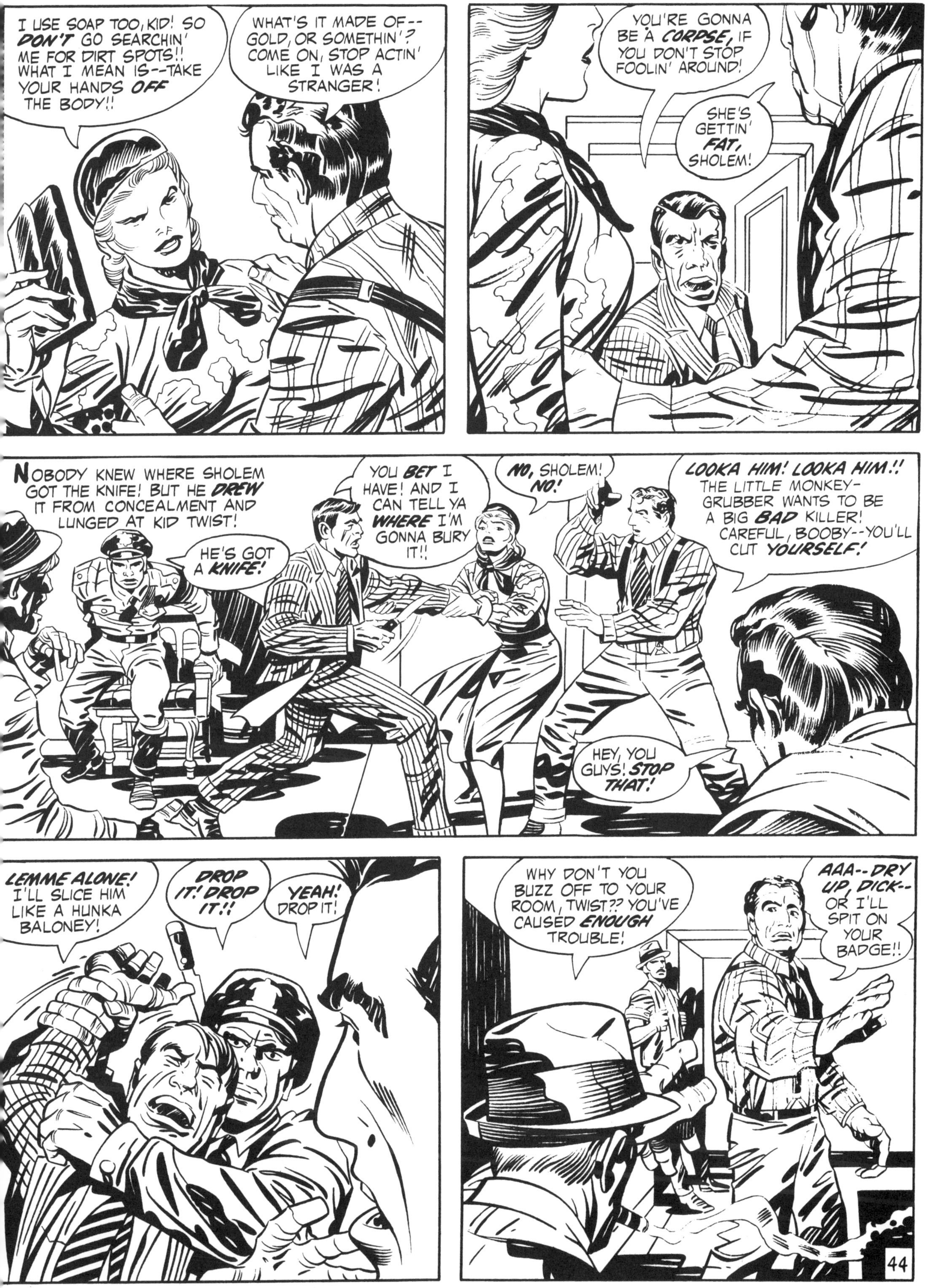

I USE SOAP TOO, KID! SO DON'T GO SEARCHIN' ME FOR DIRT SPOTS!! WHAT I MEAN IS--TAKE YOUR HANDS OFF THE BODY!!
WHAT'S IT MADE OF--GOLD, OR SOMETHIN'? COME ON, STOP ACTIN' LIKE I WAS A STRANGER!
YOU'RE GONNA BE A CORPSE, IF YOU DON'T STOP FOOLIN' AROUND!
SHE'S GETTIN' FAT, SHOLEM!
NOBODY KNEW WHERE SHOLEM GOT THE KNIFE! BUT HE DREW IT FROM CONCEALMENT AND LUNGED AT KID TWIST!
HE'S GOT A KNIFE!
YOU BET I HAVE! AND I CAN TELL YA WHERE I'M GONNA BURY IT!!
NO, SHOLEM! NO!
LOOKA HIM! LOOKA HIM!! THE LITTLE MONKEY-GRUBBER WANTS TO BE A BIG BAD KILLER! CAREFUL, BOOBY--YOU'LL CUT YOURSELF!
HEY, YOU GUYS! STOP THAT!
LEMME ALONE! I'LL SLICE HIM LIKE A HUNKA BALONEY!
DROP IT! DROP IT!!
YEAH! DROP IT!
WHY DON'T YOU BUZZ OFF TO YOUR ROOM, TWIST?? YOU'VE CAUSED ENOUGH TROUBLE!
AAA--DRY UP, DICK--OR I'LL SPIT ON YOUR BADGE!!

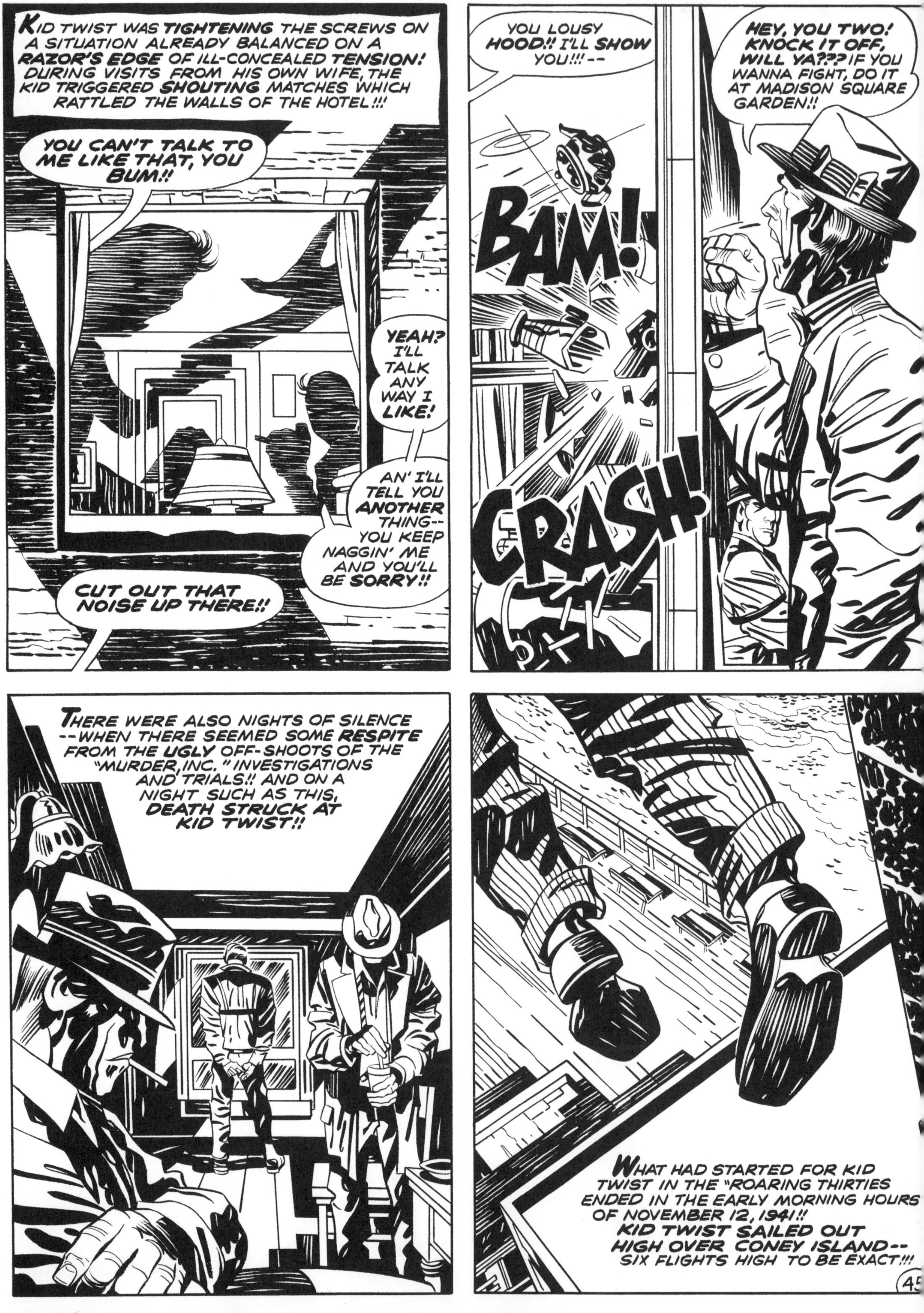
KID TWIST WAS TIGHTENING THE SCREWS ON A SITUATION ALREADY BALANCED ON A RAZOR'S EDGE OF ILL-CONCEALED TENSION! DURING VISITS FROM HIS OWN WIFE, THE KID TRIGGERED SHOUTING MATCHES WHICH RATTLED THE WALLS OF THE HOTEL!!!
YOU CAN'T TALK TO ME LIKE THAT, YOU BUM!!
YEAH? I'LL TALK ANY WAY I LIKE!
AN' I'LL TELL YOU ANOTHER THING-- YOU KEEP NAGGIN' ME AND YOU'LL BE SORRY!!
CUT OUT THAT NOISE UP THERE!!
YOU LOUSY HOOD!! I'LL SHOW YOU!!! --
BAM!
CRASH!
HEY, YOU TWO! KNOCK IT OFF, WILL YA??? IF YOU WANNA FIGHT, DO IT AT MADISON SQUARE GARDEN!!
THERE WERE ALSO NIGHTS OF SILENCE --WHEN THERE SEEMED SOME RESPITE FROM THE UGLY OFF-SHOOTS OF THE "MURDER, INC." INVESTIGATIONS AND TRIALS!! AND ON A NIGHT SUCH AS THIS, DEATH STRUCK AT KID TWIST!!
WHAT HAD STARTED FOR KID TWIST IN THE "ROARING THIRTIES ENDED IN THE EARLY MORNING HOURS OF NOVEMBER 12, 1941!! KID TWIST SAILED OUT HIGH OVER CONEY ISLAND-- SIX FLIGHTS HIGH TO BE EXACT!!!
45

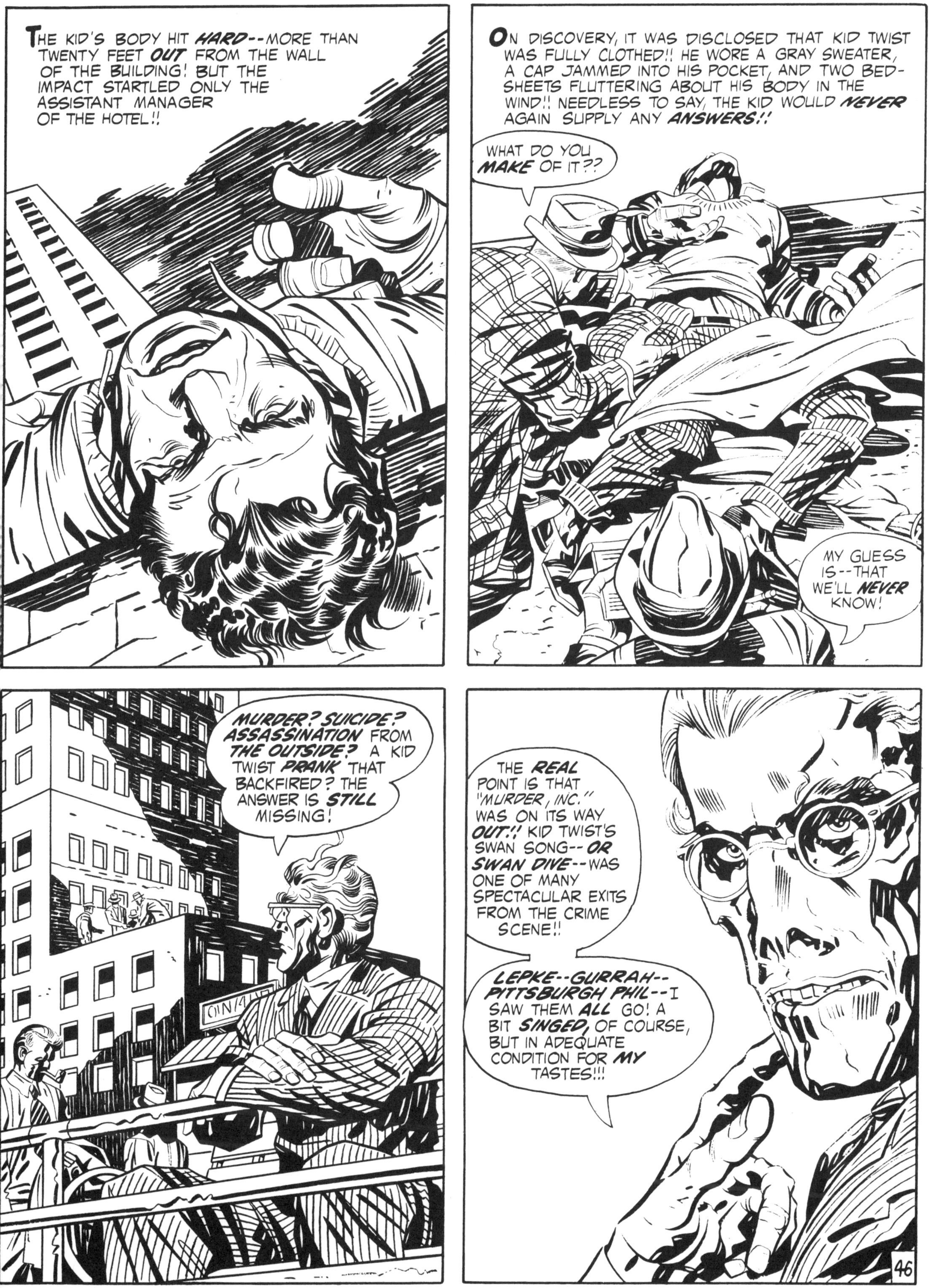
THE KID'S BODY HIT HARD--MORE THAN TWENTY FEET OUT FROM THE WALL OF THE BUILDING! BUT THE IMPACT STARTLED ONLY THE ASSISTANT MANAGER OF THE HOTEL!!
ON DISCOVERY, IT WAS DISCLOSED THAT KID TWIST WAS FULLY CLOTHED!! HE WORE A GRAY SWEATER, A CAP JAMMED INTO HIS POCKET, AND TWO BED-SHEETS FLUTTERING ABOUT HIS BODY IN THE WIND!! NEEDLESS TO SAY, THE KID WOULD NEVER AGAIN SUPPLY ANY ANSWERS!!
WHAT DO YOU MAKE OF IT??
MY GUESS IS--THAT WE'LL NEVER KNOW!
MURDER? SUICIDE? ASSASSINATION FROM THE OUTSIDE? A KID TWIST PRANK THAT BACKFIRED? THE ANSWER IS STILL MISSING!
THE REAL POINT IS THAT "MURDER, INC." WAS ON ITS WAY OUT!! KID TWIST'S SWAN SONG--OR SWAN DIVE--WAS ONE OF MANY SPECTACULAR EXITS FROM THE CRIME SCENE!!
LEPKE--GURRAH--PITTSBURGH PHIL--I SAW THEM ALL GO! A BIT SINGED, OF COURSE, BUT IN ADEQUATE CONDITION FOR MY TASTES!!!
46

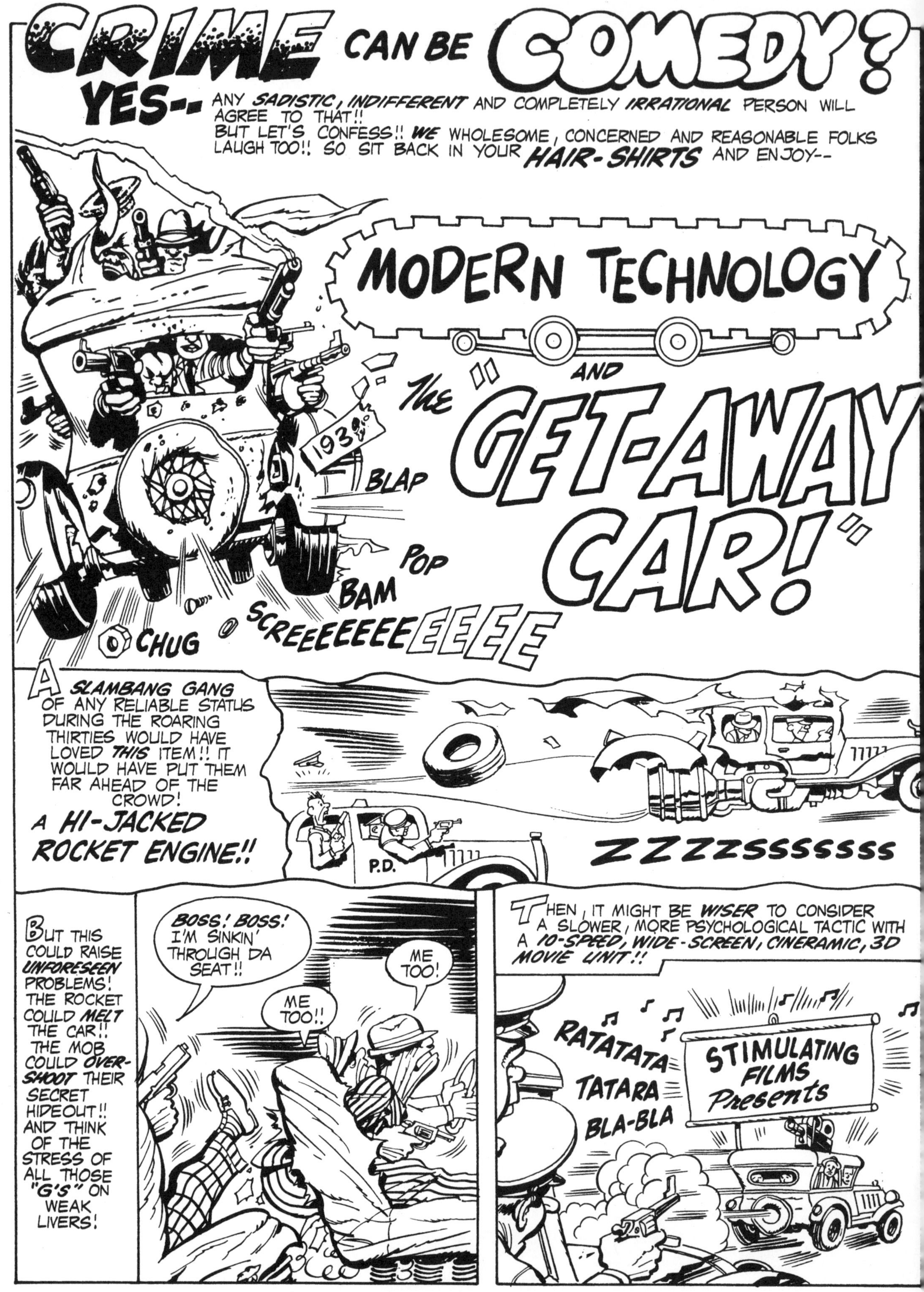
CRIME CAN BE COMEDY?
YES-- ANY SADISTIC, INDIFFERENT AND COMPLETELY IRRATIONAL PERSON WILL AGREE TO THAT!! BUT LET'S CONFESS!! WE WHOLESOME, CONCERNED AND REASONABLE FOLKS LAUGH TOO!! SO SIT BACK IN YOUR HAIR-SHIRTS AND ENJOY--
MODERN TECHNOLOGY
AND
THE "GET-AWAY CAR!"
1930
BLAP
POP
BAM
CHUG
SCREEEEEEEEEEEE
A SLAMBANG GANG OF ANY RELIABLE STATUS DURING THE ROARING THIRTIES WOULD HAVE LOVED THIS ITEM!! IT WOULD HAVE PUT THEM FAR AHEAD OF THE CROWD!
A HI-JACKED ROCKET ENGINE!!
P.D.
ZZZZZSSSSSSS
BUT THIS COULD RAISE UNFORESEEN PROBLEMS! THE ROCKET COULD MELT THE CAR!! THE MOB COULD OVER-SHOOT THEIR SECRET HIDEOUT!! AND THINK OF THE STRESS OF ALL THOSE "G'S" ON WEAK LIVERS!
BOSS! BOSS! I'M SINKIN' THROUGH DA SEAT!!
ME TOO!
ME TOO!!
THEN, IT MIGHT BE WISER TO CONSIDER A SLOWER, MORE PSYCHOLOGICAL TACTIC WITH A 10-SPEED, WIDE-SCREEN, CINERAMIC, 3D MOVIE UNIT!!
RATATATA
TATARA
BLA-BLA
STIMULATING FILMS Presents

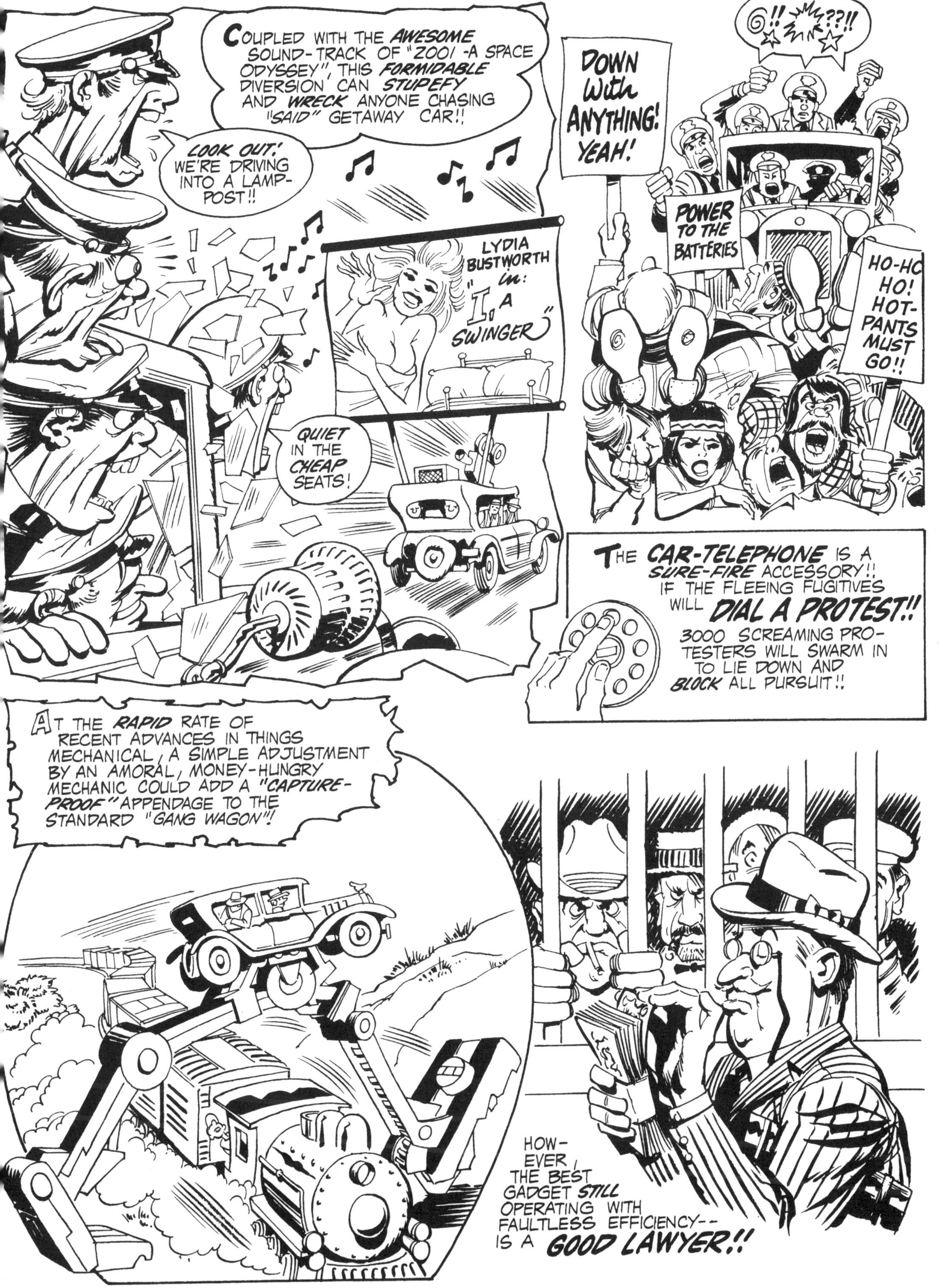
COUPLED WITH THE AWESOME SOUND-TRACK OF "ZOO1 -A SPACE ODYSSEY", THIS FORMIDABLE DIVERSION CAN STUPEFY AND WRECK ANYONE CHASING "SAID" GETAWAY CAR!!
LOOK OUT! WE'RE DRIVING INTO A LAMP-POST!!
LYDIA BUSTWORTH in: "I, A SWINGER"
QUIET IN THE CHEAP SEATS!
DOWN With ANYTHING! YEAH!
POWER TO THE BATTERIES
HO-HO HO! HOT-PANTS MUST GO!!
THE CAR-TELEPHONE IS A SURE-FIRE ACCESSORY!! IF THE FLEEING FUGITIVES WILL DIAL A PROTEST!! 3000 SCREAMING PROTESTERS WILL SWARM IN TO LIE DOWN AND BLOCK ALL PURSUIT!!
AT THE RAPID RATE OF RECENT ADVANCES IN THINGS MECHANICAL, A SIMPLE ADJUSTMENT BY AN AMORAL, MONEY-HUNGRY MECHANIC COULD ADD A "CAPTURE-PROOF" APPENDAGE TO THE STANDARD "GANG WAGON"!
HOW-EVER, THE BEST GADGET STILL OPERATING WITH FAULTLESS EFFICIENCY-- IS A GOOD LAWYER!!

### JACK KIRBY

A true giant in the world of comics, Jack "The King" Kirby began his comics career in 1937 at the age of 20. During comics' Golden Age, Kirby (along with his partner Joe Simon) drew and/or created innumerable features, including Captain America, the Young Allies, the Sandman, the Newsboy Legion and Manhunter. During the 1950s, Kirby and Simon continued to pour out stories and concepts, including *The Fighting American* for Crestwood and *Boys' Ranch* for Harvey, as well as creating the romance comics genre with their groundbreaking title *Young Romance* for Prize Comics. In 1961, the first issue of Marvel Comics' *The Fantastic Four* — a collaboration between Kirby and Marvel editor-in-chief Stan Lee — cemented Kirby's reputation as comics' preeminent creator. Throughout the 1960s, Kirby and Lee laid the groundwork for the Marvel Universe that flourishes to this day. Kirby returned to DC in 1971 with his classic "Fourth World Trilogy" — THE NEW GODS, MISTER MIRACLE and THE FOREVER PEOPLE — which was followed by THE DEMON, OMAC and KAMANDI. After a brief return to Marvel in the mid-1970s (during which time he created *The Eternals*), Kirby shifted his attention to the animation industry, where he worked until his retirement in 1987. That same year he joined Will Eisner and Carl Barks as the first inductees into the Eisner Awards Hall of Fame. Jack Kirby passed away in 1994.

### VINCE COLLETTA

Vince Colletta began his comics career in 1952, starting out as a penciller before switching his focus to inking. After establishing himself as a mainstay artist for the romance genre, he went on to contribute work to nearly all of Marvel Comics' new superhero titles in the early 1960s, inking primarily over Jack Kirby's pencils on such titles as *Daredevil*, *The Fantastic Four*, and a long run on the Mighty Thor feature in *Journey Into Mystery*. He followed Kirby to work on the Fourth World books for DC, and went on to provide inks for a wide variety of other titles, including BATMAN, SUPERMAN, GREEN LANTERN, WONDER WOMAN, and SUPER FRIENDS. Colletta also served as DC's Art Director from 1976 to 1979. He passed away in 1991.

### MIKE ROYER

Mike Royer began his comics career assisting the legendary Russ Manning in the 1960s on *Magnus, Robot Fighter* and *Tarzan* for Gold Key. In the 1970s he went on to ink and letter Manning's *Tarzan* and *Star Wars* syndicated newspaper strips. During this same period, Royer also pencilled and inked stories on his own for the Warren anthologies *Creepy*, *Eerie* and *Vampirella*. However, his best-known works are undoubtedly his numerous collaborations with Jack Kirby on THE NEW GODS, THE FOREVER PEOPLE, MISTER MIRACLE, THE DEMON and KAMANDI for DC Comics, as well as *Captain America, The Eternals* and many other titles for Marvel Comics.

Following his partnership with Kirby, in 1979 Royer began a long association with the Walt Disney Company, where he worked in the creative department of the Consumer Products/Licensing division. In 1993 Royer left his staff position to freelance for the Disney Stores creative group. He continues to freelance for various companies from his home in Oregon.

EXPERIENCE THESE TWO-FISTED WORKS FROM THE MIND OF
# JACK "THE KING" KIRBY

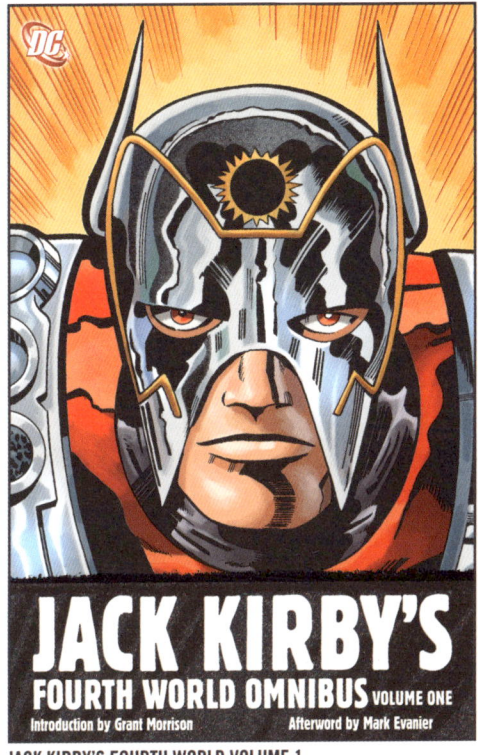

**JACK KIRBY'S FOURTH WORLD VOLUME 1**

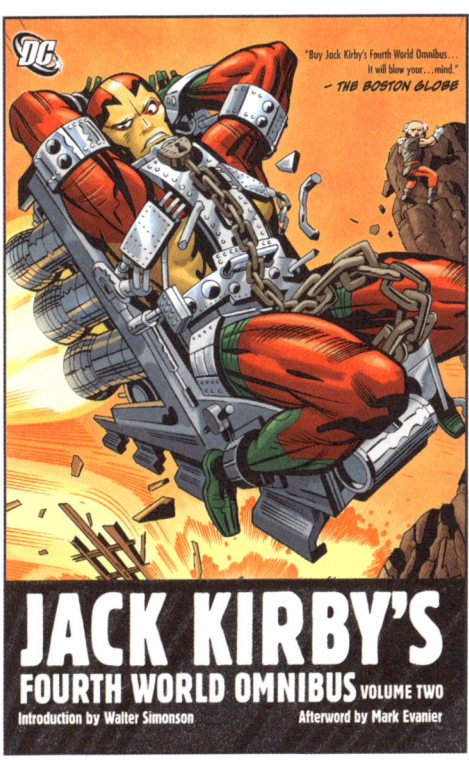

**JACK KIRBY'S FOURTH WORLD VOLUME 2**

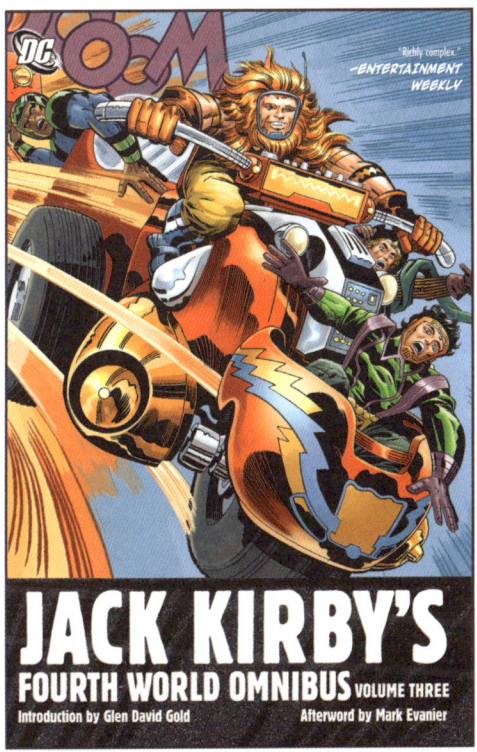

**JACK KIRBY'S FOURTH WORLD VOLUME 3**

**JACK KIRBY'S FOURTH WORLD VOLUME 4**

EXPERIENCE THESE TWO-FISTED WORKS FROM THE MIND OF

**JACK "THE KING" KIRBY**

DC COMICS
CHALLENGERS OF THE UNKNOWN BY JACK KIRBY
INTRODUCTION BY PAUL KUPPERBERG
AFTERWORD BY JOHN MORROW
CHALLENGERS OF THE UNKNOWN BY JACK KIRBY

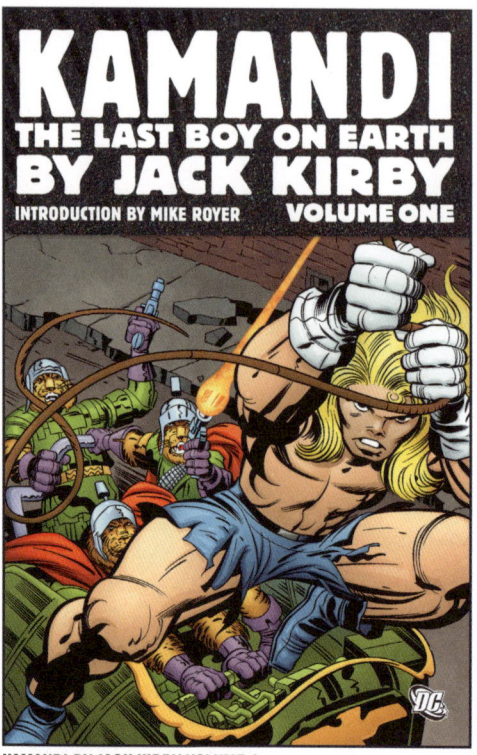

KAMANDI
THE LAST BOY ON EARTH
BY JACK KIRBY
INTRODUCTION BY MIKE ROYER
VOLUME ONE
KAMANDI BY JACK KIRBY VOLUME 1

DC COMICS
THE JACK KIRBY
OMNIBUS VOLUME TWO
STARRING THE SUPER POWERS
INTRODUCTION BY JOHN MORROW
THE JACK KIRBY OMNIBUS VOLUME 2

JACK KIRBY
ARE WE ON THE OUTSIDE OF THE
SPIRIT WORLD
REINCARNATION!
FOTO-FEATURE!
WHAT SHOCKING STORY DID THE GIRL UNDER HYPNOSIS TELL THAT PROVES … "MEN CAN LIVE FOREVER!"
SPECIAL! FORBIDDEN RITUALS OF THE… "SECRET CALIFORNIA CULTS!"
"THE WORLD WILL END IN 1983!"
THE MOST INCREDIBLE PREDICTION EVER MADE BY A MAN WHO SAW THE FUTURE 500 YEARS AGO!
PROPHECY! REINCARNATION! HAUNTING! BLACK MAGIC!
SPIRIT WORLD